BLACKWATER

Also by James Henry

THE DI JACK FROST PREQUELS

Morning Frost

Fatal Frost

First Frost (with Henry Sutton)

JAMES HENRY
BLACKWATER

riverrun

First published in Great Britain in 2016 by

riverrun
an imprint of
Quercus Editions Ltd
Carmelite House
50 Victoria Embankment
London EC4Y 0DZ

An Hachette UK company

A CIP catalogue record for this book is available
from the British Library.

HB ISBN 978 1 78087 977 2
TPB ISBN 978 1 78087 978 9
EBOOK ISBN 978 1 78429 981 1

10 9 8 7 6 5 4 3 2 1

Typeset by CC Book Production

Printed and bound in Great Britain by Clays Ltd, St Ives plc

For my mother.

'A paranoid is someone who knows a little of what's going on. A psychotic is a guy who's just found out what's going on.'

– William S. Burroughs

PROLOGUE

10.45 p.m., Friday, New Year's Eve, 31st December, 1982
Blackwater Estuary, Essex

Though they couldn't have been travelling at more than six knots, the din when they unexpectedly beached the boat was horrific. The older man's panic subsided once the racket of the small outboard motor was silenced and he realized they weren't going to sink; that they had in fact run aground. Now all was quiet. And eerily dark.

'Jesus, weren't expecting that,' his younger companion said, shaken.

Boyd grunted. He flashed the torch uncertainly around them. He couldn't see a thing in this fog. The boat gave unsteadily as he moved to the stern, water lapping gently at the hull. They must have hit a sandbank.

'Right, Felix, you go first,' he said. The boat rocked as his companion hauled one of the two rucksacks on to his back.

The late-night tide, being a high one, must have drained

1

quickly, as if a plug had been pulled. He sensed they were far from their planned destination and cursed quietly. He should have known the boat was too small to hold its own against a strong ebb tide. They had been travelling for what felt like hours; a more powerful engine would have had them here quicker, before the tide had run. But where was 'here', exactly? There were no lights visible on the shore. He had thought originally the foul weather would give them extra cover under which to land, but he had not foreseen the possibility of getting lost.

'You comin', Jace?' Felix called, already ashore and invisible in the icy darkness, though he couldn't have been more than a few feet away.

Boyd hauled the second army rucksack on to his back, making the waist straps secure, almost toppling with the weight. He let out a groan. Fifty kilos was, unsurprisingly, fifty kilos.

'Come on!' Felix called again, his footsteps crunching over what must be oyster shells.

'Right, here goes.' He drew in a breath that was pure sea mist before clambering off the tender and – Christ! – into freezing-cold water up to his waist. The boat had swung with the tide and he'd misjudged which side to jump. The sudden ice-chill caused a wave of panic; he waded desperately towards his companion's torch, fearing for his cargo, which, though vacuum-packed, he couldn't risk getting damp.

'Fucking 'ell, mate! What you doin', garn swimmin'?' The small torch beam bounced erratically in his direction.

'Piss off!' Boyd spat breathlessly, infuriated at the piercing cold numbing his groin. Regaining his composure, he looked desperately around him, but could see nothing. 'Where the fuck . . . ?' he muttered. Turning to the right, he could just make out faint lights twinkling in the mist, like dimmed Christmas-tree lights, but that was . . . too far away? He'd anticipated lights to the west, not to the east. This wasn't good – they must be way off course. He reached into his snorkel-jacket pocket for the compass, his numb fingers unable to differentiate the various objects: lighter, knife, keys – there, he had it. But he'd left his torch behind. Fuck. It was only a torch, though, and he wasn't going back.

'Give me that!' he snapped quietly, though the caution was unnecessary – he could have screamed and nobody would have heard. He flashed the torch beam on the compass, the sudden brightness off the glass hurting his eyes and causing him to blink rapidly. 'Brightlingsea? Must be . . .'

'We lost, skipper?' He felt his accomplice's warm breath at his ear.

'No. Just further east than I thought. And very, very late. The tide must have carried us. Poxy boat. We're off East Mersea – on the mudflats, at least half a mile from the beach and two miles east of where we should be. We haven't a hope of making the meet tonight – or seeing anyone else, for that matter.' He turned sharply, directing the torch into the young man's brown eyes, the pupils shrinking in alarm. 'There's only you, me and one hundred kilos of high-class party powder.'

Saturday, New Year's Day, 1983

1 a.m., Saturday, Colchester CID, Queen Street

The telephone's sudden ring jolted DI Nick Lowry awake and he knocked over a mug of coffee. Lowry, thirty-nine, ex-Divisional athletic and boxing champion, was too big for the 1950s wooden desk he'd slumped asleep on, and he started as the cold liquid reached his prone elbow. Realizing where he was, he yawned and scratched his dark brown hair, glancing sheepishly at his younger colleague, opposite, who was scribbling notes under a grimy Anglepoise lamp.

The telephone had stopped ringing. He checked his watch. He was late. Very late. He'd been expecting a call from his in-laws – hours ago – to summon him to collect his son from their house. They'd taken him to a panto in London starring Rod Hull and Emu. He'd told them he'd be working late so they should call him at Queen Street once they got back to their place in Lexden. Perhaps that had been them on the phone – but why so late? Traffic, snow, accident – the possibilities raced through his mind in ascending order of potential danger and parental panic rose in his throat. Shit, why did he have to nod off!

'Made a mess there,' DC Daniel Kenton tutted, without looking up from his paperwork, his glasses sliding precariously close to the edge of his nose. Kenton was twenty-five and far too young to be wearing specs that made him look quite so studious. University educated, Kenton was considered to be exactly what the force needed in the modern age, according to Essex County HQ. And, though County's dictate on progress was not always Colchester Chief Superintendent Sparks's view on progress, in young Kenton they did in fact meet, for Kenton could box, and box well. Not that you'd guess it to look at CID's most recent recruit. He flicked back his too-long foppish hair in a vaguely feminine way; Lowry thought him too big a lad to carry it off. Kenton probably thought it made him look intellectual.

'What were you doing, letting me doze off like that?' Lowry yawned, shuddering involuntarily in the cold of the Victorian building. 'What's happened to Matthew? I should've heard from him ages ago!'

'Don't panic. Your son is in Lexden with your wife's parents. The night sergeant took the message. They've only just got back. Fog on the A12.'

Lowry grunted with relief. 'What are you even doing here at this time of night? No New Year's Eve parties for you?'

Kenton looked up from his writing, taking off his glasses

to reveal handsome, boyish features. 'No. Making the most of it now things appear to have quietened down, so I'm getting the paperwork on the Mersea post-office job out of the way.'

'Right, well, no point me hanging around here,' said Lowry flatly, getting up. Just then, the phone started to ring again.

Kenton was meticulously fitting the cap on what Lowry knew to be an expensive fountain pen – a graduation present. 'Aren't you going to answer that?' he said. 'The night sergeant knows you're still here. It can't be anything as bad as last night.'

Lowry glanced at the obstinate phone vibrating on the desk. Not the in-laws, then. His mind flickered back momentarily to the violence of the previous evening. He snapped up the receiver, glaring at the satisfied Kenton as he did so. 'Lowry.'

'At last,' the night sergeant replied. The line was terrible, as though there lay a continent between them instead of a single storey. He could only make out the last word: '. . . body.'

'Beg pardon?' Instinctively, he reached for his cigarettes, forgetting he'd given up as of now.

'A car's run over a body. The vehicle was travelling at speed. On the Strood.' This was the local name for the causeway between the mainland and Mersea, an island that lay seven miles to the south of Colchester. It was often hit by high tides, which could cut the five-thousand-strong populace off from the mainland for up to three hours at a time. 'Wait, why are you calling me?' Lowry asked. 'Get the Dodger's boys out. They can handle an RTA, surely . . . I know it's late, but still.'

'The Mersea lads are on it, but this ain't no RTA – the body is lying in six inches of water. It's missing its head. And an arm.'

Lowry swallowed hard. 'The body's headless?' Kenton caught his eye.

'Yep, shaved clean off . . .'

Lowry hung up.

'Problem?' Kenton asked disingenuously.

1.10 a.m., Colchester General Hospital, Lexden Road

Jacqui wriggled on the bed and hoicked down her uniform. The mattress let out a sigh, signalling her lover's imminent departure. The lights remained off. She swung round and felt with her toes on the cold, tiled floor for her shoes; the room was pitch black. She could just make out the luminous marks on her Timex watch. Her break was nearly at an end – she'd have to make for the nurses' station straight away, no time for a cigarette. She heard the distinctive sound of his trouser zip, always the final step after realigning his shirt and tie.

'One day we'll have to try it with the lights on.' She laughed quietly. But there was no response – instead, a vertical slash of light appeared as the door to the private room opened.

'Got to go. Bleeper,' came a whisper from the darkness, and without a pause his slender frame slipped through the crack in the door.

'Of course. Saved by the bleeper,' she muttered to herself. She knew what they were doing was risky, but it was still curiously convenient how the bleeper always seemed to go off as soon as they'd finished. She sighed and slid off the bed.

Reclipping her hair hurriedly, she crept out into the green-lit corridor, closing the door softly behind her. She padded along and turned into the dark hospital ward, her heart racing as the thrill of what she had just done resurfaced amid the sterile normality. She stopped short of the light of the nurses' station to adjust her tights.

'Jacqueline,' an authoritative voice barked behind her, causing her to jump. She turned and saw the dour, familiar face of the ward sister.

'Yes, sister?' she replied demurely. The sight of her brought her up cold. She fiddled nervously with her wedding ring.

'Where have you . . . ? Never mind. Private Daley is in Resuscitation.'

One of the young soldiers.

'Cardiac arrest,' the sister added. 'You are needed there.'

Jacqui turned to leave.

'Nurse, your tunic,' said the ward sister.

Jacqui adjusted her uniform, feeling herself flush and hoping that the ward sister wouldn't have spotted it in the low light. The other nurse on duty looked up knowingly from the station desk. Jacqui ignored the smirk forming on her lips.

The sister turned on her heels and marched off at a clip. Jacqui refocused her mind and recalled the injured young soldier admitted during the hectic hours of the previous night. He seemed little more than a boy; she'd almost laughed when she heard he was a soldier. He was nineteen, apparently, but lying there unconscious in a nightgown, bum fluff on his soft cheeks, he looked barely out of puberty. The boy was now in the best possible hands, the very same hands that, only minutes earlier, with a different sense of urgency, had pinned her to a hospital bed. At least, she thought, hurrying past the ward sister towards her patient, Paul had a genuine call this time.

2

1.15 a.m., Saturday, The Strood, Mersea Island side

The Land Rover groaned to a halt, throwing Jason Boyd's unbelted accomplice towards the dashboard with an unpleasant crunch. Ten feet in front of them was a police vehicle, a jam-sandwich Cortina, parked side on where the Strood road met the East Mersea road. Visibility was almost nil, and Boyd hadn't seen the other car until they were practically on top of its languidly rotating blue light. He threw the vehicle rapidly into reverse and backed up to a respectable distance.

'Fuck!' he said under his breath. Fog or no fog, he should have seen the blue light.

'Nearly cracked me head open,' Felix moaned, rubbing his forehead.

'Well, you should belt up, then,' Boyd retorted unsympathetically. 'Clunk click and all that bollocks.' The fluorescent police tape was now just visible, floating in the mist before them. But not much else. Beyond the police car the thick night made the causeway invisible.

'This is all we need,' Boyd sighed, lighting a cigarette.

'Nuisance,' Felix added.

'Nuisance? Contact with the Old Bill? More than a nuisance, you plum.' He shook his head in the dark cab.

'Where's the panic, Jace? We just say we're trying to get home across the Strood . . .'

'Er, yeah, mate; with what we're carrying, we better bloody hope so. Maybe the smell of us will put him off hanging around.'

Boyd fidgeted uncomfortably in his mud-covered jeans, now beginning to dry but itching like hell. After trekking across the mudflats for what must have been two miles, they were exhausted; even with a map, it took an age to find their Land Rover in the pitch-black winter. The plan was to land under cover of darkness around six, and be in Colchester by seven; even if they'd got ashore on time, he'd still not allowed enough time for walking by foot – if they ever did this again, the whole approach would need a rethink.

The Land Rover's ancient idling diesel engine stuttered suddenly, as if choking on the wet, prompting a uniformed officer to materialize out of the gloom.

'Fuck! He's coming over!' Felix exclaimed.

'Well, just say we've been bait-digging, and then stopped off in the pub,' Boyd said, half wondering if it was worth a try if they were questioned.

There was a rap on the glass. Boyd wound the window down and smiled. A torch beam scanned the cab and settled on Boyd's face. 'Happy New Year, officer. Problems?' he asked, squinting in the light.

'I'm afraid I have to tell you to turn back.' The policeman, young and thin-faced, looked chilled to the bone. 'There's been a fatality.'

'Not surprised, in this weather,' Felix replied.

'Where are you boys heading this time of night?' the officer asked.

'Colchester,' Boyd answered coolly. 'We're just on our way home. We're not from Mersea.'

'We've been bait-digging,' Felix said.

Boyd cringed and added quickly, 'We stopped at the pub, just to warm up, like, before heading off.'

'Which one?'

Luckily Boyd remembered passing the pub. 'The Dog and Pheasant . . . we only had the one.'

'Sure, sure. Need to warm up on a night like this. Well, go back there and knock up old Bob, and he'll let you stay the night. Say there's been an incident and the only way off the island is shut.'

'Thank you, officer,' Boyd wound up the window hurriedly. 'Friendly for a copper? Makes a change. That's that, then,' he said to Felix. 'Well, we can't hang around here drawing attention to ourselves. There's nothing for it. To the Dog and Pheasant.'

1.45 a.m., Mersea Road

'Blimey, it's a real pea-souper,' Kenton said above the roar of the engine, flicking the wipers on full. Although visibility was poor, he continued accelerating into the dark as they left behind the residential outskirts of Colchester and the orange glow of the street lamps.

'A pea-souper is a fog. Or smog, to be more accurate, a smog caused by industrial waste, denoted by its colour. Clever lad like you should know that. This –' Lowry rummaged in the glove compartment for some mints – they might give you sweet breath but, sadly, they did nothing to keep you awake – 'this is just a mist. A cold one, I'll grant you.'

The mist thickened as the road dipped through Donyland Woods.

'Slow down, for Christ's sake! You can't see!' Lowry cried, agitated. He was a bad passenger. Especially in Kenton's cramped orange sports car.

'Quitting smoking making you nervous, guv?'

The Triumph accelerated out of the dip.

'No, it bloody well isn't. Just slow down. There's no hurry.' It felt surreal, travelling in a convertible in these conditions. He was trying his best not to suggest that Kenton might consider fixing the roof.

Kenton eased off a fraction, 'Not made any New Year's resolutions myself.'

'Wouldn't bother.' Lowry was giving up for health reasons,

having developed a hacking cough. He didn't give a fig that it was New Year, although the winter weather made it worse. No, it had been just a night like any other, albeit a busy one.

'Always room from improvement, guv, quality of life—'

'Don't start banging on about quality of life at this time of the morning. Get out of the police force if you want quality of life . . . and don't call me guv. How many times do I have to tell you? I'm not Dixon of Dock Green. Though I'm starting to feel as old as him.' Lowry looked across at his driver. 'Actually,' he continued hesitantly, 'I have been thinking about trying something new . . .'

'Yes, giving up the fags.'

'More than that . . .'

'Not complaining about my car?' Kenton prompted, the damp air catching his hair as turned to his passenger.

'Me not complaining about this heap will improve *your* quality of life, not mine. No. I've decided I need to take up a hobby.'

'A hobby? What, as in stamp collecting? Making model aeroplanes? That sort of thing?'

Lowry couldn't make out his colleague's expression in the dark, though he realized he needn't fear being ridiculed. Daniel Kenton, for all his joking, was as sound as a pound – if anything, he'd understand.

'Not quite so sedentary, no, although now I'm getting on a bit, it's time to pull out of the gaffer's boxing team. No, something outdoors.'

'Cycling?'

'No. Birdwatching.'

'Ornithology? Crumbs. Sounds a bit ... well ...'

'A bit what?

'Well ... Poofy? Was it the wife's idea, guv?'

'"Poofy"?' Lowry said, surprised that someone so educated would use the term. 'No – I haven't even told her. It's just an idea. I caught a programme on the telly and liked the thought of the fresh air, really. No more to it than that – not sure that qualifies me for a change in sexual preference.'

'Sorry, sir. No offence. I was just wondering what the chief will have to say about it,' said Kenton. 'Ditching the boxing is one thing – I mean, you're getting on and all, but ...'

'It's none of his business.' A vision of Stephen Sparks, the station's pugilist chief superintendent, loomed across Lowry's consciousness.

Kenton knew not to push him further. He was a good lad, Lowry thought, as he watched the tree limbs pass by, stark and white in the lights of the car, occasionally clawing ominously through the fog. Sparks, on the other hand, was not so agreeable. Lowry hadn't really considered the effect this change in direction might have on the chief; as far as Sparks was concerned, the social side of the force was as crucial as the policing itself, if not more so. And Kenton's observation was accurate enough: Sparks would more than likely view this harmless, gentle pursuit as on a par with being caught soliciting in public conveniences. But, in truth, he no longer cared; all his life he'd done things for other people. The boxing had started with his father. Even when the old man left them, Lowry had carried on, his need to impress him seamlessly replaced by the fuel of anger. And then the police force – and the shine had gone off that now. When did it happen? If it weren't for his wife and Matt, he'd have thrown in the job years ago . . .

The Triumph drew to a stop. Kenton killed the engine, and silence descended on them.

'Though, if it's fresh air I'm after, there's bags of it to be had travelling around in this thing with you,' Lowry said, dispelling thoughts of sports and pastimes as he pulled himself out of the car on to the ice-cold causeway. 'Watch your step,' he said to no one in particular, flicking seaweed off his newish shoes. He spun his torch from left to right. On either side of the road there were narrow walkways bordered by two-bar wooden fences that ran the length of causeway. The motorist had hit the body as he came off the island. Lowry shone the torch to the right. Was it conceivable that the body had been brought in by the tide? He stepped up to the fence and looked into the murk of the salt marsh beyond the causeway. He couldn't see the marshes, but he knew they were there.

'Could the body have slipped between the gaps of this fence?' he asked, more of himself than anyone else. He gauged the space between the bars – just short of a foot. Yes, probably.

'The tide was a high one, guv,' said a uniformed officer who had suddenly appeared beside Lowry. 'Fully over the first rail.'

'Sorry, and you are Constable . . . ?'

'Jennings, guv, West Mersea.' That would be why his face was unfamiliar, Lowry thought. He couldn't keep up with the treadmill of Uniform – they tended not to stick at it so much these days; impatient for promotion. He stepped back from the rail and moved towards the huddle of silhouettes standing underneath an arc lamp in the middle of the road.

The body was male and clothed. It lay sodden and limp on the road. It reminded Lowry of a drunk he'd once found in the pouring rain in the middle of a lane near Tiptree.

'Do you have a cigarette on you, son, by any chance?' Lowry asked. The officer shook his head. Lowry shrugged. 'Where's the Dodger?'

'The sergeant clocks off at nine, sir.' The respect accorded to the station sergeant, a robust sixty-year-old who had manned the Mersea Station for more than thirty years, pleased Lowry. He crouched down and regarded the blanched corpse; his experience hinted it had been in the water for at least twenty-four hours. They needed to get the body to the lab; Lowry gave the signal and stood.

A torch bobbed towards him in the blackness.

'There's nothing more we can do tonight.' Kenton approached, looking ashen under the spotlight. 'West Mersea police have already scoured the road. No sign of the head.'

'Sod the head for now.' Lowry turned round in the darkness. 'How did this get here?' he said, tapping the corpse with a now-damp loafer. 'Did it float in on the tide?'

1.50 a.m., Saturday, Colchester Garrison HQ, Flagstaff House, Napier Road

CS Stephen Sparks was cursing inwardly. They should have left the dinner party half an hour ago with the last guests, when Antonia had signalled she was ready, and not have had another brandy, as he'd insisted. Blast! The night had been fun, until now. Brigadier Lane stood in the hallway of his spacious quarters, speaking quietly into the telephone and occasionally shooting a glance in Sparks's direction.

To a casual observer, the brigadier and Sparks might appear to be friends. Over the years, a genial relationship had developed between the two middle-aged men, fostered by social occasions like this evening's lengthy dinner party. But the surface bonhomie masked a fierce rivalry. They held similar positions within Britain's oldest-recorded town – Sparks was chief superintendent and Lane was garrison commander – and, while they didn't compete in their professional lives, each had a deep-rooted need to outshine the other. It was channelled furiously through sports, particularly boxing. Both men had shared a passion for boxing since boyhood and were keen to instil the love of the sport into their respective commands; so, for the past ten years, local policeman and serviceman had met in the ring to batter the hell out of each other. Competition reached such a pitch that, in the Jubilee Year of 1977, the Colchester Services Cup was born, a prize which now glinted tauntingly from the brigadier's trophy cabinet.

Sparks eyed the surrendered cup they'd lost the previous year before swigging the last of his brandy and replacing the glass heavily on the table. This telephone call could only be bad news. Sparks knew that Brigadier Lane tempered his deep, booming voice only for matters of a serious or upsetting nature. The policeman's young fiancée shot him a pleading look: *must we stay longer?* He ignored her and watched as the brigadier replaced the receiver, his head bowed.

'That was the hospital,' Lane announced as he re-entered the room. 'Young Daley . . .' He rubbed his impressive beard, reluctant to say more in front of his wife and Antonia. But Sparks could read his expression and acknowledged what must have happened in silence. Shit, he'd never expected the lad to die. He'd only jumped off a wall, for Christ's sake. He shook his head woefully.

'The other boy has regained consciousness, according to a Dr Bryant,' the brigadier continued. 'We'll have him transferred to the garrison hospital straight away.'

Abbey Fields, the military hospital. That's the last thing we need, thought Sparks. Once the army had him, the police would never get access.

'Really? Surely it's best not to move him. Why not leave him in the General?'

'Army takes care of its own, Stephen, you know that.'

Yes, only too well. It was because the soldier had been in a critical state that the civilian police had successfully overruled the military police – Lane's Red Caps – in the first place. The brigadier's wife got up off the sofa and moved to comfort her husband. As if he cares, thought Sparks – the embarrassment is all that brute will be worried about. And the fact he's lost a good bantamweight fighter. Daley had a lethal upper cut.

Sparks rose, along with his fiancée.

'I'm very sorry, John.'

'Not your fault,' the brigadier replied. Though, of course, Lane would hold him responsible for allowing yobs to run riot in the high street on New Year's Eve. 'Have you caught the little sods yet?' he demanded.

'We're making inquiries. This, of course, ups the ante . . .'

'Murder?' piped up Lane's wife, wide-eyed.

'Let's not be too hasty,' Sparks urged. 'There'll be a full investigation.'

'Damn right there will,' Lane put in.

Sparks held out Antonia's coat for her to put on. Yes, he thought, but don't you go poking your oar in with the local

Gestapo. The last thing he wanted was MPs crawling all over this.

'Right, we must be off. Thank you for a lovely evening.' Handshakes and kisses were exchanged. 'I'll check in at the station on the way home and call you first thing in morning, John.'

Sparks ushered Antonia to the door, his hand a little too firm in the small of her back. 'Lovely evening, thank you,' he repeated forcefully as the bitter night air filled the hall. Lane nodded in silence on the threshold, and his wife smiled wanly, aware that the unwelcome news had ruined a pleasant evening.

'Did you *have* to practically push me out of the front door?' Antonia shivered as Sparks fumbled with the cap for the de-icer in the VIP parking bay. 'What was all that about, anyway? What did she mean, "murder"?' She wrapped herself tightly in her long fur coat.

'Typical New Year's Eve trouble – a ruckus between the locals and a bunch of squaddies,' explained Sparks.

'And someone was killed? There's always fighting in town over Christmas, but good heavens, what's the place coming to?' she said, appalled.

Sparks bristled. 'Yes, but this time a dozen or so yobs chased two lads and cornered them at the castle. They jumped from the north wall, not knowing it was a twenty-foot drop. Both are in hospital, and one just died.'

They sat in the Rover in silence. Sparks turned on the blower to de-mist the windscreen. Antonia brushed her lush blond hair from her face.

'Do we really have to go to the station tonight?'

Sparks ignored her and picked up the radio handset. 'Get me Lowry,' he said.

2.45 a.m., Colchester CID, Queen Street

'Ah, there you are. Just seen Kenton slope off. Where've you been?' Sparks said loudly. As usual, the chief seemed oblivious to the late hour, marching around bright-eyed and energetic in his attic office, as though it were a fresh spring morning. This ability of his to be wide awake at all times grated on Lowry. 'The night sergeant has filled me in on the obstruction on the Strood.'

'Kenton'll be back out there, on the mud at dawn, don't worry. And I've just been phoning to check on my son. He's sleeping over at my wife's parents.'

Sparks reached for a bottle from the small, tatty cabinet. The chief wasn't interested in Lowry's domestic arrangements, nor, it seemed, in the body on the Strood.

'We have a problem,' Sparks continued. 'Drink?'

Lowry nodded and took the generous measure of the chief's favourite malt offered to him. Sparks was in civvies: a neatly tailored suit in Prince of Wales check, a white shirt and a navy tie at half-mast. When out of uniform, the older man, with

25

his cropped hair and bulky frame, didn't look like a copper, especially in a get-up that wouldn't look out of place on an East End gangster.

'Cheers.' He raised the glass. 'What's happened?'

'The soldier boy who fell off the wall in Castle Park is dead.'

'Oh.' Lowry didn't need an explanation. In this town, a soldier's death was a cause for concern.

Colchester was one of the country's largest garrison towns. This had been the case since the Roman invasion in AD 43, and every policeman in Queen Street knew the history, to varying degrees. In military conflicts across the ages – the Civil Wars, the Napoleonic Wars, the First and Second World Wars and, most recently, the Falklands – Colchester had played a significant role in housing the country's soldiery. Many of the men who had taken Port Stanley had been based there and had only recently returned home. But the war had been over for six months and already the civilian population, who had welcomed home the servicemen as heroes, now ignored or even resented them for what they saw as their boozy belligerence. The police were acutely aware that maintaining peaceful relations between squaddies and civilians was a fine balancing act. Any harm caused by one side to the other would set the town on edge.

'Oh, indeed.' Sparks put his feet up on the desk. Lowry took in the quality of his superior's expensive leather soles. 'So, have we got any of the little fuckers who did it yet?'

'But he fell.'

'I'm sorry?' Sparks raised his eyebrows.

'I said he, the soldier, fell – or jumped. They both did.'

'Nick, don't cock around over the detail. Answer me – have we got them?'

'Stephen, I know you're pals with the Beard, but you know it was an accident. The coroner will give death by misadventure . . .' Lowry paused to check his boss's face. The nostrils were not flared, so he wasn't angry – either that or he'd been drinking. 'Uniform were on the scene in a matter of minutes and said there was no one else in the vicinity.'

Sparks swung his feet off the desk so abruptly it startled Lowry. 'Stop all this bollocks!' he barked. 'Do we have them?'

'No,' he answered truthfully.

'But you know who the likely candidates are, right?' Sparks pulled out a pack of Embassy Number 1. 'Here.' He tossed them over. The cigarettes beckoned to Lowry from the worn oak desk.

'I've given up.'

Sparks nodded as though impressed – although he wouldn't be – before retrieving the pack and taking a cigarette out with his teeth. 'You must know who chased after those lads.'

'How?'

'Ah, do me a favour – a ruck in the town centre? How fuckin' hard can that be? You know the locals. Bring 'em in and ask a few questions, and we'll take it from there, eh?'

Lowry got up to leave.

'Where are you going?'

'Home to bed.'

Sparks nodded. 'After the hospital.'

'What, now?'

'The other lad has come to. Lane will be looking to shift the boy to their place at Abbey Fields. You know as well as I do, it's easier while he's on our turf. Toddle off to the General.'

4

3 a.m., Saturday, Colchester General Hospital

Jacqui Lowry stood in silence as her husband consulted with her lover across the dead soldier's corpse. She assumed a mask of indifference, fighting back the notion that her sin was somehow exposed for all to see by the stark hospital lighting, like invisible ink under ultraviolet light. As Paul explained to her husband the complications that had caused the soldier to go into cardiac arrest, she tried to ignore the way he pushed his soft, wavy blond hair away from his face. This gesture, which she had adored up to now and found part of his boyish charm, seemed affected in the face of her stoic husband of ten years. And the sculpted beard, which she'd always considered a turn-on, looked vaguely effeminate next to Nick's now-stubbled jaw. She pinched herself. It was guilt that was making her feel this way.

Ever the professional, Nick had taken no notice of her when he entered the room. A polite nod was all she got. He looked tired. She was tired, too. Not for the first time did she reflect that shift work and long hours were the prime causes of all that was wrong with their relationship.

Nick, for reasons best known to himself, picked up the dead man's hand and examined the fingers, or the fingernails, by the looks of it. Paul edged behind him. Oh, God, please don't do that! She noticed a sly grin creep across her lover's face – ever so slight, but it was there. Don't mock him, please! She was surprised how stung she felt, and scowled sharply. Paul gestured to her that he would back off as Nick lay the soldier's arm carefully back down, then took both his wife and Paul by surprise by asking Paul, 'Have you ever been to Castle Park?'

'No, I've never got round to it. I gather it's quite impressive. The largest Norman keep in Europe, built on the foundations of a Roman temple.'

'That's the castle itself. The accident occurred in the grounds – which are Victorian.' Nick clearly took pleasure in trumping Paul with his superior local knowledge. Jacqui's skin prickled with discomfort; she prayed she'd not gone red. 'Anyway, I want to see the other man – Jones.'

'It's very late. Can't it wait until the morning? I'm not sure that—'

'He's awake, isn't he? I'm sure he's dying for a chat.' His expression clearly showed that this request was non-negotiable, and it was the doctor's turn to colour, which he did, brightly.

With a resigned sigh, he brushed past Jacqui and left the room, her husband following.

'I'll manage from here, thanks.' Lowry held his hand out towards the doctor's chest at the door of the patient's room. The young doctor had been very helpful and, given the time of night, struck Lowry as remarkably spry. In all his time in hospitals he had seldom come across a doctor so alert as this fellow. Not in the daytime, let alone in the middle of the night. 'Hey, doc, I'm surprised they let you try to grow a beard. Isn't it a health-and-safety risk?' Lowry joked just before the doctor left. He was sure the guy had conditioner shit in his hair. He switched on the small table-light and gently prodded the man in the bed.

'Hey, wake up, sonny Jim.'

'Wha-what time is it?'

'Don't worry about what time it is. You've been in bed plenty long enough.'

Lowry rubbed his jaw thoughtfully. The soldier looked at least twenty-two, maybe older, which surprised him. Usually, town-centre punch-ups involved teenagers – boisterous new recruits mouthing off on a payday, annoying the local lads and stealing their girlfriends. Jones was slight but of a firm, wiry build, and he looked vaguely familiar. Was he one of the Beard's fighters? He knew the dead lad had been.

'How long have you been stationed here, son?'

'Six months.' He blinked rapidly, slowly coming to.

31

'Any trouble before?'

Jones struggled to pull himself up in his bed. His arm was bandaged, as was his head. Lowry adjusted the pillows and passed him some water.

'Thanks. No, no trouble. Clean as a whistle.' Suddenly, his face lit up. ''Ere, you're Lowry, ain't you?'

Lowry nodded slightly in acknowledgement.

'Seen you fight. Pretty tasty. You took the Cup, year before last.'

'You're in the Beard's team?' He'd be around a bantamweight, so there was no chance their gloves would have come into contact.

Self-conscious in his hospital gown, Jones answered shyly, 'Yeah, I've had a bout or two – not in your league, mate.'

Lowry smiled and took the compliment.

'Didn't lay anyone out on New Year's Eve, though, that's for sure,' Lowry said. 'So, what would you put this mishap down to?'

'New Year's celebrations gone a bit far, y'know.' Speaking with a north Essex burr, the man now seemed more relaxed; a connection had been established. 'Off duty, this time of year, get a bit carried away with the booze.'

'Where are you from originally?'

'Hereabouts. Brightlingsea.'

Lowry didn't comment. He knew the place to be a small port, east of Colchester, known for its sailing enthusiasts. His silence prompted the wounded soldier to ask for a smoke.

'Sorry, I just quit. Tell me, wasn't it a bit early to be that plastered?' Lowry picked up the chart at the foot of Jones's bed. He hadn't been at the scene itself on New Year's Eve but knew it had occurred at approximately nine p.m. At the time, it was just one among many incidents reported across the town centre, incidents that would continue into the early hours of the morning. He flicked over the page, and saw the admission time of nine thirty p.m.

'What time did you hit the pub?'

'When it opened at midday.'

'Which one, and who were you with?'

Lowry pulled out his notebook and listened to the man's description of events. Jones, Daley and several others – Lowry noted the names – had kicked off their celebrations in the Bull pub on Crouch Street. The Bull was a cavernous old coaching inn and, significantly for the squaddies, the first cheap pub on the other side of Southway, the carriageway that sliced across the bottom half of the town, with civilians to the north and the main cavalry barracks, the grand red-brick buildings, to the south. Once he was the other side of Southway, a soldier could start to loosen his military shackles. A few pints in the dark, smoky interior of the Bull gave wary young recruits enough Dutch courage to push up Balkerne Hill and on to the town centre, with its Georgian houses, to the hub of the town's nightlife. In this case, they'd had a few in the Bull, a few more in the narrow halfway house of the Boadicea on Headgate, and then on to the Wagon and Horses, a soldiers' favourite at the top of North Hill. From there they left their friends and made their way down the length of the high street on their own.

'Why leave your pals behind in the Wagon and Horses?'

'They wanted to settle in there for the night and we wanted to get down to the Golden Lion to meet two girls.'

The Golden Lion was an 'alternative' pub at the far end of the high street, full of teenagers of all sorts: punks, goths, skinheads and the like. But not soldiers. The Lion was also the nearest pub to the castle.

'Unusual place for two soldiers to go, wouldn't you say?'

'Ordinarily, but I'd been there before I signed up, like. Knew these birds would be there.'

'You're now going to tell me that this whole incident was over a couple of punk-rocker girls?'

'I can't remember, mate.'

He was lying.

Nevertheless, Lowry said, 'I want the names of the girls, and descriptions of your pursuers. As best you can.'

'All right.' Jones yawned. 'Lesley Birch, blonde and cute; and her mate Kelly; don't know her surname.'

'Addresses?'

Lowry noted them down, both Papillon Road in St Mary's. Victorian terrace on the other side of Balkern Gate, up from Crouch Street. The young soldier let out a groan, as though he'd just remembered why he was in hospital.

'So how did the trouble start?'

'Can't remember. Had a few too many beers. We were probably gobby, it being New Year's Eve an' all. Locals use any excuse to take a pop at a soldier. And there were only two of us.'

'How many of them were there?' Lowry's pen was poised over his notebook.

'At least half a dozen. They'd never have the balls to take us on one on one.' This was said proudly, though the bravado was thin. The soldier's pale face and red-rimmed eyes betrayed a young man who'd had a nasty shock.

'So there was a fracas in the Golden Lion and you two scarpered. Why run through the castle grounds?'

'Thought we'd lose them. Close by, and dark in there, innit?'

'Too dark, it would seem.' Lowry bowed his head and closed his notebook.

'You're not wrong.' Jones rubbed his leg and grimaced. 'How's me mate, though? Daley? Nobody's said a word.'

Lowry chose not to break the news of his friend's death: that could wait. The lad looked shattered and needed rest. If this lad wasn't lying – of course he had seen who had chased him – Lowry was not fit to be a policeman, but this policeman was knackered. It could wait.

'We'll come to see you in the morning. You get some sleep.'

5

7 a.m., Saturday, Great Tey village, eight miles west of Colchester

Jacqui Lowry slipped silently into the warm house. She flicked on the kitchen light. Pushkin stirred in the cat basket on top of the fridge freezer. Running a cracked fingernail across the kitchen worktop as a pan slowly warmed on the hob for hot chocolate, she played back the scene from a few hours earlier with Nick and Paul. Bizarrely, it reminded her of when she'd first met Nick, twelve years ago at the hospital, then a good-looking, fit, young detective in a sharp suit. Yes, he'd been immaculate even in the small hours as he hovered over a teenager close to death from suspected poisoning. He stood out, with his sharp dress sense, still fixed in the mod style of the 1960s while everyone else was embracing the flamboyant, hairy 1970s. He was striking, clean and well groomed, with the handsome face to match, but it was his tenderness towards the fifteen-year-old girl that had won her heart. It was what she craved for herself, and she wanted Nick then with every fibre of her body. He was oblivious to her, concerned only with the girl's recovery, which only inflamed her desire. He was still by the teenager's bedside when she finished her shift, but she had felt compelled to slip him her phone number as she left the ward. They went on their first date two nights later, to the nearby Hospital Arms, after she'd finished a late shift. At closing time, Nick walked her the short distance to her parents' house in Lexden, where, at the foot of the garden path, he delivered a heart-stopping kiss, both passionate and tender.

Jacqui poured the milk from the frothing pan and sighed. Nick still wore the mod suits and button-down shirts, but now they just looked out of place and old-fashioned; outmoded symbols of another time and place. The passion and tenderness were equally remote – at least between the two of them.

Upstairs in the bathroom she placed the mug of hot chocolate on the side of the basin and ran the bath. The hot water would take a good minute to feed through. Looking in the mirror, she removed her make-up to reveal the same tired eyes that greeted her after every shift. And, once again, the same as every morning and evening, she wondered why she still did it. As a young staff nurse in her twenties, she had vowed never to end up the way she was now. As a trainee, she had observed the older nurses and witnessed how shiftwork took its toll; most were constantly too tired to do anything about their slipping figures and unhealthy lifestyles – too tired even to care. She pitied them and resolved never to let the same thing happen to her. But then she met Nick Lowry and forgot her concerns for a while. And so the years passed by, they had a son and settled into comfortable dullness. Until, that is, a young intern made a pass at her two years ago. She thought nothing of it to start with and ignored his advances, but then she looked in the mirror and realized she'd become that middle-aged staff nurse she'd always scorned. So she thought: What the hell.

Lowry rolled over in bed. He heard the plug being pulled out of the bath and the water gurgling down. Not for the first time did he think it odd that Jacqui had taken to having a bath before she got into bed. Gone were the days when she'd jump straight in and nuzzle up to him after a shift, freshening up when she woke, at around midday. Maybe it was a dig at him because he'd promised to fit a shower and hadn't? The hot-water pipes in the roof made a hell of noise, enough to wake him. Maybe that was what she wanted. The red LCD display flashed at him from on top of the bedside cabinet with the unwelcome news that it was gone seven. The headless corpse had floated across his subconscious for most of the four hours he'd been in bed. As was often the way, while a visceral scene from one case imposed itself upon him he'd be trying to second-guess another – in this instance, how it was that two soldiers could have been inside the castle grounds at nine o'clock when the gates were locked at six.

Nowadays, Jacqui would sometimes sleep in the spare room if he was still in bed when she came home, especially at the weekend. He heard her pad out of the bathroom and pass on down the hall. He'd need to get up soon and put a call in to the desk sergeant; he wanted to link up with the WPC who'd been first on the scene at Castle Park. No doubt they could arrange with the groundsman to give them access before the park opened to the public.

But not just yet. He'd had a night troubled with strange dreams of floating corpses, and now craved a few minutes of peaceful shut-eye until it was time to get up.

8.05 a.m., The Strood

It was gradually growing light. The mist showed signs of lifting across the marshes as a greyish-crimson light streaked across from the east, but it was bitterly cold. The uniform sergeant had been given clear instructions by Lowry and was barking orders through the icy damp at the huddle of officers looming by the Danger When Tide Covers Footway sign. Kenton, leaning against a Panda car and reduced to the position of observer, felt redundant. Sergeant Barnes's voice carried across the mudflats, disturbing birds who were chattering energetically somewhere in the gloom. The assembled officers split into two groups, and half a dozen men in greatcoats set off precariously along the mainland sea wall, dodging the mudpans hidden by sedge grass, while another six moved to tackle the sea wall on the island itself.

Sergeant Barnes walked stiffly towards the Panda car, which

was parked up on the curb. Kenton moved to greet him by the railing.

'Like a needle in a haystack,' Barnes said, rubbing his hands together briskly.

Kenton looked out across the channel and observed a tea-colour trickle flowing through the mud banks. The tide must be on the way in now, he reasoned, given the hour.

'Not sure what your gaffer expects us to find out there,' the sergeant continued. 'A head ain't going to be sitting waiting for us on those mudflats.'

'We won't know until we look,' Kenton said, having little idea himself. He only knew that Lowry wanted evidence to support the theory that the body had washed in with the tide, so as to rule out it having been deliberately dumped where it was found.

'And looking is mainly what we're doing – through bin-oculars from the shore. That mud out there is waist deep.'

'How long do we have?'

'High tide's not for a good few hours, but it fills quick. If there's anything lying on that mud, now's the time to see it.' The sergeant's helmet strap looked painfully tight, and his face, red with exposure to the elements, had a tortured expression. His fulsome moustache looked stiff with cold.

'Righto. I may as well lend a hand.'

'No need, detective, this is just routine. A job for Uniform.'

'Nonsense – I'm an extra pair of legs.' He'd overheard members of Uniform describe him as soft. When he'd asked Lowry why this was, the inspector had replied it was because he 'speaks nicely'.

'Have you got binoculars?'

Kenton shook his head.

'Then there's not much point; you'll only tread the same path. This really is a job for Uniform.'

The sergeant clearly didn't want Kenton under his feet, but Lowry had been keen for him get out and learn more about the terrain. How could he ever graduate from being the new boy if he was unable to participate? Training courses had taken up much of his time at Queen Street, and he was keen to put his knowledge into practice. But there wasn't much he could do; he was outranked.

After forty-five minutes in the cold, which passed like an eternity, a Green Flash tennis shoe was found in the reeds. It matched the one shoe found on the corpse's feet.

8.25 a.m., Lexden, West Colchester

Ninety-eight, ninety-nine, one hundred! Sparks jumped upright from his press-up position on the deep-pile bedroom carpet and banged his chest aggressively, producing a stentorian cough.

'Darling, must you do that?' came a sleepy reproof from underneath the quilt.

'It's Lane's rotten cheroots from last night,' he said over his shoulder, reaching into the mahogany chest of drawers for a clean vest. 'Never hands out the Cubans,' he muttered to himself. 'Not to me, anyhow – too tight-fisted.'

'Whatever it is you're doing on the floor – it shakes the bed so.' Antonia's luxurious blonde mane was all that was visible to indicate her presence in the bed. 'It is the weekend.'

'Press-ups, Antonia. They're called press-ups. One hundred every morning.' He flexed his biceps in the full-length mirror. Not bad for fifty-four, he thought to himself. 'Until those cowboys have removed their gubbins from the basement, you'll have to grin and bear it.' He lifted the covers to reveal his fiancée's white, fleshy behind and gripped it firmly. 'And once the gym is ready, you could do a lot worse than give it a try.'

She squealed in mock annoyance. Sparks adored Antonia, which was fortunate, as the wedding, his third, was a mere six weeks away. Valentine's Day: how he'd let himself agree to such a saccharine arrangement he had no idea – he still cringed when he was asked the date. But she was twenty years younger than him, and he liked to indulge her. Indeed, he could hardly believe his luck. She came from a well-off family, had a double-barrelled name and, potentially, a plump inheritance – an exceptional trophy for a regional chief of police who had just been through yet another expensive divorce. They had met at a champagne bar in Cowes the August before last; he had been crewing for the police team and she was on the lash with a bunch of toffs who couldn't hold their drink. Bored with the immature Hoorays she'd dated in her twenties, she appreciated his maturity and physique and he her figure and connections. For a moment he considered a bit of horseplay but thought better of it and pulled the blanket back down. There was too much to do.

Firstly, Lowry troubled him – dicking about with those toerag squaddies: so unnecessary. Though Sparks and Lowry had spent a lot of time together, at work and socially, Sparks could not say he knew his detective inspector. To Sparks's mind, Lowry was the model CID officer: physically impressive, handsome, polite, hardworking, well turned out. He had it all. But, on the odd occasion, the chief did wonder; he was such a quiet man, Sparks felt he didn't know what made him tick. The first time this occurred to him was when Lowry was promoted. It was the year Elvis died – seventy-seven, or was it seventy-eight? – and all Nick had said was, 'Jacqui will be pleased.' Make DS in CID at thirty-five, you're the bee's knees, the business, the face in the town; you get the respect from the underclasses without the weight of bureaucracy that comes with the upper ranks. That was it, though – 'Jacqui will be pleased' – not a smile, not a thank you, not a damn thing. Why was the man so remote? What did he have to be so buttoned-up about? Who did he think he was?

The chief dressed quickly. Maybe he had set too much store by Lowry's enthusiasm as a boxer. The man's dedication to the division was admirable – had Sparks, over the years, allowed that to shape his opinion of Lowry? Boxing. Boxing was also very much on his mind, for tomorrow was the first fight of the year. Overzealous or not, he could at least depend on Lowry in the ring.

-6-

9.35 a.m., Saturday, Colchester Road, West Mersea

A deep blue winter sky stretched above the marshland, out of which a blinding low sun burned off the remainder of the mist and gave definition to the filling estuary.

'Bright one, eh, Jace? Could do with some shades!' Felix remarked, flicking down the sun visor as the Land Rover trundled down the East Mersea Road to hook up with the main island artery that would take them on to the Strood and across to Colchester.

Boyd filtered into the road they'd been unable to use the night before, behind a dingy trailer. The mudflats glistened in the early-morning light like cooling chocolate. 'Wonder what that's all about?' he said to himself as they passed a man in a trench coat, surrounded by several uniformed police, examining the wooden guardrail.

Whatever it was it had pushed them back further. Boyd wouldn't admit it to Felix, but this delay worried him. Last night, when they'd picked up the Landy from the barn where they'd left it, he'd shrugged off his concerns, especially after the ordeal of bobbing around on the Blackwater for hours. All he'd wanted was to get on dry land. Even getting turned back by the police seemed a blessed relief at the time. Now, in the cold light of day, things took on a different perspective. They were late. New Year's Eve had been and gone without the bang many had expected them to deliver, and Jason Boyd was feeling decidedly edgy.

9.45 a.m., Castle Park, Colchester

The castle was a two-minute walk up from Queen Street police station into the centre of town. Colchester town centre, like all old settlements, sat on a rise, and the castle to the east commanded an unbroken view of the northern suburbs beyond its grounds. On the plateau surrounding the keep itself were elegant Victorian gardens, shaped within ornate ironwork and with careful topography. The northern edge boasted a large bandstand that was still used throughout the summer. Lowry jumped up on to it for a better view. The sharp sunlight caused the light dusting of frost on the manicured grass to sparkle. The grounds below sloped dramatically down to reach the border of the north wall, which was a Roman construction, part of the original settlement, which was shallow on this side but masked a treacherous twenty-foot drop on the other. Anyone who chose to run headlong down this steep incline on a dark icy night must've been pretty determined. Your average pub brawl could get nasty, reflected Lowry, but it would have to be pretty extreme to induce anyone to take this kind of kamikaze path.

He didn't have long to assess the situation – he needed to be at the mortuary in half an hour to discuss the headless corpse with Robinson, the pathologist – so a quick perusal would have to do. He didn't fancy trying to run it himself.

'Inspector!' a WPC called up to him. 'Inspector Lowry, I have the groundsman here. Wanting to know if he can go.'

'Right.' He hopped down. A man of about sixty in a park keeper's uniform shrugged apologetically at Lowry. 'Sorry, guv. I have to sort out the park before opening the gates.'

'Sure. Thanks for letting us in,' smiled Lowry. 'Tell me, do you often get intruders in the park?'

'Occasionally, in the summer. We sometimes find beer cans and the like. It's probably teenagers.'

'If you were to come from the pub, the Golden Lion, how would you get in?'

'Over the west wall.'

'And is it difficult to get over?'

'Not really. I could manage myself if I 'ad to, so no problem for a pair of soldiers.' He scratched the back of his head, pushing his grey cap forward. 'Tragic, what happened.' The WPC had filled him in on the soldier's death.

Lowry nodded in agreement but said nothing.

46

The man continued, 'Do you want me to show yer the wall?'

'No, thanks, the constable here will manage.' The grounds-man nodded and hurried away towards the castle.

'He didn't want to hang around,' Lowry said to the WPC, who'd been on duty the night the soldier fell and at the scene shortly after.

'No,' she agreed, moving off briskly towards the lower park. 'I'll show you where I found them.'

'Whoa, there!' Lowry said hastily, almost grabbing the sleeve of her uniform. He wanted to run the show here. 'Let's start from the west wall, or thereabouts, and follow the route they would have taken.'

They walked to the north-east corner of the castle. The east wall below them was within view, beyond a row of poplars. The distance the lads would have covered was, he reckoned, a good five hundred yards – all downhill.

'Is the death suspicious, sir?'

'Call me Lowry, please.' The ivy-clad wall was about chest height, easy enough to vault. He turned to his colleague. 'It's sensitive. The military connection makes it sensitive.'

She stood a little way away, underneath the poplars.

'Right,' he said. 'Let's follow their trajectory. Lead on.'

Lowry almost lost his footing on the slope; the ground was frozen solid. The frosted grass slipped like silk against the soles of his leather shoes. The tall WPC was ahead of him, looking rather ungainly as she tried to keep her balance.

'Jesus,' he said under his breath. 'Tell me the sequence of

events again. You arrived on the scene at what – just after nine p.m.?'

'Yes.' She didn't slow down or turn to address him, forcing him to try to keep up. 'My unit was on patrol, and a passerby had found Private Jones clinging at the gate on Ryegate Road, yelling for help from inside the park. The other one – I forget his name – we couldn't see him from the road. It's dark in here at night.'

'Was Jones intoxicated?'

'Drunk? I don't think so – I didn't really ask if he'd been drinking, to be honest. He was in a lot of pain and was whisked off as soon as the ambulance arrived.'

'Of course. The gate on Ryegate Road was locked?'

'Yes. I climbed over. WPC Walker remained in the car.'

'And what was your immediate response on arriving on the scene?'

The WPC paused. She looked at the frosted grass. 'It was very dark. The path was unlit. I found the other soldier at the bottom of the wall about two hundred yards down the path. He was seriously hurt. Unconscious.'

She and Lowry meandered cautiously across the park until they reached the perimeter, where they followed the Roman wall to their left. The ground had levelled out but started to rise again towards the far corner, where the soldiers had fallen. The ruined wall was as low as four feet in places and as high as twenty in others, though this was not apparent from the castle side, as the contour of the grounds swept up to meet the ruins. You could only work out the true height from the other side, where a footpath ran along the base of the wall.

A brick wall ran down the east side of the hill and cut the Roman north wall off at the point of the greatest drop. A large oak tree was situated at the apex of the rise, masking the drop behind it. Lowry crouched at the edge and looked at the path below. It would be like jumping out of a first-floor window: dangerous but survivable. Perhaps.

He stood up to meet his colleague's pale blue eyes.

'Funny place to make your escape, wouldn't you say?' he asked.

The woman, who he now noticed was taller than him, removed her cap, revealing short, bleached-blond hair. 'Is it? If you're running in a blind panic, would you notice? Would you stop to think?'

'In a blind panic, I guess not.'

'I'm just surprised they didn't break their necks on the way down,' she said.

'These boys have seen active service in the Falklands. I guess their training equipped them for it.'

'So, if they're such brave soldiers, why were they so scared of a bunch of lads from the pub?'

'Seems a reach, I admit.' He started back towards the castle. 'But most people are frightened of something, no matter how tough they are.'

10 a.m., Saturday, Beaumont Terrace, Greenstead Estate

Boyd swung the Land Rover left off the main road, looking for an address he'd memorized three nights ago.

'Keep your eyes peeled for Beaumont Terrace. All these council places look the same and it's easy to miss the poxy road name. It's like a goddamn maze.'

And this one *was* a labyrinth. On the east side of Colchester, the Greenstead Estate was the biggest in the area and still growing. Not that Boyd knew it personally; it was by reputation only: dealers claimed it had all the makings of a junkie's mecca.

'Right. At fucking last.' He sighed wearily.

'Houses look smart – which is more than you can say for the motors,' Felix said, eyeing a Hillman on bricks. 'Sure this is the right place?'

'Hmm. These houses may be pretty new, but most of the people inside haven't got two pennies to rub together.' He grimaced. 'London overspill. They shove 'em down here, but to do what?' And though the knackered Land Rover was a good ten years older than most of the rusting jalopies lining the street – even those without wheels – he was conscious that it might attract attention, being more at home on a farm, so he parked a couple of doors up from their destination.

'Come on,' said Boyd. He popped open the Land Rover door and made his way towards the house across the empty concrete drive. A sharp bang made him jump.

'Jesus, Felix, don't slam the door like that! You trying to tell every bastard in the street we're here?' Boyd occasionally forgot how dim his partner was, until Felix did something to remind him. Why Fred had insisted that Jason have him tag along was beyond him. If they got caught because of this wally, well . . . He pressed the doorbell, but of course it didn't work so he rapped on the patterned glass, nervously looking behind him as the rattle echoed in the street. The seconds passed slowly; no movement from within.

They were late and they hadn't been able to get hold of their contact – he'd tried calling from the Dog and Pheasant. He didn't expect an answer last night, being New Year's Eve, but did think he'd have better luck this morning, but no. What should they do? Boyd drummed his fingers on the door frame. Fuck. Fuck. What were they going to do with a hundred kilos of gear? Hiding such a quantity, keeping it dry and out of harm's way, not to mention avoiding the police . . . Still, that's what they were being paid for: the risk. That's what middlemen do. Fuck . . .

The door opened a crack.

'At fucking last,' said a voice with a wide Essex accent from behind the chain guard.

'Freddie?' Boyd asked, unconvinced.

'Freddie? No, Freddie ain't here.' The door opened more fully. It was Stone. Jesus. In his twenties, thin, with a mesh of permed hair, Derek Stone looked like a typical casual with his white Tacchini tracksuit, but he was in fact some sort of musician and played in a jazz club. 'Come on through,' he said, stomping off down the narrow hallway, beckoning with a hand raised behind him. Why wasn't Freddie here? Boyd hesitated. Stone was okay, but he was weird . . . He wasn't happy about this. But before he had a chance to consider their position, Felix had gone in too.

'Any chance of a brew?' he said cheerily, following Stone. 'I'm parched.'

Boyd looked incredulous as his partner disappeared gaily down the hallway. He had no option but to follow. They were led into a spartan kitchen at the back of the house.

'So where's Freddie?' Boyd asked.

'He's not here,' Stone said. 'He was here at seven o'clock last night, as arranged. You're well late. So I'm here instead.'

'So, you got the money?' Boyd demanded, dumping the rucksack on the lino floor. 'Here's the gear.'

'It ain't here.'

'What's the score, then?'

Stone plonked the kettle on the hob. 'We were giving you

up for lost. Thought you'd been nicked. So we were about to split – lucky you turned up, like. We'll get you yer readies, but you'll have to wait.'

'Who's "we?"'

'Philpott – he'll be along in a bit,' he said, leaning against the kitchen units, his arms folded across his chest.

Philpott? Who the fuck was he?

'You're mighty late, ain't ya?'

'Yeah, well . . . we ran into difficulty, but we're here now. It's all there.'

At least Stone was here, someone they knew. Freddie had mentioned bringing him in to help out.

'Yeah, you'll have to wait,' Stone repeated needlessly. Was he trying to wind Boyd up?

'So we were late – big deal!' Though he knew it was a big deal: New Year's Eve was New Year's Eve. He had to front it out. 'Have you checked out the state of the North Sea lately? Why isn't the money here? You're fucking here, aren't you? So where's our fucking cash?'

Stone made a placatory gesture. 'Look, you'll get your money. I need to go and make a call. Sit down and make yourselves at home.'

Boyd looked around. This wasn't anyone's home – it was a squat, an empty house used for dealing. As if Freddie'd've hung around here.

Stone slipped a denim jacket on over his tracksuit.

'Where you off to?' Felix asked.

'Told you, I need to make a call, to see about your cash . . .' Stone smiled, and said, 'So, yeah, calm down, man, job done. Take a breather, eh?'

'Okay, okay,' said Boyd. 'Have you got any grub? I'm famished.' He was beat. He pulled out a chair from under the kitchen table.

'No, mate, sorry, but don't worry. Just wait here while I make a couple of calls. Everything'll be fine.'

Now it was a couple of calls. Boyd was too exhausted to argue.

10.05 a.m., Southway, Colchester

WPC Jane Gabriel had felt awkward in Castle Park with the CID inspector. She was shy and reserved around authority figures – even with the aunt whose idea it had been that she join the police force (and she was family). When Lowry had asked for her 'immediate response' on finding Private Daley at the foot of the castle wall, he had been searching for a clue, a suggestion as to what had happened, anything to form a picture, to confirm it had been an accident. And what had she said? 'It was very dark.' She had answered honestly, and hadn't been able to think of anything more to say, anything that could help. She felt herself blush at the thought of it as she sat next to him now in the car, looking at her pale hands in her lap in unnoticed embarrassment. She wished he'd turn the radio on. All the PCs she partnered on patrol would put music on, which meant she could avoid conversation without the silence being uncomfortable.

As a teenager, Gabriel's height and striking looks had caused her to stand out at school, where, at the end of the sixth form, she had been spotted by a model-agency scout who was doing the rounds. At first, the horror of being the centre of attention appalled her, but then she rationalized that she wouldn't have to speak, just listen and look pretty for the camera. And, for all her self-doubts, there was no denying she was beautiful. She thought modelling might give her confidence and act as a counterpoint to her natural awkwardness and shyness. Everything was fine at first, and she earned decent money – catalogues to start with, eventually graduating to the catwalk. But it all went horribly wrong one autumn in Rome, when a collection was badly received. The designer threw a hissy fit, calling her performance into question. A humiliating critique of her appearance and poise led her to believe that the failure of the show was her fault. In an instant, all the good modelling had done to improve her self-esteem was shattered. She caught the next flight home and, six months later, under the guidance of her aunt, she had started to train for the police force, where she thought she might do some good. Her natural shyness might have been a problem, but she found that the uniform provided a barrier of anonymity and at the same time gave her authority. The young constables were easy enough to deal with – there was harmless flirting and the odd wolf whistle, but that was it. She was older than most, and generally taller, too, and working with them didn't trouble her. But Lowry was different – he put her on edge – or it wasn't that exactly; he'd scarcely paid her any attention. Come to think about it, that was it: he didn't pay her any attention whatsoever. It was that she found different.

Lowry pulled the car into a cul-de-sac off Hospital Road, at the back entrance to Essex General, which housed the morgue in its basement. The bright winter morning didn't make the Victorian building any less imposing. 'Okay. I'll go downstairs,' he said. 'You nip across to the accident ward and check that our boy hasn't gone anywhere, then come and find me.'

'Gone anywhere?'

'Been transferred to Abbey Fields,' Lowry explained. WPC Gabriel looked confused. 'The army takes care of its own,' he added.

'But the military hospital has been shut for years!'

'It's only officially closed – to the public, that is. Some wards are still functional. Then there's the unit at the Military Correctional Training Centre – the Glasshouse – which can provide emergency care. That's tricky to get into, too, even for us.'

'Oh, I didn't realize it was so . . . complicated,' she said.

Once they were inside the building, Gabriel took the broad tiled passageway through to the wards and Lowry the stairs to the basement.

It took Gabriel a good five minutes to get from one side of the hospital to the other, only to be greeted by a rude and steely matron who informed her that Private Jones had been wheeled out that morning by his uniformed colleagues. When asked where to, the woman, who wore a grey bun so tight it looked painful, said sharply, 'It's the army. We don't ask.'

-8-

10.15 a.m., Saturday, Colchester General Hospital, morgue

Lowry could smell the sea on the body.

'Could it have been a propeller?' he asked.

'Yes. It's possible. Though quite a size.'

The recovery of the missing tennis shoe suggested that the body had come in on the tide. They'd run checks from as far north as Harwich to as far south as Deal in Kent and no emergencies at sea had been reported. 'How big?'

Dr Robinson pushed back his spectacles to rest on his crown. 'Big enough that the curvature of the blade would give a straight cut, like this.' He moved his hand in a chopping motion. 'All propellers are contoured to enable them to slice the water efficiently and thus propel the vessel forward.'

'Or to slice a body.'

'Quite. And it has happened before.' He nodded. There had, over the years, been numerous boating accidents in the estuary – drownings, people knocked off boats, drunk fishermen clowning around, even a waterskier run over.

'This fellow hadn't been dressed for the sea though,' said Robinson, prodding the Green Flash tennis shoe sitting on top of the clothes placed to one side in a steel tray. 'The jeans and shoes are branded, but the polo top and jumper have labels I am not familiar with.'

Lowry took out the tennis shoe and Levi jeans. Inside the polo top, he couldn't make anything out other than *made in Indonesia*, but on the jumper label, above a large *L* he read *Größe/Size*. 'Germany? Wonder what he was up to?'

There was nothing to give a clue to his identity. The trouser pockets had yielded only loose change and a cigarette lighter – no wallet or driver's licence.

'Well, dressed like this, he wouldn't have survived more than a few minutes in the North Sea at this time of year. Not enough water in the lungs to suggest he drowned first. You've found the other shoe, I gather. Presumably, it came loose in the sea, the sock on this foot was almost off . . .'

'Wait a sec. These coins.' Lowry pushed them around in the holding dish with a pen, 'These are German marks. Interesting. What about the stomach contents? Wonder where he had his last meal.'

'Well, let's take a peek.' Robinson ran his hands though his thick grey hair and rolled up his sleeves.

Lowry appreciated his eagerness but couldn't confess to

sharing it. He watched him select a scalpel. 'Any amount of time in the water will soften the flesh – see? Like butter . . .'

WPC Gabriel appeared in Lowry's peripheral vision. 'Ah, there you are. Jones still there?'

'No, he's gone.'

'Oh. Where've you been, then?'

'I . . . I, err, was just finding my way across the hospital—'

'How interesting,' the pathologist suddenly remarked to himself.

Lowry swung back to see the doctor excitedly examining a blueish foot.

'This man suffered from terribly calloused feet.'

Hardly earth-shattering, Lowry thought. 'What about his stomach?'

'Patience, dear fellow, patience,' he murmured. 'You'll have my report by the evening, I promise. Call me at six.'

11.30 a.m., Queen Street HQ

Sparks flipped open the bulging manila folder of briefing notes, left for him by Sergeant Granger on Friday evening. As was his habit on Saturday mornings, he was in his office at the top of the Queen Street HQ, taking stock of the week's cases.

He sighed as he struggled to make out Lowry's spidery handwriting. Why the devil couldn't he use a typewriter? The body washed up on the Strood did not particularly trouble him, as long as it was just that – 'washed up' – and not anyone he need worry about from his own district. And if Lowry was not too finicky, as he could sometimes be, they could forget about it in a week or so . . . but the incident at the castle was another matter. He had plenty of time to work out his angle. He knew it was protocol to notify County in Chelmsford, but he'd be damned if he'd allow them to interfere on this one; he knew how to deal with military – they did not. As it happened, he would see Merrydown, the assistant chief constable, tonight at a gala dinner in Chelmsford, but he'd defer any shop talk until Monday morning. Yes, he'd buy himself some time and deal with any consequences later; no need to make an evening with his prim superior any more unpleasant than it would undoubtedly be.

He felt an icy draught from behind him and went over to check the sash window. It was closed as far as it would go, leaving a gap you could post a letter through. Why the hell could they not modernize this creaking relic of a building? He gave up on the window, annoyed by the glare of an unexpected morning sun, and glanced below to see two army jeeps trundle across St Botolph's roundabout, going south towards the garrison, where several thousand men would know that one of their number was dead.

There was a light rap at the door.

'Come,' he said absently.

'Morning, sir.'

Sparks spun round upon hearing the welcome voice of Granger. 'Granger, good news, I hope?'

'No news, but I do have the fixtures for tomorrow night.'

'Aha, yes!' Sparks clapped his hands in anticipation and relieved Granger – reliable heavyweight and three-times champion, now retired – of several sheets of foolscap. The worry about the dead soldier was parked in an instant: boxing – and it was the first fight of the year – was a military concern of a different kind. 'So what has that pompous bastard got to offer us this year, eh?'

He scanned the names impatiently. The Colchester Services league operated four broad categories: bantam, welter, middle and heavy – not strictly WBF, as it ignored the extremities at either end of the weight scale, since neither force had suitable candidates. There were a few new names in the lower bands, some of which he recognized, having been tipped off that they were promising by a uniformed recruit who socialized with military NCOs. Then he came to the middleweight category. One name was missing.

'Where's Lowry?'

'Sorry, sir?'

'Inspector Lowry – he's not on the fixture.'

Granger looked at the chief in surprise. 'Why, he's retired, sir.'

'"Retired"? How do you mean, he's *retired*?'

'I guess for the usual reason people retire. Too old?'

'I know what the bloody word means, Granger.' Sparks gave him a withering look and tossed the papers on the desk. 'I don't care if he's due a telegram from the fucking queen. Nobody retires unless I say so.'

11.45 a.m., Beaumont Terrace, Greenstead Estate

Jason Boyd checked his watch. What time had he made the call – ten, ten thirty? Shit, he didn't know. Freddie was nowhere to be found, according to Stone, but a bloke called Philpott was supposed to sort them out. He looked across at Derek Stone, who was long since back and sitting at the kitchen table, smoking and nodding his head along to the tinny buzz from a Walkman. What did he look like? A football casual. The country was awash in brightly coloured shell suits: a nation taken over by deranged clowns, like this wally opposite him.

'How much longer we stayin' 'ere, Jace?' Felix asked anxiously, spinning an empty mug on the Formica worktop. Boyd ignored him. They had no alternative but to sit tight – what else could they do? They could hardly take the gear back to where it came from . . . God, he felt exhausted – he hadn't had a decent night's sleep for days; though they'd got into the Dog and Pheasant all right, he'd spent the remainder of the night awake, fretting about today. 'How much longer, eh, Jace?' Felix repeated. Stone was tapping his feet in time with the muffled music. 'Eh, Jace?'

Boyd lunged at Stone and yanked off his headphones, catching the corner of the ashtray, which went spinning across the table and clattered noisily to the floor. 'Stop that, all right! Tapping your goddamn feet!'

'Jesus, man, you only had to—'

'Shut the fuck up, okay? Where's this Philpott geezer with our money?'

Stone straightened his tracky top and lit another fag. 'He's on his way, man, on his way . . .'

But Boyd wasn't listening. The adrenalin he'd been running on had dissipated now they'd come to a grinding halt. 'Where's the coffee?' he demanded, throwing open the cupboards that lined the kitchen walls. They yielded nothing apart from a packet of rice and a box of Frosties. 'Does anyone actually live in this house? I need a coffee bad.'

'Ain't none. No one lives 'ere; empty council place – a doss house. Got tea though? Or a lager – Special Brew?'

Boyd slumped dejectedly against the fridge and lit a cigarette. He was low on fags, too. He pinched the bridge of his nose and sighed in weary resignation.

'Wonder what it's like, you know, the gear?' Stone asked, fiddling with the controls on his Walkman. Felix glanced at Boyd, his eyes dark through lack of sleep.

'Never you mind,' Boyd snapped.

'All right,' Stone said, slipping his headphones back on, 'but if it's what I think it is, and it's a pick-me-up you're after . . .'

A rap on the door.

'There you go.' Stone leapt up to open the back door and let in a skinny middle-aged bloke with short hair and long sideburns.

'Jesus, who the hell are you?'

'Now, now,' Stone placated, shaking his perm out of his eyes. 'This is Philpott.'

'All right, mate?' Philpott thrust out a knobbly hand. He was in his late thirties or early forties, and looked worn, but hard.

Boyd took an instant dislike to him. 'You got our cash?'

The man seemed not hear and, instead, spying the dirty green rucksacks slumped in the corner, made his way over to them.

'Freddie'll be along with the money soon,' he said and, impressively, picked one up single-handedly, 'but, in the meantime, let's check that the merchandise was worth the wait, eh?'

9

Midday, Saturday, Queen Street HQ

As Lowry jogged up the stairs to the first floor he pondered on the headless corpse in the morgue; if it was a German national, what was the correct course of action to take? Although there was no ID, the foreign currency was a good enough reason to think it. He figured that he was duty bound to notify Interpol and should do so before they issued a statement to the press. He crossed the cramped main office. The 1970s partitioning of the Victorian room was a design eyesore, but it did afford CID some privacy at the front of the building, along with the benefit of the huge sash windows. Although freezing cold in winter and like a greenhouse in summer, Lowry far preferred the sunny space he shared with Kenton to the dingy inner section.

The pair nodded perfunctorily to each other as Lowry pulled out a small wooden chair and joined Kenton at the rickety desk. It was a standing joke that the furniture in their section had come from a school fire sale – it was certainly small enough, and just about fitted in the restricted space. From his desk tray Lowry took out a sheet of foolscap and wrote: *The Strood: body*. He chewed on his pen. There was precious little to add. *Severely calloused feet*: it meant something to the good doctor on a technical level, probably to do with the effect of salt water, but nothing to Lowry. In desperation, he scribbled, *Uncomfortable shoes? Likes walking?*

He stretched back in the chair. He decided he ought to consult with Sparks on what action to take.

'Gaffer in?' he asked Kenton, who was typing.

'Yes, and he's not happy,' Kenton replied, not looking up.

'He's never happy,' Lowry said nonchalantly. He stretched across to his colleague's side of the desk and swiped a Wombles mug, swigging from the contents. Lukewarm. But he downed the rest of the coffee regardless: he needed it. The years when he could easily run on four hours' sleep for several nights were over. Was it age? Or packing up the fags?

'You should go up, guv, seriously, before the press meeting.'

'That's why I'm here,' Lowry replied. 'But what's he fretting about? Is it the headless corpse or the dead soldier?'

'Neither.' Kenton lifted his gaze from the paperwork on his desk.

Lowry looked perplexed.

'It's the boxing.'

DC Daniel Kenton removed his spectacles to wipe the lenses, watching the blurred shape of his superior stride out of the office on his way to visit Sparks at the top of the building. He examined the lenses. They looked clear enough, although he felt they were constantly smudged. Maybe a trip to the opticians was in order; he'd not been since college.

Kenton had been at Colchester for a mere three months. An outstanding graduate, he had been fast-tracked through the force; after just a year in uniform he had already realized his dream to join CID. This was no easy task for one so young, and it was especially surprising that he'd been accepted at Colchester division. As a rule, Sparks turned his nose up at educated types with little on-the-job experience, but Kenton knew the real reason he'd had such a smooth ride – his college boxing record.

He breathed on the lenses again and rubbed vigorously. Although he'd prefer not to spend his spare time getting the crap punched out of him, it did keep him fit and, to be honest, he had nothing better to do. But Lowry's decision to quit had surprised him. Kenton, though proudly his own man, was surreptitiously in awe of his senior officer – a man very different from himself; a man he would never think of as a role model. It was difficult to pinpoint why exactly. On the surface, the DI was to him the coolest, sharpest chap in the building. It was strange the effect he had. Lowry was not remotely fashion conscious; indeed, sartorially, Kenton's boss was in another era entirely – but it was the way he carried it off, perhaps, and his manner, so self-effacing, never bragging or boasting about his successes, be it in the ring or on casework. Everything was done in a matter-of-fact, orderly fashion, without fuss. Yes, now that Lowry had quit the ring, Kenton had started to have misgivings himself, and he might well have jacked it in, too, had the subject not proved such a good conversation starter. When he'd caught the eye of the tall, attractive blonde WPC in the canteen queue the other day, she had asked if he was a boxer and expressed an interest in coming to the opening bout at the cavalry barracks. It had taken him by surprise: he could hardly believe that the girl who was the talk of the locker room – and known for being aloof – had spoken to him. If excitement about this year's opener could penetrate even her ice-cool exterior, then it was something worth being involved in. And it was true: the station was well and truly abuzz with talk of this year's contest and the age-old rivalry between the police and the army. It was a great tradition. But the fight and WPC Gabriel were tomorrow night, and today he had Mersea Island to contend with . . . He looked down once again at the barely legible handwritten police report on his desk. He squinted at the paperwork in front of him.

Kenton had yet to work with the island police, but he'd heard they were a law unto themselves and had operated as they did since the 1950s. It was run by a character out of a Dickens novel, Sergeant 'Dodger' Bradley, a curmudgeonly policeman on the cusp of retirement (hence 'coffin dodger') who refused to move with the times. Bradley was of the old school, where paperwork – if any were produced – remained on the island. Scant attention was paid to the new ruling on County remittances through Colchester. As the wind rattled the sash windows, Kenton was inclined to think Colchester itself hardly had the feel of a station firmly in the later half of the twentieth century.

'But I'm too old.'

Sparks frowned at his detective inspector. 'Bollocks,' he replied.

'But I am,' said Lowry wearily.

'Listen to yourself. Cooper was thirty-six when he fought Bugner.'

'He lost.'

'Pah!' Sparks batted away the objection. 'The referee was a wanker, everyone knows that. But, win or lose, you must agree it was close?'

'It was close.'

'And how old was Bugner?' He waited for an answer, though he didn't need to ask – they'd spoken of this fight many times before. Bugner was one of several bare-chested fighters, along with Henry Cooper and stars from his own police team, whose framed portraits adorned the walls of the chief's attic office.

'Twenty-one.'

Sparks nodded, then decided to try a change of tack. 'Listen, Nick,' he soothed, 'maybe you just need to have a rest, take a break?'

'I'm fine – I just fancy doing something different . . . I—'

'I've got it. Perhaps you're going through a mid-life crisis?' Of course, that was it! He remembered those years vividly himself – that difficult, restless transition into middle age, full of regret and self-doubt. Sparks reached for his Embassy, pleased to have found a logical explanation.

Lowry frowned. 'Wha—?'

'Yes, that's it. Explains all that shit about giving up smoking, too.'

'I hardly think . . . Anyway, never mind all that. The headless corpse on the Strood – I think it could be a German.'

Sparks's expression relaxed. 'The Hun, eh?'

Lowry cringed at the term. It was something Sparks's adversary Brigadier 'the Beard' Lane might say. Not that Sparks would ever accept he'd been influenced.

'So what makes you think that?'

'German coins in his jeans.'

'Aren't we jumping to conclusions somewhat?' Sparks replied. 'Maybe he'd just come back from holiday.'

'Maybe, but some of the clothing has what look to be foreign labels. One, I'm pretty sure, is made in Germany.' He paused, then added, 'So, do we notify Interpol before we make a statement? Sergeant Barnes has checked up and down the coast, and no accidents have been reported . . .'

Sparks pondered. 'Call Special Branch first. See if you can squeeze any missing-persons info from those slippery bastards. It would be a first, but go through the motions. And the soldier?'

Lowry hesitated before speaking. 'The kid's lying. He knows who chased them.'

Sparks frowned. 'Of course he does.' He stood up and turned to the window. 'This is a delicate case: I need it wrapped up pronto and slipped past the press. Otherwise, the Beard will cause merry hell.'

'You may want to ask him why he moved the surviving boy so swiftly.'

Sparks turned. 'Ah. Didn't I tell you he would do that? That's why I told you to get over there last night. Fuck it, I don't care. If he's moved him, he can hardly expect us to find out who's responsible. Pompous git.'

The two men looked at one another.

'Okay, get on to the Red Caps. They'll know where the little shit's been moved to.'

'Will do. The boy gave the name of witnesses, though: two girls. I've given it to WPC Gabriel – who found them – to check out.'

'Good. Keep me posted.'

Lowry made as if to go, but the chief held up his hand to detain him. 'Listen, Lowry. Go on holiday, or have an affair – I don't care which – anything to get your mojo back. Frankly, I don't give a toss what you do, but I want you back in the ring.'

2 p.m., Great Tey

Jacqui woke in the early afternoon. Usually at the end of a row of nights, she would follow a set routine: a couple of hours' catnap, get up at noon, mooch around a bit, take it easy and try to slip into conventional hours. But today was Saturday and she was off now until Monday, so, like ordinary people with a whole weekend to relax, she'd allowed herself to sleep in. And what was more, tonight – Saturday night, New Year's Day – she was going out.

Slipping out from under the eiderdown, she slunk lazily downstairs to make a coffee. She glanced at the kitchen clock: ten past two. At four o'clock her mother would appear with her son, and at half six Nick would be back to take over, so she could be ready in good time for her night on the town. Propped against the kettle was a note from Nick: *Will call at 4. x*

She knew there were plenty of things she should be doing, but if nobody was going to trouble her until four, then, what the hell, she'd sneak in another hour or so in bed. Tonight was going to be a big one, so she might as well get all the rest she could. She yawned, took the kettle off the hob and went back upstairs to bed with a smile.

10

3.30 p.m., Saturday, Beaumont Terrace, Greenstead Estate

Boyd was totally wired. He'd never felt more alive. Drugs – the magic, the sheer fucking magic of drugs. He sat, now with Stone's headphones on, at the badly marked kitchen table dusted with white powder. The Walkman was blasting out some jazz shit – correction: jazz *funk*, as Stone kept repeating – Level 47 or something. If he heard the twat dribble the word 'fusion' in his face one more time, he'd garrotte him with the headphone cable. It was shite, even on drugs. He pressed the fast-forward button and got up from the table.

He looked at the other two, who were burbling inanely at each other over a card game. A half-bottle of Johnny Walker now stood empty between them. Boyd felt suddenly restless. Philpott had long since disappeared; why or where, Boyd couldn't recall. Jesus, being cooped up like this was doing his head in. He stared through the grimy window at the bright day outside. He was thirsty as hell. Time had skipped on, and he couldn't believe they were stuck there until Freddie returned with their readies, as this bloke Philpott reckoned he would. Philpott. Where the hell was he?

Heaven 17 burst on to the Walkman and Boyd found himself frantically drumming his fingers on the stainless-steel draining board. '(We Don't Need This) Fascist Groove Thang' – yeah, this was better, much better! The industrial pounding resonated through his skull, and the song's strange lyrics whizzed around his head, repeating over and over and over again until it became too much. Fucking twelve-inch remixes! He tore off the headphones. 'I'm going out to get a drink,' he announced.

But first another line. He picked up the combat knife from the worktop and carved a slice of whizz from the mound on the table. It felt like more than speed – it had a strangely potent kick to it. It must be quality stuff, and no doubt whoever it belonged to would take a very dim view of them helping themselves. But it was such a small amount surely no one would notice. How much had they done – a couple of quid's worth each? He spliced a finger's length and hoovered the lot with a rolled pound note.

A1! Top dog! He felt magnificent. Felix and Stone were still blathering at one another, paying him no attention. That was it – he couldn't resist it. He was taking the shit with him. He carved off a sizable wrap into the curled note, folding it as quickly as he could, but it seemed to take forever. But the pair were still oblivious, and he smiled as he tucked the drugs into his jeans and slowly made his way towards the back door, a warm surge rushing through him and making him feel unsteady. He stopped on the threshold, suddenly uncertain. He didn't know the local terrain. Perhaps it was best if they stuck together. A bolt of paranoia hit him with the cold January air.

'Oi, you two,' he said. 'Fancy a drink?'

4.02 p.m., Queen Street HQ

Lowry placed the receiver back in its cradle. It was just gone four o'clock and already dark outside. At his back he felt the damp creeping in; a single-pane window was the only thing between him and the freezing afternoon.

He glanced at the young DC opposite, head down, his attention once more on paperwork. Lowry's mind turned over the phone conversation he'd just had with his wife. Did he care that their plan to spend New Year's Day night together had been shelved? He hated forced jollity, but he loved his wife and wanted to spend time with her. He kicked himself – he should make more of an effort. It wasn't the same as New Year's Eve, granted, but it would have been a nice start to the year. He remembered the last time they saw in the New Year together, at the end of the last decade. They'd argued: he'd wanted to stay in but she'd insisted on going to a party. He gave in, to keep her happy, and had hated every minute: the crowded room, the squealing doctors and nurses, the sheer *noise*. They had left at one, not speaking. No wonder she had arranged to go out with her pals tonight. Jacqui claimed she'd told him already that she had made plans, but he couldn't for the life of him remember. That wouldn't be unusual, by any means. As for all the shit Sparks had lectured him on, about a mid-life crisis – God! Advice from a man embarking on his third marriage to a woman half his age – if that wasn't a mid-life crisis he didn't know what was. Not trading in boxing gloves for binoculars, in his book . . .

'Blimey, now there's a look of consternation!' The jovial Sergeant Barnes had appeared in the office doorway and recoiled in mock horror. Lowry noticed that his hand was still on the receiver; he pulled it away and refocused on Barnes and Kenton, who hadn't stirred from his report.

'Ready when you are,' said Barnes.

'For what?' asked Lowry.

'The chief wants to run through the press briefing.'

Damn, he'd forgotten to check in with Special Branch. 'Give me five minutes with this fella.' He nodded towards Kenton.

'Right you are, inspector,' Barnes said, then jogged Kenton's shoulder. 'Thawed out yet, sonny?'

Kenton spun round. 'It may have helped if you'd let me do something instead of leaving me to stand there like a pillock.'

'Didn't want your nice clothes getting muddy, did we?' Barnes chuckled, shaking the detective's shoulder playfully before taking his leave.

Kenton rolled his eyes. 'As if.'

'Quite,' Lowry said, flicking through his Rolodex for the

Special Branch number. 'It's not as though that sports jacket's long for this world.'

'That's not what I . . . What do you mean?'

'Graeme Garden would be at home in that, what with the elbow patches.'

Kenton frowned.

'Lighten up. He likes you! Be thankful for it.' He dialled the number and held his hand up to silence the objecting Kenton as it rang. Lowry knew his young detective had had a difficult early morning, but he needed him not to take it too seriously. It was important to get on with the likes of Barnes, who'd been in uniform for over twenty years.

The number continued to ring. Eventually, it went through to the Scotland Yard switchboard. He was put on hold.

'All right, instead of scowling at me,' Lowry said finally, 'get on down to Mersea and tie up the post-office job from last week. Nail the witness statements. I'm going to be tied up here for the next couple of hours.' Lowry thought Kenton would like that, to be trusted to go out on his own. But if he found the likes of Barnes condescending, he was in for a shock down on the island; they kept to themselves and had no time for outsiders. Still, he had to learn. The only way to know a place was to know its people.

4.05 p.m., Great Tey

Had there been an edge to his voice? Jacqui stared at the phone as if the plastic itself were harbouring a grudge. The doorbell – it had been ringing but she'd not heard it. Matthew, she thought. Her parents had brought back her son. Of course, she was still half asleep. Sex on shift work was clearly taking its toll. She shrugged off the covers and slipped on her dressing gown. The heating was off, and the cold January afternoon had infiltrated the house.

She went downstairs and opened the front door to see her ten-year-old son, grudgingly wearing a Christmas scarf, looking tired and sulky. Behind him were her parents, who, as usual, looked like they were dressed from another time, her mother in a fur hat and her father in a homburg.

'Happy New Year!' She forced a smile. 'Mum, you've not let him stay up too late, have you? He looks exhausted!' She kissed her mother on the cheek as the three of them shuffled into the house. 'Brrr! Quick, in, out of the cold! I'm just going up to get my slippers.' Jacqui sighed and pushed the door shut, then hurried upstairs. The parquet flooring was freezing. Returning downstairs, she discovered the three of them lingering in the cheap modern kitchen, unsure what to do with themselves. This sort of behaviour annoyed Jacqui. Her parents were here at least twice a week; they might flick the kettle on. She was surprised to see Matthew hanging around, though – usually, he scarpered up to his room, nose in a comic or fingers sticky with Airfix glue. Jacqui rustled the lad's chestnut hair and smiled wanly at her son as she filled the kettle herself.

'Sit down, Dad,' she said.

Her father was old before his time; he'd never really been right since the stroke. She took down cups and saucers from the cupboard.

'Let me do that,' her mother interjected. 'You pop some clothes on.'

'It's fine, Mum. I've started now. How was last night?' The question was directed at her son, who was slouching against the kitchen units. Christmas holidays this year had been a trial; with both her and Nick working, Matt had been sent from pillar to post. It can't have been that much fun. The boy had the sulky demeanour of a teenager already. But he was still very slight; he had has mother's delicate features and, as yet, no sign of his father's build.

'It was fun, that Rod Hull does make me laugh. Awful journey back though. Your father could hardly see in that fog.'

Jacqui thought Matt had outgrown the likes of Rod Hull and Emu, but her mother had insisted. Next year they must try harder; maybe there was a friend he could stay with.

'. . . won't stay long, *Brief Encounter* is on later.'

'Hmm, really? That's not much fun,' said Jacqui absently, and moved to hug Matthew and muss up his hair. It was almost down to his shoulders. A haircut was long overdue.

'Eh?' Her mother lifted the kettle off the hob. 'It's a classic.

If I ever came across a doctor like Trevor Howard, your father better watch out.'

'The chance's of that are . . .' Her voice trailed off.

At the back of her son's neck, Jacqui noticed a large yellow blemish, and rubbed it with her thumb, causing the boy to pull away from her. Instinctively, she clung all the more, and a tussle ensued until he bolted from the kitchen.

'He's had a whale of a time,' her mother said, frowning.

Jacqui didn't believe this for one minute, but she had to balance any maternal guilt with her work at the hospital and the patients' needs. Christmas was, and always had been, a difficult time for the Lowrys, a time when their dysfunction-ality shone through. She sighed. What child would choose a nurse for a mother and a policeman for a father?

11

4.25 p.m., Saturday, East Road, Mersea Island

Kenton pulled up outside West Mersea police station. The ancient-looking police lamp above the entrance to the 1950s building glowed grubbily in the cold, damp air. He'd just come from Seaview Avenue, the address he'd been given for the witness to the post-office robbery, but had found no one home. The station was open though, and the rattly door knob yielded to the twist of his wrist. Stepping over the threshold into the tiny reception room, he had the sense of walking in on a private conversation. Behind a reception hatch, an elderly, red-faced man in uniform paused mid-sentence, while, on the visitors' bench, a whiskery old man in a fisherman's jersey sat smoking a pipe. Both stared at him.

'Afternoon,' Kenton said tentatively. The man on the bench shifted position, but Kenton declined the unspoken offer to sit down. Beside the bench was a gas fire with half of its elements out, which explained why the room felt barely heated. 'Sergeant Bradley, I wonder if I might ask you a few questions.' Kenton had never met the Mersea chief sergeant before and felt obliged to address him formally rather than use his affectionate nickname, 'Dodger'.

'About the body on the Strood, will it be?' replied Bradley, his huge forearms barely contained by the reception hatch.

'No, it's about the post-office robbery on the 27th.'

'Oh?' The burly sergeant raised a set of fearsome bushy eyebrows. 'But that were resolved. Steve Taylor and his brother did it.'

'He says he didn't do it, and—'

Bradley guffawed. 'They all say they didn't do it! You'll get used it after a few years.'

Kenton ignored the remark. 'And the witness statements don't match.'

'Really?' Bradley was unmoved. Kenton felt a blast of chill air as the door opened behind him.

'Evening, all.'

'Ah, Jennings. The detective here is querying your collar of the Taylor boys for the post-office job.'

Jennings removed his helmet and regarded Kenton suspiciously before stepping towards the fire. He and the fisherman exchanged greetings. Kenton was conscious of being an outsider, but he was convinced that the locals' complacency blunted their instincts, whereas his remained heightened. Seven hundred pounds was taken, bad enough for a provincial island community, but far worse was the violence accompanying the robbery, which left two bystanders in hospital.

'Had those Taylor boys bang to rights, sarge. Money was hidden under the bedroom floorboards.' The two officers and the fisherman laughed ruefully together at the robbers' blunder. 'Didn't even take it out of the bags!'

'See,' Bradley affirmed. 'Caught red-handed.'

'Not really.' Kenton shifted uncomfortably on his feet. The sergeant and the officer eyed the CID man, who cleared his throat and lit a cigarette. 'Money, in post-office bags, was found on the premises at a flat on Buxton Road, that's correct. But that is circumstantial—'

'Why'd they leg it when we turned up if they weren't guilty?' Jennings jumped in. Bradley nodded approvingly at his junior.

'I couldn't tell you, not having been there myself,' replied Kenton, reaching towards the tin ashtray balanced precariously on the gas fire.

'So, detective.' Bradley cleared his throat behind the reception desk. 'What exactly is your point?'

Kenton pulled out his notebook and thumbed to the page he wanted. He continued, 'The witness statements of two pensioners said both attackers were about six foot in height. The third witness, a Mr Nugent of Seaview Avenue, directly indentifying the brothers in his statement, described them, and I quote, as "Little Steve Taylor and his runt of a brother".'

'Every Tom, Dick or Harry is six foot to an old biddy,' Jennings said. 'How could they be sure?'

'How could Mr Nugent be sure, when both men were wearing masks?' Kenton countered.

84

'Stockings.'

'I'm sorry?' Kenton turned to the senior man behind the desk.

'They were wearing ladies' stockings.' Bradley smirked, but said nothing more, adjusting his elbows on the hatch sill.

'The point still stands,' insisted Kenton.

'But, detective,' Bradley said flatly, 'money was found in their home, which they couldn't account for.'

'Yes, I know that, but it doesn't quite add up?'

The local police were convinced they had their men, and would not be swayed. After a futile ten-minute conversation, Kenton left before he lost his temper. He stood in the biting cold outside Mersea police station and cupped his hands to light another cigarette. Blast! He was so annoyed by his encounter with Bradley that he'd clean forgotten to ask for his help in locating the key witness, Kevin 'Ted' Nugent, an elusive figure who had not been seen since giving his statement to Jennings last week. The arrest of the Taylor brothers, it seemed to Kenton, had been one of convenience. They may well be dodgy, but if they didn't commit this crime then two very violent men were still at large. According to the clerk of the small sub-post office, the men had assaulted two elderly customers with their rifle butts simply because they were not quick enough to step aside.

Kenton heard the door creak behind him. The old sea dog in the fisherman's jersey emerged into the cold, chuckling to himself.

'Care to share the joke?' Kenton asked caustically, his voice in the semi-darkness alarming the old boy, who stood and stared blindly into the shadows. Kenton stepped forward and joined him beneath the lantern. 'What's your name, sir?'

'You don't think *I* did the post office, does you, boy?'

Kenton approached the man at close quarters, backing him up against the *Police* sign. 'What do *I* think? I'll tell you,' he hissed in his ear. 'I think you, sir, and your ilk are in for a wake-up call. Think you can do what you like out here? Well, not any more. This is 1983 not 1883.' He stepped back to appraise the old man, who was somewhat startled by Kenton's outburst. 'And that's why I'm here,' Kenton said, more to himself than the old man.

'Okay, okay,' said the local. 'I'm just a fisherman, from the port down there, like.'

'You don't say,' Kenton said, breathing heavily. 'And what business did you have with Sergeant Bradley in there? Let me guess: he's your cousin and you were thanking him for the Christmas jersey?' He heard they were all interrelated out here.

'Close – nephew. But there's no Christmas jersey.'

Kenton decided not to tease the old chap any more. Better to have him on side.

'No, I dropped in on me way down to the boat – we're out tonight.'

'Out?'

'Fishing.'

'Of course; cold night for it.' Kenton's anger had evaporated

as swiftly as it had risen. You could barely find a more stereo-
typical sea dog. 'I'm new around here. Tell me, is there much
of a fishing community on the island?'

'A fleet of about twenty boats – beamers, crabbers and skiffs.'

'Good fishing?'

The man began to elaborate on how hard things were.
Kenton wasn't really listening but nodded in all the right
places and at the end replied, 'Very interesting. Well, I must
try the local catch one day.' He turned to go, but then stopped
dead. 'Hey, you seem to know everyone. Know anything about
this chap Ted Nugent? Lives off Seaview Avenue, though he's
not been seen for a week.'

'Aye, I know Ted. He'll be on t'boat.'

'Boat?'

'Seaview Avenue is his mother's 'ouse. 'E lives on matey's
'ouseboat, down on the 'ard. I'll show ya; it's on me way.'

12

4.35 p.m., Saturday, Queen Street HQ

Lowry stood next to Sparks at the front of the large ground-floor meeting room, facing handful of reporters, mostly from the local press, but some from Chelmsford, and an odd bloke with a pipe. Still in overcoats, they formed a sad little huddle and looked rougher than usual; a week of festive over-indulgence had taken its toll on lives already lived in a punishing arena of booze and cigarettes. Several had hacking coughs which, thirty years ago, would have landed them in a TB sanatorium.

Sparks's plan had paid off. He'd brushed over the 'unfor-tunate, accidental death' of the soldier in Castle Park before announcing that they'd discovered a corpse on the Strood and, just as he'd hoped, the press were far more interested in a mutilated stranger floating in on the tide than in a soldier jumping off a wall. Special Branch had been no help; until 'the headless German' could be identified, neither they nor

Interpol was interested. Lowry listened abstractedly as his superior warmed to his subject, no doubt relieved to have averted any awkward questions about Private Daley. It wouldn't take much to shatter the delicate peace between the military and civilian factions of the town.

'Now, I shall pass you over to Inspector Lowry, who will be happy to answer any questions.' Sparks winked at him as Lowry took a step forward. The questions came thick and fast:

'How big would the boat have to be to *mutilate* a man beyond recognition?'

'How far could the body have floated?'

'How—'

'Gentleman! Ladies!' Lowry halted the questions. 'One at a time, please.' He pointed to a female hack at the rear of the room whose hand was raised. 'Young lady at the back,' he said.

'Sticking with New Year's Eve, if you don't mind,' she began.

Sparks's shoulders tensed noticeably. All eyes were on the stocky woman with oval glasses asking the question.

'Chief Sparks, in a press statement the previous day, had referred to the serviceman's death as resulting from a squabble with local lads in the high street.' Lowry heard Sparks's angry intake of breath; he hadn't quite said that. 'Isn't nine o'clock a bit early for drunken brawling?'

Before Lowry had a chance to compose a response, Sparks had barged in front of him. 'I never said there was "brawling". I said we suspected accidental death in the aftermath of a quarrel – a bit of horseplay.'

'Was it a fight between squaddies and townies, then?' A local hack had woken up.

'The soldiers involved have no visible injuries that would be consistent with having been in a fight,' replied Lowry.

'How do you define "horseplay"?' the woman persisted. 'And why were things getting heated so early in the evening?'

'Most teenagers are in the pub by midday, ma'am,' Lowry countered.

'So it *was* a drunken brawl?'

And so it went on, back and forth, the press asking difficult questions and Lowry ducking each of them as he would left hooks in the ring.

Afterwards, Sparks stood in the corridor, fuming. He glowered at Lowry, who had been joined by a tall WPC.

'Who the fuck was she?' Sparks barked.

'No idea. Not local.'

'I know she's not fucking local, hence the smart-alec questions – it would've just washed over those cretins from the *Gazette*; most of them were too hungover to hold a pencil. Just wait until I get hold of the Beard – he'd better hand that kid back, or I'll . . .'

Sparks became aware of the blonde WPC hovering next to Lowry. The one who jacked in the Littlewoods catalogue modelling, or whatever it was, for the force. Strange move, if ever there was one. And now she was lingering silently like a spare part while he argued with Lowry: a passive stance to which he took exception. 'Yes, constable, and you are here because . . . ?'

'WPC Gabriel was there on New Year's Eve – she came to the park with me this morning,' Lowry answered. 'I told you about it.'

'And what do you think happened, WPC Gabriel?' Sparks demanded, with barely suppressed contempt.

'I think there's something peculiar about it, sir, same as Inspector Lowry does.'

'Peculiar?' He wanted decisiveness and action, not vague conjecture. 'What do you mean, girl?' The girl, and she wasn't much more than a girl – about twenty-one or twenty-two – became nervous and couldn't get her words out.

'She means we're investigating it,' said Lowry, stepping in.

'What, the pair of you?' But Sparks didn't wait for an answer – he had to call Lane. He could see the headlines now: BRAWL WITH TOWNIES LEAVES SOLDIER DEAD, or some such sensational stuff. Next they'd have crazed squaddies marauding through the streets on a quest for revenge, beating the hell out of the local riff-raff. 'Have you seen the other one again – Jones?'

'I've been in contact with the garrison, sir,' said WPC Gabriel, attempting to regain composure. 'Someone is coming back to us about it this afternoon.'

Sparks glared at her, then at Lowry. 'Sort it out, eh, Nicholas?'

The pair of you. Lowry pondered the chief's words. It seemed they were a pair, he and WPC Gabriel, for now at least. Sparks had left them loitering together in the corridor, having marched off angrily. The chief in a temper could do nought to sixty quicker than a Ferrari. The woman looked visibly shaken by his outburst. For someone so enthralled by women, Sparks displayed not a flicker of decorum around them. Lowry immediately regretted having sent Kenton off to Mersea – if the story of the squaddie's death flared up, he would need him. He checked his wristwatch: four fifty-five. The squaddie's death would make the local radio news this evening, he was sure of that. But then Lowry had never believed they could cover up this accident. It would have come out sooner or later, once the post-Christmas and New Year fug had dispersed.

'Who did you speak to at the garrison?' he asked WPC Gabriel.

She pulled her notebook from her breast pocket. 'A Captain Oldham.'

Oldham, the military police captain: the Red Cap supremo himself.

'What did he say?'

'That he'd look into it and get back to me.'

Lowry looked at his watch again. 'Okay, we'll give him an hour. If he hasn't called back by then, we'll chase him up. What time does your shift finish?'

'Err – nearly an hour ago, actually.'

Normally, he would be keen to get to know a new partner when they were thrown together on a case, so he briefly considered asking her to stop for a drink. He just as quickly thought better of it. Of course she wasn't his partner. And women made him uneasy at close quarters. Platonic friendships were a minefield – seeing numerous colleagues end up in trouble had convinced him of that. Attraction always got in the way. But he was equally firm in his belief that it helped if you could trust who you're working with, and to trust a person you had to know them to some degree. Take Kenton, for example. He might yet kill them both in his death trap of a car but, essentially, Lowry trusted him, and that could only come about through shared confidences. Even within their brief partnership of three months, a bond of sorts had been created, and Lowry knew how useful an understanding colleague could be when you found yourself in a tight spot. He regretted this accidental union with Gabriel; it was so much easier to work with a man.

Lowry looked away from the pale blue eyes that were staring at him fixedly. 'Okay, thanks for your help,' he said kindly, then walked off, leaving her in the passageway.

4.50 p.m, Coast Road, West Mersea

Kenton wished the fisherman had accepted a lift in his car. Instead, he'd been obliged to walk the mile to the port while the old man wheeled a squeaking bicycle. The chilly walk wasn't completely without merit, however, as the fisherman had regaled Kenton with tales about all the characters on Mersea Island. Kenton's favourite so far was a Victorian pastor who had composed famous hymns and written gothic novels about the island in the vein of the Brontës – fascinating, especially for a history graduate. Nevertheless, time was pressing on.

'Is it much further?' he asked.

The old chap shook his head. 'Nearly there,' he wheezed.

As they rounded a corner, Kenton for the first time could smell the sea. To his right were grandiose Victorian houses, austere in the darkness, while to his left all was black – the great expanse of the estuary was swallowed up by the incoming night. The road leading down to the harbour was punctuated with street lamps casting weak orange halos of light.

'Right, I'll leave you to it,' the fisherman said, mounting the old bike, which gave a creak. 'Just carry straight on. The boat you're looking for is *Ahab's Revenge*.'

'There doesn't seem to be much life down there,' Kenton said dubiously.

'Look for the letterbox and you'll find the walkway to the boat.' And with that, he freewheeled off, wheels stinging the road as he went.

Kenton walked on, his footsteps echoing. The damp sea mist moved gently across the estuary to greet him, not with the same density as when on the Strood that morning, but enough for moisture to sit on his overcoat and catch the dim gloaming of the street lights. A low white rail which had divided him from the darkness beyond stopped abruptly as the road levelled out. He paused under a street lamp in a pocket of wan copper light and looked seaward but could discern nothing save shingle and clumps of grass. Walking a little further on, he came across a cluster of letterboxes at waist height, just as the fisherman had said. And there it was, painted clumsily on the middle one: *Ahab's Revenge*. The shingle to his left had given way to mud, and connecting with the pavement was a wooden gangway leading off into the darkness. Kenton blinked in the mist. Patches of light were vaguely discernible out there, so he stepped on to the narrow wooden planking and headed towards them. The smell of the coast hit his senses with greater force; it always made him think of seaweed and dead crabs, a throwback to his earliest childhood memories, when his mother had taken him on days out to Southend-on-Sea.

As he moved cautiously on, the unmistakable sound of a piano floated towards him on the cold air. 'Mozart,' he muttered to himself. The lights he'd seen from the pavement came into focus as soft red and pink rectangles. Houseboat lights. Under sparse moonlight, he could just about make out three hulls perhaps forty yards apart, resting on the muddy flats. The gangway led to the one in the centre, a large vessel with a dirty white hull and a two-storey white cabin.

He stopped at the end of the gangway, which had brought him alongside the cabin, level with a door. He could hear water but couldn't see it. Did the tide come up here? There were no lights on, either inside or outside *Ahab's Revenge*. God, it was eerie out here. He had just shaken the feeling off when the light on the opposite boat went out, plunging him into darkness. Brilliant, now he felt unnerved all over again. He knocked gently on the door in front of him, not expecting to get an answer when he called out, 'Hello?' but the vessel gave a creak, as if someone had moved inside it. Then he felt the wooden deck he was standing on rock, indicating that there was somebody else on it. 'Hello, I . . .' He started to address the darkness but, within seconds, he was flat on his back on the freezing mud, his nose throbbing. Jesus, that hurt! He lifted his head briefly, thinking he could see stars. Sheering white sheets of light crossed his vision before he passed out.

13

5 p.m., Saturday, Great Tey

Jacqui Lowry admired her features, tilted in the mirror, as she released the hair crimpers. 'Better,' she said to the empty room, or perhaps to Bryan Ferry, whose voice was crooning out of the cassette player.

Replacing the tongs on the dressing table, she picked up her vodka and Coke and took a sip. '*Much* better,' she said, and allowed herself an indulgent sway to 'More than This'. She whipped up a can of hairspray from the dresser and shook it, then shut her eyes as she applied it liberally. The smell was overpowering, almost intoxicating. 'Gah!' she exclaimed. Once the spray cloud had dispersed and she'd taken another gulp of vodka, she opened her eyes wide.

'Matthew!' Her son's reflection in the mirror took her by surprise. She felt embarrassed by his intrusion into her private, dreamy moment and turned on her stool, feeling annoyed. 'You're not a baby any more – you should knock before coming in.'

He frowned, puzzled. 'Why?'

'Because. Now, what do you want?'

'Are you going out?'

'Come here.' She beckoned, holding out both hands. The boy was hesitant, but slowly approached, hand trailing along the wardrobe. 'Now, let me see that mark.' She said this kindly but firmly, and he acquiesced, allowing her gently to push back his hair to get a better look. There was no doubt about it: the mark was a fading bruise. It must've happened at least ten days ago, coinciding with the last days of term. What sort of bruise would last that long? She wasn't the greatest mother, she knew that, but she couldn't bear the thought of her son being harmed in any way. She studied him and noticed, not for the first time, an oppressed look about him, the same one she'd seen on the face of her brother, Kenny. What on earth was going on?

'Want to talk about it?' she said, reaching out to clutch his shoulders, as much to stop him from leaving as to comfort him. Predictably, he shook his head.

'You need to tell me what's going on. Otherwise, I'll have to tell your father.' If this didn't budge him, nothing would. She knew he'd hate his dad to become involved in any problems he was having at school. As a little lad, he'd been proud to have a policeman as a dad but, lately, Jacqui thought, it seemed that Nick's profession was beginning to cause difficulties; nothing concrete – more what was unsaid than what was said. The school was rough, she knew, from stories she'd heard from the girls on the ward.

'It's nothing – got trampled playing rugby, in the scrum. That's all.' He rubbed the back of his neck, attempting to add his story some credibility. She remained doubtful.

'Look at me, Matty.' He shot her a glance. 'Really?'

'Really.'

She took his hands and studied his palms, which were covered in coloured splodges. 'What's that?'

'Paint.'

'Oh, the model plane.' She knew he'd been at it off and on since his birthday in September. Enormous box and what seemed like thousands of pieces. 'Spitfire, is it?'

'Stuka. Nearly done.'

'That's it, a Stuka. Well, you've certainly stuck with it!' She smiled, her cheesy joke producing just the hint of a grin on his face. He was a determined little soul, her son. Jacqui then pondered her husband's resolve; Nick had announced an intention to pack up ciggies *and* boxing. It was hard to imagine him without either; both habits were as much a part of him as the wings were to her son's model plane.

6.05 p.m., Police Social Club, Queen Street

'The giving up smoking has been a triumph then!' Sparks smirked, puffing on a panatella. Lowry shrugged without comment and bent his cigarette end double in the enormous bar ashtray. In his penguin suit, the chief looked more menacing than usual, he thought.

Lowry was waiting in the dingy basement bar for Kenton to return from Mersea. His quiet drink and pause for thought had been interrupted by Sparks, who was on his way to a function. The chief suddenly reached over and clapped Lowry heavily on the shoulder, causing him to splutter. 'Let's hope you display the same tenacity in giving up boxing, eh?' The chief exploded in a great guffaw at his own joke, causing two young officers to look up from their pool game.

Lowry was sure Sparks had been drinking upstairs alone already, not just because of this boisterous outburst but because he never normally came in the social club. And the rank and file hated him being in here. A tense hush had fallen on the room when he walked in.

'Phyllis, two doubles, please,' Sparks chirped, not taking his eyes off Lowry.

'I can't,' spluttered Lowry. 'Jacqui's going out. I've got to be home by six thirty.' Where the hell was Kenton?

'Nonsense, you can stay for one more.'

'I've got to go.'

'One more.' Sparks pushed him back down in his seat. 'Listen, I'll let you off boxing tomorrow, but you have to come and watch – check out the Beard's new talent.'

Lowry was taken aback by Sparks's magnanimity; he hadn't expected to get off this lightly. 'All right, it's a deal.' He smiled in relief.

'But, next week, I want you back in the ring. No point chucking you in now for a pummelling, which you'll undoubtedly get, as I guess you haven't trained over Christmas.' Sparks blew an enormous cloud of smoke into Lowry's face, causing him to wince in irritation.

'No chance. I'm finished with that.'

'Come on, don't be such a big poof about it.' Before Lowry had a chance to protest further, Sparks was off on another tack. 'Now, tell me about the *peculiar* circumstances of Private Daley's death.'

Lowry didn't miss the jibe at WPC Gabriel. Not for the first time, he was appalled by Sparks's derision of the women in the force. He took the Scotch from the tiny bar, which this evening was ably manned by the station's cleaner, Phyllis. She was a huge, round-faced woman who perspired profusely, her brow too close to the spotlights above the bar.

'I'll advise Gabriel to use a less loaded term in future.'

'You do that. Until we know more, it's still an accident, nothing more, right? But it would be handy to know how it happened and who was involved – must be a couple of hard bastards. Take it you've not been in touch with the other soldier?'

'We're chasing it up.'

'Never mind; it was an accident!' Sparks boomed. 'Forget about it.'

And then he lapsed into silence. This could mean he was considering the situation, or it could mean he'd simply had too much to drink. Senior policemen had a lot of official engagements at this time of year, and Sparks was of the view that a constant level of alcohol in the bloodstream was the best way to deal with the season, not unlike the smallpox vaccine. After a moment or two he sighed and ground out his cigar in the large ashtray. He spoke in a low voice.

'Personally, I don't give a stuff what Jones has to say. I know I was a bit pissed off this afternoon, but, you know, if the Beard is playing silly buggers over the death of one of his own men, who cares?'

A fresh-faced uniformed officer appeared at Sparks's side.

'Understood?' the chief said to Lowry before sliding off his stool, clasping the shoulder of the young PC in order to steady himself. 'My carriage awaits. Think yourself lucky that you're going home – I have to face Merrydown at Chelmsford town hall.' Sparks grimaced and straightened his bow tie. 'What a life,' he added woefully. And, with that, he was gone.

'You will give a stuff, if Merrydown has anything to do with it.' Lowry remained at the bar and nudged Phyllis for a top-up before he hit the road. 'Right, Kenton,' he said to himself, 'I'm afraid I can wait no longer. Hope you're enjoying your evening with the Dodger.'

14

6.50 p.m., Saturday, Great Tey

'You're late,' Jacqui admonished as Lowry skulked into the house. She didn't really give a fig that it was ten to seven – the taxi wasn't booked until seven, anyway – but finding fault with Nick was a useful way of assuaging her guilt about her affair with Paul.

'Sorry, it was Sparks. He, um . . .' Lowry was clearly shattered, she could see that, but, nevertheless, she couldn't help herself.

'Huh? Don't mumble, Nick. I can't hear a word you're saying.'

Trish sashayed into the hallway. 'Hi, Nick,' she purred, stepping up and kissing him lightly on the corner of his mouth. 'Catch any baddies?' Trish Vane was one of Jacqui's oldest friends – they'd known each other since school – and was an outrageous flirt. Cute and curvy, Trish was very attractive to men, and had, a couple of years back, confided when drunk that she fancied Nick. Jacqui had laughed it off but was secretly proud that Nick still had that allure. She'd even teased Nick about it once, back then . . .

'Right, we're out of here. Maybe you should . . .' She was on the cusp of saying, 'spend some quality time with Matthew,' but halted herself in front of Trish. Her son was in the lounge watching television.

'Should what?'

The doorbell went. 'Nothing; it can wait. That'll be the taxi.'

Lowry stood there, not sure what to say.

'There's some macaroni cheese left over in the fridge you can reheat.' Jacqui unhooked her handbag from the banister. 'Oh, one thing. That young soldier, he wanted to talk to you again.'

'Really? What about?'

'He didn't say. But when he discovered his pal was dead, he had some sort of fit and had to be sedated,' she said sharply.

'A fit?'

'Yes, a fit.' Jacqui was on the doorstep.

'Did he say anything?'

'He was in shock, Nick. His friend was dead.'

'But did he say anything?'

'He was shouting, I don't know what . . . Jesus, Nick, his best friend had just died.'

'Wait – this is important. He's a soldier, Jacqs – news of a pal's death wouldn't usually require sedation. I mean, those boys have just fought a war—'

'I just said, *I don't know*. The boy was in shock. Damn it!

You're so fucking insensitive!' She spat the words out and slammed the door.

Lowry stood alone in hallway. Her unexpected flare-up had taken the last of his energy. He moved to the lounge; Matthew had left the room.

On hearing the door slam, his son had taken himself off upstairs. He would be thoroughly absorbed in the intricacies of Second World War dive-bomber markings by now so, for the first time today, Lowry could relax in his own company. He switched the oven on and slid the macaroni cheese in. Any resentment about not spending the night with his wife had been swiftly despatched by her razor-sharp tongue; he was grateful for the peace and quiet, intent on a night off from Colchester and all those who populated her, living or dead.

He flipped the top off a Pils bottle and pressed play on the VCR. Time to catch up on *The Gentle Touch*. He wasn't a big TV-watcher, preferring the grander atmosphere of the silver screen, but, like most coppers, he had an addiction to telly cops, and to Jill Gascoine in particular. For Lowry, she was the sexiest woman on the planet. Even her dodgy outfits couldn't dampen his obsession. He thought shoulder pads were the single most unflattering aberration in fashion history (but then, what did he know about fashion? He still favoured suits cut to 1964 styles). Even worse was the current fad for permed hair, which had even crossed over to blokes. Jill had dark, wavy hair, which he assumed was naturally curly, but even if it was permed he didn't care – she was perfect, like a

Venus or a Diana. Needless to say, he kept these thoughts to himself. He could just imagine the ridicule if he shared them at the station, and he had to keep some things sacred from Kenton. As the titles rolled, accompanied by the soporific, siren-like music, he put his feet on the pouffe and took a swig from the bottle of beer.

After the first episode, and having eaten his pasta, he paused the machine to check on his son upstairs. He found the boy was reading in bed. Lowry complimented his son on his progress with the Airfix kit, before wishing him good night and switching off the bedroom light. Lowry then watched a further episode, by which time he felt he was restored enough to engage with his new passion: birds. This required an element of reading around the subject – when best to see them, and so forth – so he went off to bed with Tony Soper's *Bird Table Book*. The Lowrys' house had a deep back garden that backed on to farmland; he was confident he could lure a few species on to a bird table and maybe to use a feeder. Like many things, it made sense to start at home.

But just as he put his foot on the first step of the staircase, the telephone rang. It was ten fifteen, so it could only be Queen Street on the other end. His mind switched on, instantly rushing back through the day, and fuck! He realized he'd clean forgotten to call Robinson for his report on the body on the Strood. He padded slowly in his socks towards the small table in the hallway, hoping the phone would stop. Of course, it didn't.

'Lowry.'

'We need you in, I'm afraid, inspector.' It wasn't the pathologist but the tired voice of Sergeant Barnes.

'Why? What's up?'

'It's kicking off in the high street.'

'What?'

'Fighting – townies and squaddies. Red Caps tried to intervene and have made it ten times worse. We need all hands on deck.'

'Excellent. Sparks?'

'He's at a ball in Chelmsford.'

'Of course he is.' He rubbed his stubble wearily. That was right: Sparks was getting his nuts squeezed by Merrydown at some official shindig.

'Okay, give me fifteen minutes. I'll have to bring Matthew. Jacqui's out.'

'Sorry, sir.'

'Not your problem.' He replaced the receiver, slipped on his shoes and donkey jacket and dashed upstairs. He crept quietly into his son's room, not wishing to startle him, and gently shook his shoulder, but Matt didn't stir. Lowry picked up the extra blanket at the foot of the bed, pulled back the covers and wrapped it around his son before lifting him, with some difficulty, off the bed. He was small for his age but a dead weight when fast asleep.

Carefully, he made his way down the stairs and out of the front door. He lay the sleeping boy in the back of the Saab and shut the car door as quietly as he could, saying softly, 'Another night in the cells for you, son. Sorry.'

10.15 p.m., North Hill, Colchester

Jacqui downed her drink and slid the empty glass across the bar. She felt free and on top of the world. The barman gave her a wry smile. He was a bit of all right, she thought. She and Trish had met up with two other girls, and the four of them had decided to try the new 'wine bar', Tramps, on Middleborough, at the bottom of North Hill. Duran Duran was on a bit too much and a bit too loud, and there were mirrors everywhere, which Jacqui could do without, but apart from that it was okay: smart without being poncey. The only downside was the ten-minute trudge up to the high street; a real pain in heels.

'What shall we do now?' Trish asked loudly.

'Go back up to town!' said Trish's sister, Emma, who was flushed and glassy-eyed. 'It's dead in here.'

'Agreed?' asked Trish.

'S'pose so,' replied Jacqui reluctantly, eyeing the barman. 'We'll be back, though!' she exclaimed as she jumped off her stool.

The fourth woman, Kerry, was a friend of Trish's but also a staff nurse on Constable Ward. Jacqui had a sense that Kerry was being slightly off with her. Did she know about Paul? Possibly. Well, fuck it, Kerry was clearly no angel herself, given that she'd been chatting up some fella in tight slacks for the last ten minutes. He was dressed smartly, but the shaven head and muscular build suggested that he was a soldier.

'The trouble with the no-jeans policy is that it's harder to separate the wheat from the chaff,' she smirked to Trish. 'Any old scumbug or squaddie can slip on a pair of Farah's.'

'And what's wrong with that?' came a Northern accent from behind her. Jacqui turned to see the fella Kerry had been flirting with bearing down on her. A squaddie, no doubt about it.

'Why, nothing, hon.' She smiled. 'It's just harder to find a bit of rough, know what I mean?'

-15-

10.20 p.m., Saturday, Chelmsford Town Hall

Sparks was bored. He could handle consecutive nights out pretty well on the whole, but this charity gala banquet stuffed full of Essex bigwigs in penguin suits was tedious beyond belief. They were in the draughty town hall, which had all the atmosphere of an aircraft hangar, and some old duffer across the table was dribbling into Antonia's face. She looked non-plussed.

They'd had only the starters but already his cummerbund was giving him gyp. It was going to be a long evening. The imminent arrival of Assistant Chief Constable Merrydown should have been enough to keep him on his toes, but too much booze had taken the edge off. The ACC herself had been delayed; why, he didn't know. Someone from the town hall was burbling in Sparks's ear about whether the police should be armed: a subject he could handle on autopilot.

The seat on Sparks's right remained empty as the main

course was finally brought out. Merrydown had yet to show. A waiter materialized and promptly topped up the wine – at least they kept it flowing freely, which was something. He gestured for the waiter to fill the glass at the place next to him.

'Yes, I quite understand the concern – the increasing flow of automatic pistols from the Continent is a problem. God help us if they ever build a tunnel,' said Sparks airily as he picked up his absent neighbour's glass and drank heavily. 'Although we'd be overrun with rabies before anything else.'

While the elderly windbag responded with more drivel, this time about 'ghastly Europeans', he glanced across the hall, and there she was, a familiar slender woman in her mid-forties with chestnut hair, elegantly gliding across the room. Sparks drank hastily from his boss's glass, but Merrydown was in no hurry, stopping at every table to say a few words and bestow her immaculate white smile, which complemented an almost Mediterranean complexion and Roman nose.

Sparks had mixed feelings about his superior. He considered her, in his own words, 'a ball-breaker of the highest order', but she was also fiercely intelligent. As a man of average intellect and questionable devotion to his job, these qualities alone should've struck the fear of God into him but, on the contrary, he rose to the challenge: the competitor in him was constantly striving to stay one step ahead . . .

'Ma'am, there you are.'

'Stephen, sorry I'm late.'

He rose, gesturing obsequiously for her to sit down before

retaking his own seat. She eyed the empty glasses. 'I see you've started without me.' She smiled. 'I don't blame you. These things *can* be rather a bore.'

Sparks apologized and summoned the waiter to refill the glasses once more.

'Now, then.' She again smiled that immaculate white smile. Her dark kohl eyeliner seemed too exotic by far for the police, let alone for Chelmsford town hall. 'What's been going on?'

'Nothing, ma'am. Nothing to worry about.'

'That's not what my spies tell me.'

'Spies?'

'Colchester is an important town. The military are, as you know, regarded as heroes. I hope the accident in Castle Park is not going to present problems.'

'Certainly not, ma'am. I know how to handle the military.'

'Yes, I'm aware of that – but there's more to good relations than boxing bouts.'

Her dismissive tone confirmed to Sparks that she had no idea what she was talking about.

'Of course there is, ma'am; but it's a different world to . . .' He gesticulated towards the candlelit hall.

'Oh, yes, I don't doubt that, out there in the boondocks, it's very different.' She raised her glass. 'Cheers.'

'Cheers.'

'But although it's the back of beyond, I see your annual crime stats still managed to make it to County. I appreciate the prompt filing.'

'We are nothing if not ruthlessly efficient. Must be our military neighbours rubbing off on us,' he joked.

'Indeed, but if only you were as successful at policing as they are at fighting wars.' She took a sip from her glass. 'Your clean-up record for 1982 is the worst in the county.'

10.30 p.m., Queen Street HQ

Lowry was at Queen Street inside twenty minutes. Though Matthew was now awake, it was quicker to carry him down to the cells, as he'd done for many years. He acknowledged the duty PC at the far end, who nodded towards the cell adjacent to him. Protocol dictated that the furthest cells were always kept empty the longest, for reasons Lowry couldn't recall, other than it enabled the night shift to doze in peace. And, for that reason, Matthew would more than likely be able to sleep, too.

He pulled back the coarse-woven coverlet on the low cell bed and lay the boy down, covering him with his own blanket before doubling up with the blanket there. (It got cold down here, Lowry knew.)

'Don't know when I'll be back,' he said to the PC, taking one of his cigarettes. 'By all accounts, there's a riot in the high street.'

'No probs, sir; I'm here till six.' He yawned.

'Cheers. I'll probably bed down here myself later. Looks pretty cosy.'

No matter how many times he'd done this with Matt – and, since the boy had been two, there'd been many – he still felt crap about it and made lame jokes in recompense. The duty constable, all of twenty, probably thought him an unusual father. Lowry made his way up to the ground floor. The night-desk sergeant greeted him with a nod.

'What's the situation?'

'Not good. At first, a solider punches a civilian in the Lamb. The civvy is left out cold, slumped in the bogs, while the squaddie makes off to the Wagon and Horses.' The Lamb was in the middle of the high street, one of the busiest places in town on a Saturday night, and the Wagon and Horses, a well known squaddie haunt, at the top of North Hill. 'Next thing, a bunch of locals storm the Wagon and Horses looking for the chap, just as two Red Caps get there—'

Lowry could picture the rest. 'Okay. Better get a move on,' he said.

'Take care, inspector.'

10.35 p.m., Colchester town centre

As Lowry rounded the corner on to the high street, chanting greeted him long before he could see anything. He passed two uniforms shoving a couple of handcuffed teenagers along the street and quickened his pace. The noise grew louder and, gradually, he could make out a bunch of figures moving frenetically at the far end of the street. A bottle broke on the pavement in front of him as a gang of youths tore by, then they veered off down a side alley. The dark forms of uniformed police officers came into view. 'Jesus!' he exclaimed, catching sight of a retreating PC with a bloodied face.

'Glass caught me, guv,' explained the constable apologetically, blood pouring from a cut above his left eye.

'What the fuck is going on?'

'We had it contained until the Red Caps turned up. They started laying it on a bit thick, sir.'

Another bottle smashed, closer this time, spraying Lowry's feet. 'Go get that cut seen to,' he said, sidestepping the shattered glass.

Just then, two black Commer vans with sirens blaring shot past, driving in the middle of the road, one with a mounted spotlight. Reinforcements from County. This was turning ugly.

He was now in the thick of things, at the point where the high street met Head Street, near where the trouble had started. All around him, people were brawling. Others spilled out from pub doorways, yelling encouragement or insults. It was difficult to work out who was on what side in the fight but, given the spark that had set things off, this was clearly a reprisal for the Castle accident. In front of him three youths in denims had a Red Cap down on the ground and were booting him mercilessly. They were dragged off by two uniformed PCs. To his left, two men with crew cuts were shoved up against a parked car by a bunch of braying yobs. The arrival of the MPs on the scene had clearly exacerbated matters, and outside the Lamb was the biggest scene of trouble – a stand-off between Red Caps and police on one side and a gang of chanting youths on the other. It was poised to get nastier.

Jacqui's heart was pumping nineteen to the dozen as she and her friends walked briskly up North Hill towards the high street, partly from exertion – going uphill in heels was an effort – and partly from embarrassment. The soldier in Tramps wine bar who had taken exception to her comments had turned the mockery on her, deriding her as 'overdressed mutton' and 'out for it' because she was wearing an above-the-knee skirt in close to freezing temperatures. The humiliation, combined with the chill air – her legs were already numb – had sobered her up with a jolt.

'Are they following us?' Trish asked anxiously.

'Don't mind if they are,' said Kerry, a spiky edge to her voice. Jacqui shot her daggers and caught a deep-red-lipstick smirk in return.

'I don't know about that,' Trish muttered. 'One of them was pretty hacked off.'

'I wonder why.' Kerry sniffed.

From behind them came a loud rallying cry and the sound of leather soles on the pavement. 'Jesus Christ!' Jacqui hissed under her breath.

'Look!' Kerry squealed, pointing ahead. 'Party on!'

At the junction of North Hill, Head Street and the high

street there appeared to be people dancing in the road. With cheers of encouragement, the soldiers in slacks from the bar ran past to join the crowd.

'Wait!' said Jacqui. 'That's no party. That's one massive punch-up.' Loud chanting rose up from behind them. 'And we're smack in the middle of it.'

Behind them, more people filled the road, as the pubs began to empty. The women had no escape. Jacqui clasped her hands to her ears to block out the shouting and to protect her head from the blows as she was knocked on one side then the other, after a moment loosing her footing and falling to the ground.

'Not so cocky now, are you?' a voice above her asked.

Blinking rapidly, she looked up to see the soldier from Tramps. 'Come on, get up,' he said.

Roughly, he pulled her to her feet and shoved her against a shop window. She could smell his boozy breath. Where were her friends? A hand clasped her breast and panic rose sharply in her throat.

'Come on; in a skirt that short you must be gagging for it.'

Jacqui struggled to try and free herself, but his grip was iron. 'Get off me!' she screamed, kicking him hard in the shin and losing her shoe in the process. Incensed, the soldier slapped her. She was stunned. All around her, people were fighting. No one noticed what was happening to her.

'Come on; a quick one round the back – said you wanted a bit of rough.'

Jacqui tilted her head up towards him. He was almost a foot

taller than she was. She held his gaze for a moment, then, with a deft flick of her tongue, she spat in his face.

'Slag!' he spat.

In an instant, Jacqui was winded and on the ground. Fighting for breath, she knew she was in trouble; biting her bottom lip, she braced herself for pain. She shrank on the pavement as he positioned to kick her. In her panic, everything switched to slow motion. And as it did, the enormous foot aimed at her face changed direction and missed, going high. Her attacker went over backwards and disappeared from view. A voice coming through a megaphone and a bright light flashing past the shop windows burst through her inertia. Another figure appeared, as if from nowhere, coming close, blocking the coloured light. She cowered and tried to scrabble away, across the pavement, but found herself up against another shop front.

'See what happens when you hit the town?' said a voice she knew, and a hand reached down to help her. The police spotlight gave an almost angelic tint to the man's profile.

Nick pulled Jacqui to standing. Regaining her poise, she straightened her skirt and pulled her hair back from her face.

'You okay?' He tried to look her in the eye.

'I need a drink,' she said sullenly, unable to meet his gaze.

'I think not. You're going home.'

'Where's Matthew?'

'At the station – I'll have someone there run you home.' Her husband's voice was soft, controlled amidst the chaos.

She was aware of her friends standing behind her, not sure what to do.

'I'm fine, Nick, really.' She didn't know whether she was fine or not – she was shaken, certainly, but wanted the situation over and to be away from here. Away from Nick, too. And, yes, she really did need a drink. Who could go home now, after all this? There were people thronging everywhere. The air was alive with sirens and shouts. Sod New Year's – this was her night out. And that fella wouldn't have done anything to her, right there in the street ... would he, seriously? She adjusted her red leather jacket and flicked back her hair. She smiled weakly. 'Really.'

Nick clutched her tightly to him. 'Go home,' he said quietly. Even in this flashing, obscure light, in the midst of the chaos of the town, she could tell he meant it.

'Okay,' she said, barely above a whisper.

16

11.15 p.m., Saturday, Queen Street HQ

'What, so you glassed a man in the bogs just because you felt like it?'

'He spilt my pint,' muttered the young soldier in a soft Northern Irish accent. With the arrival of backup units from Chelmsford, the fighting in the town centre was quelled swiftly. Now, the police were investigating the cause.

'He spilt your pint, eh?' Sparks exclaimed. 'Do you not think your reaction might've been a tad over the top?'

Lowry could see the vein in his superior's neck begin to pulse. He wondered about the chief's blood pressure, but only for a second. His wife had nearly been raped in the high street, not fifteen minutes ago. Lowry couldn't get it out of his head. What if he'd arrived five minutes later? What if he'd not got there in time? His legs still felt weak; they were almost trembling. And to think she'd wanted to carry on partying with the girls. She'd agreed to go home, but not in a squad car; Trish and Kerry would take her. He hadn't wanted a scene and so let her have her way. Her attacker, meanwhile, had disappeared and avoided capture, unlike the man before them now, who the chief circled, growing angrier by the second. The man before them had sparked something not far short of a riot by landing Jamie Philpott, a small-time crook, in Colchester General, and his dismissive attitude was making the chief livid.

Lowry recognized the ginger-haired Irish soldier from the gym; he had a prize-fighter's build but was slow on his feet and, reputedly, dim-witted. It was surprising he had made the Paras. But this was the first time Corporal Quinn had been caught in a fracas in town. It was hard to believe that this docile-seeming lunk was the cause of all the trouble.

'I thought they were big on discipline and self-control in the army?' Sparks shook his head and paced the room. Rushed away from a County bash where he'd been seated next to the assistant chief constable herself, for nothing short of a riot in Colchester High Street – no wonder he was annoyed. In contrast, the soldier before them seemed so calm that Lowry couldn't imagine him losing it over a spilt drink. Something about the situation didn't add up.

A WPC poked her head round the corner, not wishing to get drawn in. 'Captain Oldham is upstairs, sir. He's anxious to see you.'

'Anxious, is he? I'll give him anxious,' Sparks growled.

On hearing that the captain of the military police had

arrived, Quinn's passive expression barely changed – or was that a flicker of relief that Lowry saw cross his broad forehead?

'No wonder Northern Ireland's fucked, if they've the likes of you on the border,' sneered Sparks as he made to leave the room. He then spun on his heels and, without warning, landed the corporal an unexpected left hook of such force it caused even Lowry to jump. The soldier went crashing to the ground, the crack of his head on the wooden floor a sickening sound. Sparks had, in his time, lost it with recalcitrant villains, but it had been a while since Lowry had witnessed such open aggression. Dinner with Merrydown must have been even less fun than usual.

'Well, we can't keep the good captain waiting, can we?' Sparks stepped round the corner of the interview table, slamming his heel on the prone man's fingers and making him scream. 'You boys, you boys,' he tutted. 'If you will brawl, you can't expect to get away unscathed.'

As he passed Lowry, he whispered, 'He's hiding something.' And he left the room.

As to what he might be hiding, Christ only knew. Sparks himself had not the faintest idea. But that was beside the point; as long as Lowry thought there was something there, he would be diligent enough to give the man a hard time. The chief had not so much as loosened his tie since leaving the Chelmsford bash. He shuddered, recalling the moment the messenger had delivered the news – just as Merrydown was starting to show an interest in his achievements in the ring. For an instant, he had almost believed she was flirting with him. But leaving to attend to the riot, her parting haughty look of dismay at the news was emblazoned on his retina.

Sparks powered along the corridor towards the three military policemen – two tall and well built, one slight and severe – awaiting him in the reception hall. Captain Oldham's diminutive stature always unnerved him. He had the air of a Nazi torturer – small and sadistic.

'Chief,' Oldham said, perfectly calmly.

'Oldham,' Sparks responded, dropping the officer's rank to emphasize that he was the senior man.

'Off somewhere nice?' the captain remarked, eyeing the evening wear.

'Unfortunately not – I was called away from an important engagement.'

'Ah, sorry to hear that,' Oldham remarked, clearly not sorry at all. 'I believe you have one of our men.'

'Yes; Corporal Quinn; big bugger, can't miss him.'

'That's the one. I'd like to see him, please.'

Sparks hesitated. He wanted to give Lowry more time. 'Of course, but right now he's in a frightful mess. You'd think a chap that size could take care of himself. Listen, come with me for a snifter while the medics finish patching him up.'

The military captain raised a surprised eyebrow. 'In a bad way, you say?'

'Yes, he took a bit of a pasting.' He clasped the little man's shoulder and propelled him along the corridor. 'Shouldn't take them long. What's your poison?'

'He can't do that,' the soldier spat.

Lowry ignored him and picked up the arrest sheet Sparks had left on the table. The man had confessed to knowing Philpott, the man he'd hit over a spilt pint, by sight. Tensions had been running high; it was no surprise things had kicked off . . . He glanced at the paper he was holding and something leapt out at him: Quinn was in 7 Para, and barracked in the same quarters as Daley and Jones.

'You knew Private Daley?'

'I did. We were in the same unit.'

'What do you think happened that night? You know, at the castle.'

'I don't have an opinion.'

'But there must have been rumours flying around the barracks?'

Quinn shrugged. 'They say there was a ruck with some local lads.'

'Over what?'

'The usual. Birds.'

'Was Jamie Philpott one of those involved?'

'I dunno, do I? I wasn't there.'

Could this have been a revenge beating? Philpott was hard enough on the local scene but, essentially, a nobody and an unlikely threat to these guys. These weren't your run-of-the-mill squaddies; these were 7 Para; they had yomped across Goose Green – hardly the sort to flee across Castle Park because some two-bit crook was on their tail.

'So where . . . ?' But before Lowry could finish the question he saw a PC wave at him through the window, distracting him. Lowry mouthed, 'Not now,' but the PC was insistent. He reluctantly left the room.

'What?'

'Philpott's checked himself out of hospital.'

'Checked himself out? There was a police guard – I authorized it myself.'

'But he doesn't want to press charges . . .'

'Okay, let him go. He won't stray far; we know where to find him.' Philpott would want to dodge the spotlight, but Lowry was surprised he'd do a bunk from hospital if he was hurt. Philpott was known to the police, and to some degree he operated in Sparks's pocket. He might be a nobody, but he was *their* nobody. Maybe his wounds were superficial. He looked back through the small, latticed window at the bloodied soldier. So where did this leave them? Did they pass this man back to his military masters and leave them to it, forget the town-centre chaos and hope it would all blow over? Lowry signalled to the PC that the interview was over.

17

11.30 p.m., Saturday, Police Social Club, Queen Street

Sparks helped himself at the optics.

'Really, Chief Sparks, I must attend to my man upstairs,' said Oldham. 'If he has indeed been causing trouble in town, then he will be punished.'

'Come on, one more – humour me. You can have him in due course. Corporal Quinn and whoever else it was have ruined everyone's Saturday night; we might as well make the most of what remains.' Sparks was merely buying Lowry time, as sharing a drink with the captain of the military police was not what he'd call enjoyable by any stretch of the imagination. Though a fan of the brigadier, Sparks loathed the military police and the way they lorded it about the town – his town – as if they were beyond the law. And Oldham was the worst of the bunch. His two goons stood to attention in the social-club doorway, as if the bar were theirs, which only annoyed Sparks further. 'So what does "punished" mean, exactly?' he asked.

'Oh, come now, chief, you're mocking me. I know you think the military police just play at being soldiers.' Oldham grimaced as he took a slug of Scotch.

'No, seriously. I know the Glasshouse at Colchester is the nation's military prison. What goes on there?'

'You'll have to pay us a visit—'

There was a kerfuffle in the doorway as in came DC Kenton, filthy and wet. The two MPs looked set to pounce if he took another step further.

'Easy, lads,' said Sparks, 'he's one of mine. Jesus Christ, what happened to you?'

'Mind if I have a drink, sir?' Kenton asked, stumbling towards the bar.

'Where the bloody hell have you been?'

His face smeared with mud, and his usually groomed head of hair reduced to lank, ratty streaks, Kenton resembled a Dickensian pauper. And, Jesus, he stank like one, too.

'Mersea Island, checking out houseboats, sir.'

'Well, I must be off,' said Oldham, adding drily, 'It really is getting late, and it looks as if you two have plenty to chat about.'

Midnight, Aristos nightclub, half a mile from Colchester High Street

They'd got there too early. The place was practically deserted. The three of them sat on an enormous leather bench seat with a low glass table in front of them, sipping vodka martinis.

Aristos was a cavernous nightclub beneath a four-star hotel, a converted mill on the bank of the River Colne at the foot of East Hill.

The club had opened five years ago at the height of the *Saturday Night Fever* craze. Although it was tired and had the tacky feel of a wedding-reception venue, it was still the best place to go for a good boogie. The glitter ball span, its sparkle skittering across an all but empty dance floor.

The martinis had yet to kick in and the girls were feeling deflated. Jacqui and her friends had mooched down the high street, making a show of calling it a night. On parting, Jacqui had said to Nick that she didn't want to be alone – knowing this would sting him, as he was powerless to help, being tied up with what was going on – and that they were going to Trish's house. But now, having disobeyed him completely, and having ended up in a club, the surge of energy brought on by her defiance had dwindled.

''Ere, check those three loons out.' Kerry nudged Jacqui and pointed towards the raised bar, where a guy in a tracksuit and two others in denims were haranguing the barman. He looked like he was on the verge of having them thrown out. Jacqui's attention settled on one of the guys in denim; he looked a bit of a hunk.

She pushed herself up off the low seat. 'Where are you going?' demanded Kerry.

'For a chat.'

'What?!'

'Why not?' said Jacqui brazenly, and headed across the dance floor, figuring she might as well make the best of being out. Anyway, she was intrigued – the three men looked completely out of place – and she had to do something while waiting for the mood in the club to lift. The tracksuited guy was gesticulating wildly at the barman, who looked bemused by whatever it was he was saying.

Jacqui leaned in to address the good-looking one. 'What are you fellas doin'?'

'Just havin' a beer, you know.' He was looking past her into the distance, at the spinning, flashing lights, and nodding to the music – the twelve-inch of 'Passion', a weird, trancey disco hit. She stepped closer to speak to him over the music and noticed a strange, fishy smell.

'Didn't realize the dress code was so, err, relaxed,' she said loudly.

'He knows the doorman,' he shouted back, nodding towards the man in the tracksuit, who was still berating the barman and seemed to be smoking two cigarettes at once.

'You fellas don't look the regular type for this sort of place. And what's that smell? Did you just get off a fishing boat?' she joked, trying to divert the man's attention from the glitter ball.

'You what?' At last he turned to meet her eyes, but he wasn't really seeing her. She looked him over in the twilight of the club. He hadn't shaved and was grinding his teeth like anything. The overall effect was comical, but she was intrigued. 'You what?' he repeated.

'What's your name?' she asked.

By now the other girls had joined her at the bar, an oval island, and had surrounded his mate, who was wearing a Fred Perry T-shirt and appeared to be terrified by their approach. His face was a picture of confusion; he looked as if he might cry at any moment.

'Jason,' answered the first man at last. 'My name's Jason.' He downed his lager and started jigging fervently to the music. He was cute and not the least bit threatening.

'You like the music?'

'Nah,' he said, still dancing. 'I'm into the Floyd, you know?' When she looked blank he leaned close to her and started gabbling about some album – *Medal*, or something – and its amazing experimental soundscapes, or some such nonsense, with barely a pause for breath. He really did smell of the sea, and not in a good way.

'I'll have to check that out,' she said, pulling away. 'Sounds great.'

He then looked at her properly for the first time, as if only just registering that she was a woman.

'You're beautiful,' he slurred, eyes sparkling in the disco lights.

'Have you got any left for me?' She smiled knowingly.

He arched an eyebrow in an exaggerated fashion and turned furtively towards his pals. The little one, who, only a minute ago, had seemed to be on the verge of tears, was now laughing convulsively with Trish, while the one in the tracksuit was in earnest conversation with the barman.

'All right,' he said, grabbing her hand. 'Come with me.'

Sunday, 2 January, 1983

-18-

9.15 a.m., Sunday, Great Tey

Jacqui drifted across to the French doors, which opened on to the back garden and a small patio, and placed her trembling, hospital-scoured fingers against the glass. She was trying to put last night's events into order in her head but she couldn't seem to do it; jumbled images of dancing and fighting cascaded through her frazzled brain. She knew she'd taken something, and that she hadn't been to sleep, but she couldn't account for where she'd been at certain points of the night. She felt acutely removed from reality. One minute she was fine; the next, a cold paranoia crept over her. The crisp sunlight stung her eyes as she tried to focus on the curious scene in the garden – her husband hunched over a seldom-used Black and Decker Workmate and staring in concentration at a strip of wood. The lawn was a sea of sawdust.

She turned to her son. 'What's Dad doing?'

'Making a bird table.' Matthew's eyes didn't lift from his Atari game.

'A what?' she croaked, shielding her eyes from the morning light. Nick's breath was visible as he muttered, or cursed, to himself. Must be freezing out there, she thought.

'Or a bird feeder or something. I dunno – here.' Matthew patted around the sofa until he found a book, which he tossed on to the carpet. Catching her bare feet on fallen pine needles from the sorry-looking Christmas tree, Jacqui crossed the room to pick up the book with birds on the cover. She flicked through the pages, not sure what to make of it.

What on earth is going on in your head, honey? she thought, almost affectionately, and started to laugh.

Just then a volley of shrill curses came from the garden as Lowry kicked over the Workmate and launched a piece of timber to the far end of the garden. Even Matthew looked up in astonishment. 'Why did he do that?' he asked. But before Jacqui could formulate an answer, the doorbell rang.

Lowry sucked on his injured thumb. Shit, that hurt! Just when he'd thought his fingers were too numb with cold to feel anything, too. He smiled at his son, who was staring at him dolefully from inside the patio doors. Jacqui was there, too, looking pale as a phantom and with a look of amusement on her face which irritated him.

He patted his jeans for a cigarette, then remembered yet again that he'd given up. Shit. Jacqui was gesturing languidly at him. He could barely bring himself to speak to her – worry had distilled into anger over a sleepless night. Why, after the ordeal she'd been through, she had decided to stay around at Trish's till the small hours, God only knew. He felt as if he'd not slept a wink for worry, and when eventually he'd heard a taxi purr outside, he'd been instantly paralysed by inertia. After she'd stumbled up the stairs and into the bedroom, he'd hugged the eiderdown, unable to speak to her, and feigned sleep.

Now, he examined his thumb in the cold, squeezing it to see if the blood would ooze out from under the nail. These hands were only any good for punching, he ruminated, flipping the lid shut on his tool box. Anything requiring a modicum of skill or delicacy and he fell at the first hurdle. Fuck it. A robin chattered gaily from the garden fence a few feet off. 'You can fuck off, too!'

'Is that the way one communicates with nature, guv?'

'If "one" has nearly lost a thumb for his trouble, then, yes.' Lowry regarded the impeccably dressed Kenton, in his newer sports jacket, a white shirt and tie. Overall, an impressive display for a Sunday, if it weren't for the black eye. 'But you, perhaps, should focus your efforts on learning to work effectively with island communities before troubling yourself with the wildlife.'

Kenton reached his hand up self-consciously to his eye. 'I could've drowned, you know.'

'But you didn't.' Lowry opened the French doors and slipped his shoes off before entering the house. 'The Dodger has had complaints about intruders creeping around the houseboats yesterday evening, and one of his men pulled you out of the mud.'

'Can't remember much more than the incoming tide.' Kenton followed Lowry into the kitchen. 'I was soaked.'

'What were you doing down there?' Lowry rinsed his hands under the tap. Sparks had called him at the crack of dawn to lambast him about Kenton: 'The last thing I need right now, Lowry, is that old codger laughing at me down the blower because he's had to rescue a CID man from the mud – know what I mean?'

'A fisherman told me that the witnesses from the post-office job might—'

'Fisherman? What are you doing fraternizing with fishermen? And if you go further afield to interview witnesses, do it in daylight – don't creep around in the pitch black. No wonder somebody took a swing at you.'

'Hello, boys.' Jacqui sauntered in, dressed in a kimono. She smiled at Kenton and gave Lowry a peck on the cheek. He softened; his anger was already waning. She was all right, and that was all that mattered.

'Morning, Mrs Lowry,' said Kenton rather formally.

What a well-brought-up boy, thought Lowry.

His wife made to push down the plunger on a cafetière. 'Coffee, anyone?' She seemed jittery and twitchy and it looked like coffee was the last thing she needed. Why she insisted on getting so loaded after finishing a string of nightshifts was beyond him. it might release stress, but she wasn't twenty-five any more and her recovery speed wasn't what it used to be.

What was more, Lowry could see that his young colleague looked uncomfortable that Jacqui wasn't fully dressed. Her kimono was starting to ride up her thigh.

'I'll do the coffee – you get dressed,' he answered with a sigh.

Lowry's wife waved from the doorstep, still wearing her kimono.

'Dunno what's got into her,' Lowry mumbled, sinking down into the Spitfire's bucket seat.

Kenton didn't comment. The boss had never discussed his relationship with his wife, for which he was glad. The vision of Jacqui Lowry in her slinky robe was imprinted on his mind. He'd met her a few times, and had always found her attractive, but today took the biscuit – she'd looked like a slightly dishevelled 1950s movie star, and he'd found himself tongue-tied. The word at Queen Street was that Lowry was old before his time and that his younger wife was maybe too much for him. Kenton had never stooped to join in the gossip and had thought the suggestions unfair, but he had to admit it was disconcerting to find Lowry, a man not yet forty, building bird boxes on a Sunday morning while his sexy wife slid around the house in a nightdress. He reversed the Triumph through a cloud of exhaust, its engine roaring.

'Sorry.' Kenton winced.

Lowry said nothing. Smoothing his Brylcreemed hair, he reached for the hip flask Kenton kept in the glove compartment, and snuggled down into the seat as Kenton floored the Spitfire on to the main road.

-19-

10.50 a.m., Sunday, Colchester

Sparks hated waiting. He stood outside the worn, white, timber-framed chapel on Military Road, convinced that Brigadier Lane was doing this to annoy him. He strode the grass impatiently until he remembered he was in the cemetery, and that his irritable trudging may not be appropriate.

Voices from within the chapel rose in a close harmony; the service was taking place for the dead private. He lit a cigarette. He glanced at the clock, high on the wall: nearly eleven o'clock. The chapel was a strange building, a huge barn of a place better suited to Dorothy's Kansas than to housing hundreds of servicemen in prayer. Lane could have invited him to the service as a sign of solidarity instead of having him loiter around outside like some ne'er-do-well. He was the bloody police chief superintendent, after all, goddamnit. Feeling distinctly bad-tempered, he was on the brink of getting into the car and leaving when there was movement in the barracks chapel and a long line of men in green uniforms started to file out.

Sparks himself was in civvies and sporting a tan leather blouson. He'd avoided wearing uniform so as not to draw attention to himself, but it proved pretty pointless, given that they all seemed to recognize him and glared as they walked past. Now he felt naked.

'Ahh, there you are, Sparks.' Lane and his adjutant, a brawny, red-haired officer, marched across.

'Morning, Lane.'

'And what a fine one it is. Let's take a stroll. That'll be all, thank you, Major,' he said to his adjutant. The other man saluted and fed into the stream of uniformed bodies on the quadrangle. Lane forged ahead, striding past what Sparks knew to be the gymnasium, the venue for tonight's sparring. As Sparks caught up with him, he turned. 'Now, what do you think could have sparked this tiff?'

'Tiff? A shade more than a tiff, Brigadier, if you don't mind,' Sparks said stiffly. 'What sparked it off was your man taking exception to a couple of local lads in the pub.'

'Hmm, yes; Quinn. I know,' Lane mused, his hands clasped behind his back.

'He's from the same battalion as the other two – the Paras – bit on the big side for the parachute regiment, but, yes, we know he's one of them. So, given the obvious conclusions, I am here to insist we have no more of this retaliation nonsense.'

'Is that what you think this is?' Lane stopped in the middle of the quadrangle.

'Well, don't you?' Sparks said, vexed.

The military man's brow creased. It occurred to Sparks that, despite Lane's concern on New Year's Eve, he hadn't perhaps considered the matter with any seriousness.

The chief leaned forward and said in a hushed tone, 'I mean, come on, *really*. We can't have people beating the crap out of each other in the town centre, can we? Your mob follow bloody orders, don't they?'

Lane looked at him slyly, stroking his beard.

'Well, don't they?' persisted Sparks. 'I mean, the big worry is –' he inclined his head conspiratorially – 'that our recreational activities might come under the spotlight.'

'How so?'

'Our boxing bouts are reported in the *Gazette*. Suppose some smart arse decides the two are connected: "Sparring Paras not getting enough institutionalized violence in the barracks – resorting to the high street", and calls to ban the Services cup – that sort of thing. Think about it – the implications for the social side if we don't restore harmony to the streets.'

The other man considered his words. The boxing tournaments were of equal importance to both men.

'Now, look here, Sparks, it takes two to tango. Seen the state of Quinn? Yes, of course you have – Oldham collected him from you. A bit of respect for the military might not go amiss. I don't know how he ended up in that state, and I—'

'And nothing.' Sparks was beginning to lose his cool. 'Put it this way: if a Red Cap so much as spits on the pavement in future, all of this will stop.' He waved his arm, encompassing the whole barracks, when of course he only meant the gym. His raised voice had gathered an audience.

'Do I have your assurance that you'll catch those responsible for chasing my men across the park, resulting in an officer's death?' Lane responded stiffly.

Sparks tugged his blouson's imaginary lapels. 'I'm glad you brought that up.'

'Oh, how so? Progress?' Lane adjusted his cap and jutted his bearded chin forward, signalling approval.

'The other kid – the one who jumped off the wall – was lying. And when we went to interview him again, we discover he's been discharged from the civilian hospital.' Sparks watched the Beard for a reaction. 'I assume you have him squirrelled away back there.' He jutted his thumb behind him. 'The military hospital, Abbey Field.'

'That's shut, Chief Sparks. Now, wait a damn minute—'

'Only to civilians.' The frightful old place had officially closed a few years back. There were all sorts of stories – hauntings, the ghosts of nurses floating across the wards, poisonings – but, in Sparks's view, these had all been invented to keep civvies away. 'If you want this resolved, give me the kid back – he's the only one who saw who attacked them, for Christ's sake.'

'I am not aware of Jones's current situation, but I'll look into it.'

Sparks looked at him doubtfully. 'Scout's honour?'

'I give you my word.'

11 a.m., West Mersea

Kenton heard Lowry groaning as he got out of the car. His ears were bright pink. He was going to complain about the cold, Kenton knew it

'You know what they say at the station, Daniel, don't you?' said Lowry.

'About what, guv?'

Lowry pulled out a comb and swept his hair back into place. '*They*,' he said with emphasis, meaning the station, not himself: '*They* say you won't fix the roof on purpose because you feel you need to prove yourself as a man. Because you're embarrassed about the car.'

'Why's that, sir?' he replied, but he knew what was coming.

'An orange car with a 1300cc engine is, well – how can I put this delicately?'

'Not a man's car? Suitable only for hairdressers and ladies of leisure?'

'You've heard, then.'

'Well, they can say what they like. I think the car's great. It's a Triumph, and that's the engine it was built with. And I'm not trying to prove anything to anyone.' Kenton tried to sound defiant.

'And you're equally untroubled that everyone knows it was a present from Mummy and Daddy?'

That was different – he hadn't known that was general knowledge. How had that got out? Lowry knew, but he'd not say, surely. Kenton had mentioned it to WPC Gabriel – she had asked him how he'd managed to afford it, and he, forgetting what'd he'd said to the other lads and eager to prove himself not well off, had said it was a gift, not realizing then that it probably sounded worse. The car had been a twenty-first-birthday present four years ago. At the time, he'd been over the moon. Driving a sports convertible was cool, especially at university, where it was a huge help when it came to girls. But now he was in the police force – more than that, the CID – and life was a whole different ballgame. Working roof or not, cruising around in an orange car given to him by wealthy parents was doing nothing for his image. The car would have to go.

The houseboat moorings had a totally different feel in day-light. Kenton observed that the hulls were elegantly decorated in pastel pinks and yellows, and that under the sharp January sun the area was almost worthy of a holiday brochure. He had difficulty relating this idyll to his experience of creeping around last night in the pitch black.

They mounted the wooden walkway. The moorings stretched along the hard and were well spaced out, each having its own domain within the tufted grass and gullies of saltmarsh.

'This the one?' Lowry, looking incongruous dressed in a

144

donkey jacket and black Sta-Prest trousers and wearing wrap-around shades, gestured towards a large cream hull reaching several feet over their head.

'Yes . . . I think so.' He could see its name, *Ahab's Revenge*, running the length of the bow, so it must be, but everything looked so different from how it had last night. As they approached, a thick-set man with black curly hair under a woolly hat and a bristly chin resembling a sea urchin appeared by the hull.

'Morning, sir. Would you be Ted Nugent?'

'No, that's me,' said another man, who had popped up on the deck above them. He had bleached-blond hair and a tatty cardigan. 'Who wants to know?'

'Colchester CID.'

'Aye, thought it might be. Weren't me that clumped the young fella last night. I were asleep.'

'We're not here about that,' Lowry said. 'You were a witness to the post-office robbery last week?'

'I were leaving there when it happened.'

'You stated that it was the Taylor brothers?'

'Err, yeah, it were them, I think.'

'You *think*?' Kenton interrupted. 'Tell me, Mr Nugent, how certain are you?'

The blond man looked down at him quizzically from his lofty position on the boat.

'As sure as I can be . . . in such circumstances. I said all I 'ad to say to the police up there.'

'Tell me, sir. You know the Taylors?'

'Aye.'

'How tall would you say they were?'

He rubbed his jaw thoughtfully. 'I don't rightly know.'

'Roughly? Taller or shorter than yourself, say.'

'Shorter, for sure.' His companion nodded in agreement.

'The other witnesses said the gunman was a big chap, like Detect—' Kenton turned to indicate his boss, but Lowry was nowhere to be seen.

'Your fella there, 'e's round the stern with a pair of binoculars,' said the dark-haired man. Christ, Kenton thought, this isn't the time to go birdwatching. He walked furiously to the back of the boat.

'Sir, it would be a great help if you could . . .'

Lowry turned his back to the marsh and flicked his shades down. 'The light's too sharp,' he said, to no one in particular. 'You know, a fellow the other side of the estuary might think he's seen a totally different bird. Trick of the light.'

Kenton had no idea what he was talking about. He stepped aside as Lowry passed him on the walkway and addressed the men on the boat. 'Tell me, Mr Nugent, why did you give your address as 192 Seaview when in fact you spend most of your time here?'

'I'm not with you, sir.'

'My colleague has had trouble getting in touch with you to corroborate your statement. I wonder why you'd leave details of an address that you wouldn't be at.'

'It's no secret that I'm here. You found me right enough.'

'Were you here last night?'

'I was, for sure. Heard one fellow took a tumble.'

'You must be aware it's an offence to strike a police officer?'

'Weren't me, I tell ya. Can get all sorts round here at night. Anyway, he shouldn't creep around like that in the dark, unannounced, like. Serves 'im right.'

Kenton made to move forward but felt his boss's hand on his elbow. 'Maybe. We can discuss it on the way to the station, perhaps, where you'll review your witness statement of 27 December.'

'No chance; I'm busy. Got to get this varnish on the boat while the weather'll allow.'

Lowry paused for a second and looked across to the horizon. 'Put it this way: you're coming now, but you've a choice – either come as a witness or cuffed and under arrest.'

'Under arrest? For what?'

'For assaulting an officer.'

'Yeah, right, I should coco – how? On what evidence?'

'I saw you punch Detective Kenton, and I am here to make an arrest.'

'It weren't me, I tell ya!'

'It was dark, I'll grant you that, but who'll know any different?' Lowry made as if to go.

Nugent looked at Kenton, stunned. But it was as simple as that – a barefaced lie – and the man climbed down off the boat to join them on the wooden path.

Lowry walked slowly along the walkway, the boatman and

Kenton following. Something was not right. Nugent's witness statement definitely seemed dubious, but why would he make something up and risk getting himself in trouble?

They reached the road. 'Oh, I forgot,' Lowry said, 'we don't have a proper motor.'

They stared at the two-seater Spitfire. Kenton scratched the back of his head and looked away, embarrassed.

'S'all right. I'll walk,' Nugent said.

'What, ten miles to Colchester?' Lowry said, surprised.

'Colchester? Nobody said anything about Colchester.' Nugent's frown crumpled his weathered face. A small crucifix dangling from his right ear caught the light as he shook his head. 'No way, mate. I thought you meant East Road nick.'

'It's shut on Sunday,' said Lowry. 'We'll have to call a patrol car. Here, wait – where do you think you're going?' Nugent had started walking up the road. Kenton reached out and grabbed him firmly by the shoulder. The wiry man cringed under the DC's grip.

'I can't go to Colchester.'

'Why? What's the problem? You'll be back before the pubs open.'

'It's not that . . .'

'Well, what? Spit it out.'

Nugent looked sheepishly around him, and then said quietly, 'I got form, ain't I.'

'So your problem is what? You're a reformed character, surely. As a witness . . .'

'It's one thing going to see Bradley and Jennings,' he said quickly, 'but I can't be seen going down a nick the size of Colchester. I get seen, you know. People will think I'm a grass, won't they?'

'Hold on a sec. You testified that you'd seen the Taylor brothers do the job. How did you think that was going to pan out?' Kenton asked.

Nugent looked blank. 'It might've been them.'

'"Might've been"?'

'Maybe. Look, I don't know.'

'For somebody concerned about being seen as a grass, that's quite a risk to take, especially when you're not certain.'

'Hmm . . .' The man fidgeted, not knowing which way to turn.

'You mentioned Bradley and Jennings. Did they put you up to this?'

'The Taylor boys done something wrong is all I know. I ain't no grass.'

Lowry could see that Nugent must have been put up to it. The local police were after the Taylors for whatever reason – some minor misdemeanour or other – and Nugent had obliged as a false witness. It was only Kenton's diligence that had caught everybody out. 'Are you on parole?' he said after a moment.

Nugent nodded his head wearily, like a truant schoolboy.

'So why did you step forward in the first place?' Kenton asked, from two steps behind. 'Seems bloody stupid, given your situation.'

Nugent squinted in the sun. 'I didn't intend to, like. The poxy post-office clerk recognized me, an' said to the copper, "Them robbers came in just as Ted Nugent were leaving."' He looked dejected. 'I think it were them. All happened so fast, didn't it?'

'Well, think how lucky you are now, to have time to think things through. There's a phone box outside the Victory,' Lowry said. 'The detective constable here will call us a lift, and you and I can have a shandy while we wait.'

3.30 p.m., Friday Woods, South Colchester

'A bird table?'

'Yes.'

Paul snorted and leaned across to nuzzle her ear. She didn't like petting in the car in the daytime; there was something inherently adolescent about it, like kids with nowhere to go – which is pretty much what they were. She turned away and stared out of the window at the naked woodland, exposed in the glaring sunlight. Her mind was still on last night. She'd been stupid.

'Come here.' Paul yanked her towards him. And she hated to be manhandled like that. His tongue was already poking at her lips.

'Jesus, no.' She pulled back. 'Let's go.'

'What? We've only just got here.'

'I don't like leaving Matthew alone for too long,' she said, thinking of the bruising on her son's neck.

'Look, I wasn't laughing at him – there's nothing wrong with feeding birds,' Paul said apologetically. The way he said 'him', as though her husband loomed like some great unseen calamity, rankled more than if he *had* been laughing at him.

'I don't care if you were. It's Matthew I'm concerned about.'

'Could he be doing it for some new-fangled manage-ment-training drive?'

She rolled down the window, lit a cigarette and, with a withering look, said, 'Paul, Nick is a CID inspector, not some stiff from Lloyds. Sparks has them trying practically every outdoor sport available: when they're not in the boxing ring, they're rowing across the Blackwater or fishing off Clacton Pier – not building bloody bird tables!'

She felt nauseous.

'Are you all right? You've gone pale.'

She blinked her eyes rapidly. What the fuck was that? She opened the car door and retched.

Half an hour later she was curled up on the sofa, clutching the washing-up bowl.

'Mum? Mum! What's the matter?'

Jacqui could hear her son as if through a tunnel, but she didn't dare open her eyes. What on earth had she taken last night? She'd been fine this morning – well, not fine, but together enough to get up and see Nick's temper tantrum in the garden. She started to laugh, which prompted her teeth to chatter uncontrollably. Then she had another flashback, of

Paul lunging at her in the car, trying to stick his tongue down her throat. That had happened less than an hour ago. Then she'd been sick and insisted he take her home, saying she had pre-menstrual cramps. If only. She started to retch again.

'Mum, are you okay?'

'Fine, honey, just let me have a snooze. Just catching up on lost sleep.' Flashbacks. Fuck. The first made sense – a nightclub. Last night crept back into her consciousness. She'd been dancing, dancing like crazy with some guys they'd picked up at the bar. She'd taken something in the loo. Coke? Jacqui could never remember feeling this dodgy after doing stuff (and she'd done a lot, from LSD to methadone – sometimes a mix). And the memory loss was a new one, too. Maybe she was just too bloody old to hack it these days. Anyway, whatever it was, she'd only had a couple of lines, but it had been enough to send her into orbit. God knows what had happened to those blokes she was with. They'd been high as kites when she met them.

-20-

7 p.m., Sunday, Butt Road, South Colchester, towards the cavalry barracks

'Would you really have arrested him?'

Lowry and Kenton were walking quickly up the deserted road. Having dealt with Nugent, they had then been deluged with the huge volume of paperwork resulting from the Saturday-night arrests, which took up the remainder of the day. Before they knew it, it was gone half six, and they – or Kenton, at least – was required elsewhere.

'Yes.'

Kenton was surprised. He didn't believe Lowry would lie in a court room. 'I suppose he must have done it . . . he knew who I was.'

'It was dark,' Lowry said. 'You came to with your wallet? My guess is whoever hit you had a look, saw you were a copper then left you to wake up.'

153

Kenton paused under a street light but was intelligent enough not to feel angry and humiliated. He was grateful to Lowry for driving down there this morning, on a Sunday, for taking the trouble to back him up. But . . .

'Be more careful.' Lowry stopped ahead of him and turned round. 'C'mon; don't dwell on it. At least in the ring tonight it'll be bright – you'll see them coming.'

At that moment, though, they stepped out of the only patch of light they'd see until they got to the ring. Butt Road, just south of Southway and home to Colchester's first permanent barracks, was poorly lit, as if purposely to keep it hidden. Commissioned after an outcry at the dreadful sanitary conditions during the Crimean War, the cavalry barracks were modelled on those at Aldershot and were reputedly the finest example in the country. The imposing two-storey buildings with tall, substantial chimneys were in a deep-red brick, which rendered them black in the dark silence, lending the barracks a creepy, gothic feel. And silent they were, as most of the garrison's inhabitants would already be in the gymnasium, where Lowry and Kenton were now heading.

And there it was, moonlight reflecting off its steep slate roof. Set within the brick walls were deep, bevelled windows behind which shadows flickered wildly, betraying the activity within. The building had always reminded Lowry more of a workhouse than a place of recreation.

'Christ, it's cold,' shuddered Kenton as they drew close to the doors.

'You'll soon warm up.'

A shout of exaltation ripped through the night and was met by another cry from somewhere in front of them. Lowry's mind was taken back to the night before and the shouts of anger in the high street, and he wondered if they should have postponed the boxing for a week or so, until the situation calmed down, before embarking on this round of sanctioned violence. Too late now, he thought to himself, and pushed open the door.

A heady mixture of sweat, testosterone and uproar affronted their senses. In the centre of the cavernous building, beyond a sea of closely clipped heads, was the spotlit canvas itself, over which rested a cloud of cigarette smoke. Lowry paused on the threshold, his heart beating rapidly. Jesus, he thought, I used to be part of this. *I am this.* Only, now, he was at one remove from the whole affair, psychologically as well as physically. He felt an enormous sense of relief.

'Something up, guv?' Kenton had walked into the back of him.

'Nope, Daniel. Just savouring the moment.' He looked to see if his colleague had registered the friendly sarcasm, but the young DC's mind was firmly on the fight now: he frowned and looked steadily ahead. Lowry saw in his eyes a look he recognized – stoic and determined to do what had to be done. It was the essence of duty. He had been like that once.

Kenton headed for the changing rooms, Adidas bag slung over his shoulder, while Lowry made his way to the ringside.

He nodded to those he knew and pushed towards the front of the crowd of eager young faces shouting and hooting in anticipation. He wondered if the dead private had been fixed to spar tonight.

He made eye contact with Sparks, who was standing with a clipboard, addressing a lad of about seventeen who was jogging on the spot. Lowry nudged his way further through the throng.

'Glad you deigned to come, Nick!' Sparks shouted, struggling to make himself heard above the clamour.

Lowry looked across the ring to catch sight of a flurry of banknotes changing hands. They ran three bouts per contest, starting with the lighter-weight fighters, usually the younger, untried lads. The betting on them was lively – speculative and sometimes lucrative.

'Gary here is from the cadets.' Sparks clasped the lad by the shoulder and thrust him forward. 'Might not look much, but he's hard as nails.'

Lowry held out a hand and wished the boy luck. The boy in turn shot Sparks a quick look, as if for permission to take his hand. Lowry could see the apprehension in the kid's eyes. 'First fight?' he asked.

'First proper fight, yeah.' The inflection on the word 'proper' said it all. Tussles in the corps were all the action he'd seen – and they would be nothing compared to tonight.

'And his opponent?' Lowry asked Sparks.

'Over there, by the far corner.' Sparks jerked his chin

towards the other side of the ring, where a tall, acne-ridden youth surrounded by green uniforms was just visible between the ropes. The army lad had the height and therefore the reach, but a long neck, too; land a square punch and his brain would spin. If their boy could keep moving, he stood an even chance.

'Gary's quick,' Sparks said, as if reading Lowry's mind. Gary was puffing into his gloves, zoning out, focusing – just as Sparks would've told him. No emotion, no feeling, all mental resources funnelled into the physical delivery, the perfect punch: that was the chief's philosophy. Lowry could feel himself being swept up in the excitement of the fight. He surveyed the enormous gym: there must be close to five hundred men jostling in here, at least seventy-five per cent of them based on the barracks. He couldn't detect any unusual undertones in the atmosphere; if there was bitterness about the death of the para and the disturbance of the previous evening, it was well masked. A roar of excitement went up as the two youngsters climbed into the ring, and Lowry was carried forward by the crowd moving closer to the ringside.

In the absence of a microphone, the referee hushed the crowd by holding a bell above his head before introducing the combatants. The police cadet was unmoved by the enormous cry of support for the gangly army boy. Sparks had trained him well, Lowry mused, glancing at the commander, who was now hanging on the ropes. Kenton had appeared behind him in shorts and robe. And wait . . . Who was that with him? A shock of blond hair caught the light. Was it . . . ? Yes, it was the tall WPC who'd shown him the scene of the crime at Castle Park. Lowry felt a stirring of emotion akin to . . . what? Jealousy? No, surely not – he was glad the boy had a date – but did it have to be . . . Suddenly, the bell rang and a roar went up – they were off. Sparks's man threw caution to the wind and steamed in, pummelling his opponent. The army lad, surprised, staggered back. Cries of outrage went up. Lowry caught sight of the Beard, raging puce on the other side of the ring, and laughed. It was hard not to enjoy the atmosphere.

Then Lowry felt a tug on his sleeve and turned to see a solemn constable. The man had the cold on him still. 'Sorry to disturb you, inspector,' he said, almost shouting.

'What is it?' Lowry said loudly, knowing that whatever it was signalled the end of his evening. But he couldn't hear anything the lad was saying. 'Speak up!' he cried, still trying to follow the fight, which was getting tasty.

'Murder!'

The word scorched Lowry's ear, taking him firmly away from the ring.

8.10 p.m., Sunday, Beaumont Terrace, Greenstead Estate

Lowry stood back from the house, as was his way, taking in everything on the periphery of the crime scene before approaching the immediate vicinity of a death. There was sleet in the air, which was caught in the car's revolving blue roof lights. The houses on this terrace had only recently been built and were much newer than the cars that lined the streets. Vehicles often told him a lot about an area and, unsurprisingly, there was nothing newer than a K plate here, and there was even a tatty Land Rover predating both alphabetical plate systems just up from the house he was heading to.

Greenstead was already the borough's biggest housing estate, and they were still building – hadn't stopped since the mid-1950s. Lowry knew this part of town too well, having lived just a few streets away as a teenager.

'More new 'ouses. These ones can't have been up more than five minutes, and already they're killing each other in 'em. Bleedin' east-end trash.' The young constable held open the garden gate, grimacing against the sleet. Lowry didn't know him and met his comment on the residents with silent disapproval. He gently pushed open the front door, and a carpet of mail greeted him. This was probably a rental property. He remained outside on the doorstep a moment longer.

'Who made the call?'

'Bloke next door – smelt gas from the kitchen. He was in the shed fiddling with his homebrew – the smell must've wafted across the fence.'

'The back door was open?'

'Yes. The kitchen hob was on full blast.'

Lowry took a step inside the house. The building itself may have been relatively new, but already the carpet was dirty and the skirting boards scuffed. This house was nobody's home, that was for sure.

'Anyone been in the kitchen?'

'Only me.'

'Who let you in?' Lowry regarded the body, slumped at the kitchen table, its head face down in a plate of food.

'The front door was open.'

For the first time, Lowry took a good look at the constable and saw that he'd been wrong to judge him earlier. He was terrified.

The remains of an Indian takeaway on a tray sat in the pool of blood, which covered half the table. Lowry removed a glove and, with one arm across his donkey jacket to keep it clear, leaned over and took a sniff. Spicy.

'Vindaloo,' he said with satisfaction.

'Sorry, guv?'

'Curry – and a hot one. One I'm rather partial to.' He looked around the messy kitchen and located what he was after – a brown paper bag. Wanting to be on his own, he strategically dispatched the constable to pick up the mail, reminding him to be careful and note the addressees and frank marks. Then he took the brown bag and pulled out a takeaway menu: The Way to the Raj. 'Shehab's,' he murmured. He knew the place well enough to be on first-name terms with the owner. He placed the menu back in the bag and turned and scanned the work surface: there were two more dirty plates and several takeaway containers. Numerous Special Brew cans also littered the place, one on the floor by the deceased's foot. And there was something else underneath the table. He bent and retrieved a rolled-up one-pound note. He regarded it for a moment then ran his gloved finger across a section of the table. A line of white powder crested his finger. He lightly took a dab with his tongue, and ran it over his teeth. The taste was familiar.

Content that he'd committed a snapshot of the scene to his memory, he approached the body. Taking hold of a tip of each ear lightly in each hand, he lifted the head from the plate and sat the body back in the chair, revealing a slashed jugular. The arms of the body hung limply. He noted that the wall immediately behind the body was free of blood – no spray or marks. And there was only a neat puddle on the floor. He looked at the hands. They were grubby, with traces of mud and dirt, but no blood. Lowry was confident there had not been a struggle: the man had known his attacker, or perhaps had decided to top himself after one last, last binge, except there was no sign of the weapon.

He was disturbed by a scenes-of-crime officer at the back door.

'All yours.' He gestured towards the dead man, who promptly slumped forward into the half-eaten curry.

Out in the street, residents had gathered, aware that something was up. Lowry was buttonholed by a man in a dressing gown.

'What's going on?' the man, in his mid-fifties, rasped in his ear.

'A fatality, I'm afraid.' Lowry watched for his reaction in the light from the open doorway. The man was eager to know more – probably a neighbourhood busybody. Just the type the police love. 'Tell me, sir – you strike me as an observant man – that Land Rover over there; who does it belong to?'

'Land Rover? Bleeder's taking up Mrs Fleetwood's parking space. First noticed it yesterday evening.'

'Thank you, and excuse me for a moment. If you saw anything out of the ordinary, have a chat with the constable there.' He pointed to a marked Cortina, blue light rotating in the dark.

'"Out of the ordinary"?'

'You know,' Lowry replied, fishing out a pocket torch from his donkey jacket. 'Strange comings and goings, cars parked where they shouldn't be, unfamiliar faces, that sort of thing.' He walked over to the Land Rover.

It was locked. Mud spray reached up to the door handle. He flashed the torch through a window, but he couldn't see much. Crouching, he ran the light across the top of the vehicle's dashboard. Then he examined one of the rear tyres. Something caught his eye and he reached forward to extract some kind of black thread hanging from the deep tread. He looked at it curiously, then flashed the torch up into the wheel arch.

'Sir.' The intrusion startled him.

'Yes, constable. What is it?'

'There's another one upstairs.'

'Another one?'

'Person, sir. Deceased.'

Lowry levered himself up from the cold road.

The young PC had gone upstairs to relieve himself and discovered the second corpse. Lowry reflected that young officers often failed to search a crime scene properly – the shock of coming face to face with a gruesome corpse could render an inexperienced officer incompetent. It was understandable.

Lowry followed the PC back into the house and up to the bathroom. The naked bulb hanging from the ceiling rose gave the all-white room a scorching glare that stung Lowry's eyes. The victim, it seemed, had been attacked while he was on the lavatory. The features and fatal wound were hidden from view – the prone figure was wedged between the lavatory bowl and the bath. The victim's jeans were bunched at the end of a pair of hairy legs, a wallet poking out of the back pocket. Blood lay undisturbed across the bare tiled floor – a lake of it, almost reaching the doorway.

'Do you think he's dead?'

Lowry had forgotten the lad behind him. 'No, I imagine he's looking for the loo brush,' he said. They stared at each other for a second, the constable wide-eyed with horror. 'Nip downstairs and ask that SOCO to pop up, will you?' Lowry said.

The PC nodded and left. Lowry climbed into the bath to avoid the blood on the floor and pulled the victim's wallet from his pocket.

Shortly afterwards, Lowry left the house.

Inside the wallet there were two pound notes and a driving licence: Derek Stone, thirty-two, 19a Artillery Street. Lowry didn't waste any time. Having left the SOCOs to it, he drove over to the south side of town, cutting up through Brook Street, on to Barrack Street and turning right into Artillery Street. The Victorian terrace houses were close set and the numbers hard to see in the dark, so he bumped the Saab up on the kerb and walked up the street, his leather soles echoing in the cold night.

The house at 19a, it turned out, was a flat on top of a hair salon, halfway down the street. Lowry buzzed on the door, which rattled loosely. No response. It gave a fraction when shoved, indicating it was on the latch, so he was able to enter easily. The stairs led straight up to a two-bedroom flat. Checking the bedrooms first, Lowry's immediate observation was that both rooms had recently been occupied. The larger bedroom contained a saxophone and, judging from the military certificates on the wall, whoever lived there had a connection to the armed forces.

Monday, 3 January, 1983

8.15 a.m., Monday, Maldon Road, West Colchester

'Have a great day, Matt.'

Lowry's son did not reply, nor lift his gaze from the Saab footwell. It was too dark to make out the boy's expression, but it didn't take a CID inspector to deduce that the lad was not as keen to be dropped at his friend's house as he had been when it was first suggested, before the weekend. It was back to school tomorrow, and Nick thought Matthew would enjoy some company of his own age, having so far spent most of the break in his bedroom or with his grandparents.

'Why do you have to leave me here so early?' he complained.

'I need to get to work. Sorry, Matt.'

'You're always at work.'

'Busy time of year, I'm afraid.'

'And Mum's always in bed.'

Lowry felt a pang of guilt. Jacqui had returned to bed yesterday as soon as he and Kenton had shot off to Mersea, leaving

Matthew to his own devices all day. Okay, so she'd been at Trish's after the attack . . . but had she really needed to stay out that late? He glanced at his son, who was fiddling with his duffel bag. He and Jacqui had to talk; he couldn't allow things to lumber on like this – he knew this was a symptom of something far more complicated. He replayed her reaction when he had pulled her to her feet in the street, there in front of half of Queen Street. He'd let things slide for too long. And, at the very back of his mind, he wondered why it had been Jacqui, out of the four friends, who had been singled out.

Lowry returned to the present. 'Have a great day, mate,' he called, realizing too late he'd repeated himself.

Matthew grunted and forced the heavy door of the Saab open and climbed out.

'Matt . . .' Lowry reached across but the car door slammed on him. He sat and watched the boy tramp, head down, bag weighing heavier on his shoulder than it really should, towards the detached house of his best friend. It saddened him to see his boy start the new year this way; he had thought getting the boy to pack a football in his duffle bag would get him in the spirit. When Lowry was young, each year had given him the chance to excel in yet another sport, and there was the added bonus that it got him out of the house, away from the screaming and shouting. He should spend more time with Matt. Maybe he could take him birdwatching? He held out little hope that Jacqui would get into it, but his son might. He swung the car round clumsily and made for Artillery Street.

Lowry returned to Stone's flat for a second look alone, undisturbed, before Forensics arrived at nine, pulling on some gloves as he entered. The living-room curtains had been drawn and pale winter light fell on an array of throws and rugs which looked Middle Eastern. The room looked bleaker by day than it had under artificial light, despite the various ethnic knick-knacks and cushions. It was musty and smelt of stale cigarettes. Lowry didn't linger, passing instead into the main bedroom. Curled photographs on a cheap dressing table showed a young, uniformed Derek Stone with short back and sides – a far cry from the corpse in the Greenstead bathroom with his shoulder-length permed hair and tracksuit. On the wall above the dressing table was a creased poster of Chet Baker and Stan Getz: musicians from another era. As a proud photo from his sprucer days indicated, Stone was a military bandsman. His personal effects were slight: records scattered on the floor, an ashtray bursting with roaches, rizla papers, matches, empty Scotch bottles. However, the chest of drawers could have belonged to another individual entirely with its neat piles of crisply folded T-shirts and jumpers. Even the socks and underwear looked as if they'd seen an iron. That's the army for you, Lowry thought.

He moved across to the bed – a camp bed, also impressively neat, the *Jaws* duvet cover pulled taut – and knelt down beside it, sliding the albums on the floor to one side. He found a rucksack and, behind that, a shoebox, which he pulled out. Inside were nylon stockings. He removed a handful to reveal a revolver, a semi-automatic and some cartridges. Still wearing gloves, he examined the revolver: a Webley; without a doubt, it was an ex-army service revolver. The other weapon, the Browning, too. He replaced the guns underneath the stockings and returned the box to its hiding place behind the rucksack.

The second bedroom was empty but for a bare mattress and a limp Rucanor sports bag. Lowry peeked inside but found nothing. There was a Spurs mug by the mattress. He picked it up and sniffed: tea. A cuppa with milk could grow mould within a week – at a guess, this was three, four, maybe five days old.

He returned to the main living space. The room's stuffy odour was cloying. Instinctively, he made for the large windows that looked out on to the street, but he doubted they'd been opened since the summer, and he wasn't going to open them now. They were badly smeared from the outside, as though someone had started cleaning them but given up halfway. It was time for him to get going. He would leave the firearms for Forensics to discover. There was nothing unusual in finding revolvers such as a Webley in the homes of ex-servicemen, though, more typically, they'd be in a display cabinet rather than under the bed, beneath ladies' undergarments and along-side live ammo.

9.30 a.m., Queen Street HQ

The murders on the Greenstead Estate had put a spin on the Bank Holiday – bringing all the senior members of the force in.

'*Ex*-army, you say?' Merrydown's stress on the 'ex' was loud and clipped, causing Sergeant Granger to wince as he placed a coffee in front of her. Granger was supremely hungover – Sparks even caught a whiff of alcohol from across the desk – having got drunk after the fight. The ageing sergeant, having been forced out of retirement and back into the ring, received a severe hiding from a younger, fitter opponent, and chose to obliterate the experience in the Grenadier pub, which always had a lock-in after such events. Fortunately, Merrydown seemed not to notice – perhaps that fine Roman nose of hers filtered out unpleasant aromas emanating from the riff-raff.

'Yes, ma'am, he was made redundant in 1980,' Lowry, sitting next to her, answered.

Merrydown twitched her nose.

Sparks reached across the desk to grab his coffee. 'Yes, it's true, the army do give redundancies. There are fifteen regiments in Colchester, and each has a band. But the army's cutting back; there's little use for them. Other than for display purposes and doubling as stretcher bearers in conflict, they're not up to much; they've spent more time standing in for striking dustman and the like during the last decade than playing music.'

Lowry looked at him doubtfully. Sparks had a tendency to

show off his dubious knowledge of the military in front of the ACC.

But it seemed to be enough to impress Merrydown, who said, 'Hmm, really? Well, it's a relief, I suppose, given you already have one dead *active* soldier on your hands.'

Lowry went on to give details of the scene at the Greenstead house: the traces of drugs in the kitchen, the lack of a murder weapon. The chief placed his rancid coffee back on his desk and winced in disgust as Granger exited the office. His trusty batman had been intoxicated even before he'd turned up to the boxing match last night, and, the state he was in now, he couldn't even make a decent coffee. He turned to the assistant chief constable, who held her coffee cup affectedly, her little finger out as she listened intently to Lowry. Sparks wondered about her: posh and clever, she was always one step ahead of him. He never knew what she was thinking. The kohl eyeliner, which on Saturday he'd found alluring and exotic, like someone in an advert for Turkish Delight, only added to her mystery. He hadn't reached such a senior rank without having a certain acumen in judging human nature, but the ACC unnerved him.

'So, Stephen, what do you think?' she asked.

'A third man was at the house, as there were three plates out,' Sparks said, catching on quickly. 'And the evidence would indicate that the dead men knew their attacker – there was no sign of a struggle.'

'Well, get on it.' Merrydown crossed her legs, running her

hands down a navy skirt, and sighed. 'A drug-related double murder is the last thing we need.'

'Drug-*fuelled*, without a doubt,' corrected Sparks, reaching for his cigarettes, 'but not necessarily drug-*related* – that's different. Colchester doesn't have a drug problem.'

Lowry glanced at him in that sceptical way he always did whenever he made a bold statement.

'Stephen, don't be so defensive. You know as well as I do that the county is awash with amphetamines.'

'Awash? I know they're back, but we've just carried out a full clean-up operation the length of the Colne. Successful raids of barges moored at Wivenhoe and Rowhedge have closed down avenues into town and the university.'

'I'm not interested in floating hippies dispensing pot to students,' Merrydown said sharply. 'This is a different matter altogether.'

It was no use him interjecting. Merrydown had turned her attention back to Lowry and was now patronizing him with well-worn facts about speed now being the drug of choice. Since the recession had hit, use of amphetamines had been on the up: you got more for your quid and the buzz lasted longer than cocaine, which had fallen out of favour as the middle classes tightened their belts. And since amphetamines had been banned on prescription in the US only two years ago, there was plenty of stuff still flying around among chemists in the know. Speed had always been here, to a degree, even in the police force, until six or seven years ago. Sparks had no need of it himself, but had known it got his staff through shifts back then, and hadn't questioned it. After all, his father had been in the Battle of Britain and had always maintained that the RAF only won because our boys had a better grade of whizz than the Luftwaffe.

'I shouldn't need to ask, but your people are clean, I trust, Chief Superintendent?' asked Merrydown, as though reading his mind.

'This is 1983, ma'am, not 1963.' Sparks said firmly.

She seemed unsatisfied by this and turned to Lowry. 'Inspector, you're closer to the men on the ground – are they using?'

'Speed has never been that big a deal,' Lowry said.

'If people are getting killed, then it's a big deal.'

'Hey,' Sparks cut in. 'We just agreed this murder wasn't drug-related.'

'No, we didn't,' she snapped. 'You said that. For all we know, it could be the start of a drug war.'

'I don't think so, ma'am,' Lowry said. 'I found an automatic pistol in Derek Stone's flat last night. If he was going to Beaumont Terrace looking for trouble, he'd have gone armed.'

A short silence fell in the chief's attic office. This assertion seemed to pacify Merrydown. 'Okay. Maybe you're right. Now, from one intoxicated state to another – what on earth are these drunken riots in the town centre? Have we made our peace with the army?'

'We're making progress on that front,' said Sparks evasively.

'And have you identified who it was that started this whole mess on New Year's Eve? What does the other boy say?'

Sparks looked hopefully towards Lowry, but now it was his turn to be evasive. He volunteered nothing more than a weary shrug.

'Well? There were two, weren't there?'

'His unit has moved out.'

'What!' Sparks was aghast. He hadn't known about this.

'South Georgia. Part of the peacekeeping mission, it seems.'

'You *are* kidding?' She glared at Sparks with such anger that, for the first time in his life, he felt intimidated. 'So you've let that bearded buffoon of an action man whisk away the only witness from under your very nose! You bloody fool!'

-23-

10 a.m., Monday, Queen Street HQ

Sparks slumped dejectedly into the worn leather chair. Lowry almost felt sorry for him – almost.

'Thought that went rather well,' he quipped, trying to lighten the mood. 'But isn't "drug-*fuelled*" pretty much the same as "drug-*related*"?'

Sparks arched an eyebrow. 'Fuck off. What about the army shambles? That's your fault.'

'What?' Lowry said, surprised.

'I said I'd get you that lad for questioning by going direct to Lane. But no, the self-reliant, stubborn Lowry wanted to manage things on his own. Although, in this case, he got some bimbo in uniform to do it for him.'

'Okay. I misplayed it. I'm sorry. It seemed a simple thing. I never thought the man would leave the country.' As the chief searched for his cigarettes, Lowry leaned over to pick up the nearest of Sparks's two phones and dialled a number he knew well: Tony Pond. He checked his watch; Pond would be at his car lot by now. The Christmas Bank Holiday is always a busy one. The line connected after a crackle. He'd see what his snitch could tell him about the riot before updating the chief on Greenstead. With a curse, he realized that he should have made this call last night. He was not on top of his game.

Sparks lit a cigarette. 'Who are you calling?'

'Pond.'

Sparks, who already looked like he'd been chewing a wasp, shook his head in further disgust.

'Come on – if anyone knows anything, it'll be Pond,' Lowry said, encouragingly. Although the chief always referred to Lowry's snitch as a 'no-good spiv', it was he, Sparks, who had introduced them.

Eventually, a surly cockney accent answered the phone.

'Tony!' said Lowry.

Pond's tone on recognizing the inspector's voice brightened instantly. 'Well, Happy New Year to you, Mr Lowry. Trust you've been enjoying the seasonal festivities?' He chuckled darkly.

'It's been a ball so far. What have you heard?'

'Heard, inspector? Not a thing. I've spent a quiet one with my old mum at Frinton. Haven't heard a dicky bird. Best to be out of town this time of year, avoid any unpleasantness, don't you think?'

'And what unpleasantness would that be?'

'Ha ha. I wasn't here, I'm telling you. But word on the

street is the riot was payback for the young lad who died in Castle Park.'

Lowry glanced at Sparks, who was leafing through the forensics report on Stone's flat. 'And what do you know about that? Who was it that chased them across the park?'

'Drawn a blank, have we?'

'So far. I assume it must be local, given the repercussions.'

'Maybe not this time, inspector.'

'What do you mean? Come on, help me out here,' he said.

'All right, all right. This is what I heard. Three men were seen talking to two lads outside the George in the high street. One of the lads fits the description of the dead fella in the paper.'

'Description of the three men?'

'Big blokes. Not local.'

'Anything else?'

'That's all I got.'

'Sure?'

'Sure. If I knew more, I'd tell you, wouldn't I?'

'Cheers.' Lowry hung up. Sparks looked at him expectantly. 'He's heard that the fracas on New Year's Eve wasn't local lads.'

'How does he know that?'

'Who knows – he talks in riddles. I'll swing by the George later – he says that's where they were spotted in conversation with the two soldiers. Anyway, on to Greenstead.' Lowry sat back down and prised a mint out of his pocket.

'Yes – tell me something good, now that Merrydown's gone.'

'The Land Rover found in the street in Greenstead came from Mersea.'

'How can you tell?'

'Seaweed: traces on the tyre tread and up under the wheel arch. I reckon it must've been just either side of high tide to spray all the way up there.'

'Brilliant. Well done.' Sparks leaned forward eagerly. 'Anything in the vehicle itself?'

'A bundle of clothes covered in mud in the back. And two pairs of trainers, also covered in mud.'

'Two pairs? I thought we were working on the basis there were three people involved? That's what you let me tell that harpy—'

'Two were from Mersea. We have nothing concrete to suggest how many were in that house on Sunday; but, odds are, Stone's was the third plate. Then again, might have been two, three or ten. But we've made a start. Two men came in from the coast – more than likely from Mersea. One of the dead men had been in the Land Rover – the prints match. The mud and smell on the clothing indicates they waded ashore, suggesting that they arrived in unconventional, possibly covert, fashion. Given the substances found at the scene, it's a fair guess that drug smuggling was involved and that the murders are the result of a deal gone wrong.'

Sparks banged the tip of a cigarette on the desk and flipped shut the manila file on Stone's flat. 'Fair assessment. And the musician on Artillery Street – what do you reckon about him?'

'This bloke was a buyer, a small-time user – not a smuggler. He's a size ten shoe; the trainers in the Landy are both eights. So it looks like he was at the house, not in the Land Rover.'

'What? Stone was the customer?'

'No – *a* customer, not the main man by any stretch, given the state of his flat. He went there to buy, I'm guessing, but he had no cash on him, so any transaction must have already taken place. I think he's small fry who got caught in the crossfire.'

'So it says in the report. But it also says that the flat has another occupant: nothing to go on but an empty sports bag.' Sparks rocked back on his creaky chair, hands behind his head. 'It's a mess.'

'It's a bit more complicated than when Pond and Philpott were moving weed up the Colne to supply students, years back,' Lowry agreed.

The chief looked at his second-in-command. He sounded calm, although, given the situation, he should be feeling anything but.

'Philpott,' Sparks mused with distaste. The same man who had provoked the brawl on Saturday night. 'Moving away from dealing dope seems to have given him new ambitions. He's gone from being bonged off his nut in Rowhedge meadows to sparring with paratroopers.' He rubbed his knuckle reflectively. 'Where is he?'

'He checked himself out of hospital.'

'I'd like to know why he thought annoying a soldier the

size of Quinn was a good idea. But I doubt he had anything to do with the speed – tyke that he is.'

'He's your boy, so say they word and we'll pull him in.'

Sparks sighed. 'Get him in. Send Uniform. We better have a word.'

The chief spun round in his chair and propelled himself towards the window. It was a cold, bleak winter's day; typical grey January weather. Although they'd only just arrived in 1983, he'd already had enough of this year. He wasn't going to bollock Lowry over losing a witness – there'd been no reason to expect Jones to disappear altogether – but, all the same, Sparks resolved to make some changes. He would, himself, take a more active role in policing and not remain stuck up here in this attic, away from the action. There was no denying that lamping that soldier had got his blood up. A gull strutted along the black wrought-iron railing on the window ledge, its beady eye regarding him warily.

'Amphetamines don't send people wacko – or do they?'

'What, speed?'

'Yes. Not familiar with it myself. All I know is what I've seen in films – those little mods in *Quadrophenia* popping pills that make them dance funny.' He banged on the window pane. The bird cried out but stayed put.

'It was all pills in those days, not powder, nabbed from the chemist. Who knows what's in this shit,' said Lowry. Though he knew from the dab he'd taken from the kitchen table at

Greenstead that it contained something familiar. 'We'll have to wait for the toxicology report.'

'Good-o. In the meantime, scoot over to the island and see what you can sniff out about the Land Rover. Check in with the Dodger – that wiley old toad knows everyone's comings and goings.'

'Kenton is on it now – he's beginning to get a feel for the place at last.'

'Is he?' Sparks snorted. 'Not sure I'd agree – he came in the other night like the Creature from the Black Lagoon. How's he coming on, anyway? He's been here nearly three months – his review is next week.'

'It's a bit different to what he's used to,' Lowry conceded, popping another mint into his mouth, 'but it takes time to settle in out here. When you're used to the thrills of Surrey . . .'

'Nevertheless,' Sparks interrupted, spinning round to face Lowry, 'the lad fought well last night. He had a touch of the magic potion in his swing. I was worried he'd be distracted when I saw that blonde piece from Uniform hanging around, but he took that pencil neck in the fifth.'

'I'm glad,' Lowry said, and stood up to leave, not wanting to get caught up in boxing chit-chat.

'Middleweight wasn't such a success, though.'

Lowry's weight. He crunched down hard on the mint.

'Yes, in your absence, I had to field Granger – now, he *is* past it.' Sparks paused and frowned. 'What the fuck's wrong with you?'

Lowry had put his hand to his mouth. Something had cracked other than the sweet. He'd lost a crown.

'Eurghh!!' Sparks said dramatically as Lowry removed an incisor from his mouth. 'I told you – stick to the cigarettes. It doesn't become you, not smoking.' He laughed loudly for the first time that year.

There was a light rap on the door.

'Come.'

A fresh-faced uniform entered, clutching a piece of foolscap. 'Important message for Inspector Lowry. News on the owner-ship of Beaumont Terrace.'

Lowry snatched the paper from him. 'It's a council house,' he said to Sparks. 'The last tenants were evicted in October. It's been unoccupied ever since. The neighbours complained of squatters in December, though.'

'Excellent.'

The PC stood there.

'You have more?'

'A lady's scarf has been found at the scene. Forensics picked it up first thing when they went back to the house for a fresh look. It'll be here later today. And there's unopened post going back to October. We're checking two names; they should give us—'

'Forget the post – the people we're after aren't letter writers.' Sparks dismissed the PC and addressed Lowry. 'Maybe the third person is a woman?'

'Perhaps. We need people banging on doors. There must've been some activity in that house before Sunday.'

'Organize it, then.'

'With what? All our uniforms are currently wading in the Blackwater estuary, looking for a German's head.'

'Forget "Strood man",' Sparks said. 'There's a body, but no case. Leave it. Her ladyship didn't even mention it. Use that bird who was at the fight last night – if she's into hanging round gyms and watching sweaty blokes punching the living daylights out of each other, there might be a future for her in CID.'

'Lucky her,' Lowry remarked cynically. 'I'll bear that in mind.' He had plans, though; he'd be off to Mersea himself at some point, depending on what a certain bad-tempered Bengali restaurateur, unwittingly the last-meal chef for two men on Greenstead, had to say first.

24

10.30 a.m., Monday, Mersea Island

For the second morning on the trot, DC Kenton found himself on the way to Mersea. With him, he had the registration number of a blue 1955 Land Rover Defender.

The weather had returned to the dismal conditions of New Year's Eve, a thick, icy fog enveloping the land. Driving through it was slow and disorientating, like finding your way through a thick, grey soup, with no point of reference. And, of course, it was freezing in the convertible; despite wrapping up in gloves and a scarf, Kenton's extremities were numb.

But while he was cold on the outside, inside he had something of a warm glow. Last night had been a success: he had won his fight and remained unscathed, and WPC Jane Gabriel had come to watch. It hadn't exactly been a date, but when she'd mentioned it in passing in the canteen queue, he'd been keen immediately. Unusual, as most female officers tended to run a mile from boxing matches, but there she'd been on the night, a shock of blonde serenity amidst all that sweaty turmoil. He had been surprised to see her, as she didn't look the type for that sort of thing; she was a bit . . . how would he describe her? Fragile? Yes, fragile. But attractive, definitely. She even came for a celebration drink afterwards. His head throbbed, vaguely reminding him of the one-too-many he'd downed in the buzz of victory.

Blast! Instead of following the road round to West Mersea, he'd taken the left fork by mistake. He cursed the Spitfire's wipers, which were hopelessly inadequate at clearing the viscous sea mist from the windscreen. He slowed even more so as not to miss the right turn that would put him back on track and prevent him ending up in East Mersea. The mist gradually cleared as he rasped along the soft spine of the island. A murder of crows on a dormant field lifted abruptly into the murky sky as he passed. It was Lowry, of course, who'd told him that the collective noun for crows was 'murder'.

He swung a left to the seafront and found himself passing the Nugent home on Seaview – the home that Ted had left because his mother insisted he do something for himself, although painting houseboats and crabbing seemed to be the sum of it. As he passed the house, he noticed on the drive a white Ford XR3, which, the first times he'd visited, looking for Ted, he'd never seen. It had a large set of ladders on the roof and didn't look like the kind of car Nugent's mum would own. He slowed to crawl just as a busty blonde in a tight T-shirt at odds with the time of year came out of the house. She stared straight at him before climbing into the XR3 and driving away.

Kenton took the next left. Onerous though it was, he had to call on Bradley at home – the Mersea station wasn't open until the evening on a Bank Holiday Monday. He lived in a sedate close lined with chalet-style bungalows just around the corner from Nugent's house.

Although the Mersea police were responsible for filing their own reports, as a part-time station they required back-office support, hence Colchester's assistance in validating their paperwork. Kenton's involvement in the robbery that had taken place at the end of the year was part of this arrangement, but as the case began to look more and more dubious he'd found himself drawn in ever deeper – which would, inevitably, make him unpopular with the Mersea-based force. He stood, nervously shuffling his feet on Sergeant Bradley's doormat. He dreaded the prospect of asking the sergeant to open up shop to check out a possible Land Rover sighting.

The door opened to reveal the station sergeant in a string vest. Kenton stepped back. 'Sorry to disturb you at home, sergeant, but the station is—'

'Closed.' He scratched his expansive gut. 'I take it it's urgent?'

'Arthur! You're lettin' the bleedin' cold in! Shut the bloody door!' This shrill voice came from a stout silhouette at the other end of the hallway.

Dodger Bradley rolled his eyes wearily. 'You'd best come in, then.'

Kenton squeezed past the rotund Mersea sergeant, who appeared reluctant to retreat across his own threshold.

'Morning, Mrs Bradley.' The sergeant's wife, dressed in a pink overall, reminded Kenton of a school dinner-lady. She nodded sternly from the large kitchen.

'Suppose you'll be wanting a cuppa?' she said, in a tone suggesting this would put her out immensely but also that she would be offended if he refused.

'That'll be grand, Mrs Bradley, thanks. Nippy outside.' From the ceiling hung spider plants spilling from macramé pots, and at the far end of the house there was a conservatory which housed several large weeping figs.

'Lovely kitchen,' he ventured.

'Don't make yourself too flamin' comfortable,' Bradley snapped, his shoulder resting on the kitchen door-jamb. 'I presume there's a reason you're 'ere?'

'There's been an incident on the Greenstead Estate – a murder. We think those involved might have come from here. We're looking for the owner of a blue Land Rover.'

Bradley grunted. 'A Land Rover? Every other motor's a Land Rover on East Mersea, and between 'ere and Colchester, for that matter.'

'This one's an old one: thirty years or so. Plus, it had a tow hook. I was thinking it might've come from the boatyard.'

'Sounds more like a farmer's to me,' said Bradley dismissively.

'The vehicle has traces of seaweed on the wheel arches.'

Bradley raised a bushy eyebrow. 'Jennings pulled in a couple of drunk young fellas over the holiday, trying to launch a speedboat on the Strood at high tide for waterskiing. Bloody mad, this time of year.'

Kenton looked at him expectantly. But it took a stern glare from his wife for him to act.

'All right, all right, I'll call him.' He wandered off into the hallway, scratching his backside. Mrs Bradley shook her head woefully, pouring him a tea.

'Sooner he retires the better. Though what I'll do with him, heaven knows.'

'Loves the job, eh?' Kenton remarked. Mrs Bradley just tutted and got up from the kitchen table, busying herself with a mountain of laundry that was spilling out of the machine. Then Kenton had an idea. 'I was just over the road, as it happens, before coming here. I noticed a young blonde lady leaving one of the houses. She drives a white sporty Ford?'

'That car ain't hers,' barked Mrs Bradley. 'That no-good boyfriend of hers, Kevin Nugent – it's his.'

'Kevin Nugent?' he said disingenuously.

'Yes,' she puffed. 'Everyone knows him as Ted.'

'And what about Mrs Nugent?'

'He's trying to push her into a home, I reckons.'

'What does Ted do?'

'He's an odd-job man – painting, decorating, messing around on boats and generally getting up to no good.'

'Who's up to no good?' demanded Sergeant Bradley, who had appeared in the doorway, buttoning a blue uniform shirt.

'Ted Nugent,' said his wife.

The Dodger shot a glance at Kenton. 'Aye, I heard youse been troubling him. I'll be on to Sparks if our witness is being harassed.'

'Inspector Lowry says he's unreliable,' Kenton replied, uncomfortable at being reprimanded, especially by a man in a state of semi-undress.

'I'll second that,' the sergeant's robust wife added.

'Don't you go starting to meddle; it's not your place,' Bradley said. Kenton wasn't sure if this was directed at Mrs Bradley or at him.

The ageing sergeant continued the business of buttoning his shirt, muttering about the weather and asking Kenton how bad the fog had been, but making no mention of his call to Jennings. It occurred to Kenton that he might be going senile. Just as he was thinking this, Mrs Bradley prompted loudly, 'What about the Land Rover?'

The Dodger looked momentarily lost, and then said, 'Oh, aye. Jennings turned back an old Land Rover matching that description on New Year's Eve. It was after that body washed up.'

11.30 a.m., Colchester CID, Queen Street

Lowry sat deep in thought, poking with his tongue the hole where his front tooth should be. Before him on the desk blotter was an array of squiggles and descriptions of the three men who, on Sunday evening, at around seven p.m., had bought a takeaway from the The Way to the Raj, at foot of East Hill.

One of the three was Derek Stone.

The curry house, purporting to be Colchester's oldest (there were at least three which laid claim to this honour), was owned by Shehab, an obstreperous Bengali. However, Shehab knew his clientele, and in his opinion none of the men was military, and only Stone was local. Lowry replayed the conversation he'd had earlier that afternoon back in his mind.

'Him I see before –' Shehab had prodded Stone's photo – 'many times.'

'What about the other two?'

'Not local. But Essex boys.'

'How do you know they weren't local?'

'I know.'

'Army?'

'Not army.'

'How can you be so sure?'

'Not army hair. But not women's hair, like him.' He meant Stone.

'And why do you think they're not local – if they know him, and are from Essex?'

'Mr Lowry, sir, I know this country and the customers of this town,' he'd said, his short beard jutting out proudly. And then, indignantly, 'Much swearing at prices, but not from the one with woman's hair. He knows there many cheap places. No need to come here and shout. I say as much.'

Shehab had a reputation for being a bit pricey. 'Essex boys. Silly people,' he'd said. 'Pig farmers. One pay and wander off, leaving wallet. I give to dopey friend.'

Lowry switched on the Sony Walkman he'd found at Beaumont Terrace, presumably Stone's, as it was covered in his finger-prints, and plugged in the headphones. Some awful electronic music with brash vocals filled his ears; not what he'd expected a jazz saxophonist to be into. He turned the volume down.

Colchester was awash with Stone and his type: ex-servicemen, aimlessly drifting around town. The first place to start would be with Stone's service record, but those were classified. The best route was a chat with Oldham, to see what he knew or was prepared to say.

Lowry looked up and was startled to see WPC Jane Gabriel standing before him on the other side of the desk. He hadn't heard her come in with the headphones on. He pressed the pause button.

'Sorry, am I interrupting something?'

'No, not at all.' He smiled.

'Oh . . .' She put a hand to her mouth. Lowry was moment-arily confused, then remembered his missing tooth.

'Sorry to give you a fright.'

'Are you okay?'

Lowry waved it off. 'Sure.'

Gabriel smiled faintly. He noticed that, although she was nicely turned out, the uniform hung off her shoulders and the collar gaped at her slender neck; she was skinny as a rake.

'We've not been able to question Jamie Philpott.'

It was said with such discomfort and awkwardness that it made Lowry cringe. The chief, ever mercurial in his decision-making, had, he felt, made a mistake in assigning Gabriel to him. She looked so bashful standing there, unsure how to hold herself. He signalled for her to sit down, attempting to put her at ease.

'Why?'

'He's not at home.'

'Not at home,' Lowry repeated. 'No matter; we'll place his address under surveillance. Don't worry, not you – we'll get Plain Clothes to do it.' Then, in what he hoped was a friendly tone, he said, 'So you're a boxing fan?'

'I . . . I was intrigued. To see what all the fuss was about.'

'Did it live up to expectations?'

'Frankly, I found it all rather unpleasant.' Her expression changed to one of dry antipathy. Lowry raised an eyebrow; so, there was an assertive edge to her he'd not yet seen. 'Well, maybe next time you should ask to be taken somewhere more appealing, like the cinema. That film with the alien that looks like a potato seems popular . . . Anyway, the chief says you're to assist CID, given the dire straits we're in. Are you happy to do that?'

'Yes, of course.'

'Good. Welcome aboard – it's a blast.' He stood up and reached over to the coat stand for his donkey jacket. 'I'm off to meet DC Kenton on Mersea Island. I wonder if you might have a word with one of the girls Jones claimed he was with before the accident. A Miss . . .' He scrabbled for his notebook.

'Lesley Birch, Papillon Road.'

'That's her.'

'I've tried three times. No response.'

'Have you talked to the neighbours?'

'To confirm she's the occupant, yes.'

'What does she do?'

'I'm sorry . . . ?'

'For a living? She might have gone to ground at the weekend, but it's Monday now: pretty much everyone respectable is accountable for on a Monday. Work, college, job centre – chances are she'll be at one of them. Go and find out.'

'But it's a Bank Holiday?'

The thought had not occurred to him; the holidays had blurred.

'So it is. Give it one more try, anyway.'

And, with that, he left the office.

25

11.45 a.m., Monday, Queen Street

WPC Jane Gabriel was left smarting. Briskly, she exited HQ and hurried down the front steps, pausing to regain her composure in the biting air.

Being a Bank Holiday, Queen Street was deserted. Two PCs passed her on the station steps, giving her a cursory glance. It was then she realized – damn! – she had forgotten her cap. Never mind, she could quickly walk back home to New Town and get it. It wouldn't take more than ten minutes.

Walking the length of the high street, she thought about the night before, regretting her decision to attend the fight. Maybe she should have liaised with her fellow female officers first? To be fair, though, she'd heard the WPCs gossiping feverishly beforehand about who was fighting, so she was a little surprised to turn up and find only a handful of women present, all of whom looked as if they were there under duress. Her mistake had been to ask DC Kenton, which she'd only done because he'd stood next to her in the queue at the canteen. She'd known he was competing – strange, because he looked more like an overgrown schoolboy than a boxer, with his wavy hair and old-fashioned clothes. She certainly hadn't planned to spend the evening with him, drawing raised eyebrows from the many Queen Street supporters there. She'd even found herself holding a sweaty towel for him at one point.

Maybe that's why Lowry had been short with her. Perhaps he considered her behaviour inappropriate. She'd caught his eye across that smoke-filled hellhole and seen what she'd thought was surprise, but maybe it had been disapproval. All in all, it had been a very unpleasant evening: two hours of primal roaring, followed by a dutiful drink with a sweat-covered Kenton, who, in his over-excited state, drank far too much and was oblivious to the fact that she was annoyed. It was the last time she'd be going there as his 'date', or anywhere else, for that matter.

Midday, West Mersea port, Mersea Island

Lowry thanked the coastguard for turning up and opening the lifeboat station. It was a voluntary service, and he'd had to rouse from his slumber the rosy-cheeked lad who was on call. He was a little the worse for a heavy night at the Victory, the huge pub opposite the boatyard, but keen to help nonetheless.

He thumbed through the crumpled logbook. 'It's been quiet – not much happening this time of year. Too flaming cold.'

'Not pulled anyone out over the last week?'

'Not that I can see.'

'Vessels in distress, or lost?'

'That'd be the harbourmaster more than us.' The young lad looked apologetic. 'Wait – here. January the first . . .'

Lowry stepped closer.

'Oh, it's nothing,' he said, disappointed.

'What was it?'

'A tender – it was found adrift in the channel. Empty.'

'A what?'

'A tender, like a dinghy – a small boat for carrying people or supplies and stuff to a larger boat. This one probably came untied from a yacht.'

'Is it here?'

'In the boatyard? Yeah, I guess . . . though I don't know exactly where.'

'Know where it was picked up?'

'Yeah.' He turned round and tapped a finger on the map behind him. 'Roughly here.'

'Would it be possible, if someone had, say, come ashore and left that boat on the mud, for the tide to carry it out again?'

'Definitely.'

'Am I right in thinking the shoreline varies between shingle and mudflats?'

'Yes, below the tide line.'

'Might you have a chart?'

'Behind you.'

Pinned on the cabin wall was a detailed map of the estuary. The coastguard walked over and ran his finger along the shoreline, which was shaded variously yellow or brown.

'We're here,' he explained, 'and the mudflats start here.'

'Okay. I think I might take a stroll in that direction along the beach. Where's the best place to start?'

'Take the Monkey Steps down to the beach, just back up the road there, about five hundred yards or so.'

'Can I get all the way round to the country park on East Mersea? I'm meeting a colleague there.'

'Cudmore Grove; that's here.' His finger travelled the length of the island's shoreline from the westernmost to the eastern-most tip. 'It's a fair old walk – good hour, I reckon.'

'That's all right, I've got time.' Lowry thought it would be worth it, to get a measure of the coastline. 'Tell me – comings and goings in and out of the estuary: how easy is it to move in and out unnoticed?'

'That all depends.'

'On what?'

'Who's looking – at this time of year, visibility is poor, so with the naked eye you can't see a lot, even here in the harbour – let alone out there – but with radar the coastguard can easily cover this stretch of coast and spot pretty much anything bigger than a dinghy.'

Outside the lifeboat station, Lowry popped the Saab's boot open. To his mind, the muddied clothes and trainers found in the back of the Land Rover told a story. He ran his thumb over the soiled denims; there were traces of salt up to the groin. He didn't need a forensics expert to tell him that the owners had been wading across the mudflats off West Mersea. There was something else, though: a viscous, sandy-coloured mud that was unfamiliar. He took a closer look. It wasn't from the arable fields of East Anglia; he'd never seen mud like it on the numerous occasions that some farmer or other had unearthed human remains. He closed the boot and surveyed the boatyard. It was deserted, the only movement a lacklustre breeze that seeped through the riggings of the boats, tickling the lanyards. It would take an earthquake to rouse this place out of season; a couple of figures tramping across the mudflats up the coast wouldn't cause a ripple.

The Monkey Beach was so called because, in the eighteenth century, smuggler-hunting customs officers, insultingly nick-named 'monkeys' by the locals, had their lookout post nearby. It was also the island's primary tourist attraction, with its broad sand-and-shingle beach. Lowry descended the zigzag steps from the main road and passed an ancient wall, so skewed it looked ready to topple at any minute. He began a slow, plodding walk across the damp sand towards a breakwater in the distance, where the shingle would afford a firmer footing. Behind him were the harbour and the oyster sheds; to his left, the road, flanked by large Victorian houses; and to his right, the Blackwater, looming within a ghostly white mist.

Lowry played with his thoughts as he meandered along the beach. Given the state of the clothing and trainers in the Land

Rover, the tide must have been out; low tide fell at midday and, more significantly, at midnight. He was traversing the south side of the island, where the Blackwater drained into the North Sea. Though this wasn't the only place there were mudflats, from the charts it looked the most obvious place to land.

12.05 p.m., St Marys, Colchester

WPC Jane Gabriel had discovered from a neighbour who had been putting out milk bottles on Papillon Road that Lesley Birch worked just round the corner at Videodrome on Crouch Street, and that the store was open today.

A bell rang as Gabriel entered the store. The place was empty apart from a man with sideburns and wearing a raincoat, furtively considering the top shelf, a row of *Electric Blue* and *Emmanuelle*, no doubt. Clocking her police uniform, he hastily grabbed something from the horror section and made for the desk. Gabriel walked to the counter and stood next to him; he had a blue card headed *The Evil Dead* in front of him. Never heard of it, she thought. A woman in her late teens with a dyed-black wedge haircut returned from the storage room behind the desk.

'Seventy-five pence, please.' She slid across a cassette. 'Back tomorrow, before six.' While the man rummaged in his coat for the money, she addressed Gabriel openly. 'You look too cool to be a copper.'

'And you look too smart to be serving raincoats on a Monday afternoon.'

The girl shrugged as the man deposited a pile of silver and left hurriedly. 'I go to college on Tuesdays and Wednesdays.' But she offered no more; she was confident enough not to feel compelled to explain herself, Gabriel assumed.

'Recognize these men?' She held out two passport photos of the servicemen.

Lesley Birch nodded sullenly.

'Were you out with them on New Year's Eve?'

'Early on.'

'Until what time?'

'About seven.' She pulled a Silk Cut from a pack on the counter and casually offered one to Gabriel, who declined and instead pulled out her notebook.

'Where did you see them?'

'In the Boadicea – centre of town, on Headgate.'

'Jones said he was with you at the Golden Lion on the high street?'

'No, he wasn't with us. But that's where we go – I am a student, after all.'

'Who's "we"?'

'Me and Kelly.'

'How well did you know Private Daley?'

The girl looked away, touching the corner of her eye lightly, cigarette smoke curling up her face. Gabriel couldn't work out whether she was upset or embarrassed. Possibly neither.

'We got on better before the war – you know, the Falklands. There was a gang of six lads, all really close, and we all used to go out, me an' Kelly an' the girls. You know, drink on payday, messing around, as you do. They had so much dosh, living in barracks, like, never having to shell out. A shame . . .' She cocked her head slightly, recalling happier times.

Gabriel knew of horrors out in the South Atlantic from the papers but hadn't come into contact with anyone who had had first-hand experience. 'What was different after the war? Were any of his regiment injured or killed?'

'No, they all came back.' She took another drag on her ciga-rette. 'But one quit the army, another's posted in Germany . . . and now Daley. Nothing stays the same, does it?'

'So where were they heading that night?'

She exhaled smoke in a jet from the corner of her mouth. 'Dunno, but they were pretty edgy.'

'Edgy? Scared, or nervous?'

'Anxious. They were up to something –' she held up her hands – 'but don't ask me what. Looking for someone. Going from pub to pub, couldn't settle, like.'

'Did they mention any names?'

The girl scrunched her nose in that way young girls do, reminding Gabriel that she was, for all the make-up and cigarettes, a girl just out of school.

'Nah. I asked – thought maybe we could help – but they said we didn't know them, whoever *they* were. They were from out of town is what Jones kept saying, like.'

'Maybe they were trying to impress you?'

'Nah, I doubt it. They might have been to the Falklands, like, but they were pretty clueless about anywhere else.'

'Did Jones say anything else?'

'Nah, just that they were looking for these fellas from out of town.'

'Fellas? You're sure it was plural?'

'Positive. Whoever it was, they were only down for the night.'

Gabriel thanked her for this vital information but added sharply that it was a pity they hadn't spoken to her before now.

'We've been trying to get hold of you all weekend. We've been to Papillon Road several times.'

'It's a student house – what can I say? We all went home to our mums and dads to get fed over the holidays.'

-26-

12.15 p.m., Monday, Queen Street HQ

'What? Speak up, man.' Sparks stood in his office, clutching the telephone receiver and frowning angrily.

'I said, your CID boys are making life difficult.' The voice was so soft he could barely make it out. 'They scare the life out of one of my witnesses, and dismiss him as unreliable. The young one, Kenton, says they've got another lead. But then he's seen watching 'is 'ouse!'

'So? What the fuck? That's what they do. Be straight and stop dicking me about. I've got enough problems without nonsense from you.'

'But I can't file me crime stats for December while there's a question mark over the robbery.' Dodger Bradley's voice was almost a whine, and Sparks despised whining.

'Jesus, what the hell do you want me to do about it? How long have you been running that nick?! The case is back open. If you think the witness is credible, stick to your guns.

But tie up the loose ends, will you? Then we won't have to bother you, will we?'

'The trouble is our chap's got form.'

'For what?'

'Armed robbery. He's on parole.'

'Well, maybe he's turned over a new leaf – putting money into the post office instead of taking it out without an account.'

'You know how ex-cons are. He won't want to be fingered as a grass.'

'Well, make your flaming mind up, but stop complaining to me about it. Jesus!' Sparks slammed the phone down. 'Peasant.' God, that woman had put him in a bad mood. She'd called again to remind him that he had to improve his clean-up record.

'What?' he barked at the bulky form of Granger, who was standing tentatively on the threshold to his office, as he had been throughout the phone call. 'Come in, come in. I've not got all day.'

Granger stepped forward, a large envelope in his hand. 'Lab results on the drugs at the Beaumont Terrace murder scene.'

'That was quick.' Sparks tossed a cigarette in the air and caught it between his lips, an unconscious habit of his when he was stressed.

'Assistant Chief Constable Merrydown insisted the lab give it top priority, so . . .'

Of course, the ACC, sticking her oar in again. Hell's teeth, once she got her claws into you, that was it, she just wouldn't leave it alone. So much for his and Lowry's confidence-instilling chat this morning.

'Well, what of it?' he muttered as Granger handed over the manila envelope. He lit the cigarette and sat down with the report. He was aware of Granger lingering. 'Is there something else?'

'Would that have been Sergeant Bradley on the phone, sir?'

'And what if it was?' He looked up disdainfully, seeing not an officer but a middleweight well past his prime, as had been demonstrated the night before.

'It's just that—'

'Just nothing.'

Sparks did, on the whole, like Granger, finding him reliable and dependable, while many of those around him were not. But he did have a tendency to try to interfere in areas he shouldn't. And Mersea was one of those areas. His sister was married to Dodger Bradley, and he was inclined to stick up for his beleaguered brother-in-law.

'The post-office robbery, that Detective Constable Kenton is—'

Sparks met Granger's watery, tired eyes. 'I know what you're going to say – just because I said that to *him*,' he said, glaring at the telephone. 'But there are more serious matters to attend to, don't you think?'

The seal on the envelope was unbroken – meaning that Merrydown hadn't seen the report before him. He tore it open. The compound scientific names were of little interest; all he cared about was the summary – the effect on the drug user. Straightforward amphetamines were nothing to get hot and bothered about . . . blah, blah, blah, yes . . . yes . . . Hello. What was this?

The compound structure of this substance has the potential to lead a user to exhibit patterns of psychotic behaviour. Instances of hallucination and delusion are likely to increase proportionately with increased intake of the substance. Memory loss is common, and can range from hours to, in extreme circumstances, days. Gaps in short-term memory can occur both as a side effect, for several days after use, or when the user is under the influence of the drug; instances of the latter may confuse the individual, rendering him/her severely paranoid and a danger to themselves and those around them.

1 p.m., East Mersea beach

Lowry held the binoculars and scanned the grey blur where the horizon should be. The point where the sky met the sea was hard to judge: sea mist sealed the two like a greasy smear. According to the coastguard, the tide was on the way in but, right now, it was out for what looked like miles.

'Fuck, it goes out a way,' he muttered to himself.

'Sure does.'

Lowry turned to see a man in a Barbour jacket with dark, wavy hair. He struck the detective as handsome in a classic, chiselled sort of way.

'Not much to see out there,' the man said.

'Quite.'

'Are you Customs?'

'No; CID, as it happens. Why did you think I was Customs?'

'Not that many people as smartly dressed as you would be peering out to sea on a day like today.'

Lowry shrugged and scrunched back on the shingle. 'You're right. And yourself? A twitcher?'

'Hah!' The man flapped his hands forward in his Barbour pockets. 'Sort of. I'm responsible for the park as a whole – including the birds – but also for this.' He gestured with a sweeping motion behind him to what appeared to be a small cliff. Lowry hadn't noticed it before. The face of it was a grubby red-brown. It was as though the land had been severed abruptly, for there were toppled trees below while the roots of those remaining close to the edge above poked out precariously.

'Hell, that's dramatic – what happened? It's as though something's taken a bite out of the island.' Lowry climbed the steep shingle bank and touched the cliff surface.

'You're not far wrong: erosion. The sea is slowly eating away at the island.'

'What is this, a sort of mud?' asked Lowry, recognizing the viscous stuff from the boots he'd found in the Land Rover.

'Not really; it's London clay. And here is one of the few places you can find it on this coast. Very good for fossils.' The man played with a clump of it between his thumb and forefinger. 'Yes, you never know what might turn up.'

'I reckon you're right there.' Lowry smiled.

'Where have you come from?' the ranger asked. 'You look as if the cold's taking its toll on you, if you don't mind me saying.'

'I don't. I walked up from West Mersea, from the houseboats.'

'My, that's a good four miles. You've done well, tramping across this terrain.'

'Do you know much about the coast?'

'Only that it should be protected – birds nest there in salt marshes around those boats, in the grass. Oystercatchers, dunlin and the like.'

'At this time of year?'

'No – and a good job, too. These high tides bring in giant swells from the Atlantic. I'm surprised any of those houseboats are still there.'

'You wouldn't think it to look at it now,' Lowry scanned across the flats.

'Oh, it's not so bad now. The surges have subsided. And the tide will always go out again, as long as we have the moon!'

Lowry had taken to the ranger. He realized that this country park was exactly the kind of place he wanted to spend more time: outside, in the open air. The gloomy, damp weather didn't bother him – sooner that than a bawdy, smoke-filled gymnasium. He felt good.

27

1.05 p.m., Monday, Cudmore Grove Country Park, East Mersea

Kenton parked in the empty car park, as instructed by Lowry. He was excited and impatient; he had a lead. Climbing out of the Spitfire, he reflected on what an unusual place Mersea Island was, with its part-time police station and peculiar houseboat community. And what sort of place had he arrived in now? Although it was early afternoon, there wasn't a soul around; this really was the back of beyond.

Moisture clung to the air, and the naked trees were motionless in the bleached landscape. No wonder the park was deserted; it was more like the setting for a John Carpenter film than a country park. He could just imagine some ethereal spirit drifting in and out of the thin white trees. Suddenly, out of nowhere, something large and grey flew towards him, almost without a sound.

'Crikey,' he muttered. It was a large bird of some sort.

Just then, he heard two low voices and, to his relief, he

saw Lowry rounding the information hut, accompanied by a young, dark-haired man.

'You look like you've seen a ghost.' Lowry was laughing.

'I thought I had. Whatever it was, it had huge grey wings.'

'It was a barn owl,' said the dark-haired man. 'We disturbed her coming back from the cliff.'

'An owl? Don't they come out at night?'

'Yes, but you quite often see them in the daytime.'

'Doug, this is my colleague, Detective Constable Kenton.' Lowry stood back as the two men shook hands. 'Doug Young is the park warden here at Cudmore Grove.'

'If there's anything else I can help with, please give me a shout,' said Doug.

Lowry nodded and waved as Young left for the hut. He filled Kenton in on his morning.

'So you reckon this is the place they landed?'

'It's as good a place as any,' said Lowry, his lips now tinged blue with cold. 'The soil matches that on the clothes and trainers in the back of the Land Rover. A dinghy with an outboard motor was found adrift in the estuary with nothing in it apart from a torch compass and a plastic bottle of red diesel.'

'Adrift?'

'Which indicates to me they arrived at low tide – seeing how far it goes out here, they'd never tow it across that mud. We can check the tide times. Must have just left it there, and that's why it floated off when the tide came in.'

'That doesn't make sense, though. Why would anybody do that?'

Lowry looked up at the bleak sky. 'I reckon they were lost, don't you? Easy enough in weather like this. Even Columbus would get lost in this shit. So, what did you find out?'

'The PC stationed at the cordon across the Strood on Saturday night turned back an old Land Rover. Two men were inside. Mid-twenties.'

'Turned back?'

'Yes – it was the night they found the body on the Strood. The road was shut from one fifteen to two thirty a.m.'

'Of course.' Lowry frowned. 'How could I forget? Have you a tide timetable in there?' He made a show of looking in the car, knowing full well there was no such thing, then climbed in. 'Never mind. How did it go with the Dodger otherwise?'

'Oh, okay.' The car started gingerly and Kenton drove off, wincing as the Spitfire's exhaust caught on the earth camber of the mud-track exit. If they got stuck, he'd never hear the end of it. He didn't want to mention the robbery, or Nugent; the whole episode was an embarrassment to him. Instead he said, 'Do you think Sergeant Bradley might be going senile?'

'Very possibly, yes,' Lowry said, tightening his scarf and hunkering down in the bucket seat. He seemed preoccupied.

'Right, let's get out of this goddamn cold,' Kenton said, raising his voice as the car took off on the straight and empty East Mersea Road. His nose had gone numb – he really had to do something about this car.

1.10 p.m., Colchester General Hospital

Jacqui hurried on to the ward. She was late for her shift.

After a lost weekend, she'd slept dead for fourteen hours and hadn't managed to stir herself until gone noon. Hastily tying up her hair, she'd not had time to put on her face or even have a shower. Heads lifted from the nurses' station – shift handover was in progress – among them, Trish, her forehead concertinaed with concern when she caught Jacqui's eye.

'What? I'm only ten minutes late,' Jacqui whispered, sidling up to her.

'Not that,' she hissed back. 'I need to talk to you.'

'What?'

'Excuse me, sister, I need the loo. It's urgent!' Trish clutched her elbow and hustled Jacqui out of the nurses' station, grabbing something as she went. Jacqui was barely out of her coat.

'Jesus, Trish, what the hell's the matter with you?'

'In here, quick!' Trish ushered her into the Ladies. 'Look at this.'

She thrust the *Gazette* under Jacqui's nose. Two Butchered after Drug-fuelled Frenzy screamed the headline. Jacqui's pulse quickened as she read the article.

'It doesn't name them. It might not be—'

'Oh, come off it – it says Greenstead Estate.'

'But this was last night – it was Saturday we were out with them.'

'And Sunday morning. It's got to be them. Mid-twenties. Drugs. Jacks, we were fucking there!'

'Were we?' Then a chink of reality forced its way into her consciousness. 'I can't . . .'

'Can't what?'

'Can't really remember.'

'I'm with you on that.' Trish sighed, 'Whatever that gear was, it was powerful stuff, all right. I still don't feel myself.'

'Me neither – flashbacks all the time. I can't remember anything after we left the club.' She hadn't tried to remember was nearer the truth; she'd blocked it out, and every time she did think about it, she felt nauseous, like the time in the car with Paul yesterday (and even *that* meeting felt like it might not have happened).

'Imagine what those boys were on – they were racing faster than flamin' James Hunt when we met them.'

Jacqui returned to the article to be greeted by her husband's name, then looked up to see Trish eyeing her.

'What are you going to tell Nick?'

28

2 p.m., Monday, Queen Street HQ

Kenton stood in the corner of the chief's office next to Granger. Lowry was in front of them, patiently explaining to Sparks his theories on the Greenstead murders and the drugs coming in from Mersea. It was patently obvious he did not like the situation. Smuggling was difficult to police on this coastline, and they thought they'd stamped it out, or so Kenton had heard.

'Okay,' Sparks said sharply, 'let's assume that this is the case. Focus on finding the bloody stuff and the maniac that did those men in Greenstead. That's our priority now.' He levelled his stare at Kenton. 'Stop poking about with the post-office robbery; you've discredited their witness – bravo. So now let them get on with it. I don't want the Dodger bleating down the phone at me again.'

Sparks ground out his cigarette and glowered at the three men in the room. A pulse throbbed at his temple: the tension was palpable, and they were each personally responsible for the turn of events. 'These drugs –' he picked up a manila folder and flapped it on the edge of the desk – 'they aren't your run-of-the-mill amphetamines.'

'No?'

Kenton glanced at Lowry as he sat back down, calmly adjusting his Sta-Prest trousers as he crossed his legs. The inspector was at ease, perfectly calm. Oddly, the more intense Sparks grew, the calmer Lowry became, and vice versa. It occurred to Kenton that he'd never witnessed the two of them overheated about something at the same time. It was either one or the other; they were never both angry at once.

'No.' Sparks flipped open the folder. 'What we appear to have is a mix of amphetamine and lysergic acid diethylamide – LSD, or acid, to give it its street name – and something as yet unidentified.'

Lowry leaned forward, his interest piqued. 'Are you kidding?'

'Nope. There's not enough here to try out on a human guinea pig –' here, he gave Kenton a surreptitious glance: clearly, it would've been him – 'but the chemist reckons that in the compound the effects are unpredictable and dangerous.'

'How dangerous?' Kenton asked uncertainly.

Sparks torched the end of another cigarette with a heavy desk lighter, and shrugged. 'The lab boys are cautious: mildly aggressive to psychotic behaviour, depending on the level of intake.' He exhaled. 'Could mean bloody anything – they're just covering their arses.' He tossed the folder on the desk.

'Oh, and memory loss or blanks are practically a dead cert with this shit.'

'Well, that explains his bad mood, I guess.' Kenton flicked back his hair as they descended the tight staircase from the chief's office to the main office. 'With good cause – this is another matter altogether.'

Lowry remained quiet. He preferred not to discuss Sparks's behaviour. Whatever the disputes between himself and the chief, he didn't want to generate disrespect for Sparks in the recent recruits. However, the fact was that Sparks did not like the unknowable – it was as simple as that. Murder, he could deal with – even the possibility of West Mersea being the new gateway to drug pedlars' paradise. But present him with an unquantifiable problem – like untested drugs – and he panicked. Lowry opened the door to CID, to be greeted by a surly WPC, who handed him a manila envelope and strode off downstairs without another word. Everyone was chippy today, it seemed. The envelope read *Artillery Street*. 'I'm sorry?' he said, realizing Kenton was still talking.

'Those drugs,' Kenton said. Lowry turned to him and was taken aback by his large, pink paisley kipper tie. Somehow, he'd not noticed it.

'That your dad's?'

'I'm sorry?'

'The tie.'

Kenton held it between thumb and forefinger. 'What's wrong with it?'

'Bit early in the year for something that loud.' They entered the kitchenette. Lowry jiggled the kettle. Empty. 'The drugs? Doubt they're lethal – who'd ship in a ton of drugs that'd kill the user? Wouldn't be good for repeat business.'

'But this stuff sounds really dangerous.'

Lowry lit the hob. 'Everything has the potential to be dangerous. It's a matter of understanding. New variations of drugs are always popping up. Just because our boys can't fathom the compound with their chemistry set, doesn't mean it's anything special. Sparks was right – maybe we should try some?'

Kenton's young face was intent.

'But not today.' Lowry spooned Nescafé into the mugs. 'This'll do for now. Now, forget about drugs for an instant. Sparks brought up the post-office robbery.

'Yes.'

'Why did he do that?'

'I . . . I told Bradley you'd discredited their witness. You know – Nugent – you said yesterday—'

'Yes. Yes.' The kettle began to whistle. 'And so Bradley called the chief – odd.'

Kenton scratched the back of his neck nervously. 'I wasn't rude to him – I mean, he wasn't too happy when I turned up at the house, because the station was shut, and his wife was—'

'I'm not worried about that.' Lowry poured water into the

mugs. 'Something just occurred to me – I don't suppose you recall what firearms the gunman who did the post office used?'

'A semi-automatic and an old service revolver.'

'Are you sure?'

'Yes; I'm very familiar with the paperwork. But the chief just said to leave—'

'Let me worry about him. How sure of the authenticity of the statement are you – given the track record so far?'

'It's from the clerk's statement. He had the barrels shoved in his face, so I reckon he was pretty sure.'

'Good.' Lowry slid the paperwork on to the kitchen worktop and lay it out, mindful of a mousetrap next to the sugar bowl. 'There were shots fired?'

'Two. In the ceiling.'

'The two guns found at Derek Stone's were a semi-automatic and a service revolver. Get the striation marks matched to these. I didn't mention it up there, as there was no need bringing the Mersea robbery into it yet, given the dodgy statements—'

'Bloody hell!' Kenton beamed. 'Result!' A wave of jubilation flooded through him: this was down to *his* persistence. Fine-tooth combing the Mersea report had kept the case in everyone's mind.

'Maybe,' Lowry replied, less exalted.

'What are you doing, then?'

'The garrison – see if they can shed any light on Derek Stone.'

29

2.30 p.m., Monday, Abbey Fields, Colchester

Lowry knew enough of the military police routine to know that if he waited around in the right place for long enough he could snag the captain of the Red Caps. Screened by poplar leaves in the warmer months, the grey Victorian headquarters, usually so severe, was starkly revealed by the winter landscape. And it wasn't just the trees that were bare; the entire military district seemed deserted. The wide open playing fields, usually fraught with activity, with red-faced corporals hollering as panting new recruits jogged around the perimeter, lay empty. Only a solitary runner could be seen, in the middle distance, sprinting across crisp grass, through the line of leafless poplars. Lowry had trained on these fields many times, hence his familiarity with the area.

He'd parked close to Flagstaff House, the austere military police HQ, and, although he'd been there only ten minutes, it felt longer. He was used to long stints of sitting in the car, but not without cigarettes. After his early relapse, he was determined to give kicking the habit another shot. But if his irascible commander was a test of will – one that he'd failed so easily – it was nothing compared to a January afternoon alone in the car as the light began to fade. The thought of nicotine, and the comforting glow of a cigarette end, nagged at his patience. He forced his mind instead to think about amphetamines and the traces of speed found on the Greenstead Estate.

The toxicology report had confirmed high levels of the drug compound in the bloodstream of the two dead men. In Lowry's experience, the one reliable thing about drugs was that if you took a particular substance – speed, say – you knew how it would make you feel. Take too much of something and you overdosed, but, in general, if you knew what you were taking, then the outcome was predictable. Lowry's own tender years of popping pills and bopping along to the Small Faces in dingy local clubs attested to this. However, the effects of this unknown cocktail seemed dangerously unpredictable. Could it really send people crazy and turn them into homicidal maniacs, as Sparks was inferring? Lowry remembered rumours from the Vietnam War, about the Americans having used experimental drugs on troops to turn their men into fearless killing machines. But they was far-fetched and unsubstantiated . . .

Just as Lowry's feet were beginning to numb in the footwell of the Saab, Oldham materialized between the Doric columns framing the entrance to Flagstaff House. He pattered down the steps and headed unwittingly towards Lowry's parked car. Right, sonny Jim, Lowry thought, it's time we turned the tables.

Waiting until Oldham was practically upon him, he sprung the door open forcefully, almost hobbling the military man.

'Captain Oldham, I beg your pardon. Nearly had you there!'

'Detective Inspector Lowry.' Oldham's eyebrows converged angrily beneath his peaked cap. 'You nearly had my kneecap. What are you doing here, anyhow?'

Lowry pulled his donkey jacket tighter as he stood tall against Oldham. 'I'm after the Beard,' he lied.

'Oh, about the boxing. Congratulations on your victory, by the way.' Oldham wasn't remotely interested in the bouts and forbade any of his own command to take part; he would know about last night's result, but probably wasn't aware of Lowry's retirement.

'It's not about that, actually.'

'Oh?' Oldham straightened his cap.

'The soldier who survived the fall – Private Jones – appears to be bound for the South Atlantic, which is a nuisance.' Lowry tutted. 'He's the key witness. If there's to be an inquiry, it'll be compromised. I'm here to outline the ramifications to the brigadier.'

'An inquiry? Wasn't it an accident?'

'Yes, but that argy-bargy in the town the other night has escalated the situation. But I'm sure it's not your concern,' Lowry added dismissively. He paused for it to sink in, watching for a reaction, but Oldham gave nothing away, so he pressed on. 'Seeing as you're here, perhaps you might help with another inquiry?'

The Red Cap commander was reluctant to speak and looked to be considering making an excuse. Lowry observed his fine, almost Slavic features and olive complexion and wondered at his background. Balkans, perhaps . . .

He tried another tack: 'It would certainly placate Sparks if you could help with our other problem.'

'Of course.' Oldham exhaled deeply, a cloud of condensation visible in the air. 'What is it?'

'I'm after information pertaining to an ex-bandsman, a Lance Corporal Stone, made redundant in 1980; he played the—'

'I'm sorry,' he interrupted, relief in his voice. 'Once someone's out of the army, there's nothing I can help you with. There are simply thousands of ex-serviceman that pass through Colchester.'

'Of course, but pointing me in the direction of the dead man's regiment, with a word from you to cooperate, might speed things along.'

'Dead, you say?'

'Throat slit from ear to ear.' Lowry usually kept such information to himself, but Oldham was unlikely to tell the *Gazette*, and a few honest details might just prompt him to cooperate.

'What was his regiment?'

Lowry pulled out his notebook and gave the captain all the information he had. Oldham's tone changed, and he adopted a helpful air, describing to Lowry exactly where he should go. He even explained the rationale for the cutbacks in military bands and why Stone's job had been axed; the resources required for the Falklands had resulted in job losses on the military fringe (Lowry already knew this from Sparks, of course, but feigned interest). He jotted down the regiment details with a blunt pencil and thanked the captain. As he opened the Saab door, he felt Oldham touch him lightly on the elbow.

'The accident at Castle Park – I'm surprised that an inquiry is to be held. You think it suspicious?' he asked, with what appeared to be genuine concern.

'We think it was an accident,' replied Lowry, 'but it would be helpful to find all of those involved, to see if they're in any way responsible for the mayhem on Saturday night.'

'I see. I'm sorry about Private Jones, then; his unavailability certainly doesn't help matters.' Oldham gave Lowry a grave nod of farewell before moving off at a fast clip.

2.35 p.m., Queen Street

Sparks strode back up the road. He'd been to the fruit-and-veg stall at the bottom of the road, opposite the Mersea round-about. He didn't have to go and buy fruit – the canteen was adequate – but, after a raft of meetings, he'd felt suffocated up there in his garret. Sparks certainly prided himself on loving his job, but there were aspects he found stifling. Meetings and paperwork got to him, the more so when progress was slow and answers were lacking, as they had been today. But he'd decided that a more hands-on approach would remedy that. Get out from behind the desk and get stuck in, that was his plan. Lord knows they needed an extra pair of hands and a brain as sharp as his. Plus, he loved these streets.

Already he felt better for some air. He pulled a Granny Smith from its paper bag and demolished it quickly. He'd say this for Colchester: the fresh produce was superb, provided you stuck to the local independent shops that thrived here. Keeping a sound constitution was a passion of his. He might drink like a fish, but he ate healthily and heartily, and the busier he was, the hungrier he grew.

And he loved to be busy. For him, a certain level of crime was desirable and necessary; it allowed him to exert authority and to justify the existence of his Queen Street HQ. So long, that is, as they got results. Merrydown's words – 'worst in the county' – played constantly on the periphery of his mind. And this latest crisis – potentially lethal drugs – was the last thing he wanted on his watch. As the day wore on, and the facts sank in, he'd started to fret about the real possibility of drugs coming through West Mersea. Had he been too complacent? There'd been no real issue with class-A drugs since the 1970s. Then, along came the recession and the decline in the use of cocaine, and as a result the coastguard was less active. Had they taken their eye off the ball?

Ahead of him in the street was the blonde WPC, the one he'd assigned to help Lowry.

'Constable!' he called. She turned, her nose red with cold.

'Sir.'

'Good to see you at the fight last night,' he remarked. 'Some say women have no place ringside, but not me. If you're man enough to be on the force, then why not?'

'How about inside the ring, sir?'

Sparks studied her face for clues as to whether this was a joke, but she remained staring dead ahead. He found her inscrutable, just like Merrydown. What was it with women in the police? Why were they so bloody difficult? 'Well, this is the 1980s – anything is possible,' he said, in a mildly patronizing tone, eager to change the subject. 'So, how are you finding rubbing shoulders with CID?'

Her eyes remained stony as she responded. 'I've just interviewed Private Jones's alibi – the girl he claimed both he and Daley were in the pub with on New Year's Eve, before the accident.' She stopped on the station steps. 'She says they were meeting people from out of town – London, maybe. To do what, she didn't know.'

'You're sure?'

'That's what she said.'

Sparks smiled. If folk from outside Colchester were responsible for Private Daley's death, then the feud between squaddies and locals was over, and his life became more manageable. Excellent. 'After you,' he said jovially, ushering the woman into the station. He'd call the Beard straight away. It was progress of a kind.

30

2.55 p.m., Monday, Colchester High Street

Lowry sat in the Saab outside the George Hotel, trying to make himself heard by Sparks over the radio. The line wasn't great.

'I said, I've just seen Derek Stone's old sergeant,' he repeated. 'And now I'm outside the George to check out Pond's story about the scuffle outside.'

'All right. I was just saying – hold on.' There was a thud, and a burst of muffled conversation. '*What? You what?* Lowry, I have to go – the Beard is raging down the phone.' And with that Sparks snapped off, leaving only a static hum.

Lowry wanted to check the George's hotel register and talk to the staff. It was a long shot, but maybe these out-of-towners had stayed there overnight, or at least stopped in for a drink. Meanwhile, he had a lead on Lance Corporal Derek Stone. The regimental sergeant major of Stone's old battalion had been very helpful, thanks to Oldham having a word. Stone had found a new job of sorts, as resident musician at the

Candyman, a jazz snug on Sheregate Steps. The seedy little bar built into the old Roman wall on the south side of town was not far away but wouldn't be open for some time yet.

He entered the gloomy foyer and approached the front desk.

'New Year's Eve, you say?' The dusty, waistcoated concierge flicked through the register. Thick-rimmed Eric Morecambe spectacles slid down the bridge of his nose, catching on bulbous, veined nostrils. 'Three fellas? Together?'

Lowry realized how unlikely this sounded. 'They may not have stayed over – perhaps just used the bar?' That, too, sounded improbable, given it was New Year's Eve and the George was hardly a kicking nightspot.

The old man frowned and pushed back his glasses. Lowry was sure he was the same concierge who'd been on the desk when he and Jacqui had spent their wedding night here ten years ago, before flying off to Spain for their honeymoon. The musty decor hadn't changed either.

The concierge sighed and shrugged. 'It was New Year's weekend. We were fully booked.'

'Yes, of course,' said Lowry resignedly, already assuming this line of inquiry was hopeless. He surveyed the dismal array of decorations; the tired rows of tinsel did little to lift the gloom of the lung-red wallpaper and drab maroon carpet.

'The rooms are mainly booked out to couples – men and women. Although there was –' he looked a little embarrassed

– 'one middle-aged gentleman down from Norwich with his "son".'

Lowry rolled his eyes. 'No, forget it. Thanks.' He turned to go.

'Shame about those two young lads at the castle,' the old man croaked.

'Yes . . .' Lowry swung round. 'Wait – you didn't happen to see them, did you?' Uniform had spent the last two days sweeping the high street for witnesses. He'd strangle someone if they'd missed the George.

'Yes, I saw them. There was an argument going on in the street when I finished me shift that night. Two young lads with crewcuts and a dapper gent. Recognized the blond lad in the *Gazette*.'

'Did you not tell the police?'

'Been off the last two days. Thought nothing of it. Only saw the paper today, like.'

'Okay,' Lowry said calmly. 'I don't suppose you remember what the man they were talking to looked like?'

'As a matter of fact, I do. He had a fancy jacket and a handlebar moustache. These two young fellas were shouting at him.'

'What about?'

'Didn't stop to listen. Figured it was none of my business. But then the dapper gent, seems he'd had enough, and I saw him jab the blond one in the chest, like that.' And he mimicked a feeble prod with his index finger.

'And then what?'

'There was a kerfuffle, and some other fellas – big lads – came along, so the two soldiers scarpered. Just like that.' He clicked dry fingers.

'Did you get a look at the others?'

'Nah. I didn't hang around, like. I just wanted to get home for me tea.'

'What time was this?'

'About seven.'

Lowry tapped his pencil against his notebook. 'When you say a "fancy jacket" – what do you mean? An overcoat?'

'No, a jacket. Piping down the lapels, like him off the telly.'

'Who? Doctor Who?'

'No . . .' The man's face creased with the effort of trying to recall. 'No, he were in something else first . . . Oh, can't remember that neither. This other one, I couldn't understand a word of it; me and the wife gave up on it.'

Lowry pondered for a second. '*The Prisoner*?'

'Aye, that were it.'

There was only one man who dressed like that in Colchester.

'And one more thing – how many big fellas were there?'

'Three.'

He thanked the man for his time, and left the hotel. Before heading back to Queen Street he paused to consider two things. The first was curious and troubling. In his mind's eye, the two soldiers had been pursued by a gang – perhaps four or five men. But the witness claimed there had only been three men. Why run? Would they not stand and fight? The second was more a matter of annoyance: the man in the suit with the piping sounded very much like the man who'd tipped him off in the first place. Tony Pond.

3 p.m., The Fingringhoe Fox, Fingringhoe, five miles south of Colchester

What the hell? *What the fucking hell?* That was all Felix could think as he sat alone at the bar of the almost deserted pub. He could barely speak, nor stop his fingers from shaking; he sat with his hands firmly clasped, one over the other on the bar. He removed his left hand slowly to pick up his pint and straight away his right began to tremble as though he had the DTs. Plus, there were cuts and blood all over both hands. Blasted brambles. He was in the right place now, though; the phone box was there, just over the road. He drained his glass.

'Another one, please.'

'Are you sure?'

'Eh?' He looked up to see the round, kindly face of the landlady.

'I mean, you look washed out,' she clucked. 'A good night's sleep is what you need.'

He scanned the bar furtively. There was only an old duffer at the far end and a dog, flat out on the floor under the bar stool. Keep it together, he said to himself. 'Nah, I'm fine for one more. And another pack of Monster Munch.'

'Another pack?' She frowned.

In front of him were the twisted remains of three empty packets. *The biggest snack pennies can buy.* The TV ad flashed through his head. He was in the right place. Something was missing, but he *was* in Fingringhoe . . .

'Yeah, one more, then I'll be off.' But off where? That's right, to make the phone call. Gotta keep it together. That shit they'd taken – God knows what it was – it was giving him flashbacks. Flashbacks! You don't get *them* from speed. This stuff had messed with his memory. He wasn't even sure how long he'd been in the pub. One hour? Two? He did remember waking in the shack in Donyland Woods but was unclear on how he'd got there. And where was Jason? He had made it here on his own, having lost the others outside a curry house in Colchester. He shovelled a handful of crisps into his mouth. A curry. He'd kill for a curry right now. But that had been last night. Shouldn't Jason be here by now? Where had he got to? Fucked if he knew. But he did know the time to call – that, at least, was written down for him; yes, that he did know.

'There you go, luv,' said the landlady, her brow creased with concern. He must look really rough. He glanced at the dog, which was now sniffing his feet, which he realized were covered in mud. The dog looked up at him. Its strange, floppy face, with flaps of skin hanging over a drooling jaw, was too unpleasant to countenance in Felix's chemically unbalanced state. 'Fuck off!' he hissed. He absently scraped the mud off his shoes on to the bar stool as he suddenly recalled trekking through the woods last night to the abandoned shack.

He clutched his head – what had happened to his train of thought? The woods – yes, that's right, he remembered now – roaming around in the dark, off his knockers. The headache was coming back. He needed another line, to keep his focus; otherwise he'd go doolally. He finished the crisps and popped the bag. *The biggest snack pennies can buy.* He started laughing.

3.15 p.m., Police Social Club, Queen Street

'I am not a number, I am a free man?' Kenton repeated.

Lowry had opened up the social, and he and Kenton sat alone in the basement bar, contemplating a large, sweaty pork pie that was under a Perspex dome. The question was how long it had been sitting there, basking in the warm glow of the sunken bar lighting. Neither man had eaten today and this was all there was to be had.

'Indeed.'

'Never heard of it.'

'*The Prisoner.* I never watched it, but I know for a fact that the Prisoner never had a handlebar moustache.' Lowry picked up his pint. 'But Tony Pond does.'

'But that's the chap who tipped you off in the first place.'

'Yes. He mentioned three men from out of town arguing with our boys, but omitted to say he'd been arguing with Jones and Daley himself.'

'So, the argument he mentioned – did he say what it was about?'

Lowry considered his answer. 'No. People like Pond only ever help by degrees, but he knows I'll be back for more if necessary.'

'Do you have a theory on what it might've been about?'

'Directions to Castle Park?' Lowry quipped, and reached for the pork pie. 'No, no, not yet . . . Of course, when I tried calling Pond again just now, there was no answer.'

'Hence a restorative pint.' Kenton beamed.

'And some lunch,' Lowry said, attempting to divide the pork pie with a plastic knife. The utensil flexed uselessly. Kenton felt his appetite slide.

'Rock hard; like those Paras, so we're led to believe. Why didn't they stand their ground and fight it out? These guys are famed for their fearlessness. You don't expect them to leg it down the high street at the first sign of trouble.'

Kenton laughed softly as his boss continued to fight with the obstinate slab of pie, finally succeeding in slicing it. He was genuinely excited by the course of events and the gradually unfolding mystery, and hoped to have a hand in solving it.

'Ah, there you are!' came a familiar bellow. The chief's sudden entrance caused Kenton to dissolve into hiccups. 'Got time to lounge around, eh?'

'It's my lunch.' Lowry spoke through a mouthful of pie.

'It's gone three. What've I told you about the importance of regular mealtimes?' Sparks tutted. 'Hmm, just time for a fast large one.' He went behind the bar and reached up to the optics.

Kenton looked at Sparks, taking in his five o'clock shadow and the sprinkling of dandruff on his navy pullover. The chief turned, clutching his drink. He was smiling, but not in a friendly way, Kenton could tell, even though he didn't know him well enough to gauge all his moods. Sparks drank heavily from the glass then clunked the tumbler carelessly on to the bar and wedged himself between Kenton and Lowry.

'Now then, Nick. Please explain something to me. Exactly why did you advise the captain of the military police that we're holding an inquiry into Private Daley's death, when the idea has never so much as been raised? And given that we're supposed to be working *with* the military, not against? Of all the people to lie to, that stiff—'

'It was that stiff's office who fobbed us off about Jones's whereabouts. You can bet they didn't even check.' He brushed crumbs from his palms. 'They hold us accountable, yet don't lift a finger to help.'

'All the same, don't go making stuff up that only compli-cates matters.'

Lowry seemed unperturbed by Sparks's outburst and remained sitting stoically on the bar stool.

'And get that fucking tooth fixed – you look like Bill Sikes.'

'Err, don't you mean Fagin, sir?' Kenton suggested.

'You trying to be funny?'

'I can't get an appointment,' said Lowry, wearily tossing a pound note on the bar for the drinks and the pie. 'Hardly surprising when half the town has spent the weekend fighting

– there's probably a queue the length of the high street for missing teeth. I assume you told the Beard that those lads at Castle Park weren't chased by locals—'

Granger burst into the bar, making a beeline for Lowry and cutting him short.

'Sorry to interrupt, sir –' he gave a cursory nod to Sparks – 'but the landlady at the Fingringhoe Fox has called asking for Detective Inspector Lowry. Says it's urgent. There's a man in her pub, early twenties, covered in blood and clearly on something.'

31

3.35 p.m., Monday, The Fingringhoe Fox, Fingringhoe

It took them less than fifteen minutes to get there.

'Which way did he go?' Lowry gasped, surprisingly short of breath after a ten-yard dash from the car park to the pub.

'Don't rightly know.' The woman coughed and banged her chest sternly, as if to dislodge a small amphibian. The air in the pub smelt of woodsmoke and was hard to breathe. The fire was unable to draw in the damp, oppressive atmosphere. 'He was just sitting there, laughing. When I saw all the blood on his hands, I went to call you lot, and when I come back, he were gone.'

'What was he wearing?'

'One of them coats with the furry hoods, you know.' She flapped her hand round the back of her wide neck.

'An anorak?' Kenton offered.

''As a funny name – it were a blue one.'

'Snorkel jacket.'

'Yes, luv, that were it.'

'Anything else you can tell us about him?'

"E just sat there, rocking and laughing to 'imself,' she said, pulling on a ceramic beer pump, 'and eating crisps. Packet after packet. Like some sort of loon.'

'Told Dougal to fuck off 'n' all.'

'I beg your pardon?' Lowry turned to see a red-faced man in a flat cap perched at the far end of the bar.

'Me dog.'

Lowry switched back to the woman. 'How long ago did he leave?'

'Ten, fifteen minutes ago. Like I said, 'e were still 'ere when I called. Something weren't right.'

'Because he had blood on his hands?'

'All over his fingers. I did right, though, didn't I? You came running, eh?'

'Yes, madam, we did,' Kenton said kindly, 'but what did you think was up?'

'Eh?'

'Other than the blood on his hands – was there anything else?' Lowry added quickly.

'Oh. He was filthy and looked as though he'd not slept in weeks. And . . .'

Lowry looked around. There wasn't a soul to ask other than this witless landlady and the beetroot at the far end of the bar.

'And what?' he prompted.

'His eyes. His eyes was glassy, like he were on something.

And, you know, I read in the paper about that awful business in town.'

'Thank you. You did well to call us. It might be nothing to do with that, but we need to rule it out. If only we knew where he was heading.'

'Follow his trail!' the florid drinker hollered.

'Excuse me?' said Kenton.

'Mud from 'is shoes. Look!' He pointed. 'Ain't that what you detectives do?'

Outside the Fox, the cold bit deep. The adrenalin rush of the dash from Queen Street had subsided, and Lowry felt the beer he'd drained resurge uncomfortably. He'd not been to Fingringhoe in many years. It was a small village, made up of little more than a church, a manor house and the pub. Its sole contribution to the local economy was shipping sand out of the quay along the Colne.

'Think about it, guv; he'll surely be making his way back to Mersea, where he came from.'

'Yes, across country, I know. But it doesn't make sense. Why, if he's our man, would he go to all the trouble of travelling rough and staying hidden only to stop at a pub halfway? It's not as if he's on a nature ramble.'

'Maybe he developed a thirst?'

'Or was waiting for someone.' Lowry looked across to the folly, a brick tower attached to the grounds of the old manor house. According to folklore, it had been built to disguise a bear pit, though his grandfather maintained that it had been used by the army as a lookout for smugglers because of the view it commanded of the Colne. He ran to the gate and along the path towards the folly door.

'Do you think he's the man we're after?'

'Covered in blood and on drugs? I think it's more than possible, don't you?' The folly was shut, the entrance overgrown.

'What's between here and the island?' Kenton called breathlessly behind him.

'Fields, marshland and frozen mud.' He rattled the heavy wooden door – locked – and, stepping back, squinted despondently at the top of the tower, from where a spray of doves now fled.

'Helicopter would spot him easy enough.'

'Not in this fog.' Lowry paced the gravel, annoyed. 'It's sitting too low. Got any cigarettes?'

'Glove compartment.' Kenton didn't question his chief's need for a smoke, but he did wonder on the call for a helicopter; surely it would be more effective. And the fog did appear to be lifting over the marshes, slightly. Lowry walked back to the car, still in front of the Fox, and bent over the Spitfire door to get the cigarettes. Having lit one and taken a deep drag, he stepped across the narrow country road to a break in the hedgerow, next to a telephone box. Kenton followed, mindful of the drainage ditch, which his boss had just effortlessly leapt.

'Or maybe he's heading for the channel from the quay,'

Lowry said, thinking aloud. 'Either way, Mersea will have a better vantage point. We'll catch him there, and anyone who's helping him.'

Lowry weaved through the brambles, thorns catching on the sleeve of his coat. They studied the landscape for signs of a possible fugitive. The ploughed field on whose perimeter they stood eased gently towards the salt marsh several pastures beyond, and the channel itself was just discernible, a dull glint in the distance under a swirl of mist which encompassed the land like a protective covering. Kenton pulled his anorak tight as they made their way back.

'Hey, what's that?' A bright red, rotund bird flickered in front of him through the hedgerow.

'That I do know – a bullfinch. As a lad, I saw them everywhere here,' Lowry remarked. 'Funny, they're here all year round but they're only seen in winter, when the landscape is leafless. If only a man in a snorkel jacket was as easy to see as a bird.'

'Is Mersea really our best bet?' said Kenton. 'It'll be tricky to cover the beach with any degree of accuracy . . .'

'We don't have much choice. It'll be dark soon.' Lowry turned to face him, front tooth missing and unlit cigarette hanging from his bottom lip. 'Of course, it's a gamble. Everything is.'

Felix watched the men retreat through the hedge. Weird, that – men in suits, in a place like this; not farmers, surely. Policemen, maybe? Nah, he was just being paranoid again.

Drug-induced paranoia had already led him to the field. He hadn't liked the looks he was getting from the landlady in the pub.

He gave an anxious chuckle, which caused a pain in his side. Oooh. He did feel funny. Very funny. He looked towards the bleak horizon, trying to steady himself. A wave of exhaustion began to consume him, taking his legs first, which turned to jelly, and passing straight through to his head. He dropped to the ground and allowed sleep to take him, feeling safe in the knowledge he was in the right place, if not in the right circumstances – but that could wait until he'd had a little rest . . .

-32-

3.50 p.m., Monday, Colchester General Hospital

Jacqui drifted through her shift on autopilot, in an inattentive fashion, which was not her way usually – she was a good nurse, and the one thing she did care about was her patients. She wheeled the washing trolley into the next bay, preoccupied with the events of Saturday night; or, more specifically, her inability to recall them. The report about the two dead men in the paper had shaken her up, but not enough to awaken her memory. Not since her teenage years had she experienced such a complete void. She played back the night's events as best she could: the drink with the girls at Tramps, the walk up North Hill, being attacked by the drunk soldier who had followed them up to Head Street, Nick intervening, telling her to go home, and her indignantly (and foolishly) deciding to go on, then the trip to Aristos . . . What time had that been? It had still been early, she was pretty sure of that, as it had been practically empty apart from those guys at the bar. She

245

remembered the dance floor, the revolving lights . . . then going to the loo, giggling with that young fella, who promised her a high she'd never experienced before – that glint in his eye, manic, out of control. It should've been a warning, but it had only served to entice her; that temptation to escape—

'. . . Excuse me, nurse. Ow! Not so hard. *Oww!*'

This. To escape *this*. Just for a night. Jacqui was suddenly back on the ward with her hands underneath a seventy-five-year-old man, his creased face crumpled further by discomfort.

'Sorry, Mr Moore, sorry,' she soothed. 'Nearly done.' She turned back to the trolley. One thing she was fairly sure of: she hadn't slept with anyone. She'd had her knickers on when she got home and they were as pristine as when she'd slipped them on before going out. She sighed, and pushed the trolley out into the aisle. Paul had entered the ward. Though he could at times be annoying, he was safe and reassuring, like the hospital itself, just so long as he didn't get too serious. She mustered a half-smile and moved to the next bed.

4 p.m. Mersea Police Station, East Road

Kenton could tell that Bradley was unimpressed by being dragged in here on a Bank Holiday; the Mersea sergeant sat, arms folded and devoid of facial expression. He was flanked by two similarly blank PCs. The five of them were crowded into the small back room of East Road station. Lowry finished explaining how things stood and stubbed out the last of Kenton's Bensons.

Sergeant Bradley grunted. He caught Kenton's eye, but his look betrayed nothing; it was as if they'd never met, let alone shared a cup of tea at ten thirty that morning, Bradley in his string vest.

'So, inspector, you're telling me that you have wilfully allowed a murderer on to Mersea Island, endangering the lives of our women and children?'

Lowry took a deep breath.

'No, Sergeant Bradley, *we* –' he enunciated the pronoun strongly – 'have done nothing of the sort. *We* are merely looking for a man to help us with our inquiries. Let me remind you that the murder in question may involve drugs that were smuggled through Mersea, right under *your* very nose.'

'I resent that implication,' Bradley barked. Lowry looked sternly at PC Jennings, who shuffled his feet. 'In any case, you are still putting the island's population at risk.'

'Oh, fuck off, Dodger!' Lowry was losing patience. He pushed back the cheap plastic chair, which made an unpleasant screech, and flicked his fingers between the slats of the blind. 'It's practically dark out there *now*. It would've been pitch black by the time we'd scrambled a helicopter. Look on the bright side – if we catch him here, it makes you look good.'

Dodger Bradley grunted and moved away from the table. Kenton looked at his boss. Lowry was the same as ever: determined. Though at first Kenton had thought his boss's logic was flawed, he now agreed with him – even if the coastguard could've got a helicopter out in fifteen minutes, the visibility would have been to poor. It was practically dark by the time they'd got to Mersea. The fog was not receding at all; if anything, it was pulling afternoon to a quicker close, cloaking the marshes. Kenton toyed with his now-empty cigarette packet; he didn't quite understand Lowry's mentality, but thought him instinctively right and was keen to learn.

'I don't see how you think he'd get over here, meself. From Fingringhoe? Only way'd be by boat.'

'He could wade across at low tide?' Kenton asked, thinking of the other morning, when on the Strood, watching Uniform hunting for evidence along the sea wall.

'Not a chance; mud'd swallow 'im up at low tide. Only way on is the road at low tide, or a boat at high tide . . .'

'There you go, then – make sure you cover the Pyefleet Channel.'

'Okay, what do you need?' Bradley asked resignedly. 'We don't have that many hands. Will you be getting back-up from Sparks?'

'Nope. All you need to do is alert the coastguard. Anything tries to make off from these waters, we nab it.'

'All right, then,' Bradley said, with the air of a man who'd do anything for a quiet life. 'I'll talk to the coastguard – we can keep tabs on any vessel moving out until, say, dawn? We have two boats; that should do it. One thing, though.' A shadow crossed Bradley's brow.

'What?' Lowry asked.

'That other business.' Bradley nodded indignantly at Kenton. 'I thought that was why you were here – because I fired a rocket up Sparks's arse.'

Lowry laughed coldly. 'That post office has been done more times than the chief's taken rectal rockets from County. We've no interest in that now – stop getting hung up on it.' He was aware of Kenton's offended stare but continued anyway. 'All we're trying to do is our job; if you don't need our help, then fine, we'll leave it up to you.'

Bradley stroked his unshaven jaw. 'All right. Jennings, grab your life jacket.'

33

4.20 p.m., Monday, Mersea Road

As the car hurtled back towards Colchester, Lowry wondered if he'd made a mistake. He was thinking about the radar the coastguard had mentioned to him this morning. He loved the idea that they could simply swoop on any vessel coming to and going from the island. But what if their man had other plans? He could slip away along the north shore and quickly reach Brightlingsea or the caravans at Point Clear. They'd never find him there.

Of course, he might not even be the man they were after, but every instinct of Lowry's told him this was a killer retracing his steps. He imagined him fleeing the scene of the carnage at Greenstead and heading for the place of guaranteed escape – the coast – following the river and so avoiding the main roads. The route would take you south through Rowhedge, and along the woods to Fingringhoe, but from there, where? Bradley was right: it was nowhere near the causeway, and getting across the mudflats on foot and at low tide was perilous at best. So why had he left the Land Rover behind? Again, Lowry returned to the premise that it was all unplanned. Something must have gone very wrong – a deal gone sour, an act of madness, then panic.

'I didn't know you lived at Fingringhoe?' Kenton had interrupted his line of thought.

'What?'

The car slowed to a melancholy growl as they approached the Abberton junction on Mersea Road.

'I said, I didn't know you lived at Fingringhoe. You mentioned it back there. I always thought you were a Greenstead boy.'

Lowry was caught unawares. He seldom talked about his problematic family: it was of little interest to him and he was therefore taken aback when anyone else took an interest.

'Originally, yes, from the village. My mother moved to Greenstead when I was a teenager.' When his father did a bunk, he thought.

'Nice place – picturesque.'

Lowry smiled as the car jolted forward. 'Picturesque' was the word his mother had always used to describe the place, though he himself had different memories: of cycling to the Rowhedge docks with his paternal grandfather that last summer he was there, hauling timber until he was fit to drop. The Lowrys had always worked at the docks; Colchester, back then, had been an industrial town, and the family shipping business had flourished – timber, predominantly, coming in, and sand going out. It was decided that Nicholas, when he was thirteen, should get first-hand experience of the business, so he spent his summer holiday unloading timber, a backbreaking yet formative experience. He enjoyed the open air, the camaraderie, the honesty of the work. But that all stopped when his father severed all ties and he ended up on a council estate with his abandoned mother. The experience, while unpleasant, toughened him up enough to survive one of the roughest comprehensive schools in the area, where he'd excelled at sports – boxing, in particular. As the chill wind rushed through his hair and they entered the brick-and-tile outskirts of Colchester, leaving the countryside behind, he realized that his growing passion for birds and nature was an effort to realign himself with some happier, childhood self who had flourished in the open spaces of Fingringhoe.

'Yes. It was – is – a lovely place, especially in the summer,' he conceded.

As they the pulled into the station car park, Lowry was in a brighter, warmer world, until the precariously wired police radio sputtered into life to inform them of new evidence discovered at the Greenstead house.

4.30 p.m., Fingringhoe

Felix woke abruptly.

The hard earth he had collapsed on, its ploughed furrows

cast in frost, had eventually forced enough discomfort into his shoulder blade to pierce his exhaustion. This first sensation was followed by the sharp pain of biting cold at his extremities: his nose and fingers were numb, but the cold in his feet was the worst; thin socks and cheap trainers gave next to no protection. He propped himself up on his elbows and took a deep breath of cold, black air. It wasn't quite pitch black, though; the moon was up there somewhere, illuminating the layer of mist that swept across the field. It gave just enough visibility for him to remember where he was. He staggered to his feet. His head felt like lead and the vile taste in his throat made him think he was going to vomit – it was probably only the cold that stopped him. He needed water.

In spite of the aches in his body, his mind felt clearer than it had in days, but now his thoughts were climbing over each other to get his attention. The tide must be up by now. He needed to get to the dinghy before it grew dark; otherwise, he wouldn't find it. A cry of laughter drew him to the pub behind the hedge. He made his way gingerly towards its glowing orange light, stopping at the phone box on the roadside. He pulled open the door and slumped inside. He should try the numbers before making his getaway. As his numb fingers groped blindly for some coppers, he thought about how bad things might be. For one, he didn't have the money they were supposed to get for the drop. But had the drop even taken place? He struggled to make sense of what had happened – he remembered the house, arriving with

Jason, being late. Getting bored. Taking a dip into the drugs. He found a two-pence piece in his pocket. The drugs. He thought vaguely about where they might be and in the same way wondered what had happened to Jason. He felt a pang of guilt: Jason wouldn't get far without his wallet. And what was he going to do now? He opened his friend's still-damp wallet. In it was a slip of paper with two series of numbers written on it. These were important – he'd seen Jason get them out before, when they were stranded in the pub. One was a Colchester number: the house he'd been at.

His finger, swollen from the cold, only just managed to dial. The number rang. He waited. It rang and rang. He hung up.

The other number ran to the paper's edge, where the damp had made it illegible. But there were plenty of digits all the same, so he picked up the receiver again . . .

. . . and then hung up in despair. He'd never felt so alone. He'd done all he could. He might as well try for home and wait.

5 p.m., Queen Street HQ

Lowry was at the point of calling it a day and was just back at HQ briefly to pick up Saturday night's arrest reports from the desk sergeant. He needed time to think, and that was best done at home.

A scarf lay in a transparent polythene evidence bag on Lowry's desk.

It looked familiar. He thought Jacqui had one similar. Similar, or was it the same? He could see the Top Shop label. Hadn't she been wearing one like it when she went out on Saturday? A chill ran through him. Forensics had found the garment in the tiny front garden at Beaumont Terrace. He touched the edge of the bag. Maybe there would be a scent on it . . .

'The bullets match.' Kenton entered the office eating a banana, his complexion still burnished from the cold. They'd been back at Queen Street at least half an hour, but the temperature inside was only marginally higher than outside.

'Sorry?' Lowry's mind was on his wife.

'The automatic found at Stone's flat. The bullets match those in the Mersea post-office ceiling.' Kenton handed the forensics paperwork across the desk. 'And fingerprints matching those taken from the mug at Stone's flat were found there, too.'

'Even better.'

'Yes, a clean set, but they don't match those of the man murdered alongside Stone.'

'That would figure. The other dead man was one of the smugglers, without a doubt.'

He pushed thoughts of Jacqui aside and returned to the theories that had floated through his head while strolling across the beach this morning. Small-time drug-dealers rob a post office to get the cash for a big deal. Two men pulled off that job, and Stone was one of them. The other one's fingerprints were on a mug found in Stone's flat, but who was he? So far, there were no more clues. He had spoken briefly to the girls who worked in the hairdresser's beneath Stone's flat. They said they'd seen Stone regularly, but had never spoken. He was often on his own but sometimes with company (often male – but they couldn't say one way or another whether there was anyone else living in the flat).

'So, some progress to cheer the chief up,' Kenton suggested. 'He seemed out of sorts earlier.'

'Yes, "out of sorts" is a fair assessment. He's got a lot on his mind, and the one case that was solved – the post-office job – you've spilt wide open.' Lowry paused to swig some coffee. 'Have we looked for a car?'

'A car?'

'Stone was holed up in Artillery Street . . . He'd have to get back there from Mersea . . . Speak to Barnes: Uniform need to check out the area – someone might have seen them pull up. Start with the hair salon underneath his flat.' Lowry rose. 'Right, there's nothing to be done on Greenstead for now, so I'm up top to see Sparks, then off home – but could you have a word with Uniform about prodding a few of Jamie Philpott's known associates? I find it hard to believe he's just disappeared.'

As he passed the coat stand, he slipped the bagged scarf discreetly into his coat pocket.

34

5.30 p.m., Monday, Queen Street HQ

DC Kenton sat with the phone glued to his ear, waiting for the man on the other end to return. He stared at his reflection in the black rectangle of the window. The day was far from over, and the harder he worked, the less success he seemed to achieve, and hanging on the telephone for a second-hand car dealer wasn't exactly helping them find Philpott. He doodled pictures of cars on a notepad underneath the name Barnes and sighed: something else he had to do. He considered himself diligent, but the prospect of obeying Lowry and going cap in hand to Uniform for titbits on a lowlife like Philpott filled him with gloom. Despondently, he glanced up at the window again and his heart quickened. In the glass he saw WPC Jane Gabriel coming his way with a colleague from Uniform in tow. The twinge of excitement grew and he absently swapped the telephone receiver to his other hand and patted down his hair.

''Ello? 'Ello?' a cockney voice said down the phone. 'You there, mate?'

'Err . . . Can you hold on a sec?'

''Old on? 'Old on for what?'

Gabriel was almost at Kenton's desk.

'I've been waiting a good five minutes for you, so please allow me the courtesy of a minute.' He placed the phone on the desk, conscious that he was risking losing his man, but for the moment he didn't care.

'Hi,' said the soft voice behind him. 'Is Detective Inspector Lowry here?'

It was obvious he wasn't, so was this just an excuse to come and talk to him without inspiring gossip?

'No, he's up top.' Kenton turned and thumbed towards the chief's garret. 'Anything I can do?'

'No, it's okay . . .' Uncertainty passed across her face. The WPC behind her tugged her sleeve.

'Are you sure?' Disappointment seeped into Kenton's voice.

Gabriel hurriedly gave an account of having bumped into Sparks on the street, and of a subsequent phone call from a witness he didn't know, but it appeared unrelated to the Greenstead murders, so was of little consequence to Kenton. Instead of listening to her, he watched her mouth, the flick of a curl on her top lip – so sensuous.

'Well?' she asked, jolting him out of his daydream.

'Err . . . we think we're close to finding the Greenstead murderer.' He smiled, trying to appear authoritative.

She frowned, then glanced at the telephone receiver lying on the desk, a tiny voice coming from the earpiece. Her colleague whispered that they should go.

The two women marched off, as if they had lost patience. Feeling slightly foolish, Kenton picked up the telephone and engaged with the surly car dealer on the other end. He had no truck with rudeness, but he didn't want to let this chap go: he'd promised a good price on the Spitfire. He was resolved to sell it, for if he wanted to ask Gabriel to go on a date, it was unlikely she'd be happy to go in a car she was too tall for.

'Someone is scaring Leslie Birch.'

Lowry nearly collided with Jane Gabriel, who stood at the bottom of the stairs alongside a stocky WPC. Lowry couldn't remember her name but knew she didn't stand for any non-sense. She had once clouted a Red Cap for hurling abuse at her in the high street.

'Leslie Birch?'

'The girls who met Jones and Daley on New Year's Eve. One works in the video shop. WPC Hughes, here, just took the call.'

Lowry paused to recollect: Jones had given him the name, from the hospital bed. Lowry had been so consumed by the murders in Greenstead that the details of the incident on New Year's Eve had slipped to the back of his mind.

'According to Birch, a man barged into the shop, furious, demanding to know why she had been talking to the police,' Hughes said, indicating Gabriel. 'The same man had been after her on Sunday, too – she reckons he saw WPC Gabriel sniffing around on Papillon Road.'

'Did she know him?'

'Vaguely – she was ambiguous. Probably frightened.'

Lowry frowned. 'Did she know him or not?'

'She thinks he was a friend of the dead soldier,' Gabriel said.

'Any description?'

Hughes flipped open her notebook. 'A big man, looked like he'd been in a fight and stank of drink,' she said matter-of-factly.

'Narrows it down – in a town fit to burst with men full of booze,' Lowry said, 'and where the whole place has taken to beating the crap out of each other.'

'He was Irish,' Hughes added, 'and probably a soldier.'

Lowry nodded. 'In the same regiment as Jones, no doubt.' It sounded like their man from Saturday night's brawl hadn't got the message. Lowry wouldn't be going home early, after all.

The WPC had more: 'He told her that if she spoke to the police again she could tell them Sparks was for it – "Dead Meat", he said – and pointed to his face.'

'Did I hear my name mentioned?' came a booming voice. The chief had appeared on the stairs behind Lowry. The WPCs looked embarrassed.

'Sounds like that lad you took a swing at the other night has come over all tired and emotional,' Lowry said.

'What is it about the festive period? Seems an excuse for everyone to turn into a big girl.' Sparks looked indignantly at Lowry, and then at the two women, clearly oblivious to their discomfort.

'Should we call Oldham? Put him to some use for a change?' Lowry suggested, thinking of how helpful he'd been earlier that day.

Sparks shook his head. 'No chance – he'll whisk him off before we get a how's-your-father.'

'I thought we were all for cooperation?' the inspector pushed.

'There's a time and place for that. I thought you'd have realized that by now,' Sparks said sharply. 'So, do we know where this poor drunken lamb of a soldier is now?'

Hughes piped up. 'After he left the shop, the witness saw him enter the Bull pub, sir.'

Sparks clapped his hands. 'Well, we'd better get on down there!'

Lowry hesitated. 'There's no need to go mob-handed – I'll handle it.' Then, after a moment's consideration, he added, 'I can't think of better place to question an inebriated soldier harbouring a grudge against the police.'

-35-

6 p.m., Monday, Crouch Street

The police must not be seen to shirk the military area of town; this, Lowry knew. What better place to reassert their authority than the Bull, the huge pub just across Southway, used by locals and army alike. It was right on the edge of the civilian side of town, and just a stone's throw from the video store further along the road.

Sparks had been determined to come along but Lowry had managed to persuade him against it. There was still an uneasy truce between squaddies and civilians and, while they needed to take things in hand, it was vital not to go too far. To have a chief superintendent turning up on military turf and reading the riot act to an off-duty NCO he had recently clumped could easily spark off tensions. A disgruntled Sparks eventually backed down, and Lowry set off with Kenton and the two WPCs.

The pub was in darkness apart from the lights behind the

long bar, making it difficult to work out how many were in the shadows. The Bull was an old-fashioned drinker with sawdust on the floor and little in the way of home comforts.

'Not a place for the ladies,' Kenton whispered as they crossed the threshold.

'You go to the rear, in case he tries to make a bolt for it,' Lowry said. He turned to the WPCs. 'You two wait at the door.' He headed towards the bar, where a familiar-looking silhouette was perched on a stool. He sidled up. 'All right, soldier.' The cavernous bar fell quiet.

The man took no notice of Lowry, continuing to drink silently, the pint glass resembling a child's beaker in his huge fist. Lowry turned to the barman. 'What've you got in the way of sherry?'

The request made the soldier laugh in a boyish, scoffing manner, throwing his head back to reveal a shaving rash. He gave Lowry only a cursory glance, but it was enough for him to see dilated pupils, the youthful face afflicted with menace.

'Having trouble deciding what film to rent, were you?' Lowry said, alluding to the outburst in Videodrome. Quinn remained silent. 'I must say, I'm surprised you're out and making a nuisance of yourself already.' His eyes now accustomed to the darkness, Lowry scanned the other drinkers, who looked to be mainly civilians. The soldier was on his own, it seemed.

'I was out there, you know,' he stated simply. By 'out there', Lowry knew he meant the South Atlantic, and though they'd all heard it many times in the last twelve months in similar circumstances, there was no appropriate rejoinder he could think of. Not that Lowry was unsympathetic towards servicemen such as Quinn; they had his admiration. Silence was a mark of respect in his book.

The barman doubtfully raised a bottle of Harvey's Bristol Cream, and Lowry nodded.

'Not a mark on me – until now.' The soldier pointed to his eye, should Lowry have missed it.

'That's unfortunate,' Lowry said.

He shrugged. 'Colie is a dangerous place for a soldier, these days.'

'Oh? And why would you say that?'

'Those lads at the castle.'

'An accident.'

'Some say.'

'And what do you say?'

'I knew Jones.'

Lowry nodded and sipped his sherry from a chipped schooner. He knew this from Saturday night. Now lost in some reverie, the man had obviously forgotten their conversation (though not the beating dealt out by Sparks). Jones must be the connection with the girl at the video shop.

Conversation resumed around them; the punters assumed a brawl had been averted.

'Did you see Jones with Leslie Birch and another girl on New Year's Eve – the night of the accident?' Lowry wondered whether there might be some feud over an ex-girlfriend.

Quinn said nothing, though he swayed ever so slightly. The man was doing his utmost to maintain an air of control and sobriety – something one had to do in the military.

'Come on, you must have – why hassle the girl now?'

'She's got no business talking with the likes of you.'

'Why?'

Quinn pushed his empty glass forward and grunted to the barman, but Lowry reached for it to prevent the barman refilling it. 'Why?' he repeated. 'You know Leslie, don't you? How? Why threaten her? Did you see her with Jones on New Year's Eve?'

'I did not see Jones on New Year's Eve,' he said firmly, but not mentioning the girl.

'Do you know Leslie Birch?' Gabriel had come into the pub.

'Who?' Quinn was confused, lost to the booze.

'Okay, how about Philpott?' Lowry wasn't giving in yet. 'You said you knew him, the bloke you thumped on Saturday night? Care to elaborate?'

Corporal Quinn turned and looked at Lowry as if for the first time, noticing his missing tooth but saying nothing. Lowry could see him sizing up his options and, keen to avoid another punch-up, said softly, leaning forward, 'The back and front is covered – make a bolt for it and we'll have you. So, tell me – you knew the man you hit the other night, didn't you?'

'Philpott.'

'Yes, Jamie Philpott. Remember him?' Lowry said. 'Did you see him on New Year's Eve, too?'

'Nah.'

'So why'd you punch him? Was it really because he spilt your drink?'

'Time of year, too much booze,' he said, without irony.

'One final question: who were you with on New Year's Eve?'

'I didn't see no one on New Year's.'

'Oh? And why was that?'

The barman had served him another pint, and Quinn took the pint glass gratefully, and said with relief, 'I was in the Glasshouse, weren't I. You can check with Captain Oldham if you don't believe me.'

'What do you make of that then, sir?' Shadow covered Gabriel's face as they stood outside the pub. The pavement was slushy with sleet.

'Not sure what to make of it,' Lowry admitted.

'Lesley Birch said they were a tight-knit bunch.'

'Who were?'

'Jones, Daley, Quinn and some others. Yes – they were quite a crew until the Falklands.'

'And some were killed, no doubt.' Lowry padded his jacket for cigarettes on reflex.

'No, not that any were killed, more that they're not in the army any more—'

'Did she mention anyone else, a name we're not familiar with?'

'No, I—'

'Go back; get their names. If they're that close, who knows what you might unearth.'

She stood uneasily, awaiting further instructions, thinking he meant now.

'Tomorrow is fine,' he said. 'Good work.' He smiled in the dark. He needed time to think. He asked her to notify DC Kenton, at the rear of the pub, that they were done here, and said goodnight.

Although the police had not pressed charges, it struck Lowry as unusual that the military authorities had allowed Quinn out following his involvement in the weekend's unrest. Two broad-shouldered men with crewcuts passed him to enter the pub. Lowry heard the hiss of a whisper as they pushed the heavy door open. There was something missing, some connection out there they weren't seeing, he was sure . . .

6 p.m., Southway

Sparks had left Lowry to it and gone home. He badly needed his bed; he had another big do tomorrow. He needed a break, he conceded. He swung the heavy car lazily on to Lexden Road, and thought of Antonia curled up on the sofa in the lingerie he'd bought her for Christmas. He smiled to himself in the dark; yes, take her and the brandy up to bed. The year had got off to a bumpy start, with no sign of a breakthrough on Greenstead – he needed to clear his mind to enable him to focus better. On the passenger seat he had the football fixtures for the North Essex league to mull over. The police team had performed adequately, but only adequately at the end of the year – middle of the first division. Football was a perfect diversion from the current barracks aggro: the army were not permitted to compete, as it was a county league. No, here it was other police teams and his arch-rival, the fire service.

The fire brigade were the reigning champions and the police team had not won a match against them in two years. Those Trumpton tossers had the perfect fitness regime – running up and down ladders while on duty and jawing all night, propped up at the brigade bar, when not on call, and regular drills in between. Untroubled by the complexities of the often sedentary art of crime solving, they were in a different league, fitness wise. Sparks's boys might be able to go ten rounds in the ring, and even row across the Blackwater in respectable time, but ninety minutes on the football pitch was a different matter.

As he pulled up to his Lexden townhouse, his mind was pondering the need for young, energetic talent on the left wing. A youthful face sprang to mind: Dodger's boy at Mersea, maybe? Jennings. The lad might not be all that bright but he was young and had young, long legs. He'd call the Dodger at home immediately.

'Hi, honey.' His fiancée's silky voice greeted him from somewhere inside the warmth of his home. He wiped his shoes and frowned. There was the risk that Bradley would bring up that other business, though. Young Kenton had been disturbing the natives. It was all well and good bringing college boys into the force, but the well educated often lacked the moral diversity required in a well-rounded police officer. That, and the inherent problems of mixing those who think too much with those who don't at all.

He briefly entered the lounge to indicate his intentions to Antonia, who smiled alluringly at the prospect of an early night (in fact, he found her eagerness a little daunting), then made for the recently kitted-out office at the front of the house and popped open his address book. Locating the Dodger's number, he sank down into the leather recliner and stared at his Siamese fighting fish in the newly installed aquarium. Often, he'd sit here, as now, without the light on, entranced by the fish, so elegant.

'Ah, hello, Gertie; the Dodger there?'

"E's not, as you well know.'

'How's that?'

"E's out on the boat.' She cleared her throat. 'At sea.'

'Really? What on earth for, this late in the day?'

'Beats me. Thought you'd know, being the boss an' all.' She cleared her throat again. 'Better be careful he don't hit an iceberg – bleedin' cold enough for one out there, night like this. Inspector Lowry was here . . .'

What the hell was going on? He leaned closer to the tank. The fish fluttered like silk scarves in the wind.

8.15 p.m., Queen Street HQ

Lowry took the stairs two at a time up to his office in an effort to stretch his stiffening legs, Kenton trailing behind him. As they entered the foyer, they were greeted by the night sergeant sitting in the glow of a desk lamp like a lone nurse on a sleeping ward.

The lights on the first floor flickered uncertainly to life to dimly illuminate the deserted, untidy office. The encounter with the soldier had come at Lowry sideways, but it also brought to mind that he'd not got hold of Tony Pond. Maybe he'd try him at home tonight, give him a rattle for dicking them all around.

'So, what do we have?' Kenton asked, interrupting Lowry's thought processes.

'Nothing. Jealousy, perhaps: Quinn had a crush on Birch and, though for different reasons, is looking for her, like us, and finally finds her on Sunday and discovers that the police are asking questions about Private Jones. He puts two and two together and realizes she was out with Jones while he was banged up on New Year's Eve . . . The agonies of young love.'

'What about Quinn knowing Philpott?'

Lowry picked up a missing-persons fax from County HQ he'd only just noticed lying on the desk. 'Colchester's not such a big place – the fact that he knows Philpott, or denied knowing him, means little. The fact that Philpott has gone to ground is possibly more significant – jumping out of a hospital bed

270

after being glassed. It leads me to believe he's been up to no good. What do you think?'

'I've never had the pleasure, so I couldn't comment . . .'

'He's still not at home, that much we know, which is more of a concern.' Lowry sat down at the desk, his calves protesting as he did so, and flicked on a desk lamp. 'Now, what do we have here?'

Before him was a grainy photograph of the man found slumped in a plateful of vindaloo with his throat slit on the Greenstead Estate. The man had been identified: Jason Boyd, twenty-five years old, Brightlingsea. He waved the fax at Kenton, but realized he was no longer there. 'Where'd he go? Never mind.' Boyd had been unaccounted for since Friday morning, but it was not until he was missed at work again today that concern grew, and the fact that he'd not turned up at teatime prompted his mother to contact the police in Brightlingsea. The desk sergeant there immediately contacted Queen Street. 'Everyone is accountable on a Monday,' Lowry remarked to himself, realizing it was the second time he'd said that today. 'Even on a Bank Holiday.'

36

9.15 p.m., Monday, Brightlingsea

Home of Olympic-standard yachtsmen and world-renowned oysters, Brightlingsea sits at the mouth of the River Colne, some ten miles to the south-west of Colchester, facing the East Mersea shoreline. For a town of its size, it was remarkable for its inaccessibility; it was surrounded by salt marsh and there was only the one narrow lane in and out. Lowry cursed as the Saab cut through the wet darkness. Poor visibility was draining his tired eyes.

Informing relatives of the death of a member of their family was something Lowry undertook himself wherever possible. He believed it was his duty as a senior officer not to allow younger, inexperienced officers into this most intimate of intimate situations. A bad delivery of the news would do neither party any good. And, wherever possible, it had to be done face to face. Lowry was in no way ghoulish, but, statistically, murder was most likely to be carried out by one or more of the victim's nearest and dearest, and initial reactions to news of a death could be vital. In this instance, however, the news would not be delivered face to face. Joanna Boyd had guessed the nature of his telephone call, though was shocked by the circumstances of her son's death. She was a fishmonger in her mid-sixties and had imagined him to have been drowned at sea.

Once he was out of the damp mist, the small brick cottage in the town centre was easy to find. He knocked and introduced himself, and Mrs Boyd offered and then busied herself making tea.

As she pulled the tea cosy tight over the pot, she said, 'Greenstead? What the devil was he doing in Greenstead?'

'I'm afraid it might be drugs-related, Mrs Boyd.'

She tutted, as though Jason had been caught nicking from Woolies' pick 'n' mix. 'His father won't be best pleased.'

It crossed Lowry's mind that she hadn't really registered that her son was dead. 'And where might Jason's father be?' He moved to take his mug of tea.

'He's gone.'

The phrase just hung there. Lowry knew all there was behind those few words. Mrs Boyd shuffled from the tiny kitchen to a rocking chair in front of the hearth that looked as if it might collapse. 'But he won't be best pleased that Jason's lost his boat.'

'A boat has been found in the Blackwater. It might be his boat?' Lowry was becoming increasingly convinced that the woman was not all there. 'Tell me, Mrs Boyd,' he went on, 'what prompted you to call about Jason's disappearance?'

'His boss at the garage. He works on the place on the Clacton Road, selling cars. Busy weekend, this one.'

'But you said to Brightlingsea police you'd not seen Jason since Friday but were unconcerned, is that right?'

'He were off with his friend, Felix, up to no good. Simple, that Felix Cowley. I remember telling him not to put to sea with . . .' The woman bowed her head. Recalling the last time she saw her son had finally brought the reality crashing through.

'I'm sorry.' Lowry looked for a tissue, but the woman retrieved one from her cardigan sleeve. Allowing her time to compose herself, he took in his surroundings. A nautical theme ran throughout: pictures of yachts and men with boats adorned the walls. He was surreptitiously looking for a photograph of the dead son but was instead confronted with one of a confident, bearded fellow. The errant husband? Despite having lived in the district his whole life, he'd seldom had occasion to visit Brightlingsea, even within the police. They were a community unto themselves and closer to the sea than to any of the neighbouring towns. It was, strangely, more remote than Mersea.

'My son, my son!' Joanne Boyd wailed, tilting the aged rocking chair. Lowry would allow a respectful amount of time to pass and then drive her to the County Hospital morgue to identify her son. And at least he now knew the name and hometown of Boyd's accomplice: Felix, the man who had slipped through his fingers at the Fox, would not in all likelihood be making for Mersea, as he had suspected, but across the quay, back to his home in Brightlingsea.

'I know this must be hard for you, Mrs Boyd,' Lowry said, 'but might you be able to tell me where Felix lives?'

10.35 p.m., Great Tey

Her scarf was lying on the table. Jacqui felt her legs go as she entered the kitchen. Shit – she'd completely forgotten about it. Nick sat there with a drink underneath the bright fluorescent-tube lighting. He looked tired but not angry. She would have to front it out.

'Evening, stranger.' She walked into the room breezily, slipping out of her coat. 'Oh – can I have one of those?'

She could do with a drink, take the edge of this hangover cum interminable comedown – and he had the good stuff out: amontillado.

'Be my guest.' He raised his glass cordially. 'Good day at work?'

'Long and exhausting,' she said, pulling her hairclip out and shaking her hair free.

'You slept like a log all yesterday – I thought you'd have recovered. Matthew told me, before you ask.'

The ice-cold sherry glugged generously into the glass. They'd both been smitten with sherry since a week in the Costa del Sol on their honeymoon, though she'd long stopped asking him not to keep it in the fridge, in the same way that she'd stopped inquiring how he knew things. Taking the glass from the table, she stepped back and leaned against the kitchen draining board, putting some distance between herself and the scarf.

Nick stretched out his legs. He still had his shoes on. She wondered fleetingly where he'd been – they were covered in mud.

'How was your day?' she asked, finally.

'Busy.'

'Hmm.' She bit her bottom lip. She would tell him, but he'd have to ask. To be honest, she actually wanted to tell him – but she was spooked and still tired and was desperate to get to bed. She had lost count of the number of times she'd repeated to herself she would never ever touch drugs again.

'So, how was it at Trish's on Saturday night?'

'Fine.'

'Remind me again where she lives?'

He knew damn well where she lived: in the Dutch quarter, among the squiggly lanes that ran across the back of the high street. What to do? What to do? There's lying and there's lying.

'And you went straight there, right?'

She twisted uncomfortably against the kitchen units. 'No.' She couldn't risk being found out – he'd never trust her again.

'Where did you go first?'

'Aristos, at the bottom of East Hill.' She looked at the chequer-tiled floor. It needed mopping.

'And what did you get up to?'

'Took a load of speed with some blokes we – Trish – met.'

The flint of Nick's lighter, and the sound as it skittered across the table. He loved her and he would protect her, surely – pull her out of all this crap?

'I don't remember anything. Honest. I was with Trish the whole time.'

'Why?' he asked.

'Why? Well, I didn't want to—'

The slap on the table made her jump.

'Why didn't you go home like I said you should, Jacqui?!'

'I . . .' The anger in his voice scared her. Nick never shouted.

'I told you to go home, but no, you wanted to be comforted by your friends, which I agreed to – fair enough – but then to stay out? On the street, after what happened?'

Jacqui frowned. Who cares? she thought. Why's he going on about that? She *did* go out – so what? Her scarf, linking her to a place where two people were killed, surely that's the—

The legs of his chair scraped back. She forced herself to look at him as he made his way towards her. What was that expression? Not anger.

'Look, I'm sorry. I didn't do it to annoy you – I did it to forget, to forget about what had happened. You know?' She met his stare. Pained – that was it. 'Wipe it away, so, you know, a line of speed – never hurt anyone.'

'You have no respect for me,' he said flatly.

She could smell the sherry on his breath and slipped away from the kitchen units. Picking up the bottle to top herself up, she turned round. 'I don't know what you mean. Why would I want to come home to an empty house? You're never here; always on the job or boxing with that psycho boss of yours.'

He shook his head and smiled.

'What?' she said, confused.

'Forget it.'

'Am I in trouble?'

'I know you were with Trish the whole time, like you say.'

'You know?' She met his gaze, which was fixed on her but said nothing. 'How?'

'I spoke to her.'

'You spoke to . . . Why, you . . . let me sweat like that!' Relief was swiftly replaced by humiliation and she started to tremble. No, she was not going to cry.

'And the taxi rank in town.'

'What did they say?' Now she was genuinely curious.

'I heard you come in, so I checked the taxi rank for all trips around three that morning. You shared a cab. Jesus, Jacqui, I thought she might for once act responsibly and think of someone other than herself.' He shook his head solemnly, then downed the beaker of sherry. 'Can't Trish get a steady boyfriend? Cavorting around town like she's nineteen. No wonder Andy had had enough.'

Jacqui nodded in agreement. She'd been living off her best friend's divorce as an excuse for reckless behaviour for the last year. Andrew Vane, an accountant in town, had run off with his secretary, who was half his age. 'What are you going to do?' she asked eventually, not understanding his change in mood but sensing she was off the hook.

He raised his eyebrows blankly. 'Nothing yet. That's why I spoke to Trish first.'

'When?'

'When I came on the ward this evening. You were on a break. Surprised she didn't say?'

'Oh. Sorry.' She felt a pang of guilt. She'd been to see Paul. Trish had left by the time she returned.

'I told her to say nothing until I'd figured this out.'

'But Nick, they're bound to find out! When you find out whoever did this – they'll say we were there! You'll get into trouble.'

Nick topped up his drink. 'If we ever do. And even if we do, their memory is likely to be so frazzled they won't remember a thing. The killings took place at least sixteen hours after you left, judging from the time they went to Shehab's. You're safe.'

She went to hug him. 'I promise I'll never do anything like this again. Promise. Promise.'

'Easy.' He broke off the embrace, forcing her to stand upright. 'I need you to think and stay calm. I will need to talk to someone at Aristos . . .'

'I will stay calm, promise.'

'I'll need you to think hard about what went on.'

Jacqui felt the harshness Nick put into the word 'think' was a sign he was trying to stay calm. She needed to distract him.

'Nick, there's something else. It's Matty.'

His expression softened slightly 'Matt? What about him?'

'I think he's being bullied at school.'

'Bullied? What do you mean? It's been school holidays for the best part of a fortnight.'

She hurriedly explained the mark she'd found on her son's neck and watched another worry sag her husband's shoulders as he drank his sherry.

'You're on an early tomorrow?' he said at last, wanting the day to end.

'Yep.'

'Don't worry. Everything will be fine.' He smiled wanly.

'Let's have another,' she said.

'No, no.' He shook his head. 'I need to think. I'll be up soon.'

The telephone rang in the hall. 'Leave it, eh?' she said. 'Probably only Trish.' She didn't want to talk to Trish yet; she needed to corroborate with her friend first. But he made towards the phone. 'Or, worse, my mother – I said I'd pop over tomorrow evening.'

It was time to go to bed – quit while she was ahead. She drained her sherry and put the glass down on the kitchen unit. 'Night, then. Don't be long.'

'Sure.' He smiled thinly. 'It'll be fine.'

She prayed he was right. What if it made the press? What would happen to them? She'd be out on her ear, no question. She kissed him on the forehead and left the kitchen, vowing to herself she'd never take another drug as long as she lived.

*

Lowry stared at the cheap beaker. Matthew, being bullied? It had been the Christmas holiday; was she sure? Surely it was rugby? He couldn't bear the thought of his son, his pride and joy, being hurt in any way. He topped up the beaker. He didn't believe it. She was manipulating him, to get herself off the hook. It hurt to realize how transparent it all was. He was fast coming to the conclusion that she was taking the piss – or there was something very, very wrong. She'd nearly been raped, and yet it was water off a duck's back to her. Was she blanking it out, as a way of coping? But he couldn't deal with that right now; he had to come out the other side of the Greenstead murder first, and that meant keeping Jacqui out of it.

He could, conceivably, keep Jacqui's involvement under wraps. If it weren't for the scarf . . . He'd have Uniform check all the nightclubs in town so that it wouldn't appear obvious that he'd singled out Aristos, which he himself would visit. He would also check that the descriptions of Boyd and Cowley tallied with those given by Shehab, and take it from there.

After leaving Mrs Boyd, he, with the assistance of Brightlingsea police, had called at Felix Cowley's address. Nothing – an empty flat. From this, Lowry wondered if Cowley had headed for open water: Fingringhoe was close to the Colne estuary due east, which led to Brightlingsea on the east bank and East Mersea to the west, and beyond that to the mouth of the Blackwater and the North Sea. Logically, that must mean Cowley had escaped out to sea, if he hadn't returned home; had his intention been to go inland, there would have been easier, more accessible paths. Bradley was out along the Mersea coastline now; there was every chance they'd pull him out of the water . . .

He pushed himself up from the table with an effort. He was in a tight spot, no doubt about it. And he couldn't say he'd been there before – he hadn't. Did he inform Sparks of Jacqui's involvement in the case? Doubt niggled at him, and he decided he'd think about it again in the morning, with a fresh mind. He picked up the scarf and pulled it out of the bag and smelt Jacqui's perfume. She really didn't understand why he did what he did. Everything – always – had been for her. He could only laugh – to keep his sanity. A sudden surge of anger powered through him and, instead of flicking off the kitchen light, he punched it hard, splintering the plastic housing and leaving the house in darkness.

Standing in the pitch-black hallway, the answering machine blinked red at him from the telephone table. He remembered that the phone had rung earlier – West Mersea police, maybe? There were two messages. The first was the dentist. Could he come first thing tomorrow morning, at eight forty-five? There'd been a cancellation. Great. Next was a tired-sounding Trish. Tired and, yes, anxious. Hell, let her be anxious, the mess she'd led them into. He flicked the phone the V and followed his wife up to bed.

Tuesday, 4 January, 1983

37

6.15 a.m., Tuesday, Dutch Quarter, Colchester town centre

Frost sparkled on the roof of the Mini under the street lights' weak glow as Trish Vane scraped away the ice on the windscreen. Cold shards flew off, catching her eye. God, how she loathed early shifts in winter; it would be at least another three months before she left for work in daylight on an early. No matter how long she'd slept, it still felt like going to work in the middle of the night. She couldn't endure another year of this hell. Though she probably would.

The exhaust spluttered intermittently while the Mini's feeble heater did its best to thaw out the car's damp interior. 'That'll have to do,' she said to herself, giving up on clearing the screen completely and jumping inside the car. Slamming the stick into reverse, she realized she hadn't done the rear window. Sod it, she thought; there was nothing there to crash into. Flying out of the drive and roaring forward, she found she could still barely see and grabbed her scarf from the passenger seat and started rubbing frantically at the wet interior glass. Flicking the wipers on and over-revving, she clumsily knocked the gear stick into third, still clutching the scarf.

'Jesus Christ, women drivers!' said a hoarse voice behind her. Her heart froze, not unlike the crystals spraying before her eyes. 'Keep driving, there's a good girl,' said the voice, and she felt something cold against the nape of her neck, which she could only imagine was the nose of a gun. Foot trembling on the clutch pedal, Trish drove the car timidly out of the back streets.

'Where now?' She had reached the junction on North Hill.

'Wherever you've stashed it.'

'Stashed what?' Trish said this with conviction, but knew, somewhere within her, it had something to do with Saturday night. Christ, what on earth had she done?

9.15 a.m., Queen Street HQ

'Nothing. A big fat zero.' Sparks slammed the desk, sending a flutter through the pages of his morning report, which detailed the previous evening's incidents and arrests. Kenton flinched in his peripheral vision, but the object of his outburst – Lowry – did not. 'What the fuck do you think you're playing at, having those berks poncing up and down the Blackwater in the middle of the night? I have to pay those blighters overtime!'

'He might still be on the mainland, then,' Lowry mumbled. He'd at least had his tooth fixed.

'Might he?'

'Both smugglers come from Brightlingsea. Cowley may have tried to get back there from Fingringhoe, across the channel. And from there—'

'What, after killing his partner, Boyd? He'd still head home?' Kenton asked.

'We can't be certain that he'd head there – or that he even killed Boyd and Stone, at this stage – but he was seen at the Fox, and Boyd's mother said Cowley was simple, so—'

'Well, let's hope so,' the chief said. 'Clumsy to have lost him, in any case. That's the second man you've lost in as many days,' he remarked, casually this time. 'Anyway, glad you got your tooth fixed before tonight.'

'It's only temporary.' Lowry put his hand to his jaw, then asked, 'Why, what's happening tonight?'

'Ladies' night, remember, at the Queen's Head?'

'Not going.'

'Course you are.'

'I'm not. Is that all? I've a briefing to do, so if you don't mind . . .' Lowry rose to go.

'You're really not going? We always go together.' Sparks was crestfallen. Something *really* must be up with Lowry; he knew it. Giving up boxing and smoking, and now the Lodge.

'Not on a Tuesday night, I'm too busy. Besides, the food is awful there.'

Sparks pulled his creaking chair up to the desk. The food was poor, but so what? It was part of the tradition. He felt a twinge in his gut at the prospect of yet more rich seasonal fare. He stretched back on the chair to alleviate the grumblings in his stomach. 'All right,' he said, 'toddle off to your briefing.' They both turned to go. 'Not you, Kenton. Wait here a sec.'

Sparks rubbed his abdomen – maybe he should skip tonight, too? – and stared down at his desk, a manila file catching his eye. 'Oh, yes, Lowry, that reminds me – your dead German; the autopsy's done. Stomach contents: turkey.'

Lowry, who was already at the door, asked, 'Do Germans eat turkey over Christmas?'

38

9.30 a.m., Tuesday, Queen Street HQ

Lowry wandered back down to the main office. The Dodger had found nothing in the estuary, Felix Cowley was still at large, and all that was on Sparks's mind was ladies' night? God, that was the last thing he needed – he wanted Jacqui as far away from Sparks as possible. Besides, he had plans. There was a meeting of the Colchester ornithologists tonight, and a lecture on raptors; Doug Young, the ranger from East Mersea, had told him about it. But he was damned if he was about to share that with Sparks. He may as well announce he'd taken to wearing women's underwear.

He put the autopsy report to one side on his desk – turkey or not, the German was low priority – and instead tried to focus on the briefing meeting and on coordinating resources to find Cowley. And on whether there was a connection between Boyd, Cowley, Stone and the now-elusive Pond. The garage that Boyd had worked at on the Clacton Road was one of Tony

Pond's concerns. Pond, Pond, Pond: he was always turning up, like a bad penny. It was about time Lowry tried to get hold of him again, find out what his game was. As he sat down and flicked through his tatty Rolodex, the phone trilled.

'Yep.' He scribbled the number of the garage on a Post-it note.

'Detective Inspector Lowry?' a silky, clipped voice asked.

'Speaking.'

'Merrydown here.' The assistant chief constable. 'I'm in town later this morning and I wondered if we might meet.'

'Of course.'

'Super. I'll see you in the Old Library café at eleven.' And she was gone. It was the first time she'd ever telephoned him and, unsurprisingly, he hadn't recognized her voice – it had been so formal and polite; she had even omitted her Christian name, as a man would do. What could she want with him? Whatever it was, it couldn't be good. It was a nuisance, in any case – he wanted to get on to Pond, and it was already gone half nine, and he had a briefing . . .

39

10.15 a.m., Tuesday, Queen Street HQ

Kenton returned to the CID office with two coffees. Bizarrely, after Lowry had left the chief's office, Sparks had unexpectedly asked the young DC whether he was free to attend a Masonic ladies' evening. He even suggested Kenton take Gabriel, having seen the WPC in attendance at the fight. Kenton had declined, claiming truthfully the lack of appropriate attire and short notice, but he was nevertheless touched to have been asked and said next time, for sure. With Jane, imagine that! He placed one coffee before Lowry, who looked puzzled.

'Thank you,' Lowry said, taking his coffee. 'Did Uniform have any joy looking for the car round Stone's place?'

Kenton's expression was blank. 'Car?'

'Yes, after pulling the job on Mersea? Never mind. Ah, there you are,' he said, looking over Kenton's head. Damn, Kenton suddenly recalled, he was supposed to talk to Barnes yesterday. He'd clean forgotten when Gabriel had turned up.

'I've set up the incident room, as you suggested, sir,' came a familiar female voice from behind him. 'Sergeant Barnes is waiting.'

Kenton turned to see WPC Jane Gabriel outside the office, her delicate, pale fingers lightly holding the doorframe.

'Right, let's go.' Lowry rose, slipped on his suit jacket and exited the office swiftly. Had Kenton missed something? Since when was Gabriel involved in setting up briefings? He grabbed his blazer – the briefing room below was possibly the coldest room in the building, without so much as a fan heater – and hurried after them. He trailed behind, suddenly not feeling part of things. The blonde WPC was shoulder to shoulder almost with Lowry, her bearing upright, confident; she seemed replete with the trust his boss had clearly put in her. Maybe if Sparks has concerns about Lowry's state of mind he should ask Jane Gabriel ... Or was he overthinking the situation between the two?

In the interview room, xeroxed pictures of the two dead men from Greenstead were pinned to the noticeboard, alongside an OS map of Colchester and the Blackwater. Lowry walked to the front and the room fell into silence. Gabriel accompanied him and stood to one side. Kenton remained at the back, like a spare part.

'Morning, fellas.' Lowry rubbed his hands to warm them up. 'Now, you'll be pleased to hear we have now identified both victims of the Greenstead Estate murder.' He slapped one of the large black-and-white images. 'On our left, we have thirty-two-year-old Derek Stone, retired army Lance Corporal saxophonist. On our right, we have twenty-five-year-old Jason Boyd, second-hand car salesman and part-time fisherman. Now, what do these men have in common?' The question was rhetorical.

'Here's what we know about Stone: a redundant army musician who plays in a jazz band under Sheregate Steps. Part of a small alternative community that dabbles in class-A drugs as part of a lifestyle, but not really out to trouble anyone – or not that we know of. We also know from bank records that Stone squandered his redundancy money and was on the dole. Sergeant Barnes, anything else?' Lowry addressed the bearded uniform sergeant.

'A Browning automatic pistol was found at Stone's flat on Artillery Street. With two clips,' said Barnes.

'Go on.'

Kenton knew Lowry had discovered the pistol himself, and yet here he was, deploying Barnes, a uniform sergeant, to inform the team. It was Lowry's way of stepping back and allowing others to come to the fore. He was reticent to the point of shyness when it came to taking credit.

'It's a standard-issue officer's pistol. Though Stone was an NCO, it's not uncommon for the rank and file to possess firearms,' Barnes continued. 'They pick them up all over the place, souvenirs and the like.'

'Does it work?' someone in front of Kenton asked.

'Very much so,' Lowry said. 'We have conclusive evidence

that the gun was used in the Mersea Island post-office job.' A murmur went around the room. Kenton felt himself colour.

'Which leads us to believe there's a connection between this raid and the drugs murder. Sergeant Barnes, in the first instance, can you get banging on doors around Artillery Street – Stone must have had a car.'

Kenton looked at his feet as Barnes affirmed that he would take immediate action.

Lowry stepped close to the board to consider Stone's photo. 'This info also tells us that Stone wasn't expecting trouble that night on Beaumont Terrace. Which supports my theory that he was a minor figure in all this – if he thought he was in danger of getting his throat slit, he'd have gone prepared, and taken the Browning.'

Kenton knew this, but there were grunts of approval in the room. Gabriel looked particularly impressed, he thought.

'Right, this other man, Boyd, worked at a car dealership three days a week and as a fisherman out of Brightlingsea the rest of the week, which involved some night work. This man lands a vessel at Mersea Island on New Year's Eve – with one accomplice, presumed to be Felix Cowley, who is still at large, and a cargo of drugs on board – and plans to meet Derek Stone here.' He jabbed at the south-west corner of Colchester on the map.

A uniform came through and handed him another photograph.

'This is the third man, Felix,' Lowry said, holding the

photo up for all to see. 'He left Brightlingsea port on Friday morning with Jason Boyd, on a small boat with an outboard, bound for where, we do not know, to come back to a deserted Mersea beach late that same night with unknown quantities of amphetamines. The landlady at the Fingringhoe Fox confirms that this was the man who visited her pub yesterday afternoon.'

Lowry was now in full flow. He commanded the entire room's attention and drew everybody in. An imposing presence, smartly turned out in a pristine white shirt and dark, slender tie – always the same outfit – he made everyone around him feel vaguely underdressed; even those in uniform made a point of adjusting their navy ties and collars. And Lowry had a spark to him today that Kenton had not seen in his short time here. When the pressure mounted, the experienced inspector was fully engaged, and his enthusiasm was infectious.

'We need to widen the net. Felix is likely to be running scared. There are only a limited number of ways out of here.' Here, Lowry circled the marshes on the map with his finger. 'I'm confident he'll pop up soon enough. But, remember, it's by no means certain that Felix is the murderer; he knew Jason Boyd well, they were close – and he'd have had easier opportunities to make off with the drugs, if that was his intent, than to wait until he got to Greenstead – so I want a refocused effort on discovering what happened on that Sunday in Colchester. We have no idea of how big a consignment of the drugs was brought ashore, but the amount must've been sizeable – nobody would bother with getting two men, a boat and a Land Rover to move a ten-quid wrap.'

'Yes,' Kenton interjected from the back of the room. 'And as the sighting of Felix Cowley indicated, he was travelling light – meaning whatever was smuggled in is still out there somewhere.'

Lowry winked at him from the other end of the room, something he'd never done before. Kenton was relieved he'd been let off the hook for failing to advise Barnes to mobilize Uniform but at the same time he felt he was being patronized. And Miss Prim was still standing there contentedly, as though her elevated status were perfectly natural. Orders were issued to sweep the East Hill area of town again, door to door – the route from The Way to the Raj to Beaumont Terrace on Greenstead Estate – and then everyone was dismissed.

Kenton waited as Uniform filed out. To his relief, Gabriel exited with her uniformed colleagues. Lowry signalled for him to wait behind.

'Sir?' he said, when they were the only two left in the room.

'I need you to have a word with Tony Pond,' said Lowry.

'I thought you knew him well, guv?'

'Yes, but I've been called away unexpectedly.' Kenton couldn't read his expression; Lowry was usually open about his movements. Maybe it was personal? His boss continued: 'I'll give you his home number, but he's more than likely at his showroom on Clacton Road, though it's more like a field . . .'

'Not Racing Green?'

'That's the place. Go there and see what more you can get out of him about Boyd. And while you're there, chuck these at him, too –' he reached into his jacket – 'to jog his memory.' He passed over two photographs. 'Tell him we don't think for one moment he chased those lads, but the time for being mysterious is over. Find out how he knows them. And if he proves difficult, mention we know from the concierge at the George he's been lying.'

-40-

11.10 a.m., Tuesday, Old Library Café, off the high street

Where was she? He could ill afford time out for coffee, even for someone as important as the assistant chief constable herself. He'd left a note at the front desk, so that if there were any developments they knew where to find him and to fetch him immediately. He sat in the corner of the empty café by the window, mulling over the direction he'd given at the briefing. The key was to catch Cowley, he knew that. There was every chance that, if the lad was as simple as Joanne Boyd had made out, then he would try for home. So his decision not to rake the land by helicopter had turned out to be the right one – he'd avoided alerting the entire marsh that a manhunt was in progress. But they *had* to pick him up soon – there was nowhere for him to go.

It was one hell of a start to the year. A radio in the background warned of snow. The weather couldn't make up its mind what it was doing. Correction: it was always bloody freezing; the sky was just somewhat inconsistent in what it had on offer. He'd felt a sharp wind funnelling down the high street on his way here. A coffee machine let off steam, cutting off the broadcaster. He stared glumly down at his black coffee. He still had Jacqui to worry about – but the worry alternated with anger.

The door to the Old Library café opened and in walked a tall, elegant woman in a fur coat. Lowry stood and gave a slight wave. The ACC raised a hand in response and smiled.

'Ma'am.' Lowry nodded as she came over. She was fractionally taller than him, something he'd not noticed until he'd helped her out of her coat, which must have cost more than his monthly salary.

'Morning, inspector,' she said lightly, as informally as it was possible to be when addressing someone by rank. Such officiousness was fine by him; authority was authority, it was simpler that way. (Sparks didn't count.) Merrydown had always been resolutely official and as straight as the pleat in the navy skirt she now ran her fingers along. The coat had thrown him, though – she always wore a beige mackintosh when she was at the creaking Queen Street offices. The waiter, who'd been borderline rude to him, was at her side in an instant. The woman who held sway over the county's boys in blue had a certain aura.

'Busy start to the year for you Colchester lads, isn't it?' She smiled again, revealing perfect teeth.

'I was just thinking the same myself,' he admitted.

'How are things? Moving forward?'

'Progress is being made.' He took this as his cue and cleared his throat, then summarized the major cases, painting as positive a picture as he could. Merrydown was easier to impress than Sparks; her expression suggested she was pleased with the progress they had made since her visit the previous morning. She inquired about the background of the Brightlingsea men, and he veered between sketchy and knowledgeable, and she didn't ask about the fighting on Saturday night. Sparks believed that her concern in a case was driven by the airtime it was given: the punch-up had failed to make the grade, whereas the murder at Greenstead had made it on to the national channels, and he assumed, for want of a better reason, that it was why she'd requested the meeting. He mentioned that they were after Pond and Philpott, mostly to see if these men were on her radar, but as he talked on, Lowry had a vague sense she wasn't listening; her eyes darted here and there, and she gave several flicks of her hair. He grew self-conscious and started gesticulating with his hands to make a point – something he seldom did, even before an audience – then decided to quit while he was ahead, and finished by commending Sparks's grasp of the situation. He knew it would pay to do so.

'Ah, yes, Chief Sparks,' she said sharply. 'How is the lord of Queen Street?' She looked Lowry in the eye for an instant.

'He's . . .' Lowry paused. 'He's well.'

'Is he going to marry that girl?'

'Antonia? Why, yes – soon, I believe.' Unusual question, Lowry thought. 'Have you met?'

'Yes. Briefly.' She stirred her coffee slowly, her attention on the swirl in the cup. Where this was going?

'Do you think Chief Sparks is modern in his outlook?'

This was a trap, he was sure. 'I'm not sure what you mean,' he said.

She looked up from her cup. 'In his approach to policing?'

'As modern as the rest of us. His are the ways we know.' His tone was deferential. He would not be drawn into whatever game she was playing.

'Yes, of course,' she said, unimpressed. 'You've only ever been at Colchester.'

That wasn't correct, but he remained silent, then asked, 'Is it something specific I can help with?'

'No, it's nothing specific. They tell me you're very bright. I thought you might have a view, perhaps, on how Colchester division fits into the modern world. Is it abreast of current thinking?'

Lowry had no idea who 'they' might be. 'We're aware of developments in the law, such as the Justice Act passed last year, if that's you mean? The treatment of young offenders—'

'Never mind,' she said, as if giving up, then, 'Are you any closer to resolving the New Year's calamity with the soldier?'

This caught him out; he thought he'd successfully glossed over it. 'We think there were outsiders involved.'

'Ah. That'll mean no more outbursts in the high street, then.'

'I think not, ma'am. But we are still investigating what happened at Castle Park.'

'Hmm . . . You must be at a stretch, what with the murders in Greenstead?'

She produced a pack of cigarettes and extracted one with long, elegant fingers. Lowry scratched the back of his neck.

'We've drafted in a WPC.' It was all he could think to say.

'A woman?'

'They usually are.'

She arched an eyebrow. 'Whose idea was that?'

'Chief Sparks's.'

'So how's it working out?' She appeared genuinely interested.

'Terrific – they're getting on like a house on fire.' He was rapidly losing patience. 'Tell me, ma'am, why did you wish to see me?'

She sipped her coffee delicately. 'When a town is experiencing as many difficulties as this one, I feel it prudent to open channels with those on the ground and find out what's really going on.'

'I see.' She was questioning Sparks's ability to handle the situation. 'Well, I'm always here.' He tried a smile.

'Christmas is a funny time,' she said, oblivious, 'especially for the services, spending time away from home. I had a brother stationed in Germany. He married a local girl . . .' Her voice trailed off.

'Really? Tell me, what do they do eat there for Christmas? Turkey?'

Merrydown gave him a blank look. Lowry, about to explain further, was distracted by an urgent rap on the window. It was a young PC. Lowry beckoned him inside. 'You'll have to forgive me, ma'am,' he said.

'Not at all. I'm intrigued.'

The PC burst through the café, blurting. 'They've found him, sir!'

'Who?'

'Fella in a boat in the Blackwater, sir. Sergeant said I was to tell you immediately.'

'Quite. Ma'am?' Lowry waited for permission to leave.

'Of course, and thank you; you've been very helpful.'

Lowry rose, not knowing in what way he possibly could have been. As he reached the door, she called out from their table: 'Goose, inspector. Goose is traditional.'

11.20 a.m., Clacton Road

'We spoke yesterday evening.'

'Mr Kenton, was it?' A stocky man wearing a black overcoat, who reminded Kenton more of a bouncer than a second-hand car salesman, made his way across the frozen field crowded with gleaming Fords and Vauxhalls. Chances are he's both, Kenton thought, losing his hand in the huge sheepskin glove offered him.

'Yes, that's me.'

A sharp wind sliced through the forecourt bunting. Beyond

the fluttering pennants there was a Portakabin, inside which another man in a suit marched back and forth, a telephone receiver in one hand and its cradle in the other. This man was the main reason Kenton was here, but not the only one; he had bitten the bullet and come to Racing Green Autos in order to trade in the Spitfire.

'Yeah, sorry about that – I've only just started working 'ere.'

Kenton turned his attention back to the car salesman before him. In his mid-fifties, the squat gent sported a sculpted grey bullet-head haircut and, between the lapels of his overcoat, a bright paisley tie (one not dissimilar from his own, he was dismayed to realize).

'Oh?'

'The gaffer's an old pal – he was short of staff when a couple of his regulars were no-shows.'

'A couple?'

'Two fellas from Brightlingsea.' The salesman clasped his gloved hands. 'Bit parky still, ain't it? Now then, it's a Spitfire, right?'

'Yep,' Kenton said, keeping one eye on the Portakabin. 'Here she is.'

'Cor, bit on the bright side, ain't it?' He whistled.

'It's topaz orange,' Kenton said defensively.

'You're telling me.' He started to pace around the car, tutting. He lifted the broken roof limply.

'I mentioned the roof on the phone . . .'

'You did, son, you did. That's easily fixed round back. But that colour . . .'

'What about the colour?'

'What was you hoping to trade it for again?'

'The Mark 2 Capri.'

He shook his head woefully. 'I can't go any more than a monkey.'

'I beg your pardon?'

The cabin door opened and out came a man in a suit with piping on it – Tony Pond.

'Five hundred nicker.'

'Is that all? You're having me on.'

Pond stood on the steps, adjusting his cuffs.

'The colour's your problem, innit? Girls' colour, and the birds ain't got the readies.'

Kenton ignored the stocky man and made his way across the forecourt to prevent Pond climbing into a white XJS. 'Mr Pond, might I have word?'

Pond held his up his hand. 'I don't dabble in the day-to-day – Mr Palmer is my man on the forecourt.' The bullet-head beamed behind him.

'I'm sure that's so,' Kenton acknowledged, 'but it's Mr Palmer's predecessor I'm interested in.' He held up his ID.

'Ah, of course. I didn't recognize you.' Pond frowned and scratched the back of his neck. His impressive handlebar moustache appeared to move independently as he spoke. 'You'd better come in, then.'

Inside the Portakabin, Kenton laid two photos on the cheap desk while Pond poured coffee into polystyrene cups.

He turned and froze, the cups steaming in his hands. 'Those two, er, gentlemen, have never worked here,' he said.

Kenton leaned over the desk, and feigned having made a mistake. 'Oh, how clumsy of me. This is a different investigation.' He scooped up the pictures of Private Jones and Private Daley, all the time watching Pond's reaction.

'Fuck, fuck, fuck!' Pond's sudden outburst of swearing was accompanied by him dropping, or throwing, a scalding coffee over Kenton's legs. 'Shit, I'm so sorry! I scalded myself . . . Shit, shit! Here.' He fumbled with a tea towel. Kenton mopped away the liquid as pain began to throb across his thighs. He tried to compose himself.

'Now, where were we?' asked Pond.

Kenton sensed he'd been out-manoeuvred; spilling the coffee had been a diversionary tactic.

'Your employee, Jason Boyd—'

'Yes, terrible what happened to him. I heard the news.' He relieved Kenton of the tea towel and wiped his own heavily ornamented fingers. 'We reported him missing, you know?'

'Yes, we're aware of that.' Kenton sat down on one of the plastic chairs, to make it plain he had no intention of leaving. 'That's why I'm here. When was the last time Boyd and . . . ?'

'Cowley. He just washed the cars. They were expected here on the Saturday. I left it a day, thinking they were likely to be hungover, but when I still couldn't get hold of them on Monday, I called Boyd's old dear. I've said all this already.'

'Of course, of course. But there's something else,' Kenton said, unable to stop fidgeting; his legs were wet and uncomfortable: 'We – I mean myself, Chief Sparks and Detective Inspector Lowry – know you've got a history of small-time drug-dealing. So, bear with me, this is just routine question—'

'Ha! This shit on the Greenstead Estate?! That's a far cry from selling a bag or two of weed to students.' Pond rocked back on his far grander chair on the other side of the desk.

'Drug dealing is drug dealing: it's the contacts rather than the contents a jury will be interested in.'

'Stop fucking with me, boy.' Pond lit a cigarette and fixed Kenton with a scathing stare. 'So, what's the plan – you're going to arrest me? On the basis of what? After all those years you've ignored the weed floating by under *your* very nose – something I've never been nicked for. How's that going to look to a judge?'

Kenton hated this sort of misplaced smugness. Sparks and Lowry had allowed this minor collusion to fester; for how long, he had no idea. On some level, he felt it would serve them right if it all came crashing down. There was a whiff of corruption there, as with the Mersea post-office job – the kind of thing Kenton couldn't abide.

'Times change. The pressure is on from County,' Kenton said loosely, in a manner that suggested it wasn't worth the energy to argue; there were far greater forces at work. 'This is a big deal. Nobody's safe when we're faced with an incident on this scale.'

Pond leaned forward across the desk, his face contorted with menace. 'Do you really think if I was involved I'd call Boyd's old dear when he'd not turned up for work? Of course she's going to call you lot.'

Kenton remained unruffled, picturing how he imagined Lowry would play it. 'I don't know what you'd do, Mr Pond, but anyone wrapped up in this mess should consider their options very carefully.' He rose to leave.

'I've heard about you, college boy. You've got no idea how things work in this town. Next time, tell Sparks to send me the organ grinder, not his monkey.'

'The organ grinder says to let you know we've spoken to the concierge at the George.' He peered out of the Portakabin window. Pond's salesman was gushing around a young woman who looked to be interested in the Capri he himself was after. 'I am indeed only the messenger, but this won't go away. Next time, it won't be me asking nicely. Good morning to you, Mr Pond.'

'All right, all right. Come back here a minute.' Pond lit a cigar.

Kenton paused.

'But don't take me for a fool, all right? Those pictures. The men in the pictures.'

'The two soldiers?'

'Yes, the two soldiers – of course they are – I spoke to Lowry about them.'

'But you never said you yourself had seen them – we know you saw them because the concierge at the George spotted you,' Kenton pointed out.

'And why's that, do you think?' He sighed. 'To avoid having dicks like you banging on my drum, perhaps?'

Kenton waited for more.

'Look, the way it works is I throw the rozzers the odd snippet, show them I've got me ear to the ground. But I don't want to be bothered by 'em unless it's absolutely necessary.' He glanced out of the window. 'It's bad for business.'

'Well, let's just say that this time it *is* necessary.'

'If you say so.'

'I do. Daley and Jones – you know them?'

'Know them, no. But I do know who they were after.'

'Who?'

'Boyd and Cowley.'

'What for?'

'Ooh, could it be for a good shag up the arse?' he jeered. 'What do you think? Drugs. It was New Year's Eve and they wanted to score, just like everybody else.'

Kenton sat down. 'Why did the soldiers ask you about them?'

'One of them had looked at a motor here; he recognized me.' Pond rubbed a dark jaw, and puffed on his cigar. 'They knew Jace and Felix worked for me. On Friday night, I bumped into them outside the George, and it was all this "Where's fucking Jason?" stuff.' He held his hands up theatrically.

'What sort of mood were they in?'

'Pissed off. Frantic. I'd guess they were buying on behalf of half the garrison, given the anxious looks.'

'So when you realized Boyd and Cowley were missing, what did you think had happened?'

Pond held up his hands in defeat. 'I'm not involved, right? But I'm guessing that it's either Boyd or Cowley dead in Greenstead, along with Stone?'

'You know Stone?' Stone's name was the only one that had been made public. But Derek Stone was unknown to the police. The fact that Pond knew of him was a surprise.

'By name only.' Pond lightly stroked the tip of his moustache. 'Jamie mentioned him.'

'Jamie Philpott?'

'The very same; so I figure, given the blood at Greenstead, it's only a matter of time before you lot work out those two worked here, so I'm waving my hand in the air and saying they're missing, all right?'

'Wait – how did you know that Boyd and Cowley were selling drugs? Did Boyd confide in you?'

'Nah. Jamie asked me if I wanted in on a big deal. He said there was a delivery due New Year's Eve – a pal of his at the Candyman had tipped him off. Jamie P. wouldn't have the wherewithal himself, you understand. And then when Boyd and Cowley asked for the 31st off work, I grew suspicious. I asked Felix what they had planned. He said a fishing trip. Not the sharpest tool in the box, that one.'

'Weren't you interested in a cut, even then?'

The Portakabin shook in a gust of wind. They both looked up as the roof stirred uncomfortably.

'I'm an honest businessman,' said Pond plainly. 'Besides, I'm not interested in new-fangled party drugs.'

'I'm sorry?'

'What they were flogging. Philpott and I used to do a bit of weed back in the day – before your time – but nothing like this sort of shit.'

'What about him, then – Jamie Philpott?'

'What about him?'

'He's wrapped up in this with Stone?'

'You'd have to ask him that.'

'We can't,' Kenton said, vexed.

'Why not?'

'He's disappeared.'

Pond considered this for a moment. 'Has he, indeed? Maybe he managed to cut himself a slice of the action? He's been hanging out at the Candyman off his nut on something a fair bit since the good Chief Sparks brought a halt to the dope coming in through the Colne; dipping into the jazz scene up in town – amphetamines, coke: you name it, he'll try it.'

'Jamie took a pasting on Saturday night.'

'So I heard on the grapevine. Hmm.'

'What?'

'Just thinking . . .' He rubbed his jaw thoughtfully. 'If half the garrison was intent on getting loaded on New Year's Eve, but instead of them being able to score, one of their procurers ends up dead in Castle Park, they'd be pretty narked to see ol' Jamie the following night, mincing around, touting some gear?' Pond let out an enormous cloud of cigar smoke, which filled the top half of the Portakabin. 'Colchester ain't such a big place. There's not that much gear pinging around.'

'I suppose that makes sense. They might think he was mixed up in it somehow.'

'Too bloody right. I reckon they might've lynched him. I'd say he'd got away pretty lightly with a thumping, wouldn't you?'

Kenton's mind was whirling. 'Bloody hell,' was all he could think to say.

'I should say so. Can I ask, if you don't mind, how much gear there was at Beaumont Terrace?'

The police still had no idea. The drugs hadn't been there, but 'substantial' was what everyone at the station was thinking. Pond took Kenton's silence to mean he wouldn't say.

Pond continued: 'One imagines it was a lot. Any idea where it is?'

The young detective couldn't help but shake his head ever so slightly.

'To be honest, I'm not surprised you've got problems.'

'Do you think Private Daley's death is related to this drug deal?' Kenton couldn't help asking.

Pond shrugged. 'You're the policeman, aintcha?'

41

11.45 a.m., Tuesday, Brightlingsea port

Gabriel ran down the jetty, the collar of her raincoat flapping against her cheek as she went. Barnes was lumbering along behind her. She hadn't noticed just how windy it was on her charge to get down here, which had seemed to take for ever, through endless narrow lanes – but she felt it now, all right.

The police launch was buffeting against the tyre bumpers in a petulant sea. The captain offered up his hand, which she took gratefully, and stepped awkwardly into the boat. A PC dispatched from Brightlingsea constabulary was already on board, arms wrapped around his greatcoat.

'What are your sea legs like?' the pilot asked as she climbed down.

'Sea legs? Will I need them?' she asked uncertainly. Gabriel couldn't remember ever having set foot in a boat before.

'Reckon so.' He grimaced through chapped lips. 'It's whipped up a good 'un.'

The young PC looked distinctly unhappy. Gabriel took slow, cautious steps towards the prow of the boat.

'Wow.' Before her was a scene both frighteningly dramatic and piercingly beautiful. The sea glowed bright beneath a sharp, low sun, which was gradually being swallowed by a huge bank of dark cloud tumbling in from the east. She shielded her eyes with gloved hands. The clouds moved slowly but steadily, as though made of iron, pushed by the ferocious wind. She couldn't remember a sky having such a spectacular array of colour; bands of blue, purple and orange stretched across the horizon, slowly compressed by the darkness above, their edges alight.

The boat gave a jolt and they were off. She took a few awkward steps back and gripped the stern as they moved out into the estuary. The sunlight and colour abruptly disappeared as the cloud sealed the edges of the horizon. Now she could appreciate the true strength of the wind; the white horses racing across the sea become perilously visible. Not that a visual aid was needed; her face stung with cold and spray as they gained momentum.

'This is not going to be fun,' the PC next to her shouted. The craft banked portside, and she felt her stomach turn. Oh, my heavens, was she going to be sick? 'Keep your eyes out front and it won't seem so bad,' her companion added kindly.

Gabriel tried to stay focused, but all the beauty was gone, replaced with an endless, grey, hostile wall of water. 'How the hell will we find him in this?'

'Not many idiots try and sail a dinghy in these conditions. Must be a good force seven . . . Wait! Look!' Barnes cried.

Gabriel craned her neck and was lashed with spray in return. She couldn't see a thing.

'Look right out there – just a speck!'

Sure enough, amidst the grey turmoil was a dot of white. And that was all, just a dot. The PC scrambled to the wheelhouse.

The launch adjusted its course and accelerated powerfully, almost throwing Gabriel to the deck. The hull of the vessel rose sharply, then slammed down with such force she felt the thing may split in two, shattering her with it. Again the boat surged upward. She braced herself as her feet slid on the wet deck, and as they traversed the swell, she quickly realized that this first violent movement wasn't going to be a one-off. If she was going to be sick, the moment had passed; she was now too busy keeping herself upright.

'What have we here?' the PC shouted in her ear excitedly. He must've been all of eighteen, and very keen. The boat slowed and she realized she'd had her eyes closed. The motion eased to a queasy side-to-side rocking. Before them was a sailing dinghy, with no sign of crew. The main sail flapped angrily. 'Right – let's see if we can grab it with this.' He produced a long wooden pole and leaned cautiously over the side. Sergeant Barnes helped steady him.

'Gotcha!' the PC exclaimed, and tugged the dinghy in. The noise of the loosened sail was deafening. 'Keep hold!' the young policeman yelled to Barnes, before leaping over the side and into the captured boat with a coiled rope. Spray stung Gabriel's cheeks as the smaller vessel crashed against them. The policeman disappeared under the sail to fasten the rope, then tossed it back to Barnes, yelling something they couldn't make out.

'He knows his stuff!' Barnes almost screamed with admiration as the younger policeman lowered the sail, the smaller boat rising and falling in the rough swell.

Once the sail was stable, Gabriel noticed a shape in the bottom of the boat, covered by a tarpaulin. Her heart raced. As the PC went about busily securing the rigging, the shape began to move, and Gabriel nudged Sergeant Barnes. A very pale man raised himself into the storm. Gabriel couldn't help herself: she went rigid with fear as a corpse-like man struggled to his feet. Though she knew she was in no danger, the figure in front of her was so shocking in appearance she felt she might vomit in panic and scrabbled back hastily to allow Barnes room to help the skeletal Felix Cowley on board.

5 p.m., Colchester town centre

When a drenched, fragile WPC Gabriel returned to Queen Street, a gentle wave of relief washed over Lowry. The young woman had obviously found the experience draining – she looked exhausted – but the recovery of Felix Cowley from the Blackwater had a more effusive effect on Sparks, who was positively jubilant. This was a major result. Cowley wasn't in great shape. He had narrowly avoided pneumonia. Unable to get much sense out of him, they heeded medical advice to let him rest overnight – but in the Queen Street cells. The loss of Philpott from the General Hospital was still on their minds, and Sparks was adamant. However, Lowry had ordered the duty PC to move the electric heater to Cowley's side of the barred door to at least try to keep him warm; after all this hassle, he didn't want him expiring overnight. Having overseen the PC grudgingly move the heater, he and Sparks then left the station, and it was with lightened moods that the pair made their way through the town centre on foot as the first snow of the year began to fall.

'I gather you had coffee with the ACC,' Sparks said casually, his breath catching in the streetlight as they made their way towards the old city wall. The uneven cobbled pavement was slippery in places as the snow began to settle on patches of ice. Their footsteps, which at first echoed along the glistening alley, were soon muffled as the snow grew heavier.

'I did. How do you know?' Not that it was a secret.

'I know someone in the police. Sneaky bastards have eyes everywhere.'

Lowry didn't respond. Instead he asked, 'Are you sure you've got time for this?'

'Of course. Besides, I think it does good to show my face on the streets every once in a while – show 'em who's the daddy.'

'Jeez, you watch too much telly.'

'C'mon, Nick, what did she want? What did you talk about?'

'You.'

'Me? What the fuck did she want to know about me?' They turned off at Sheregate Steps; they were steep and treacherous on an evening like this. The number of people who had come a cropper navigating their way down these slippery stones was one of Colchester's least noble statistics.

'Whether I thought you were "modern".' Lowry stopped outside a dark wooden door within an enclave, halfway down the ancient passageway. Even during the daytime, most would pass the Candyman jazz club and remain unaware of its existence.

'"Modern?" What the fuck does that mean?' Snow had settled on the chief's eyebrows.

'Beats me. Shall we?' They stepped inside. The place was darker than the alley they'd just left, and the cigarette smoke clawed at their throats, causing an involuntary cough from both, hardened nicotine addicts as they were. 'What're you having?'

'Better take it easy – I'll be driving through those pissy lanes later. Vodka tonic,' Sparks said, wincing in the smoky gloom.

'Two large vodka tonics, love. I thought you were looking forward to ladies' night?'

Sparks shrugged and surveyed the scene around him. 'You blowing me out has taken the wind out of my sails somewhat. Would've been nice to see Jacqueline, too. How is she?'

Lowry paid for the drinks. 'All right.' He'd not spoken to her since their conversation the night before and was not

particularly keen to say any more to Sparks. Instead, he signalled to the waifish girl behind the bar and asked, 'Lester in?'

Sparks's good humour had evaporated as swiftly as it had
arisen. When, thanks to Granger, he'd first got wind of this
tête-à-tête between the ACC and Lowry, he'd hardly minded
at all, but now, on hearing Lowry's oblique response, he
was furious. Talking about *him*? Modern? What the fuck was
Merrydown on about? Now he'd stopped to think about it,
why was she talking to Lowry like that, behind his back? Not
that he didn't trust Lowry – he did – but her? No chance. She
hadn't got to where she was by being Felicity Kendal. She was
not to be trusted. Indeed, she had, only this afternoon, called
Sparks to warn him about her niece, Gabriel. And though
Merrydown was sweetness and light about the whole thing,
and apologized that he was kept in the dark about the connection, it was still underhand. Sparks was going to mention
it to Lowry, but now thought better of it . . .

He grabbed his drink from the bar and took in his surroundings. He used to listen to the odd jazz record once upon
a time and he knew this place from his days as a DC in the
sixties – his glory years. A desk job wasn't what he'd signed
up for, but that's what it had become, and although the
sports that he engaged in compensated to a degree, it didn't
quite replace life on the streets. 'This place hasn't changed,'
he said, nodding to a leathery old goat at the far end of the
bar. 'He was in here when this was my patch, in sixty-seven.
Don't think he's moved. Certainly hasn't shaved.'

Lowry raised his glass and took a swig. The low ceiling caused both of them to stoop. 'Not much of a stage,' he said, indicating the far end of the bar, where a skinny, long-haired youth was messing with a snare drum.

'You don't need a big stage with jazz, Nick. There's no need to strut about like they do with that crap you're into – the music does the job for you.'

'Didn't know you were into jazz, chief—'

'Evening, gents.' A man so skinny that it was a wonder a turtleneck was made that would fit as snugly as the one he sported had drifted over. 'Superintendent, welcome. It's been a while.'

'Lester,' Sparks acknowledged. 'There's been a mishap.'

'Derek.' He nodded, tutting. 'Shocking business.'

'When was the last time you saw him?' Lowry asked.

The club manager waved a cigarette indolently. 'Thursday. He was supposed to be here on Sunday – but he didn't show up.'

'How did you hear about what had happened?' Sparks asked.

'I can't recall – was it in the paper?'

'Did you not inquire as to his whereabouts? He's in the house band – didn't you wonder why he hadn't turned up?' he persisted.

'How does one ever hear anything?' the man half replied, his attention drifting towards the guy fiddling with the snare drum, who had been joined by a short black man with a trumpet.

Sparks was out of the habit of being dicked about. He was sure Lester Pink had a drugs habit. What it was, he had no idea, but there was no way a man could be this skinny without poisoning his body with something. Maybe he was on it now, which would explain his disrespect. He downed his drink and muttered to Lowry, 'See if you can jog his memory – or, if not, unsettle it.'

Sparks marched over the trumpet player. 'Evening,' he said.

The musician gave a cursory nod but then carried on chatting to the man at the snare drum.

'Oi, Satchmo,' Sparks said politely. 'May I have a word?' They both stopped what they were doing and stared at him.

'Armstrong played the cornet,' the black guy said.

'I'm sorry? What did you say?'

'I said –' he paused – 'Armstrong predominantly played the cornet.'

'Did he? Did he really?' Sparks looked at the low, yellow ceiling as though in thought, tapping his foot playfully as he did so, then stared at the man straight and said, 'Well, I don't give a fuck whether he blew down Liberace's bone flute.' With a sudden jerk, he shoved the trumpeter against the back wall. Due to his small size, this didn't require the effort Sparks put in, and the push caused several framed photographs of hallowed jazz musicians blowing earnestly to shatter.

'Now, Derek Stone. Know him?'

'Yes.'

'Yes?'

'Yes, he plays with us. He hasn't been turning up. Turns out he was murdered.'

'Did he take drugs?'

'Erm . . . occasionally.'

Sparks shoved him hard against the wall.

'Hey, man,' came a soft voice, followed by a tap on his shoulder. 'There's no need for that.' It was the drummer.

'Come here,' Sparks beckoned, as if to confide in him. As the man leaned forward, Sparks spun and deftly headbutted him on the bridge of the nose. The drummer toppled and Sparks felt momentarily stunned. The trumpeter, still in his grip, had gone limp against the wall, pulling Sparks forward. He was trying to whisper something.

'Sorry, son – didn't catch that?'

'He'd gone to score – Del had – on Saturday night. He'd gone to score on Saturday night.'

'Fab.' He yanked the man upright. 'Anything else? Any girlfriend? Who'd he hang out with?'

'I don't know. I don't know.' Sparks squeezed the man hard again. 'Wait; he had a mate who'd drop by – Ted.'

'Ted? Ted who?'

'Nugent. Comes from Mersea. Bleached-blond hair. You're hurting me.'

Satisfied, Sparks released him and marched back to the bar, where Lowry and Lester Pink had been watching the display. 'That's bang out of order, Mr Sparks,' Pink protested, seeming now to have been roused from his dreamland. Sparks squared up to him and he instantly shrunk back.

'The trouble is, Lester, people ponce about. Call me

old-fashioned, but I believe that if a policeman, especially a senior one such as myself, asks for information, he's entitled to an answer.' Sparks gestured towards the musicians, where the trumpeter was fussing over the drummer, who was still lying on the floor. 'Not a load of arse. Know what I mean?'

'We done?' Lowry said, and placed his empty glass purposefully on the bar. They left in silence.

Sparks was irritated by Lowry's lack of comment. As the cold night air punched his lungs outside on the cobbled street, he said, 'Was that "modern" enough for you?'

42

6.30 p.m., Tuesday, Queen Street

Lowry said goodnight to Sparks on the station steps. He watched his superior march off at a brisk pace in a swirl of snow and disappear round the back, towards the car park. Sparks's slapping about of the trumpet player was his second violent display in under a week. Lowry was not averse to violence here and there, where necessary, but he couldn't help but think that Sparks's behaviour was unwarranted. Neither the musician nor Corporal Quinn had deserved it, and both were easy targets. Maybe the chief was beginning to feel his age, and irrational bursts here and there were a means to reassert his authority before it was too late.

'Maybe it's not me who's having a mid-life crisis,' he said to the shadows.

Still, they had made progress, tactics notwithstanding. It appeared that Derek Stone *was* small time. He'd gone to score on New Year's Eve, and ten grams of speed was hardly a major haul requiring a beach landing. No, he was of little interest – even less now he was dead – whereas Ted Nugent was suddenly very much back in the frame, having seen Stone the night before he was murdered. He doubted there could be two people with the same moniker. The trouble with crims on parole was that they could never seem to untangle themselves from the fraternity net . . .

Sparks's Rover pulled out from the side of the building and a pale palm waved from inside. Lowry crossed the road and made his way up towards the high street. He thought back to Kenton, grumbling at Sparks's remark, when he first started, that he looked like Dennis Waterman (which had offended Kenton deeply) – and, ironically, how Sparks's conduct at the Candyman had been a beautiful reenactment of 1970s policing, as portrayed in *The Sweeney*. He'd have to bung Pink a score to compensate for lost clientele: a bunch of students had witnessed the whole thing and fled in horror . . .

As he walked down East Hill, his thoughts turned to his next destination: Aristos nightclub. He'd considered telling Sparks about Jacqui's involvement in the case but had decided against it after his little outburst in the jazz club. It would only cloud the issue further. And, anyway, as Lowry kept telling himself, the scarf was found in the garden, which meant she may never have even entered the house.

The club was not open tonight, but he'd called ahead and requested that the staff who'd been on duty on Saturday night open up for him. Two sirens shot past as he walked into the reception of the Colne Hotel, beneath which sat Aristos. A clerk guided him through some double doors and downstairs to the club, where a curly-haired man in a black open-necked shirt greeted him and flicked on all the lights.

'Of course, the main entrance is outside the hotel. The way you came in is strictly for VIP guests,' the manager, Stu, said. 'Over there's the main bar.' He pointed towards a raised oval bar on the other side of the dance floor. The bar, shrouded in darkness, was ringed by chrome barstools. Nightclubs were not the sort of place Lowry frequented, but even to his untrained eye, this place was straight out of 1977. 'So, the guys you're talking about were sat there, right in the middle. It was pretty early. They were, like, some of the first in.'

'Was this them?' He held up pictures of Jason Boyd and Felix Cowley.

'That's them. There was another dude who came on his own, chatted, then split. Much later.'

'This him?' Lowry held up a picture of Stone.

'Not sure . . . It was dark, and, like I say, he wasn't here long.'

'Look at it closely?'

'Wait a sec. I know this guy – he plays horn at the Candyman?'

'He did. Was he here?'

'Yeah, yeah, he was here later, after the birds had joined them.' Lowry baulked at the description, knowing it included Jacqui.

'And what sort of mindset were the men in?'

'They were loaded, all right.'

JAMES HENRY

'How did they behave?'

'Like people off their faces do: really chatty, arms waving everywhere – not out of control, though; sort of hyper-excited.'

'Any aggressive behaviour?'

'No.'

'What were they up to? Mixing with the crowd when it filled up?'

'Nah, they kept to themselves. Just sat there yakking at each other until these birds turned up.'

So, not actively selling, just using, thought Lowry.

'So, they just sat there?'

'They were rooted to the spot until the ladies dragged them up on to the dance floor.'

'And then?'

'I watched them briefly. The men were all over the place – almost comical – completely on a different planet. The chicks were in time. There was this cute, dark one who was quite a mover. But then I lost them as the place started to fill up.'

Lowry surveyed the club. It had an expansive floor space with a capacity of several hundred. He started to picture Jacqui gyrating in the middle with another man, but stopped himself. He couldn't remember the last time he'd seen her on a dance floor – probably a Masonic do such as the one Sparks was attending tonight – although he had no doubt she was the woman the barman was referring to.

'Was Stone a regular?'

'Nah – not his scene. And neither were the other two you

327

showed me; this place wasn't their sort of groove. And they weren't exactly choice clientele either.' He flicked a tiny piece of lint from the sleeve of his pristine shirt. 'We'd just relaxed the dress code to drum up a bit of business, otherwise these chancers would never have got through the door.'

Lowry moved on to the empty dance floor.

'How late were they here until?'

'I couldn't tell you, but the lights come on at ten to two.'

'You shut at two.'

'Two, that's right, else we have your mob down on us – but the dregs can still be in here at twenty past.'

Dregs, Lowry thought with a heavy heart. A fragment of a scene twirled in his head: Jacqui draping her scarf around the neck of now-dead Jason Boyd. He snapped his mind shut.

'Thank you, you've been more than helpful,' he said, and left, hoping not to have to enter the club again for a long time.

7.45 p.m., Abberton village hall, south of Colchester

Lowry arrived late for the lecture and sat at the back of the draughty village hall. He tried to shut out all the events of the last few days and engage with what the man standing at the front was saying about peregrine falcons.

'Of course, it could be dismissed as nature's strange irony that such a powerful hunter should have the most fragile of eggs. But no, this is not nature's doing, it is man's. Agricultural pesticides continue to kill and damage our wildlife. DDT has been banned for nearly ten years in the United States, yet here it is still widely used.'

Doug Young, the park ranger, spoke eloquently about the challenging circumstances Britain's raptors faced. A slide of a magnificent falcon with its grey, noble head was replaced by a chart showing a complex table of chemicals. Lowry shifted in his seat. He had come here to find beauty and peace, but instead it was turning into a forensics lecture.

Afterwards, Young came over to him as he was leafing through a collection of RSPB leaflets by the hall entrance.

'Detective Inspector Lowry, I'm so glad you could make it. How did you find the talk?'

'Unfortunately, I was late, Mr Young, and caught only the science.'

'Ah, yes. It is rather depressing.' He held his hands before him, fingers crossed, like a man of the church. 'But it's important to get the message out.'

'Absolutely.' He smiled. 'But I've yet to see a peregrine and was hoping for some tips, rather than to discover that farmers are destroying their chances of rearing young.'

'Of course. And you shall.' He leaned forward and whispered conspiratorially. 'We have a breeding pair not ten miles from here.'

'Really? Where?'

'Fingringhoe.'

'I was there yesterday,' said Lowry, surprised.

'But not on the marshes, I'll bet.'

'No, the village. So, presumably, the marshes are out of danger, being away from farmland?'

'Hmm ... They're not entirely hazard-free for the birds. As I'm sure you know, most of the vast area of marshland is part of the ranges.'

'Yes, of course, the firing ranges – the army uses the land for shooting practice.'

'Exactly.'

'What do you do? Wait for the red flag to be lowered before entering?'

'Not necessary. The range sergeant is a decent sort; he'll call if they spot the birds making an appearance during operations, and at other times he lets us use the command hut – makes a perfect hide.'

'A telephone call from the ranges?'

'Yes, they have a line even out there.'

'Is that so? Thank you, Mr Young.'

Wednesday, 5 January, 1983

43

9 a.m., Wednesday, interview room one, Queen Street HQ

Lowry looked at the pitiful excuse for a man sitting behind a worn wooden table in the otherwise empty interview room. He knew instinctively that this sorry specimen was not responsible for the mayhem over the last few days. Cowley sat, teeth chattering, in the same filthy clothes he'd been wearing when they pulled him out of the water yesterday morning. When quizzed, the duty PC assured Lowry that the heater had been on full blast throughout the night.

In the far corner of the interview room, a bucket sat collecting droplets from a leaking pipe that ran overhead across the back wall. Sparks refused to have it attended to, presumably enjoying the idea that the dripping was a form of torture for suspects.

'Get him a blanket, for Christ's sake,' Lowry muttered crossly to the WPC on the door. The first-floor room was bitterly cold – he himself had kept his scarf on.

He sighed and flipped open the buff folder which contained a medical record for Felix Simon Cowley. The individual before him was not a well man, by any stretch, and at first glance didn't look capable of tying his own shoelaces. And judging by the paperwork in front of him, that might not be all he wasn't capable of, for the medical report was from Severalls, the asylum to the north of the town, up on the Essex plains. However, Cowley did have some awareness of the situation: Gabriel had told Lowry the day before that the lad had confessed to smuggling drugs on to the mainland. He was vague on detail: from whom, and what, was still a mystery; all he could confirm was that they'd landed with two army rucksacks containing 'stuff' and a change of clothes. No mention of the two dead men had been made. They were middlemen, couriers.

'Th-thank you,' Cowley said, glancing up with wide, dark eyes at the WPC, who'd draped a coarse blanket across his shoulders.

'Can you tell me why you're here, Felix?' Lowry asked, sliding a pack of Player's across the stained table.

'Where's Jason?'

'Jason? Was he with you?'

'Yes. We went out on the boat, then—' He stopped himself, hand over his mouth.

'No, no, it's okay to talk – we won't hurt you. To help us find Jason, it's better that you tell us all you know.'

Cowley took a cigarette with a filth-streaked hand. Lowry reached over to light it. Barely twenty years old, the wretch looked haggard and worn out. He drew deeply on the cigarette and then looked at the glowing tip and nodded towards the buff folder. 'They never let me have them in there.'

'No, I'm not surprised,' Lowry said.

'I don't want to go back. I want to go home.'

'Is that what you were doing in Fingringhoe? Trying to call home?' They'd matched some prints from the phone box to Cowley, who must've been under their very nose when Lowry had tried to get into the tower.

'I don't know who I called,' he replied, puzzled.

'How could you not know who you called?' This was going to be painful. Felix Cowley had been sectioned at the age of sixteen with severe psychological disorders, not helped by the fact that he'd seen his mother burn alive in a cottage in St Osyth. If anyone should avoid dabbling with recreational drugs, it was this lad. God knows what was going on inside that head.

'I want to go home.' Cowley's eyes were glazed like those of an alcoholic twice his age: slightly bulbous and held in place by a jelly-like film. Home would be Brightlingsea. The file indicated next of kin to be a father and a brother.

'We'll see about that,' Lowry said diplomatically, 'but first let's get these questions answered, to help find Jason.'

'I want the lady.'

'What lady?'

'The police lady what give me the blanket.'

Lowry turned, surprised, to look at the stout, silent WPC on the door. 'What, her?'

'No – the one on the boat. She gave me a blanket, too, but the man with bad breath and a beard took it away.'

Gabriel and Barnes.

'Constable, see if WPC Gabriel is available,' Lowry said over his shoulder.

'Tell me, while we wait for the lady to come, about being at sea in the dark. Must have been scary?'

Cowley frowned and tried to roll his eyes, but couldn't for some reason and blinked rapidly instead. 'Jason was so cross. We'd got lost in the fog and it was so cold. Soooo cold. And then the mud! We had to walk forever, carrying the stuff across the mud.'

'I'd have thought a couple of local lads like yourselves would know the way from Brightlingsea . . .'

'We started out from Brightlingsea, out of the estuary – where we met, well, you know, out in the sea, a bigger boat. I don't know nothing about it, though.'

'I believe you, honestly,' Lowry said, watching the boy squeeze his cigarette tightly between thumb and forefinger. This lad was an innocent, just a mule, he was sure of it, but he was all they had. 'But c'mon, how can you tell me you made a telephone call and didn't know who you were calling – did you just have a number?'

Cowley fumbled inside his denim jacket. A wallet? Somebody had slipped up on the front desk. From inside the leather pouch, which had certainly seen better days, he pulled a creased slip of paper, carefully unfolded it and passed it to

Lowry. Two numbers. One Colchester – Greenstead, probably – and one longer number with a code Lowry didn't recognize. 'Saturday' was scrawled across the top.

'It says here *Saturday*. You called on Monday.'

'We got lost.'

'Okay. Between getting lost on Mersea and the time of the phone call, can you tell me what you were doing, where you were?'

''Ouse in Colchester.'

'When you got there, how many people were at this house?' Lowry reached across and picked up the wallet. Inside was a familiar-looking green document – a driving licence.

'One bloke.'

'Called?' he prompted. The name on the damp licence was Jason Boyd.

'Del, or Derek.'

'That it?'

'No, later, a geezer in his thirties turned up, called Jamie. That's when it all started to go wrong.'

Bingo. Kenton had already called Lowry to relay his conversation with the obliging Pond about Jamie Philpott. But just to be sure: 'This Jamie – light-brown or blondish hair, late thirties, skinny, long sideburns, about five foot ten?'

'Yeah, I guess.'

'So, Jamie turns up; then what?'

'We were waiting to be paid so we could spilt and get home. When the door goes, we think it's . . . it's someone with our money. But it's this Jamie bloke. It's him that cracked open the gear. We were knackered, too, you know; hardly slept. Bored of waiting.' He rubbed his filthy forehead. 'Seemed like a good idea, you know, a little dab. Next thing I know, I'm here.'

'You must recall something of what happened in between? That's one hell of a gap, between Saturday afternoon, in a kitchen on the Greenstead Estate, to Tuesday morning, floating in a gale off the North Sea.'

'I'm telling you, that gear was lethal.' Cowley looked at the wallet, which seemed to be a trigger. 'Jason wouldn't have let 'is guard down if it wasn't for that nuclear whizz. That's his wallet.' Cowley had a faraway look, as if trying to reach into a childhood memory rather than recall a drugs binge on a council estate at the weekend. Then he snapped his head back. 'Left it behind with me in the curry place. Jason would normally never do that.'

It was unclear whether he meant leave him or the wallet.

'How did you get left behind? Weren't you just collecting a takeaway?'

'Went for a leak. I came out and they'd gawn. The Indian bloke was waving Jace's wallet at me . . . I couldn't work out which direction they'd gone in . . . It's not like I don't know Colchester – I do, like – but when it's dark and you're on stuff, you know . . . you get . . .'

'Disorientated?'

'That's it. Disorientated.'

'But when was this? Sunday?' he prompted.

'Yeah, maybe . . .' But he looked vacant; he had no idea.

'You went to a nightclub on Saturday – remember dancing? Under the glitter ball?'

'Yes! We did, on Saturday – well raring, we were!' It was as though a switch had been turned on. 'After doing a couple of lines, Jace gets up and says he's off for a drink – thirsty, like – and we all pile out with him. Can't remember much, but you're right, we ended up in a club . . . yes, and then went back to the house – that would be Saturday, all right.'

'So, you, Jason, Stone, Philpott, got back to the house in the early hours of Sunday morning?'

'Yeah, but not Philpott; he peeled off somewhere . . .' That much was true. Jamie had had his hands full in the high street.

'So, was it just the three of you, or was there anyone else?' He knew he was leading the man and cringed as he awaited his response, especially as a WPC was present.

'There were two birds with us, walking up the road.' Cowley scrunched up his face. 'They were making a hell of a racket.'

Lowry tensed; he heard the WPC shift on her feet. He had to ask. 'These women, were they in any way connected to Stone?'

'Nah, just a couple of tarts.'

'They returned to the house with you?'

'Nah, couple of prick-teasers; got as far the front door, then changed their minds. Stone tried to drag 'em in, there were a bit of a skuffle out the front of the house, then they cleared off.'

'And what did you do then – go to bed?'

He rubbed his eyes. 'I wish. Nah, we were up until it got

339

light – then I must've conked out. Then . . . then I remember waking up and being starving. Everyone was hungry. But we were knackered, though . . . so we just got straight pissed.'

'Drinking?'

'Yeah – booze, to make us sleep. A couple of Special Brews.'

'Why didn't you eat?'

''Ad nothing, did we? That 'ouse was empty. All the shops was shut, being Sunday . . . so we had to wait for the Indian to open. Later.'

'So you had nothing at all until then?'

'Apart from beer and then some whizz when we woke up, to get us moving a bit.'

Lowry looked the man in the eyes. He was amazed that he was in one piece. The human constitution at that age was incredible.

'Time?'

'I couldn't tell you, but it was dark by the time we left the 'ouse – must've slept most of the day, I s'pose. Had the fear a bit, by then, too . . .'

'I can imagine. Who else were you with when you went for the curry? Jamie?'

'No, Jamie had disappeared up to the high street after we tucked into the gear . . . the night before, I think . . .' He scrunched up his face in thought. 'Or did he come back . . . ? It's all so fuzzy.' He clasped his face with his dirty hands. 'That shit was weird.'

'Weird in what way?'

'I ain't, like, good with words. But one minute you feel great, like you could climb a mountain, and the next you're just in a different world . . . or it's like everybody else is in it and you're looking in on them. In an instant, like.' He clicked his fingers. 'Then you get the fear like you've never had and just want to hide.'

'Sounds grim. I—'

'But then someone says something and you're back on a high – like switching on a light, and you just want to dance and laugh. For a while, before –' he tapped his head slowly. – 'before the gaps – like massive black 'oles. In me memory, like. Can't remember a friggin' thing.'

Having had the toxicology report from Sparks, Lowry was not surprised to hear this. He asked what had happened after he'd got left at the curry house, and Cowley managed to recall that he'd tried for a taxi to Fingringhoe. For reasons unconfirmed, the taxi had dropped him in the middle of nowhere, possibly near Donyland Woods, where he spent an uncomfortable night – here, his eyes grew wide – with only horrific hallucinations to keep him company. At dawn, he felt safer and thought he might've slept for a few hours.

'But if you live in Brightlingsea, why not get a taxi home?'

He scratched his grubby head. 'There was only a quid in Jace's wallet. That wouldn't get me home, so I reckon I thought I might get to Fingringhoe and take me dad's old boat across the channel,' he said uncertainly.

'In the dark?' Lowry asked, incredulous.

'Dunno what I was thinking, do I?'

There was a light rap on the door. Lowry gestured for the WPC to answer it. Gabriel was outside in the corridor. He would leave her with Cowley – she had fished him out of the water; maybe she'd squeeze something more out of him now – while he focused on catching Philpott. It was beginning to seem like all of Colchester's lowlife knew of this shipment . . . Just how much of this stuff could there be out there?

Lowry explained to Gabriel what he knew so far. He spoke softly in her ear, so close he was almost touching. He felt her twitch. 'And be cautious. If you play your cards right, you can prise information out of him he doesn't know he has. Forget the drop, where they picked up the gear – that'll be over his head – focus on what went on in Greenstead. Play dumb about the murders for now. He knows more than he thinks.'

She nodded.

'Okay. Easy does it.'

Felix looked the blonde woman opposite in the eyes. They were pale blue and couldn't meet his. Nevertheless, he preferred her to the mod policeman. She mustered a smile and then busied herself with his file. His file: that was a joke. But he'd use it, goddamn it, to save himself getting banged up – rather Severalls than Chelmsford or, worse, fucking Broadmoor.

'Do you think you're unwell, Felix?' the WPC asked kindly.

He knew he wasn't right, sometimes. 'Err . . . Well, I've

342

taken some funny stuff, which has left me feeling a bit peculiar, miss.'

'But surely not since you've been in here? We pulled you out of the water yesterday afternoon?'

'It was right odd stuff. Never had the like.'

'Did you take much?'

'Can't rightly remember. Only took it because we were bored waiting for the pick-up.'

'Do you know who you were waiting for?'

He hugged the blanket tightly. 'No, I don't know anything. Jason don't trust me with important stuff.' That much was probably true. Even now, in this freezing police station, Cowley marvelled at how little he really knew. They all said in Brightlingsea he wasn't right in the head since his mother died. Maybe he wasn't – how would he end up here, like this, otherwise? He wiped his nose on his sleeve. The one thing he knew he mustn't do was mention Freddie. Jason had said that, and Freddie himself had said that – and, anyway, Freddie said to always do as Jason said. Jason would always look after Felix no matter what . . . But then, where was Jason, and Freddie, for that matter?

'Where's Jason?' he asked.

The lady policeman frowned, creasing her pale, smooth forehead. She looked sad.

'I can't say for now, I'm afraid.'

Her change of expression triggered a ripple of anxiety in Cowley, which quickly began to build. Her use of the word 'afraid' had pierced his fragile mind. It was as if he'd been told how to feel.

'My pills.'

'Pills?'

'Took 'em out when I emptied me pockets. I need them.' Not having them increased his anxiety.

The woman stood up. She was tall. 'I'll get them for you, Felix. Don't worry.' She smiled down like a kind goddess. 'Is there anything else I can get you?'

'Some pencils?'

'Pencils?'

'I like to draw. Calms me down.'

-44-

10 u.m., Wednesday, Queen Street HQ

'Sit down, sit down,' Sparks commanded, smoking a cigarette behind the desk on which his feet rested. The chief's trousers had slipped up his calfs, revealing a dense matt of wiry hair. Kenton, wishing to distance himself from such a view, leaned back as far as he could on the wooden chair. Sparks was reading something intently in his lap.

For what felt like an age, neither spoke. The chief's expression was obscured by his leather soles, propped on the desk, but Kenton could hear him suck on his cigarette. The street noise never made it this high, and Kenton realized how peaceful it must be up here, and with a view, too. Sparks made a noise that might have been a chuckle. Kenton thought that, finally, some acknowledgement was coming his way for his casework, or perhaps it was another pat on the back for his bout on Sunday. It couldn't possibly be about Lowry this time, could it? After a while, Sparks stubbed out his cigarette and sighed loudly.

'Where do you see the future of the police heading, son?'

This question struck him has unusual. The chief was not one for small talk, not with the likes of him, anyhow. Promising.

'Err . . . I hear word of computerization in the Met and the West Country. I suspect that may influence how we collate information and forensics—'

'Eh?' Sparks poked his head to one side, appearing from behind his shoes. 'What are you on about, son?'

'I thought, when you asked about the future, you meant—' he said, confused.

'No, no, no. Computers? Only children and bearded freaks have time for that nonsense. Besides,' he leaned across to the electric heater at the side of the desk, 'I think getting some fucking central heating in this godforsaken rotting building is higher on the priority list. No, I'm talking about men.'

Kenton looked at him blankly. Sparks's interest in men usually only extended to their ability to thump each other.

'Guys like you and me. Lowry, even.'

It seemed an odd remark: the three of them had zero in common other than all being policemen that liked to box, and even there, one, of late, had decided to hold binoculars rather than to punch anyone. He had no idea what the chief was on about.

'Sorry, guv, I'm not with you.'

Sparks took his feet down and tossed a copy of *Asterix and the Secret Agent* on the desk – the source of his chuckling.

'Look at women. They wanted equal pay, they got it; they want equal opportunities, they've got that in spades – we've even got one running the fucking country. How the fuck that ever happened will remain a mystery – that, people will ponder for all eternity. What next? A black guy in number ten?' He shook his head and tutted.

Kenton nodded his head dumbly.

'Well, think on it; it's a fact.'

Kenton nodded again.

'So, in addition, there's a type of woman who will use her feminine assets to progress her career in any way she can.'

'Sir?'

'What I mean is – I'll be direct – have it off with the boss, or –' he shot Kenton a meaningful look – 'someone in a position of power.'

'Sorry, sir, I don't see where this conversation is heading,' Kenton said, confused.

Sparks held an authoritative finger in the air. 'Alternatively, if the woman's a bit of a . . . you know –' he flopped his hand about – 'but still ambitious, she might try and fuck you over instead.'

'Sir, please can you explain? I'm lost.'

'Very well. WPC Gabriel has made allegations against you.'

'Allegations? What do you mean, "allegations"?' Kenton paled.

'Wait a minute; what's the term she used?' As Sparks scrabbled around among the papers on his desk, Kenton sat shell-shocked; he couldn't begin to understand what was being suggested. 'Allegations' sounded formal. What had she said?

'Harassment?' Sparks looked up at him doubtfully.

'What does that mean?'

The chief frowned. 'I'm not sure it really *means* anything – a form of discrimination, perhaps? But this is the police force, so it doesn't apply.' He reached for his cigarettes, belatedly offering Kenton one before adding, 'Ordinarily.'

'How so?' said Kenton, dizzy and still uncomprehending. Was he in trouble or not?

'The police force is a man's arena, and as such any woman prepared to play in this world has to be prepared to take a few punches, much like inside the ring.' Kenton's heart jerked at the recollection of Gabriel watching him fight. 'Figuratively, of course – we can't go knocking them around; that would be wrong.' He paused. 'But, ordinarily, the odd grope, an arse squeeze on a night out, is acceptable.'

Sparks didn't elaborate on whether the woman in question should be complicit in such behaviour, but Kenton felt sure he was about to find out. This whole thing was ridiculous.

'Hang on, sir, this is about WPC Gabriel, yes? But it was only yesterday you asked me to take her to a Masonic bash!'

'Correct, son, but if the girl – woman – in question happens to be the troubled niece of the ACC, it's probably best to adopt a hands-off policy, don't you think?'

'Yes, sir,' Kenton acquiesced.

'Good lad. We'll say no more about it then; consider

yourself reprimanded and leave the girl alone and save your magic potion for the ring.' He reached for his comic book. Deflated, Kenton made to go. 'Oh, and good work on the West Mersea post-office job. Lowry tells me the gun implicates Stone, the fella found at Greenstead, as one of the robbers. Good work, son. If you hadn't cross-examined the Dodger's paperwork, we wouldn't have him. I shall personally be visiting Sergeant Bradley later today and advising him to get his house in order.'

'How was that? Promotion in the air?' Lowry asked jocularly.

Kenton sat down opposite like a punctured balloon, his luxurious wavy hair, usually carefully swept back, now fell unheeded across his eyes.

'Dan, you okay?'

'How could she? *How could she?*' he muttered, staring into nothing.

'The chief?'

'No, no, no.' Kenton felt himself pulse red with humiliation.

'Hey, what's up?' Lowry leaned forward in concern.

Kenton couldn't face his boss like this; he didn't want him thinking him weak. Maybe he'd been foolish. Or naïve. Either way, he shook his head involuntarily – as if that would shake the last half-hour away.

'Nothing's up. Everything is fine.' He managed to compose himself – mind over matter.

His phone began to ring, the shrill tone a violent intrusion on his thoughts. 'Doesn't matter,' he said, taking a deep breath and picking up the receiver. 'CID. Detective Constable Kenton speaking.'

'That number you gave us.' It was a British Telecom engineer – Lowry had asked him to try to trace the number Cowley had found in Boyd's wallet. They'd tried to call it and got an 'unobtainable' signal, but as some of the final digits were smudged, it was difficult to read. But the area code was unfamiliar to them all.

'Yes,' he said, collecting himself.

'It's not a known BT number.'

'But there might be a digit or two missing – it was smudged?'

'I have tried every permutation – didn't take long – adding one, even two numbers to the string you gave.'

'So it's not a telephone number?'

'I couldn't say that for certain. It could be a defunct, unlisted number. An old line, out of use.'

'What does that mean?'

'Unlisted means we – I mean here, or maybe at Dollis Hill – have no record of where or whose it might be. An extra digit would give the quantity of numbers for an unlisted line, but as I say, I've tried every combination. That's not to say it's been cut off – numbers can be issued then cut off—'

'Who would have an unlisted number?'

'The government?'

'How about the military? Could it be an army line?'

'Yes, that's entirely plausible.'

Lowry, on the phone now himself, pointed upstairs. Sparks beckoned again.

'I'm telling you, this man is not our murderer,' Lowry said.

It was mid-morning, but to Sparks it felt like the end of the day.

'He's just a half-crazy kid involved in something way over his head. His psychiatric report makes no mention of violence. He's just a bit disturbed.'

'Disturbed? I'm beginning to grow disturbed myself. He's sitting in our cells practically with blood on his hands – if we don't arrest him, there has got to be an extraordinarily good reason for it.' The chief was conscious of raising his voice.

'He's mentioned Jamie Philpott. Philpott was at Beaumont Terrace.'

Kenton's head turned. 'As did Tony Pond – asked him if he wanted in on a drugs deal.'

'Have we pulled Jamie in?' Sparks asked. 'What does he have to say for himself?'

'He did a bunk from the hospital Saturday night and has not been seen since,' Lowry said.

'I heard that Jamie Philpott has never been arrested,' Kenton said disingenuously.

'He's been known to peddle dope to students, but he's never been nicked.' Lowry glanced at Sparks. Corruption wasn't widespread in Colchester, but there were, it was acknowledged, a number of men roaming the streets who should perhaps be behind bars. Philpott was one such character. It wasn't so much that the line between police grass and small-time hood was blurred – it was more that there was no line: to be of any value as the former, one had to be a player or dabbler in the criminal fraternity.

'I hear you,' Sparks retorted, 'but I can't see a minnow like Jamie Philpott being behind all this mess. Murder and smuggling this sort of thing? Different league altogether.'

'But turning over a post office with Stone to get some cash to buy into a deal is credible, to my mind,' Lowry suggested.

'Yes . . .' Sparks let the word linger. 'And that spat between Philpott and the squaddie surely had something to do with the Castle Park incident?'

'Maybe there's a connection between the two,' Lowry said, glancing at Kenton.

'What?' Sparks said with dismay. 'Between a soldier's "accidental" death in Castle Park and a drugs murder in Greenstead? How do you arrive at that?'

'Jones and Daley were looking for Boyd the night the accident happened,' Kenton announced.

'Whoa, there!' Sparks exclaimed. 'What you're saying is fucking serious. Soldiers trying to buy drugs?'

'We've got multiple bodies,' remarked Lowry. 'It's already serious.'

Sparks held up his hand. 'All right, all right. Get round to Philpott's gaff, pull the little shit in.'

'He's gone to ground – we've had his place in the Stanway under surveillance for forty-eight hours.'

The chief absorbed this information. 'So, doing a bunk from hospital wasn't down to a dislike of hospital food. If he's in something this deep, no wonder he's disappeared . . . But he's a show-off, a smart-arse.' Sparks lit another cigarette. He'd known Jamie for years – indeed, it was he who had overlooked his and Pond's dope dealing until County had insisted on a clampdown a few years back, when Philpott was told quietly to 'stop'. 'He'll show. Impossible to keep a lid on that cocky bravado. The only reason he'll have gone to ground is because of the pasting that gorilla gave him in the town centre. Even men like him have pride. Try his mum's place in Tiptree.'

The two detectives nodded but made no sign of leaving. 'Is there more?' asked Sparks.

'Cowley had Boyd's wallet on him,' said Kenton. 'It contained a phone number that—'

'Hold on a damn second!' Sparks stopped pacing, cigarette smoke continuing to swirl ahead of him. 'You're saying he had one of the dead men's wallets, and you still think he didn't kill him?' He was incredulous.

'He picked the wallet up at the curry house on East Hill. The owner said Boyd paid and left it behind while the other was in the lav. Cowley tried to ring the number in it from a phone box.'

Sparks shook his head in dismay. 'What do the telecom

353

engineers have to say? Do they know whose number it is? Can they trace it?'

'Yes and no,' Kenton interjected. 'It's not a recognizable number – even allowing for a missing digit or two, but—'

'This is beyond fucking belief. We have a looney calling someone he doesn't know on a non-existent number.' He rubbed his creased forehead. He was up for a challenge, but this took the biscuit.

'The engineer said, if a digit was added, it might turn out to be an old discontinued government or military phone number. Stands to reason, given . . .' Kenton paused mid-sentence.

Sparks followed the young DC's eyeline. Gabriel was at the door. Sparks waved her away dismissively. He continued to tread the centuries-old floorboards, which occasionally sighed under his weight. '"Might turn out to be"? Can you hear yourself? You're saying add a couple of numbers to a string of digits and you *might* have a number that's discontinued?! Which *possibly* could be used by the military? Jesus. Forget it, for Christ's sake. Cowley doesn't have the sense he was born with, you say so yourself. It could be a bank account number for all we know.'

'It's incomplete. But it's worth knowing—'

'If it's incomplete, it's useless.' Sparks was not prepared to countenance some flimsy army connection so swiftly after the Castle Park incident. 'Lowry, does the simpleton know *anything* of any use? Where is he, anyway?'

'He's on the first floor, in interview room one,' Lowry said.

'He knows a little, but not much, and he's terrified of being locked up again. I left him with Gabriel. She was there when he was pulled out of the water yesterday and I think he's taken a shine to her.'

'Hmm, he's not the only one,' Sparks said, noting Kenton staring forlornly at the door. 'Anyway, let's keep things in perspective: we're not investigating the army, are we? Remember, we're going to get hold of Philpott, and I haven't seen him on the fucking parade ground of late, have you?'

A uniform entered the room unbidden.

'What is it?' Sparks barked.

'Assistant Chief Constable Merrydown is on the phone.'

-45-

11.30 a.m., Wednesday, incident room, Queen Street HQ

Kenton couldn't help but smile to himself as Sparks left the room like thunder, trailing expletives. The young DC, too proud to let on, was still smarting from the lecture he'd received earlier and was delighted to see the chief hauled away like that. Lowry, meanwhile, was contemplating the OS map pinned to the noticeboard.

'I'm sure there's a military angle,' he said. 'All this land here is used by the army for firing ranges. I'd not thought of it until last night.'

'Why didn't you mention it just now?'

'While he's pacing the room like a caged lion?' Lowry rolled his eyes, and Kenton laughed. 'Listen, Cowley was here, at Fingringhoe, and just over here are the marshes.'

'What's our next play?'

Lowry squinted, jettisoning smoke at the ceiling. He certainly seemed more relaxed when he was smoking. 'I need to get to Tiptree. Philpott has been gone too long.'

'Shall I come with you?'

'No. You track down Ted Nugent on Mersea – he's the other piece of the jigsaw – but try not to frighten him, and remember to dodge the Dodger. And what was all that stuff about earlier, anyway? You seemed upset. Want to talk about it?'

Kenton shook his head. 'Nope. All fine. Do you think there really is a connection between the Castle Park incident and the Greenstead murders?'

'Could be.' Lowry ran his hand through Brylcreemed hair and adjusted his slender tie. 'Who knows?' He picked up his donkey jacket to leave. 'You sure you're all right?' He clasped Kenton on the shoulder in a conciliatory way.

Although his boss was quiet and often distracted, Kenton thought he felt others' troubles keenly.

'Yes; storm in a teacup. No big deal.'

'Okay. Meet you back here at two.'

Kenton slouched out of the incident room. His face said it all. Lowry reflected how young, fresh faces are less able hide their emotions, which always lie just below the surface, without any sagging, lined skin to obscure them. Gabriel entered the room silently. It didn't take a genius to work out that whatever was wrong with Kenton involved her, but Lowry wasn't going to pry.

'Right!' He rubbed his hands together. 'Let's motor.' He tossed her the keys, catching her eye briefly as they left the cold room. Her clear blue eyes betrayed nothing. Life still had to make its mark on her, he thought, and sighed inwardly. He didn't consider himself one of the world's natural philosophers, but as they left the building, he found himself musing on the way every upset will add a line here and a crease there until one gradually builds up a mask of resistance, until, in the end, no one can ever tell.

Midday, Tiptree village, nine miles west of Colchester

They'd followed Maldon Road through the softly undulating white countryside. Neither had spoken. The wind sprayed snow lightly across the road. As she fumbled for the wipers, the police airwaves crackled intermittently: a granny arguing with Woolworths staff over stealing a ballpoint; truanting school kids vandalizing a phone box; a dog off the lead terrorizing a pregnant mother in Castle Park: that was Gabriel's world – the general public and its daily grind.

'Turn here,' Lowry, said, the first words he'd spoken since they'd left Queen Street. 'What did you make of Felix Cowley?'

They were now cruising slowly through the village centre. The Tiptree police had confirmed with Philpott's mother that he was in the village; the old woman seemed relieved to hear from them, and had said quietly he would nip to the bookie's at noon.

'He's very confused.'

'He's not the only one.'

'I didn't get anywhere, I'm afraid. He needed his medicine.'

'What sort of medicine is it?'

'Lithium: some kind of mood stabilizer. I had the doctor see him. He'll be transferred to Severalls later today.'

'Good.'

'He asked for pencils, too. Drawing calms him down.'

'Well done.'

'What for?'

'You said you'd not got anywhere – but you found out he likes to draw. That wasn't in his file.' Suddenly, Lowry jerked forward. 'There he is, coming out of the newsagent's with the terrier. Pull over.'

Gabriel did as instructed, and parked in front of a café. She found the inspector's Saab heavy and uncomfortable to drive. She didn't get the thrill she'd expected from the pursuit of hardened villains – if that's the kind they were now after. She hastily grappled with the seat belt; Lowry, not wearing one, was out already.

'He's oblivious to all the world,' Lowry said over the roof of the Saab. The suspect was walking towards them, the dog in a little coat trotting next to him.

'But I'm in uniform?'

'So? If he's going to run, he'll run.'

Gabriel was bemused, but then there was a lot she didn't understand at the moment. Take this morning, for instance: Chief Superintendent Sparks had made an incredibly patronizing speech – it was his way, of course – lined with platitudes concerning a woman's place in the police force. And then there was Detective Constable's Kenton's inexplicable hostility.

'He hasn't seen us. Look at that shiner – Sparks was right,' Lowry remarked as the suspect, a man in his early forties with short brown hair and large sideburns, chatted to an old man with a walking stick.

'Right about what?'

'Licking his wounds at his mum's place – a self-respecting villain wouldn't want to be seen sporting a black eye like that on his own patch; he'll be sensitive about his reputation.'

It sounded like machismo nonsense, so she had no further comment. Philpott and his dog stopped before them at a pelican crossing and strolled across towards a park still white with yesterday's snow. Although she would've loved to be somewhere else, Gabriel decided to act positive and said brightly, 'Tiptree: I've never been here before – it seems a quaint village.'

Lowry snorted. 'Gypsies and jam is all you'll find here. Oi! Jamie!'

Gabriel jumped at his sudden bellow. The man, who was wearing a green bomber jacket, stopped in his tracks just inside the park and turned round. His face registered an agitated 'What now?' look. The terrier, sensing his master's displeasure, started yapping angrily.

'I hate dogs, don't you?' Lowry asked.

'My mother has a poodle . . .' But he hadn't waited for a response and was crunching ahead across the white ground.

Gabriel followed, catching up with Lowry as he entered the park and strode towards Philpott. A group of young boys stopped passing a football and regarded them with curiosity.

'Jamie, old son, what a sorry state you are.' Lowry tutted. Philpott was about the same height as Lowry but of slighter build: course and sinewy, she imagined, under the football scarf and bomber jacket. 'Whatever happened?'

'Fucking squaddie took a swing at me, as if you didn't know,' grumbled Philpott. The dog continued to yap.

'Can you quieten your dog, please?' Gabriel asked, feeling the early twinges of a migraine.

Philpott took her in for the first time. 'Bleedin' hell, where'd you come from? An improvement on the usual trunks Lowry gets landed with. Shut it, Jasper.'

'Why didn't you leave a note of your whereabouts when checking out of the hospital?' Lowry asked.

'Why should I?'

'We had questions pertaining to your assault,' Gabriel chipped in bluntly.

'Why question me? It should be that meathead you hassle. I'm the one who got lumped.'

'We need a witness statement,' she replied. Lowry stood by, quietly regarding the dog.

Philpott sniffed, unpleasantly drawing up phlegm. 'All right, what do you want to know?'

'Did you know your attacker?'

'By sight. Big fella.'

'Why did he hit you?'

'How the fuck should I know?'

'He says you spilt his drink,' she said. Philpott snorted in derision.

The man was repellent.

'Let's go inside for a chat,' Lowry said quietly.

'Inside where?' His eyes darted this way and that, unable to focus on either DI Lowry or WPC Gabriel.

'The car. It's chilly out here,' Lowry said. 'Besides, do you really want to be seen fraternizing with us?'

Philpott regarded the boys with the football, who had yet to resume playing. Gabriel now understood why he was looking at her so disdainfully. Lowry was in plain clothes, so it was she who was drawing attention to him – her and the foul little dog.

'What about Jasper?'

'He's wearing a coat, so will be fine outside. C'mon.'

They left the park. Wondering where this would lead, she looked at the crisp ground and was reminded of the bright morning a few days before, when she'd watched Lowry on the bandstand, surveying Castle Park. He'd not so much as mentioned the case to her since, and she wondered again at his silence on the road this morning.

Lowry ushered Philpott into the back of the car, taking the dog lead. He nodded for her to get in the front. She frowned; he pointed to the driver's side. He moved round the back of the Saab, after shutting Philpott in.

'Right,' Lowry said, climbing in. 'I'll just trap Jasper's lead in the door here, all right, Jamie?'

'Be quick about it. I don't want to be seen with the likes of her in the middle of the flaming village.'

'Sure, sure.' He slammed the door. 'Start her up, WPC Gabriel; get the blower on.'

She did as he said and turned the heater up.

'Right, Jamie, ol' fruit.' He clasped the younger man's shoulder. 'Were you, or were you not, at number four Beaumont Terrace on Saturday morning?'

'What? I thought this was about that punch-up?'

'In good time. But before we get to that – where were you at that time? Down on the Greenstead Estate trying to pick up a bit of whizz?'

'I'm not 'aving this.' Philpott tried to open the door. 'I'll be on the horn to Sparks if you don't—'

'WPC Gabriel, pull out.' She turned round to make sure she'd heard right. Lowry was perfectly calm. Philpott was a vision of panic. 'WPC Gabriel, if you will. Slowly, though. We want our little friend outside to keep up, at least at first.'

'Eh?' Philpott exclaimed in alarm. 'You bastard, Lowry!' Philpott rattled the door handle again, gripped by anger.

'No use, Jamie: child-locked, I'm afraid.'

Gabriel reversed the car tentatively. Lowry surely wouldn't kill the man's dog, would he? Jamie Philpott clearly thought otherwise; he'd gone quiet and now sat sullenly in his seat.

'Now, I'll ask again: were you, or were you not, on the Greenstead Estate on Saturday?'

-46-

1 p.m., Wednesday, Queen Street HQ

'I don't buy that for one minute,' Lowry muttered.

He and Kenton were in the corridor outside the interview room where Philpott was being held. Kenton had returned from Mersea empty-handed, having failed to find Nugent. To be fair, the island was small and Kenton knew no one there, and this, along with the handicap of him avoiding the governing police presence, who by rights should point him in the right direction, made his chances of locating Nugent practically nil. So, in an attempt to appear not totally useless, Kenton had tried to bamboozle Lowry with his theories about the murders. He was convinced that the deaths of Private Daley and of Stone and Boyd in Greenstead were directly related. The premise was simple: Stone had chased the soldiers across the park in connection with a drugs feud and, as retaliation, he himself had been murdered, along with Boyd. Kenton had read of similar drug-related killings in South London.

But Lowry remained unconvinced.

'Why not?'

'A flake pothead like Stone chasing a pair of six-foot soldiers across town? What's the worst he'd do if he caught them – give them a blowback?'

'What if he was armed? Stone had a gun – he pulled an armed robbery.'

'No.' Lowry refused to be swayed. 'Derek Stone couldn't run for a bus, let alone up and down Castle Park. Whoever it was those boys were scarpering from, it wasn't some stoner who would've tripped on his shoelace before getting to the end of the high street. Forget that theory for now.' Lowry peeked through the glass panel of the door at the bruised and unshaven Philpott. 'Let's see how this man trips up.' He pushed the door open.

As they entered the interview room, Lowry turned to Kenton and pointedly said, 'Pond's story figures – very useful; we're a step closer.'

'What's that you said about Pond?' Philpott said.

'I'm sorry,' Lowry said, pulling up a chair, 'I wasn't talking to you.'

Philpott didn't pursue it, but Lowry knew a loose line like that would play on his mind. Tony Pond was higher up the food chain than he was, and therefore more valuable to the police. Philpott watched Kenton writing something in his notebook.

'All right, I did pick up some gear from the Greenstead Estate. What of it?'

'Who tipped you off to it?'

'Derek Stone.'

'Ah, yes, Mr Stone. We'll get to him in a minute.'

Lowry might not reckon on Philpott as a murderer but he wouldn't put turning over a post office past him.

'Now, let's start from the beginning. Saturday just gone. New Year's Day.'

Philpott sighed and reached for Lowry's cigarettes. His eyes were glassy, and he had a tendency to flinch, almost a tic; Lowry'd not noticed it before. 'Okay, okay. Saturday morning, I bowl along to Beaumont Terrace.'

'With Derek Stone?' Kenton asked sharply.

'Nah,' Philpott said, not looking at Kenton. 'I'd not seen Del since the night before.'

'Was he there already?'

'Yeah – if you let me talk, I'll bleedin' tell you, won't I?' He dragged on the cigarette contemptuously. 'I got there, and Del and the couriers – the guys who brought it in – were all there.'

'Just them?'

'Yeah – three of them, sitting round the kitchen table, bored. The two lads were anxious, waiting to be paid off. There'd obviously been a fuck-up of some kind.'

Lowry slid photos of Cowley and Boyd towards Philpott, who grunted in recognition.

'So how long did you stay?' Kenton asked.

'I told you already, all I wanted was my gear, for personal use . . . but they wouldn't let me have it first off. I could tell they were on the verge of taking a dip themselves, so I twisted their arm, like, an' we had a line. They loosened up a bit after that, so I chucked them a twenty and took my lot.'

'What happened next?'

'Things began to liven up. We all went out to the Rose and Crown for a quick pint, and then I left 'em to it and shot off up the town centre.'

'And?'

'That's it. Enda story. They were off their nuts, and I was pretty perky myself.' The man's eyes were darting everywhere; Lowry detected anxiety. 'Can I go now?' Lowry wondered if he was on a comedown.

'Going back to the house: when you first entered, how was the mood?'

'"How was the mood?" What sort of gay question's that?'

Lowry stepped up to the table. 'I mean, Jamie, how were they? On edge? You knew the two men were the couriers, and they were still there. Did that not strike you as odd?'

'How the fuck do I know what they were doing there?' The swelling round Philpott's cheek squeezed his eye shut when he raised his voice.

'Have a guess?'

'Waiting for Father Christmas? The Easter Bunny?' He eased his chair back from the table. 'But I'd *imagine* they might be waiting to get paid so they could bugger off? Wouldn't you?'

Lowry had had enough. Why on earth Sparks had let this

eel continue to slip and slide around them and the town all this time was beyond him. But Philpott's time was coming to an end. He just wanted to circle him once more before springing the post-office robbery on him.

'Did you try to sell speed to Quinn?' Kenton asked.

' . . . No.'

'But you went in the pub, with the intent of selling?'

'Eh? Why d'you say that? I went round there to get my own wrap, and that was all.'

'How do we know what you bought? You might be dealing,' Lowry said.

'Leave it out.' He snatched up the Player's irritably. 'Besides, I still got it on me.'

Philpott chucked the cellophane bundle on the table. Lowry picked up the wrap and tossed it in his hand. There was more than a few nights' personal use here, by his reckoning. What was he doing, going for a stroll in the park with a dog, with this on him? He had to be on it still; his mind was still under the influence of the drug; he wasn't thinking straight. And, given however much he had in his system now was making him as irritating as hell, it didn't take a genius to figure how insufferable he'd have been on Saturday night when he was completely wired. And it wouldn't take much to provoke someone into laying the little bastard out, let alone a lunk like Quinn . . .

'Why bunk out of the hospital?' he asked finally.

'Why—?'

'Someone out to get you?' Kenton reasoned.

'Fuck off, Gaylord.'

Offended, Kenton looked at Lowry, willing him to react. Lowry sighed. 'As you know, two people were murdered in Beaumont Terrace on Sunday night, in the very house you'd visited. So –' he leaned forward and, with a clenched fist, jabbed a prominent index knuckle into Philpott's worn forehead; the villain jolted back in surprise and pain – 'can't you get it into that thick head of yours that doing a bunk like that would make you the prime suspect?'

'Wha—?!' the man bleated, rubbing his head in surprise and shock. 'I was – shit, that hurt – I was round my old dear's! If I was a murderer on the run, I reckon I'd've gone a bit further than bleedin' Tiptree! Where's Sparks? He'd not let you shove me about like this—'

'I think Sparks would be more than happy to shove you about himself, given you robbed the Mersea post office on 27 December with Derek Stone.'

'Wha—? How?' He appeared genuinely startled.

'Oh, come on, Jamie.'

Lowry was about to tap him on the forehead again but was distracted by an urgent-sounding rap on the door.

'Right.' He turned to Kenton. 'Get a blow-by-blow account of where he was the week between Christmas and New Year.' There was something about this creep that made Lowry uneasy, but he was too wound up to think clearly now, so he just added, 'And Jamie, think about it – the sentence for armed robbery versus the sentence for armed robbery and murder.'

He moved across the room and edged the door open to greet an excited PC.

'A car, sir; we've found a car!'

47

1.45 p.m., Wednesday, Hythe Hill, New Town, near Artillery Street

A blue Ford Cortina sat amidst snow-crowned builders' debris on a patch of wasteland across from Artillery Street. A skimpily dressed girl of seventeen or so with peroxide-blond hair stood next to the car with a WPC. An icy wind flapped a torn bag of cement; you couldn't tell whether the area was up for development or had been abandoned for good.

'This is Kerry, sir; works in the salon. Remembers the man in the flat above asking where he could park a car.'

'The man who lived there didn't know where to park his car?'

'He didn't own the car, sir; it was for his friend.'

Lowry looked at the girl, who was shivering. She managed a smile. 'When was this?'

'Between Christmas and New Year.'

'Did you get a look at his friend?'

She nodded her head emphatically. 'Yeah, was the winda cleaner from the week before.'

'Are you sure? What did the window cleaner look like?'

'Tanned, blond hair; untidy – could do with a trim.'

The car, a blue '76 Cortina with a vinyl roof just visible under an inch of snow, had seen better days, and looked quite at home next to a rusting cement mixer. The vehicle was unlocked.

Lowry slipped into the passenger side. The seat was pushed halfway back. The inside of the vehicle, though grubby, seemed free of any trace of its occupants. He opened the glove box, and found a post-office cloth bag holding a bundle of used notes. He thumbed through the cash: one hundred quid . . . and the boot popped open behind him. He stretched his arm across to the driver's seat; it was slid back further than the passenger seat, suggesting that a taller man than Stone, who was of average height, had been at the wheel.

'Guv! Guv!' The WPC was at the door. Lowry turned, the low sun causing him to blink. 'Come and have a look at this.'

On the rim of the boot was what was unmistakably a blood smear, dried to dark brown around the latch.

'Nothing else in there apart from a few strands of straw or hay.'

Lowry leaned into the boot. It smelt damp. He removed a glove and dabbed the dark carpet. Wet. He smelt his fingers.

'Blood?'

'Seawater. And that's not hay, it's salt marsh.'

2 p.m., Balkerne Gardens

Chief Sparks walked briskly past Jumbo, a lofty Victorian water tower and one of the landmarks of Colchester, towards the Balkerne Gate. He had heard Lowry out but, having already put two and two together, he was keen to talk to Brigadier Lane, so had put the call in to Flagstaff House. He was determined to be more proactive and not rely so much on those below him in the pecking order. Not that he didn't trust Lowry – he did – but Lowry could be ponderously slow at times and there were some things only he could deal with: the Brigadier, for one.

Lane had suggested they meet in a pub called the Hole in the Wall: a dank, dingy affair next to the Balkerne Gate. It was allegedly the oldest pub in Colchester and, as the name suggested, was built into the ancient city wall. Sparks entered and saw Lane already at the bar, scrutinizing the brandy selection. The view of his profile afforded his companion the full splendour of his huge beard. Sparks thought it repellent for a man to have such a quantity of facial hair; it couldn't be hygienic.

The two men exchanged greetings.

'I'm surprised you suggested this venue. Aren't you worried about being seen fraternizing with the police by the rank and file?'

'You won't catch the men in here.'

'Oh?' Sparks looked around the bar. The clientele included a kid wearing a studded dog collar, a girl with pink hair chatting to an old bloke in a homburg, and two men sitting in the corner, holding hands. Shakin' Stevens crackled on the jukebox. 'Why not?'

'It's a gay bar.'

The police chief raised his eyebrows. He caught the eye of the barman, a plump fellow in a bow tie, and grinned in embarrassment.

'You're kidding!' he hissed in the soldier's ear as soon as the barman turned away. If there was one thing that unsettled him more than women, it was poofs.

'Yes, I'm kidding,' Lane said wryly. 'This is an officers' pub. The easiest way to deter the men from coming in here is to tell them it's frequented by homosexuals. Then one can drink in peace.'

'I see,' Sparks acknowledged. 'But this doesn't seem classy enough for your officers.' Though one of the town's oldest pubs, it had always attracted the sort of crowd Lowry would call 'alternative'; to Sparks's mind, they were freaks.

'I know what you mean, but the clientele are harmless – too obsessed with hair dye and music to care about anything else. But it serves jolly good ale, and this isn't the only one – there's also a bar on Queen Street, but I thought it best not to meet you there – a little too close to home, no?' Lane took in a nostril of brandy and frowned before chugging it back. 'With the one hand, we actively dissuade the men from certain pubs, and with the other, we pin a list of the same pubs in the officers' mess. Keep the two classes apart and everyone's happy.'

'Segregation – good idea,' Sparks said. 'After all, it works in South Africa.'

'Exactly,' Lane confirmed.

As if to prove the point, the two men began an animated discussion about Sunday night's fight. But although they were jovial, there were undercurrents; they discussed tactics but they both knew full well the army had taken a beating because one of their best fighters was dead. And while Sparks had been evasive with Lowry, he knew the writing was on the wall – there was a drugs scandal developing and the military were in the frame, as much as he'd prefer to think otherwise.

'I'll come straight to the point, John.' Sparks drew heavily on one of the brigadier's panatellas. 'There's a possibility those two boys were mixed up in a drugs deal.'

Brigadier Lane looked dead ahead at the optics, his right eye twitching ever so slightly. 'Preposterous,' he blustered, causing spittle to catch on his beard. Sparks waited for him to continue, but the veteran soldier failed to elaborate.

Stubborn bastard, the chief thought. 'I'm afraid things are pointing that way,' he continued. 'Don't take it personally – they're just kids. You've got to remember that, regardless of his uniform, the dead lad was – what? Nineteen?'

'Eighteen,' Lane said quietly. 'Listen here, Sparks: there are no drugs in Colchester barracks.' The small patch of hairless flesh visible on the brigadier's cheeks had turned puce. For a moment, Sparks thought Lane was going to punch him. Let him try: the military man was overweight and out of condition.

'Instead of huffing and puffing, Lane, you might try and help us with our inquiries. Produce the other lad, eh?'

'Where's your flaming evidence?' the brigadier boomed, ignoring the request.

'Your lads were seen in conversation with a shady individual well known to us. They were asking after two men who were selling drugs. An hour later, one of your men falls to his death in Castle Park. Two days later, one of the men they're looking for has his throat slit. I think that's good cause for you to be concerned, don't you?'

'I know nothing!' Lane's anger, Sparks thought, was not directed at him but at his own ignorance at what may have been going on. He touched the soldier lightly on the elbow.

'I'm not suggesting you do, but the sooner we get to the bottom of this, the better for both of us, eh?' Sparks unfolded a piece of paper and placed it next to the tin ashtray. 'Is this a phone number? We think it may be a military line.'

Lane blinked and picked it up. 'It could be an old field line,' he said.

'A what?'

'An army number, but not a barracks or garrison line – in the field, a portable number; a mobile phone, if you will. It's not a number from around here.'

'Are you sure?'

'Chief Sparks, you may take me for an idiot, but I assure you I would recognize a military number.'

48

2.30 p.m., Wednesday, Fingringhoe Ranges, between Colchester and Mersea

Lowry had left the blue Cortina off Artillery Street with Forensics after having made a call to Robinson at the lab. Traces of seawater in the car boot had piqued Lowry's interest – he wanted to know everything that had been in that car, down to the last fibre. In the meantime, he'd picked up Kenton, and they found themselves out on the marshes on some far-fetched premise which the younger man couldn't quite grasp. The cold pinched as they climbed out of the car and stepped on to the frozen mud of the lay-by.

'Are you sure about this?' Kenton asked uncertainly. The woods had a deathly stillness to them. Lowry laid the OS map out on the Saab's bonnet. 'Look here. Do you see this?' He outlined the broken red line marked DANGER AREA.

'I see it.' Kenton stood close behind him.

'The military use this for practice – manoeuvres, whatever

soldiers do – shooting at things, hence it's marked off to prevent access by members of the public.'

'It's all marshland beyond these trees. What makes you think there's anything there?'

'There's an observation hut around there –' Lowry jabbed at the map, on the middle of the marshes – 'that has a phone. There's just a chance . . .'

Lowry led the way, already regretting not having appropriate footwear. In all his time in CID, he'd never spent so much time in the cold; his toes had been permanently numb since before Christmas. He trudged through the still woodlands, feet sinking into fresh snow, and on to the marsh.

'That girl . . .' Kenton said behind him.

'Which girl?' Lowry's mind flitted to his wife. He should've checked the calendar on the fridge this morning to see what shift Jacqui was on.

'Gabriel.'

'Hardly a "girl".'

'Whatever. She's the ACC's niece.'

'I see.' They'd reached a clearing, and there was no discernible footpath going forward. 'That would make sense.'

'Why?'

'I met with Merrydown yesterday. I wondered what her motive was; I thought at first she might fancy Sparks.'

'How so?'

'All her questions were about him. She's recently divorced, so Barnes tells me.'

'I can't see them as an item. Jesus.'

Lowry laughed involuntarily. 'She's way out of his league. Perhaps it's his inner depths she's trying to tap.'

'Yeah, well, he gave me a dressing-down for hassling Gabriel.'

'Ah, I thought something was up.' So Merrydown had been circling him to elicit what, if anything, was going on with her niece.

'I haven't . . . slept with her. I thought . . . Oh, it doesn't matter.'

Lowry's feet squelched in the snowy marsh underfoot. Christ, this was hard going. 'Good. Avoid screwing people you work with; it's hard to draw the line, and you can never escape them.' And then, after a pause: 'I told Gabriel to work at my desk; maybe I'll be the next one in trouble.'

'Is that why you married a nurse?' Kenton said, ignoring the last remark.

'Well, I never see her, that much is true – hold on, what's that?'

'Looks like a garden shed.' They approached it and Kenton flicked the latch on the hut door. A smell of musty wood greeted them.

'Have you got a torch?' Lowry asked.

'No – I . . .'

Lowry tutted. The hut was pitch black. 'Wait a sec,' he said, walking over to the far side. A horizontal oblong of light appeared. 'Wouldn't be much of an observation post if you couldn't see anything, would it?' Lowry had lifted a wooden flap, and secured it to the wall above. Kenton made to open another. The cold air rushed in.

'There's not a lot in here to get excited about, is there?' he remarked. There were two benches, a table and several charts pinned to the wall. A first-aid box hung next to a large OS map of the area. The floor gave slightly as the two men paced the hut.

'Who tipped you off to this place, anyhow?'

'Let's just say I went to see a man about a bird . . .' Lowry halted mid-sentence. There was a small green box mounted next to the window slit. Lowry released the tin catch. Kenton moved closer. A field telephone. He could imagine Lowry's thoughts: was this the number? But the DI stepped back from the phone and clambered over one of the benches so he was facing the open hatch.

'This spot commands a view of the firing ranges and beyond, I bet.' He riffled around in his donkey jacket, pulling out a small pair of binoculars. 'You can see the channel and the Strood from here.' He angled forward, elbows resting on the wooden sill. Kenton slid in next to him. 'Here.' Lowry passed him the binoculars.

After adjusting them, Kenton scanned the dip towards the river, noticing another shed-like structure hidden in the trees at the bottom of the valley. Beyond that, he could see silvery hints of a draining tide snaking through the white. To his right, a treeless view of mudflats, still brown, having been submerged in water during the recent snow, slipped away towards heathland. And skimming across the river bed as if on air was a car crossing the Strood, the road on which it travelled invisible in the soft winter haze.

The wooden floor squeaked behind him. In a flash, Kenton was on his hands and knees.

'This floor comes up.'

A small amount of prising of floorboards revealed him to be right. Underneath was an earth cavity.

'Let me have a look.' Lowry bent down and ran his hand around the inside. There was a powdery residue. Could it be? He dabbed his finger. Yes . . .

'Guv, look.'

Lowry looked up; Kenton was pointing to a small chalkboard on the wall.

'What?'

'A list of range commanders and dates. Here's a familiar name. Wonder what he'd be doing here?'

Oldham.

49

3 p.m., Wednesday, Queen Street HQ

Gabriel dexterously typed up her report on hauling Cowley out of the sea on Tuesday, having overcome her initial discomfort at sitting at Lowry's desk. The DI had insisted on it, so that she wouldn't be distracted by the humdrum of Uniform (his words). She didn't mind the idea at all; it was the untidy state of the desk that troubled her. For such a suave dresser, Lowry took surprisingly little care of his environment: the desk was a mess of magazines, books – most about birds, rather oddly – scraps of paper, various notebooks, three ashtrays, several seven-inch records, and photos of his wife and son.

'Oi, answer that, will ya, luv!' someone bellowed across the room. The phones of both Lowry and Kenton had been ringing since she'd arrived, but she'd felt it wasn't her place to take the call. 'Go on, it won't bite!' At last, she reached over for the telephone.

'Hello?'

'About time,' a soft but irritable female voice replied. 'Is Detective Inspector Lowry there?'

'Err, no, he's not.'

'Do you know when he'll be back?' The irritability had an edge to it. Panic?

'No, sorry. Can I help?'

'Who's that?'

'WPC Gabriel.'

Gabriel waited.

'It's Jacqui Lowry. It's about one of my friends – Trish – she's not turned up for work. I'm worried . . .' The woman hesitated. 'Can you ask Inspector Lowry to call me?'

She glanced at the framed photograph of the attractive brunette on the desk. Lowry's wife was a nurse, that much she knew, not that he'd ever mentioned her to Gabriel. Lowry was currently out on the Fingringhoe marshes. She had no idea when he'd be back.

'Are you calling from the hospital?' she asked lamely.

'Yeah,' said Jacqui absently. 'The ward sister marked her down as sick again this morning, even though she'd not phoned in, but . . . but . . .' Her voice trailed off. ' . . . I wondered if she'd got her shifts in a muddle with all that's gone on, and thought she was on a late yesterday. But we've just done handover and she's not shown up again today. She would normally call, so . . .'

'Of course. What's the best number to get you on?' Gabriel

picked up a chewed Bic ballpoint. *All that's gone on* – what could that mean?

3.15 p.m., Colchester Road

The light was fading with the onset of more snow as Sparks crossed over on to Mersea Island. He had two things on his mind. The first was the pressure from his boss: Merrydown had given him yet another ear-bashing on the telephone about the North Essex clean-up rates. This time it was the Mersea sub-division, which had not filed a stats report in months. It was bad enough to have poor results but supplying nothing whatsoever was tantamount to treason. Ordinarily, County wouldn't give a toss what the locals got up to in a rural community like Mersea, but once Merrydown knew drugs had got on to the island, she'd made a beeline for East Road's latest submission, only to find an empty manila folder. So, no crime stats and the wrongful arrest of the Taylor brothers for the post-office robbery – Dodger Bradley had well and truly cocked up, and the chief had taken it upon himself to get to the bottom of it.

The other thing on his mind was more sensitive. Having telephoned Lowry from the pub about the possibility of a field line, Sparks had returned to finish his drink with Lane and the conversation had moved to more convivial matters, such as where to get a decent meal outside of Colchester. Sparks had been impressed to hear that the army had a list of 'recommends', several of which were unfamiliar to him. One was on the island: a new oyster restaurant added to the list by Captain Oldham, who apparently owned a houseboat moored just outside the harbour. The fact that the captain was a Mersea resident, albeit only when off duty, had struck the chief as odd. Sparks had not even registered the houseboat community on West Mersea until Kenton was punched after snooping around there, but it now emerged that Oldham was one of these virtual gypsies. Sparks tried not to be swayed by his dislike for Oldham but, personal feelings aside, he couldn't ignore his instincts as a policeman. There was – dare he say it? – something odd about the captain.

3.25 p.m., Abbey Fields

Gabriel, having placed her report on Felix Cowley in Lowry's in-tray, was now on the south side of Colchester. The military side.

Lowry had left her one additional, simple task: to check whether the big Irish soldier, Corporal Quinn, had spent New Year's Eve in the Glasshouse, as he'd claimed. Having allowed herself to be fobbed off by Captain Oldham's office once before, this time she was determined to come up trumps. She had checked that the military policeman himself would be at his Abbey Fields office. She had booked an appointment, claiming she'd been tasked with setting up a liaison committee between the police and the army following the recent disturbances. (Lowry had mumbled something to that effect, hence the idea.)

She quickly ascended the steps and entered into a brightly lit atrium. Underneath glinting candelabra were lush red walls adorned with exotic animal heads, the spoils of empire. A neat little man in green behind a desk ticked her name off a register and ushered her to sit down. Nestled in a comfy armchair, she looked up at the painting on the wall opposite: an imposing figure in a pith helmet, one foot resting on an enormous tiger. Somewhere in the building a piano was being played – Mozart, if she wasn't mistaken. People say the police live in their own world, but it was nothing compared to the armed forces; they lived in another place and time entirely, or so it seemed to her.

'WPC Gabriel?' A uniformed man in olive with a bright red belt and highly polished shoes addressed her politely. 'Come this way, please.' They marched down an oak-panelled corridor towards the piano music. The soldier stopped at an open door and gestured for her to enter. It was not so much an office, more of a large sitting room, like something from a period drama on the television. At the far end, sitting at a grand piano, was Captain James Oldham, head of Colchester's military police force. His playing was beautiful. It was difficult to imagine that someone capable of performing such delicate music was responsible for such a brute presence of force in the town. She drifted closer, not wishing to interrupt his playing. Gabriel noted his thinning hair and balding pate.

'Can I assume, WPC Gabriel, that this meeting has nothing to do with arranging a liaison committee?'

His question caught her unawares but still didn't quite break the spell of his playing. 'That's wonderful,' she couldn't help saying.

'Do you know it?'

'Mozart.' She'd not played in ages. 'A sonata. Eight?'

'Very good. You must play?'

'Not in ages,' she said, feeling apologetic for reasons she couldn't fathom. 'It's not an easy piece, from what I recall.'

'Mozart is very difficult to play, even for one who's left-handed.' He span round on the stool. 'One has to be so very light.' He examined a well-manicured hand, but then, catching himself, glared up at her with eyes of watery grey that betrayed nothing of what went on behind them. 'Well?'

'I'm here regarding Corporal Quinn.'

'Hmm.' He smiled. 'I suppose that could be construed as a "liaison" issue. Though of what interest he is to you now, I can't possibly imagine.'

'Just a matter of routine.' She relaxed slightly. 'He claims to have been locked up on New Year's Eve. Can you confirm this?'

'New Year's Eve? Why are you interested in where Quinn was then? The punch-up was the night after.' Oldham had soft-looking tan skin; she wondered if he might be foreign.

'Yes,' she said hesitantly, 'but he subsequently harassed a member of the public over his concern for Private Jones, the soldier who—'

'I know who Private Jones is, thank you. But I fail to see the connection.'

'They were in the same platoon, were they not?'

He smiled at her fixedly. 'This member of the public – can you enlighten me as to who it was?'

She sensed he was niggled. 'I will if you can confirm that Quinn was incarcerated on New Year's Eve.'

He raised himself from the piano stool. 'I don't happen to know off the top of my head.'

'But you could find out easily enough.' She indicated the shiny telephone that sat on an ornate octagonal table.

'Very well.' He picked up the receiver and placed an index finger in the dial. She looked away, thinking it rude to watch, and reviewed the elegant room. It was indeed from another era. The walls were lined with oil paintings, though not of a military nature; many were seascapes. On top of a cabinet was a stuffed bird of some description. Ghastly. Probably shot. It seemed that, if they weren't shooting men, the military must shoot the wildlife to relieve the boredom, especially in foreign climates, as indicated by the tiger painting in the atrium.

'Yes, he was,' Oldham said, bringing back her attention.

'Excellent . . .' She made to go.

'And who was it that Quinn was at odds with, in the town? This member of the public?'

'Oh, we suspect it was over a girlfriend.' She didn't think she needed to give a name; it'd not mean anything to Oldham.

'A girl. It often is.' He said, unimpressed. 'Though not on

Saturday night. The chap in the Lamb? Philpott, I think his name was.'

Gabriel was uncertain what to say; she was growing acutely aware that Captain Oldham knew far more about what went on in town than she did.

'Yes, it was Jamie Philpott.' She wanted to leave.

'And what does Mr Philpott do with himself when he's not sparring with members of Her Majesty's armed forces?'

'I'm afraid I can't really comment, sir. However, I can confirm he's helping us –' she hesitated and then said – 'with another matter.'

'"Another matter",' he repeated slowly, as though weighing up the words. 'I see. I think that concludes our business.'

'Thank you, Captain Oldham.'

'My pleasure – anything in the spirit of cooperation,' he said. 'And take up the piano again – I'm imagining you'd be rather good.'

50

3.30 p.m., Wednesday, Mersea Police Station, East Road

'Well, Dodger, none of us are getting any younger.' Sparks stretched his legs, the wooden chair twingeing underneath him. Bradley sat on the other side of the hearth in the small back room of the East Road police station, twiddling his thumbs across his expansive girth. They were practically in darkness, except for the fire, which spat feebly.

'Age has nothing to do with it; you'd have to be mad to want to be out in the Blackwater in the middle of the flamin' night, this time of year.'

'Water under the bridge now – we got one of them off Brightlingsea.'

The Dodger grumbled. Sparks hoped his days on the force wouldn't end like this. There wasn't much between them if you thought about it – six, seven years?

'Now then, where's your December incident report? Merrydown has been breaking my balls about crime stats – and poor though they are, at least Colchester's were submitted promptly. Yours aren't even in.'

'Aye, well, that'll be your fault.'

'My fault? How the bloody hell is it my fault?'

'Your boy hassling us over the post-office job after Christmas.'

'Eh?'

'I tried calling you to get him to back off so we could get on with our business, but you failed to intervene, and he wouldn't let it lie.'

Sparks stood up to light a cigarette. 'You should've spelt it out, Dodger, rather than making cryptic phone calls. I've a lot on my plate – I've got a house full of bodies on a council estate—'

'Ahh, well, that's none of my business. I can't file me bleedin' reports with your mob sticking their oar in; you stick to yorn and we'll keep to ours.'

'Wish that were possible, but it just so happens that our difficulties overlap.'

'Eh? How so?'

'One of your bloody robbers was found dead inside the Greenstead house.'

'Eh?'

'We found two handguns at his flat, one of which matches that used in the robbery.'

'There you go, then. No harm done. Progress.' It was said in a tone of voice that mimicked authority – how he imagined County would speak.

The door creaked as PC Jennings brought in a tray of coffees.

'But,' continued Dodger, 'the Taylor brothers are wrong 'uns, and deserve to be banged up.'

'Christ, man, you can't go around just banging people up willy-nilly any more. You know that, Dodger.' Sparks reached for the least chipped mug. 'So that's it – you couldn't file your report because Kenton wouldn't brush the post-office robbery under the carpet? And is that really the only reason you didn't want to properly investigate? Paperwork?' he said disbelievingly. 'What was all that nonsense about hassling the locals?'

'Aye, your men have been picking on one of our boys. Lowry pulled him into Queen Street nick, then he said the youngster was watching him on Monday. Jennings, what's his name?'

'Nugent, sarge.'

'Aye, that's him. Ted Nugent.'

'So what's his problem?' Sparks asked. The name prickled; he was that friend of Stone's – from the Candyman.

'He claims harassment.'

'But he hasn't been charged – or am I missing something?'

'He's on parole – a bit panicky,' the lanky policeman said.

Sparks grunted. It was hard to make out the features of the young PC in the dim light. Jennings – yes, this was the lad he had in mind for football. 'What position do you play? Bet you're out on the wing?'

'Football? Yeah, in me day, I've—'

Sparks cut him off. 'Good, good, well, Granger will be in touch. Anyway, the lad on parole: why the jitters?'

'Maybe he thinks you'll collar him for the post-office job if the case against the Taylors falls through,' PC Jennings replied.

'Well, the situation has changed – we have Stone in the frame, for one thing – but we still have a bandit at large. I think we might have another word with the fellow with the nervous disposition.'

'I don't think that's necessary, sir. We can pull him in.' The young policeman looked at his superior, but Bradley was preoccupied with examining his fingernails. The second Jennings had been drawn in, the Dodger appeared to switch off. Old age again, Sparks thought grimly.

'Nonsense. Given we might have got the right man this time –' Sparks glanced pointedly at Bradley – 'we should have a word with someone with form in that area. What does Mr Nugent do by day?'

'Odd-job man; this and that,' said Jennings.

'He's a window cleaner, too,' Bradley added.

'A window cleaner?' Sparks rose. 'I'll have our boys pull him in so it doesn't unsettle community relations.' The young policeman was about to protest, but Sparks silenced him with a raised palm. 'No need to thank me. We're used to this sort of thing.'

'Grateful,' the Dodger said, standing, 'an' no hard feelings about the post office. Makes a change that it ain't someone on the island ripping the place off!' he guffawed.

'Well, quite,' Sparks said, regarding Bradley with distaste. 'Now, on to important stuff: I've heard there's a new place that's opened up on the front that sells quality seafood. Where exactly is it?'

4.15 p.m., Fingringhoe Ranges

The firing ranges were now sealed off. The high, green all-clear flags, now invisible in the dark, had police tape flickering beneath them in the chill evening air. It had stopped snowing. But it was the barking dogs that upset the tranquility of the place, disturbing the wintry silence. Lowry thought it was all a waste of time: the drugs were no longer here – there were traces on the floor of the shed, but it had been a holding place only. Besides, it was too dark now; a couple of feeble arc lamps running off a portable generator barely illuminated the area beyond the hut. Dogs or no dogs, anyone venturing beyond the circle of light would soon get lost on the marshes.

They'd caught Sparks on the way back from Mersea, and Lowry was pleased to see him on the scene to witness their result.

'I suppose even the military police need to keep their eye in,' Lowry suggested to the chief.

Sparks, in a flat cap and Crombie, looked at the ground, lost in thought. The possible complications of the captain of the MPs being mixed up in drug smuggling caused his shadowed brow to crease heavily.

'Don't get too excited – I'm telling you, it's not a phone number,' Sparks said.

'How d'you know? Hello, he'll be able to tell us.' Lowry gestured towards a soldier with a large moustache who was crunching towards them across the snow.

'I say, what the bloody hell is going on here!' called the soldier. He was dressed in combat fatigues and wearing a beret.

'That shed contains traces of illegal substances,' Lowry replied. 'The field telephone – we need to know the number.'

The soldier was having none of it. '*Shed?!* That is an observation platform, and what's more it's Ministry of Defence property, as is this entire area.'

'Sergeant Barnes!' Sparks called to the uniformed officer, who was issuing instructions to the dog handlers, who appeared to be having difficulty controlling their animals.

'Sir!'

'Deal with this gentleman, and find out the phone number.' Turning his back obstinately on the army man, Sparks ushered Lowry towards his Rover. 'How the devil did you find this place?'

'I . . .' Lowry almost let it slip about the Colchester Ornithological Society, but decided it could wait. Kenton, good man that he was, didn't say a word either. 'Last place anyone would look? Good view of the estuary. Just a hunch.'

'Hmm, well, an excellent hunch. I doubt they'll find anything in all this snow, though.' Sparks indicated the German shepherds as he trudged back to the car. 'Right, you two, a quick word. Shall we? Bit parky out here.' He opened the Rover's passenger door.

'That's a result,' he said when all three were inside the car.

'It was a holding place . . .' Lowry said, from the rear seat. 'Perfect, way out here.'

'How do you figure that? The army are here all the time,' Kenton said.

'But only army. They do what the hell they like when they're out of view of the rest of the world.' The irony of what he said was not lost on him, out here on the marshes, bleak and exposed for miles.

Sparks turned round. 'Let's not jump to any conclusions, Lowry.'

'I didn't say a word.'

'I know you think I'm a pussy when it comes to Lane, but I tell you, he is aware of the direction this is pointing, and now we have grounds for a direct approach to Oldham.'

Lowry, not wishing to argue, let the matter drop; he was less concerned about Oldham than with the blue Cortina. What had been in the boot of that car was what he cared about. 'It looks like Jamie did the post office with Stone. He has no alibi for 27 December.'

'Oh, silly boy . . . Why?'

'Money for drugs,' Kenton said simply.

'Shame – could've told the Dodger. Just been over there to

tick him off about his bloody records. This Ted Nugent you've been bothering—'

'Wait—' Kenton tried to interrupt.

Sparks held up a gloved hand in front of them. 'Let me finish, son. It would seem to me he's tied up somehow in this post-office job, and I get a distinct sniff that the Mersea mob don't want us troubling him.'

'You know, you might be on to something there,' Lowry said. 'I'd discounted him as just a flakey ex-con, but since finding out about the Stone connection, I've been thinking it's worth another chat. Kenton was looking for him on Monday.'

'Good, well, you have my blessing. I told the Dodger we'd pull him in, so you shouldn't get any grief – gave them some old flannel about not upsetting the community. He's been out cleaning windows, by all accounts.'

'Windows?' Lowry said.

'Yeah, cleaned the Dodger's place the other day. Why?'

'No reason.' That would be more than a coincidence, a getaway driver doubling as a window cleaner . . .

'Why would anyone have their windows cleaned in January?' Kenton asked, leaning forward between the seats.

'On Mersea Island? I can think of two reasons. One, there are lots of retired folk with nothing better to do than inspect their domiciles for dirt. And, two, they're a bunch of curtain twitchers, and for that you need clean windows. So, you two find him, and I'll tackle the Red Cap Action Man. Any more questions?'

'Yeah; what's that god-awful smell?' Lowry winced, lighting a cigarette. 'It's like something's died in here.'

Sparks flipped open the glove compartment.

'Winkle, anyone?'

51

6 p.m., Wednesday, Police Social Club, Queen Street

Kenton watched Gabriel dart out of the social-club bar, leaving a huddle of jeering uniforms behind. He turned back to his boss. Lowry was in good spirits: the forensics examination of the Cortina had not only confirmed traces of seawater and salt marsh in the boot but also mud mixed with blood. This news, however, had failed to lift Kenton's spirits. He felt a strong urge to pinch one of Lowry's cigarettes. He was out, but he wasn't a fan of filterless.

'It'll pass,' Lowry said, perched on the barstool next to him.

'Changing the subject –' Kenton turned to face his boss – 'the chief has been very hands-on this week. Is that usual? I mean, shooting over to Mersea, telling us to chase up window cleaners and what have you?'

'Didn't I tell you to pick Nugent up on Monday?' Lowry jettisoned cigarette smoke from the corner of his mouth.

'I searched high and low – every street. He wasn't on the island. Maybe he's expanding. But the chief—'

'The chief is feeling the pressure. There's a lot going on. It's not that he doesn't trust us, but sometimes things don't happen fast enough for him. And remember the new broom at County is a female broom.'

'Why does that present a problem?' Kenton asked.

'What do you say, Jack?' Lowry addressed Sergeant Barnes, who was behind the bar, now resting two hairy forearms on the Double Diamond beer mats.

'The chief is a man's man.' Barnes smiled.

'What does that mean?'

'What the sergeant is saying is the chief is terrified the nice posh lady is going dish him his comeuppance.'

'Is one due?'

'Not especially,' Barnes said, 'but we've been left to our own devices for many a year. All these newfangled things – faxes, computers, "memoranda" about improved communication – are vexing the guv'nor.'

'You're not wrong – "communication" to Sparks means Morse code from submarines, and no way does accountability come into it. That's why we're seeing him dashing about now.' Lowry took a long swig of his drink. 'That and four dead men in as many days, not to mention a ton of space speed on the marshes.'

A clack of balls fired behind. Kenton flicked back his hair and removed his glasses to wipe them. It was hot down here.

He sort of got what they were saying. 'You mean he has to prove himself?'

'You might say that.'

'Well –' Kenton flipped his tie over a lens – 'he might prove more efficient if he spent less time reading *Asterix* books.'

'You're wrong there, Daniel. We – well, Colchester – are the indomitable village.'

'He's right, you know. How's your potion?' Barnes pointed to his pint.

'Ah. That's where it's from. I wondered what he was banging on about.' Kenton had read *Asterix* but not in ages, and so hadn't cottoned on. 'And Colchester being a Roman town and fighting the army, I see . . . How funny.'

'Talking of potions,' Lowry said, playing with a cellophane bundle, which he had produced from nowhere. There was a dark glint in his eye that Kenton had not seen before.

'Wonder what's really in that stuff?' he asked.

Lowry seemed lost for a moment, looking intently at the small packet lying on the bar towel in front of him. 'Good question . . .' And he removed the small package as deftly as he had produced it. 'Who's for another?'

Kenton, who had nothing on that evening, nodded his assent eagerly. Talk continued in a wide and varied way – theories expounded, rumours scotched and personalities assessed. Kenton hungrily took in all that Barnes and Lowry had to say on anything and everything, but before he knew it, it was late and the small bar was laden with pint glasses. Eventually, the young detective exited Queen Street into the cold, shrouded in the warm glow of camaraderie. Swerving up the slippery street, his head swimming, he felt good. He loved his job, the station, Colchester, his boss – everything – but none more so than Jane Gabriel.

8.35 p.m., a boat, Blackwater Estuary

Trish woke feeling woozy. Her head was heavy – very heavy. She must've been drugged. Her abductor had urged her to drink something that tasted similar to lemonade before she was gagged and hooded. She recalled him saying it was the last chance she'd have for a drink for a while. And then the hood went on and she was pulled out of the car. Her throat was parched now.

Every limb ached. She was seated, but her hands were cuffed above her, around a pipe, her fingers curled uncomfortably beneath a low ceiling. She was disorientated, and the more she came to, the more nauseous she felt. She kicked out with bound feet but met with resistance before she managed to straighten her legs. Wherever she was being held, it was in a confined space. Kicking out again, her bottom slipped off the chair – or was it a chair? The edge was curved, suggesting a lavatory. Jesus wept, she thought, I've been incarcerated in a toilet. And a small one at that. Suddenly, it came to her. A boat. She was on a boat. She could recall clambering up a ladder and smelling the sea. But now all she could make out was the damp-canvas smell of the hood.

She thought back to leaving for work – when? This morning? Yesterday morning? – and the gun behind her head. Why would anyone want to kidnap her? She'd not been harmed, and her kidnapper had not said much, other than encouraging her to drink the drugged lemonade. She could only imagine it had something to do with the fiasco in Greenstead on Saturday night. Maybe whoever it was thought she was a witness ... God, she wished she'd gone home that night instead of out on the razz with Jacqs – as if they'd not had warning enough. Shit. Shit. Shit. She'd just tell whoever it was she'd not seen anything. For the first time in many months, she thought of her ex-husband, Andrew. Bet he's snuggled up with that tart he ran off with. Huh. She started to cry. If he could see her here now. Not that she knew where the bloody hell here was.

Thursday, 6 January, 1983

-52-

9 a.m., Thursday, West Mersea

Lowry indicated left and took the next turning, on to an avenue that led to the sea. The overnight snowstorm had passed and the roads had already been cleared, and there were plenty of people about. But Lowry's mind was not on the state of the roads or the extremities of the weather. Jacqui was bothering him about her pal, Trish – the woman had disappeared, apparently. From where he was standing, this was a blessing, but Jacqui wasn't having him dismiss it lightly; the woman had not returned to work and was not at her home in the Dutch quarter – he was a policeman, it was his job to do something. Trish had no next of kin to speak of, and Jacqui was worried. Lowry's anger had simmered silently as he heard her out. He'd decided to let things ride until he got through Greenstead, and said he'd do what he could.

In the meantime, he was keen to find Nugent. Philpott was saying nothing and was, even if proved guilty, unlikely to snitch. He and Kenton had carved up the island and each was searching within their patch. There were only so many streets and, after thirty minutes, Lowry drove past a white XR3 with a roof rack, just as Kenton had described, on an empty avenue leading down to the esplanade. Lowry slowed the Saab to a crawl, and yes, there was his man, hard at work on the upstairs windows of a grand, detached Edwardian house, his shock of blond hair standing out even at a height. A window cleaner driving a boy-racer Escort? Not the most obvious choice of utility vehicle. He parked several doors down and walked slowly back to the house. It was eerily quiet, not a soul in sight.

'Oi, sunshine, you've missed a bit!' he hollered up towards the man, who was wearing faded denims.

'Fuck off!' came the terse reply.

'Say that again?' Lowry stepped up to the ladder and gave it a hearty shake.

'Oi!' Nugent rattled down the aluminium frame. 'What d'you think you're playin' at?'

'Remember me?' Lowry flashed his badge. Nugent paused on the bottom step, water sloshing over the rim of his bucket.

'Now what?'

'We just want to chat with you again.' Lowry turned as an old dear in curlers appeared at the frosted front door, and was just about to reassure her that everything was fine when he was suddenly drenched: lukewarm water gushed down the back of his collar and the inside of the orange plastic bucket obscured his vision. Before he could recover, a violent thump flattened the bucket against his nose, sending him flying backwards into the snow.

'You all right dear?' the woman in curlers inquired.

Startled, he sat up and tugged the plastic bucket off his head. 'Where'd he go?'

She pointed to the white XR3, which at that instant thundered out a belch of exhaust fumes. 'I won't be tipping *him* . . .' the woman mumbled.

Lowry hurtled towards the car, which surprised him by reversing to meet his charge. Rather than try to evade it, he launched himself at the vehicle's boot. His sportman's agility served him well; he leapt on to the car, his toes catching the rear bumper and his hands reaching for the roof-rack bars. Nugent braked abruptly, throwing Lowry forward, his knees catching the spoiler. He managed to scramble further on to the car before it screeched forward.

Nugent swerved erratically up Seaview Avenue, trying to shake Lowry off. If only the fool had slowed down, Lowry would've got off gladly, but instinct made him cling on for dear life. At the top of the avenue, Nugent took a right turn at speed. Lowry was close to being flung off but was still clinging on as the XR3 span out of control, colliding with a VW camper van. Lowry scrambled over the roof and punched Nugent's windscreen with the base of his fist. The driver's door opened. Pivoting round, Lowry grabbed the shock of blond hair and yanked upwards, causing Nugent to howl.

'I haven't done nothing!' he rasped.

The oncoming flash of an orange sports car caught the corner of Lowry's eye as he tightened his grip on the window cleaner's hair and gazed at the puce face beneath him.

'No? You left pretty sharpish. What about your ladder?'

Kenton stepped in, pulling Nugent round and pushing his face hard against the windscreen.

Lowry lowered himself off the roof. He brushed his hands and straightened his tie. Reaching for his comb, he turned and was surprised to see a crowd of people of all ages. Where the hell had this lot sprung from?

9.35 a.m., Mersea Police Station, East Road

Nugent's dramatic reluctance to come quietly and answer a few questions left little doubt in Lowry's mind as to the man's guilt in the post-office job: he must have been the one who drove Philpott and Stone back to Colchester. But how he'd managed a double billing as both witness and getaway driver was a detail Lowry was keen to learn. Whether all three of them knew what had been held in the boot of the Cortina, he couldn't say.

In the first instance, Lowry decided to take Nugent to the local nick on East Road to get any local knowledge Bradley might have on the man, if necessary, before heading to Queen Street.

'An XR3 seems an odd choice of vehicle for a window cleaner?' Lowry said, apparently randomly.

Nugent looked suitably put off balance by the question.

'Missus said you'd been round,' Bradley added. 'Ain't seen you at it before.'

'I ain't no winda cleana . . . I'm minding me brother's business; his patch is north Colchester – New Town. He's gone to Marbella for a month and asked me to do his round. Busy time of year – lot of people take time off, so you can earn a couple of extra quid in the run-up to Christmas, like. So, as he went in the van, I 'ad to get a roof rack and, as I'd forked out on that, thought I might as well skim round Mersea.'

New Town, Artillery Street, where Stone's flat was: Lowry remembered the state of the window. 'Didn't make a good job of your pal Derek Stone's windows, did you? All smeary, as I recall. When did you have a crack at them? Surprised you'd have the time, what with turning over the post office.'

'Look – I didn't ask for this, you know; it all happened . . . by mistake. Honest.'

'I can't wait to hear,' Bradley said. 'You're the bleedin' witness!'

'I'm on parole, ain't I?' said Nugent, as if this explained everything.

'What's that got to do with the price of fish?' the sergeant spluttered. 'You damn near ran the inspector over.'

'So you admit you were a party to the robbery?'

Nugent nodded.

Lowry was relieved the man had the sense to admit defeat on that front, at least. 'But Ted, how could you be a witness to your own crime?'

'The post-office clerk said I was the last served, yeah? Which is true, but I was on me way out as the other two came in – right by the door—'

'So you were keeping an eye out?'

'Exactly. I'd give 'em both the all-clear as I left, though God know's what I'd've done if I'd seen a rozzer – thrown meself at their mercy, probably. Can I pinch a smoke?'

Lowry slid him the packet.

'And so I was the first one out the door.'

'And everyone would be looking for two men, not three.'

'Now that you mention it . . . yeah.'

'And this third man, you claim you don't know him?'

'Yeah. He slid in the back of the motor.'

'Weren't you curious?' Bradley asked.

'At first, yeah; once I was in, like, on the job, I wanted to know who I was dealing with.'

'And what did Stone say?'

'"Best you don't know, mate – you know me, and look where it got ya."'

'Can't argue with that,' Lowry agreed.

'Look, I didn't want to get involved in this shit . . . my share's still in the glove box of the Cortina, if you don't believe me.'

Ted Nugent's story was first class. On his first morning minding his brother's window-cleaning round, he had started on Artillery Road. Armed with a list of regular customers, there was one that particularly attracted him – the hairdressing salon under Derek Stone's flat, which was full of pretty young girls. He decided to start with this one.

His brother Eddie had passed on little in the way of professional tips, but there was one thing he had said: if it's a two-storey building, start at the top; that way, if water slops on to the panes beneath, it doesn't mess up glass that has already been cleaned. But Ted hadn't realized there was no connection between the salon on the ground floor and the flat on the first floor. Lowry could imagine him now, parking his ladder in front of the salon and grinning at the dolly birds inside, then ascending to the first floor to be faced with a doped-up Derek Stone in the middle of an argument and wielding an automatic pistol.

Stone, spotting Nugent, had gestured with the gun for him to descend and enter the flat. So down he went, ignoring the girls and taking the stairs up, to face a gun barrel and the penalty for stumbling across two men planning an armed robbery. Nugent confessed he knew Stone; if he hadn't, he'd have made a run for it. It's a small world, he said dolefully; they both went to the Candyman. The argument Nugent had witnessed from the ladder was about the getaway driver – or the lack of one, until then. Nugent claimed he was coerced into the job but admitted there was a ton in it for him. He claimed to have protested vigorously, terrified of the chance of getting caught, and the threat to his parole.

'Honest, that's the way it is,' Nugent pleaded. 'Like I said, me spilt's still in the motor. Have you found the car?'

'The car.' Lowry made to get up.

Nugent gazed after him.

'Yes. Time for you to identify the vehicle, and for us to move you from the island. Lowry nodded to Sergeant Bradley. 'Dodger, it's been a pleasure, as always, but I'm afraid it's time for you to say cheerio to Mr Nugent.'

53

10 a.m., Thursday, Queen Street HQ

Gabriel tapped her chipped nails lightly on the worn desk, and looked at her long, thin fingers. The piano – funny, she thought; that was second time this week it had come to mind. Oldham might be slightly terrifying, but he played beautifully. What made him say he thought she would be good? It wasn't as if he'd any cause to flatter her; on the contrary, to him, she was an annoyance. Maybe she'd get an opportunity to ask him, though. Sparks had just requested she accompany him to the barracks this morning, for what he phrased as a 'matter of supreme diplomacy'. Whatever that might entail, she had no idea, but as Lowry and Kenton were out already, it would be her going.

She stared, not for the first time, at the photo of Lowry's wife. She was attractive – too good for him. Lowry, she thought, was plain – neither handsome nor ugly – whereas the woman she saw in the photograph had fine, angular features, not dissimilar to those of Audrey Hepburn. What was it she'd said on the phone? 'All that's gone on'? What had she been alluding to?

'WPC Gabriel.'

She looked up from her desk to see a very young officer, clutching a fax.

'For you.' He gingerly handed over the floppy sheets. She laid the papers out before her and flattened them with a wooden rule. The top one was an official HM Forces cover sheet. She looked nervously about her, but of course nobody here would know or care what she had on her desk.

Before her was a list of individuals who made up Company B, 7th Parachute Regiment. On leaving Oldham's office, she had asked the man on the desk in the foyer for a full list of men in Jones's and Daley's platoon who had seen active service in the summer of 1982. She hadn't asked Oldham's permission to request the information but she had relayed the request to the desk corporal as if to suggest the captain had sanctioned it. Sneaky, but not illegal, and why would Captain Oldham withhold such a request anyway, other than purely to be unhelpful?

Besides, the police already had a list of those soldiers who had comprised Company B, provided by the brigadier shortly after the incident at the castle. She had that here in front of her. What she'd now received was an active-service log: the company as it was at the time of the Falklands conflict. The first thing she noticed was that the company had originally been based in West Germany. Not that this held any great significance for her; what she was after was the change in personnel. At the bottom there was an addendum listing the names of those – two of them – killed in action. Private Jones's friend, who worked in the video store in Crouch Street, had mentioned that some of their close-knit group had since left the army. By comparing the two lists, she would be able to identify the soldiers in question.

The lists were alphabetical: Adams, Allcott, Brookes, Cowley . . . Cowley? Cowley hadn't been in the army – not *their* Cowley, in any event. The initial was F, though. Wait, she had Felix's medical report – it had mentioned a brother as next of kin . . .

12.20 p.m., Abbey Fields, Military Police HQ

'It means nothing,' Oldham said calmly. 'Anyone can access that place, and a fool could work out the flag system – a green flag means no firing, red means duck. There was no firing over the entire Christmas period. It means nothing.'

Sparks followed Oldham's gaze towards Lane, who was perched on the piano stool. The brigadier was perturbed and in need of reassurance from the MP chief. Sparks was starting to see the Beard in a different light; his reliance on the military police to keep order and control wasn't something Sparks had fully appreciated until now. Oldham held the real power.

'I beg to differ,' Sparks said, leaving the chesterfield sofa and pacing across the Persian carpet towards Oldham's desk. 'You assume, because your signalling system is second nature to you, that all and sundry are aware of its significance, but I assure you the rest of the world, myself included, consider the Fingringhoe ranges a no-go zone.'

He let that sink in for a moment, and toyed with a small ivory buddha on the captain's desk. The information Gabriel had obtained behind their smug olive-green backs had convinced him they had the military by the balls, and thus he found himself curiously calm and confident.

'Traces of amphetamines on MOD land cannot be ignored. That, along with two of your men reputedly on the lookout for drugs on New Year's Eve. It doesn't look good.' He replaced the buddha in a different spot. My, how the tables had turned, he thought, since the young private had died.

'Ha. If what you're suggesting was correct, there would be no need for our men to stalk the high street, would there? They could just shoot up in the observation post on the marshes!' Oldham exclaimed. Sparks detected anger below the surface.

'Now, James, we mustn't be flippant about this,' Brigadier Lane interjected. 'If there is even the slightest evidence of drugs in the ranks, we must address it. Stephen, what can we do to help?'

The chief had said nothing about Oldham's name appearing on the range chalkboard; he first wanted to gauge his reaction to a little heat. So far, he seemed only mildly irritated, with a dash of contempt for his commanding officer.

'A thorough search of the barracks would be a start,' replied Sparks, 'and instant recall of Private Jones, wherever he might be.'

'Yes, but first let's be clear,' said Lane. 'Are you suggesting the traces of substances on the marshes are related to the death of Private Daley and the civilian deaths at Greenstead?'

'The traces in the observation post will be compared with those found at the house in Greenstead, which will give us our answer.'

'But what about Daley and Jones?' the brigadier asked. 'I must confess I'm slightly baffled and inclined to agree with Captain Oldham – if my men were involved in drug trafficking, why would they attempt to procure amphetamines in Colchester High Street?'

'There are four thousand soldiers here: who says we're talking about the same men? But since you mention the Castle Park incident, we have a further request. WPC Gabriel?'

Until now, Gabriel had remained silently by the door. Oldham shot her a piercing glance; she had been to see him only yesterday afternoon.

'We'd also like to interview Private Frederick Cowley, previously of 7th Parachute Regiment. We want you –' and here she looked at Oldham directly – 'to find him for us.'

'Who is this man?' Lane asked.

'He was in the Falklands with Quinn, Daley and Jones,' replied Gabriel. 'They were in the same unit. Frederick Cowley exited the army in July.'

'I can't help you,' Oldham said. 'The army does not keep a record of the whereabouts of every ex-servicemen. The bandsman, of whom the inspector was inquiring, was different – I can't recall the name, but he had stayed—'

'Stone – who had stayed in Colchester,' Sparks cut in. 'Ex-soldiers often make their home where they were posted. 7 Para have only been here since September. Where were they before?'

'Why, Germany, of course,' said Lane. 'Osnabrück.'

'Germany?' Sparks frowned.

'Precisely,' said Oldham. 'As if we can keep tabs on every damn soldier that's served in the regiment.'

'Am I missing the significance of this fellow, other than that he served in this unit?' The brigadier was struggling to keep up.

'Freddie Cowley's brother was one of the drug couriers,' Sparks said sharply.

Lane turned sternly to Oldham. 'Come, come, James, we must have something on the fellow? Would the chap's medical records help you identify him? We can have them in a jiffy, I'm sure.'

'Good work, Gabriel,' Sparks complimented her, waving Freddie Cowley's medical record at her as they exited the building. 'Very good work.'

She nodded. Sparks himself had risen in her estimation – she liked the way he handled the military commanders with such confidence, even on their own turf. 'Thank you, sir.'

Sparks was flicking through the medical report.

'Freddie Cowley's dead.'

'I'm sorry?' Gabriel said, surprised.

'Roughly six foot two, twenty-four years old, lived in Germany?'

He tapped his foot on the pavement and regarded the military buildings behind them, austere in their silence. 'Goose is traditional . . . not turkey.'

'Sir?'

'Something Lowry said. And the body discovered on the Strood had German currency on it and was around the right age, too.' Gabriel didn't know how to respond; she wasn't familiar with the case. Sparks read her confusion. 'Don't worry, no need to trouble our friends back there until we're sure. With or without dental records, we can approximate his height – the doc can estimate the head length – and even shoe size will confirm. Ring this through to Lowry and Robinson, at the lab. Funny, we thought he was German because of his clothing and some loose change. But who else would eat a turkey Christmas dinner abroad before returning to the UK, other than an ex-pat?'

'How does this tie in, sir?'

'If the man on the Strood is Freddie, then there's a connection between the drug traffickers and Daley – the Castle Park lad.' Sparks was looking earnestly at WPC Gabriel, who was marginally taller than he was. 'I figure they were trying to smuggle a ton of drugs in from the Continent, using their ex-servicemen pals to source the gear. It's all tying up . . . though the timing of this chap's demise puts a different spin on things.'

'How?'

'Because we were working to the theory that the boys were killed at Greenstead because they were a day late delivering. Kenton's conversation with Pond makes this seem plausible – the whole town was waiting to get loaded . . .'

'But Freddie Cowley was dead before the men landed with the drugs.'

'Exactly!' His suddenly raised voice made Gabriel start. 'Which indicates a rival gang. Making this whole mess even more complicated.'

'The army boys seem pretty close, sir. Even Stone was ex-army. How would anyone else know? Why would they let anyone else in? They're a tight-lipped lot.'

The chief was still looking at RMP HQ. He exhaled deeply through his nose, the condensation giving him the fleeting appearance of a dragon at rest after blasting out fire.

'It's such a shame. They were all so young,' she said finally.

He wasn't sentimental, but she had said something that was confirmation enough for his line of thought. 'You know, I think we're missing a link . . . or perhaps a chain of command? Putting Cowley's death aside for a moment, you're right. These are just boys who are used to following orders . . .'

'You think there's more senior military involvement, sir?'

'It would make sense. Tight-lipped – that's Oldham all right. When Lane announced the Paras were stationed in Osnabrück, how did Oldham react?'

'I thought he bristled slightly.' She looked squarely at the chief as he stepped closer.

'Bristled. Exactly.' Across the road, half a dozen men in military green marched briskly by. 'The Beard told me that Oldham has a houseboat on West Mersea. Uses it at the weekends.'

'Really?'

'Yes. We were gassing about food. This may surprise you, but myself and Lane do get on damn well usually, above and beyond the sparring in the ring. Anyhow, Oldham had told him of a new fish place that had opened up near the port and sold the finest oysters, just beyond the houseboats.'

'That's funny,' Gabriel replied.

'Why?'

'Detective Constable Kenton told me that the night he was attacked snooping around the houseboats he heard piano music. The captain was playing the piano when I visited yesterday.'

'Piano music? Are you sure? Kenton never mentioned it to me.'

'One hundred per cent. He didn't mention it at Queen Street because he was too embarrassed. Having been knocked down, he thought, if he said he'd heard music, people would laugh all the more.'

She watched Sparks contemplate the soldiers marching past. She couldn't tell whether he was listening, but then he turned his back on the grand building they had just left and said abruptly, 'Right, this is what we're going to do.'

As they walked towards the chief's Rover, Sparks laid out their next move. Although flattered that he'd taken her into his confidence, and feeling sucked in by his enthusiasm, which she hadn't felt with either Kenton or Lowry, she was slightly disturbed that the boss of Queen Street had decided to take matters into his own hands in such a direct fashion. She sat next to him as he dictated into the car radio precise instructions to have Captain Oldham placed under surveillance for twenty-four hours with immediate effect, and to advise immediately if he left the barracks.

'In the meantime, let's you and I check out these houseboats.'

'Check them out?'

'Yes. I'm very curious about Captain Oldham's weekend retreat. And leaf through this and radio Lowry en route.' He slapped Cowley's file at her midriff. 'Let's go.'

54

1 p.m., Thursday, Hythe Hill, New Town, near Artillery Street

Lowry watched Kenton open the Cortina boot from inside the Saab as he listened to Gabriel reel off Freddie Cowley's stats over the radio. It sounded as though they had their unidentified man; Robinson would need to confirm but, on the face of it, the headless corpse washed up on the Strood was Felix Cowley's brother Freddie. He remembered that the Green Flash tennis shoe had been a size ten, the same size as Private Frederick Cowley. Lowry was impressed with Gabriel's discovery. Though how she'd arrived at the connection was not altogether clear, nor was why she was now in a car with Sparks, heading for Mersea.

He watched Nugent's silent protests at Kenton beyond the windscreen, but his mind was on the military involvement as he now saw it: ex-servicemen sourcing drugs on the Continent and shipping them over here through civilian couriers, then on to . . . who? Who were they for, ultimately? The men who had chased the two soldiers at Castle Park? But that was at the end of the deal, when things had already gone badly wrong. To answer the question he'd need to go back further, and Freddie Cowley ending up on the road across to Mersea was his starting point.

Kenton and Nugent plodded back across the frozen mud. There was snow in the air again. Lowry wound down the window.

'I niver looked in the boot; I ain't got a clue what went in the boot. Honest.' Nugent's weathered face looked pleading.

'Ted, you have to be the most honest bank robber in the land.'

The forensic evidence pointed to there having been a body in the boot, at some point – and now Lowry was sure it had been Freddie Cowley. 'Take Ted back to Queen Street,' he said to Kenton. The morgue was five minutes away across town. If there were any clues to be had, it would be from the corpse of Freddie Cowley itself.

1.20 p.m., Colchester General Hospital, morgue

Lowry watched as they slid the shrouded body of Frederick Cowley on to the steel table. 'The situation has changed,' he said.

'So I gather.' Robinson's spectacles slid down his nose as he laid out the corpse.

'I'm sorry I didn't call you back, it's just that—'

'No need to apologize, inspector, I know you've been busy; as indeed we all have.' The affable doctor indicated two white-shrouded gurneys behind him.

'I did see the report about pooling blood which suggested that the body had rested on a firm surface and that the man was not killed at sea.'

'Such as lying in the boot of a car?' Robinson smiled knowingly.

'Yes. News travels fast.'

'Good to know. One always takes pride in one's evaluation.' He whipped the sheet back with such exuberance that Lowry half expected the body to have disappeared, as in a magician's trick.

'You'll know then that the man was a soldier, hence the calloused feet.'

'Yes . . . However, you feel I may have missed something.'

'Not at all, doc. I fear we were at fault. The body was indeed found on the Strood; however, we failed to mention that it was hit by a car. So I want to check for impact marks.'

'Clearly, there are none,' the doctor said firmly.

'How do we know until we've looked?' Lowry crouched level with the trolley and started to examine the grey torso.

'*I* have looked, inspector. I have examined the body fully and, were there any impact wounds, I would have noticed them.'

Lowry was somewhat perplexed, but said politely, 'Of course – thorough fellow that you are.'

'What speed was the vehicle travelling at?'

'I don't know, to be honest, but the policeman who answered the call said he thought the car was travelling at speed. On that road, could be forty miles per hour? Fifty?'

The doctor shook his grey head, his forehead concertinaed as he frowned over his glasses. 'Very, very unlikely. What type of vehicle was it?'

'No idea.'

'Well, assuming it's an ordinary saloon, for the driver to get more than a jolt it would have had to have hit the body above here.' He indicated the thighs. 'You'll have experienced enough RTAs to know that a half-ton car can pass over a shin or arm without fuss.'

Lowry wasn't quite convinced of the assessment 'without fuss', but that wasn't the point. 'So you're saying there would be bruising at least from here to here.'

'Almost certainly.'

Robinson flung the white sheet back over the body as theatrically as he'd removed it.

'Unusual,' was all Lowry could say.

'Yes. I'd have a word with the driver, if I were you.'

1.25 p.m., West Mersea

The houseboats rested in the grassy mud two hundred yards from the road and were accessed by narrow wooden foot-ways. Gabriel felt fraudulent. Despite special dispensation from Sparks, she was pretty sure she shouldn't be doing this.

Even if she *were* CID, she was pretty sure she shouldn't be doing this.

Sparks knew that Oldham had not left the barracks; his quarters had been under discreet observation. The chief had been dismissive with Gabriel. 'If there's nothing there, there's nothing there. But look at the facts: he's been obstructive – didn't he fob you off and let Private Jones out of the country? He was on the ranges, and he knew, like Lowry said, that it offered a vantage point over the Colne estuary to see any escaping vessel. And didn't Oldham pull Quinn out of Queen Street damn quickly – for fear the boy would speak out, maybe?'

One footway led straight to *Ahab's Revenge*. A breeze disturbed the grasses and tickled the mast riggings further off towards the port itself. The vessel Gabriel was to search was the neighbouring one – but on which side? Damn. To the right was a deep-hulled craft that looked imposing. She couldn't see a name on it. It was sizeable, grand enough for Oldham: she could see large, double-fronted glass doors opening on to a spacious deck, but still she wasn't convinced. She rounded the bow and passed along the length of the hull, dodging mud pools between tufts of grass. On the stern in ornate gold was inscribed the name *Lily's Fancy*. That didn't sound very Captain James Oldham. A weak sun sat beyond the channel, behind the old oyster sheds on the proud sandbanks. There was not a soul about. Next to *Ahab's Revenge* on the other side was a low-sitting, turn-of-the-century boat with a high-standing wheelhouse.

Discreetly etched on the stern were the words *Così fan tutte.*
This was the one. Deftly clambering a rope ladder across the
transom, she slipped into the cockpit and below eye level.
Underneath the wheelhouse was a small wooden hatch leading
to the galley below. The hatch was not locked but fixed only
by a latch.

She flicked on a torch and shot the beam inside the galley
but then switched it off – the sunlight through the port-
holes was enough. Gabriel could almost stand at full height,
which surprised her, given how low the boat appeared from
the outside. The decor was tasteful and elegant; books and
gramophone records lined the wooden interior, with lush
upholstery between the cabinets. The boat was impeccably
tidy. She passed into the galley, which was adorned with cut
glassware.

It didn't strike her as the home of a drugs mastermind.
Through the kitchenette and past storage cupboards were
two berths, one holding a three-quarter-size bed, which she
searched under and around before riffling through the ward-
robes, which delivered nothing. The smaller berth was fitted
with bunks. She ran her fingers along the flimsy mattresses,
looking for a discreet opening; again nothing. Gabriel was
starting to perspire; it was stuffy. She had to get out. As she
was leaving the smaller berth, a dull thud from the passageway
made her jump. She opened one of the mahogany doors: it was
a cupboard holding tins of food and blankets. The next one
wouldn't open: it was locked. She shook it with annoyance,

and there again was a thud. Her heart beat fast – there was somebody in there. She put her ear to the door. She heard a faint groan, and then another thud, against the door, which caused her to lurch back. Had they locked themselves in? No, wait, there was an outside bolt at the very top, presumably to secure the door when the vessel was at sea. Without hesitation, Gabriel slid the bolt and released the door.

She leapt back in surprise: a nurse?

55

2.20 p.m., Thursday, Great Tey

The two women embraced, sobbing, in the Lowrys' front room. The tall WPC stood at a respectable distance, her face lined with concern. Lowry, always a figure of calm and composure, was visibly surprised by the turn of events and hung back awkwardly, unable to speak. The chief himself, standing there in the middle of the room, still in his Crombie, was not sure what to do now that they'd arrived.

Sparks, initially jubilant in his recovery of Patricia Vane, had decided to grant the woman's request to see her best friend, Lowry's wife, before moving on to Queen Street. As a divorcee living alone in the Dutch quarter, it was a reasonable request. Also, Sparks was keen to see Lowry's reaction to what could only be described as an extraordinary situation, and ordered the inspector to meet him at his own house.

And it was extraordinary indeed. Where he had been expecting to find a ton of class-A drugs, he instead discovered a thirty-two-year-old nurse shackled to the boat's toilet. This job never ceased to amaze him.

The woman at the centre of it all, Trish Vane, was remarkably composed, considering she'd been cooped up inside a houseboat lavatory for the best part of two and a half days, ' . . . though I could hear the gulls, and smell the sea . . .' she was saying.

'Why would he want to kidnap you?' Sparks asked, not for the first time.

'She doesn't know,' Lowry's wife replied stonily. Both women were in nurses' uniform. 'Give her time. Come on, let's get a coffee.' She gestured to Gabriel to join them.

Sparks noticed that Jacqui avoided her husband's gaze. He considered her for a moment, something he'd never really done on the times he'd previously met her. Fond of women as he was, a colleague's wife was not his concern. Elfin – not his type, anyway. She was pale, so pale; almost translucent. She looked more washed out than her pal, who he'd just sprung. Something very odd was going on here. The Vane woman had said she'd been out with Jacqui on Saturday night; they'd had quite a time of it, apparently. That was odd in itself – he knew Jacqui had been assaulted in the town centre that night; what the hell had she been doing, out caning it? What had he missed? Very, very odd . . .

The women left the room, leaving the two men alone. Sparks stepped over to Lowry, who was staring out of the patio doors. '*Peculiar*. This is my definition of a peculiar situation,' he said in a low voice, thinking of the balling out he had given Gabriel earlier in the week. 'We've known each other a long time . . .'

Lowry nodded, not altering the direction of his gaze.

'And so, if there was anything I should know, you'd tell me?' He paused. 'Because, from where I'm standing, the fact that a nurse ends up on a houseboat owned by a military police captain, cuffed to a toilet cistern, after a harsh night out with your missus, is fucking *peculiar*.'

'There's no denying that.' Lowry could feel the chief's eyes burning into him. On the surface he was calm, but inside he was in turmoil. Trish. Jacqui's Trish, kidnapped. He had to remain level-headed. It had to be connected to Saturday night. Was Oldham linked to the murders on Greenstead, too? Lowry fought to keep events separate in his mind, even though he sensed that everything was connected, in a way he couldn't yet fathom. Cigarette smoked drifted under Lowry's nose as Sparks lit up. Lowry braced himself.

'What the fuck's going on out there?'

'I'm sorry?' Lowry said. Sparks's eyes were on the garden.

'That.' He jabbed the glass. 'An up-ended Workmate and timber all over the place. Some sort of DIY experiment?'

'Something like that.' Lowry was disturbed that Sparks had careered off down a path of investigation on his own, and without consultation. He accepted that the chief missed getting his hands dirty, but this seemed random. Rash, even. Gabriel re-entered the room and asked if they wanted coffee.

Lowry shot her a glance as both declined: unreadable – God only knows what she was thinking.

'Freddie Cowley's death is a game changer. He's the mastermind, arranges the deal, but he has to come back here to the UK? Why? To check the delivery went through? And then to discover what? That his gang's about to get screwed over, and then he ends up dead himself? There has to be a key player coordinating this, between civilians and army.'

Sparks nodded forcefully. 'Oldham, it's got to be Oldham – bumping off all the civilians involved in getting the drugs on to the shore.' The chief looked around for an ashtray. There weren't any – Lowry had chucked them all in the garage when he'd packed in smoking. 'Maybe it's connected to that soldier's death on the castle wall, too. A reprisal, or turf war – call it what you like. I know we thought this before . . .'

Lowry slid open the French doors, took the butt and flicked it on the lawn. 'Why would he kill Freddie? His own man from Germany, who winds up in the back of a getaway car used to rob a post office by two men keen to buy what he brings ashore?' Lowry asked.

'Possibly Oldham was behind the post-office job too,' Sparks guessed, then paused, before continuing, 'though you've yet to explain: how did Freddie end up on the Strood?'

'He was mutilated and dumped to make it look like an accident at sea, with the body being washed in on the tide. But I've sent Kenton back to Mersea. The pathologist's report raises questions regarding the discovery of the body.'

'Questions?' Sparks frowned. 'Like what?'

'It might be nothing, but the body was hit by a car travelling at speed that night, but there are no signs of impact on it. I want to check out the car driver who discovered Cowley.' He stared out at his own back garden and the ridiculous, up-ended Workmate.

Lowry had been reluctant to dispatch Kenton to Mersea again – he'd much rather have gone himself, but Sparks had demanded that he return home, for what was indeed truly a 'peculiar' turn of events. He still couldn't quite believe that Trish had been locked up in a houseboat. He shook his head. He had to focus.

'Fred Cowley was back in the country the day before the robbery, and was staying with Stone in Artillery Street,' Lowry continued. 'His father confirmed this and handed over his son's passport to Kenton. He must have been killed the day after his return.' Jacqui re-entered the room, accompanied by Gabriel, who was clutching a mug. Lowry followed his wife's movements with detachment and said, 'Philpott and Nugent are both guilty as hell for the robbery – could they be working with Oldham? Is that what you're suggesting? I can't see them working together, and I don't have Oldham as getting his hands dirty turning over a post office.'

Sparks shook his head. 'Not necessarily as a hands-on armed robber, but I'm more and more convinced he's the mastermind. Stone was in on the drugs deal and part of the robbery and is ex-army – and he was putting Freddie Cowley up in his flat on Artillery Street. The Cortina can be traced to Stone *and* Philpott, both of whom were at the house on Greenstead. Cowley's body was, we believe, in the Cortina. And Freddie Cowley can be traced back to Oldham and the rest of that unit in Germany.'

'Why kill him?'

'Money and drugs – a fatal combination. But maybe it was unintentional? Cowley fixes the deal in Germany, flies back here, has a disagreement with Oldham on the houseboat, there's a scuffle . . .'

'Cowley goes overboard, off the houseboat – at high tide,' Lowry said, considering the idea. He knew the water came up that far; the park ranger had told him as much. 'That explains why the body is wet. Oldham hacks him apart so he can't be identified – the doc reckons the arm went because Cowley had a military tattoo; an army man would recognize its significance – shoves him in the boot and gets him dropped on the causeway at high tide so it looks like an accident, by whom, we're not yet sure . . .'

There was a pause. Lowry noticed that Sparks had switched his attention to Trish and Jacqui, who were now perched on the sofa and speaking in hushed tones to Gabriel. 'You haven't said so, but I know that Jacqui was out and about on Saturday – the night of the riot.'

'Stephen, I . . .' Lowry was suddenly pulled back into the room at the reminder of his wife's connection with what had happened.

Sparks held up his hand. 'Say no more – in case you regret it. Let me finish: Jacqui was out; Sergeant Barnes saw the altercation in the high street and witnessed Jacqui and her pals going off to party against your advice, charged on adrenalin, no doubt, or on something else. I think they must have seen something that placed them in danger. A woman's scarf was found outside Beaumont Terrace; there's every possibility it belonged to her or one of her friends. I trust you've not yet seen the evidence?'

'I . . .' Sparks was offering him a way out, without lying. Lowry bowed his head with embarrassment. Now that it was out in the open, the situation his wife had landed them in embarrassed him intensely.

'Very good.' The chief patted him on the shoulder. 'At this point in time, we need not concern ourselves with fine details. Let's just say these young ladies are caught on the periphery, but it's close enough to warrant one of them being kidnapped by the murderer.'

For the first time, the possibility that it could have been Jacqui who was kidnapped crossed Lowry's mind, but, for all that implied, it did not mute his sense of humiliation. 'Why?' he said uncertainly, to no one.

'Who the fuck knows? When you're messing with that sort of drug, anything can happen. But we'll ask him politely – at first, at least.' Lowry met his stare. 'I'm bringing Oldham in.'

'We'll need to tread carefully,' Lowry said as Sparks turned to go. 'Get this wrong and all kinds of hell will break loose.'

56

4 p.m., Thursday, West Mersea

Kenton crossed the high street and walked a short way along East Road. Despite Lowry's insistence on urgency, he was desperate for some air before seeing his Mersea police colleagues again and had taken a stroll in the near-dark along the esplanade.

Visiting Cowley's father earlier that afternoon had troubled him. The old man had affected nonchalance, proclaiming he had always known his eldest had been up to no good since quitting the army. However, beneath the surface, Kenton could see the hurt. When he described how Freddie had stayed no more than half an hour to leave his passport for safe keeping before hunting out Derek Stone, the old man's disgust at the lowlife Stone was a thin veil for the pain he was feeling. Kenton had wished to inquire after Felix, but hadn't been able to bear being in the Brightlingsea council house any longer.

He took a deep breath and pushed open the heavy door to the police station. He wasn't terribly keen on being in this particular building too long either. Inside, PC Jennings stood behind the reception desk and, in the small office beyond, Kenton could just make out the bulky form of the station sergeant.

'Afternoon,' he said jauntily. He was determined to get on with these chaps.

'Not that bleedin' robbery again?' Jennings asked.

Kenton didn't want to rile them immediately, so shook his head. 'No, no. It's about the body found on the Strood last weekend.'

'Yes?'

'I'd like a word with the fella who came across the body.'

'Eh? That were me,' Jennings said. 'I saw you there, re-member? I know it was dark 'n' all.'

'Yes, yes.' Kenton stepped closer to the wooden hatch. 'I know, I do remember. But the chap in the motor who reported it, who hit the poor devil on the causeway: who was that?' Kenton was close enough to discern a shaving rash troubling the young officer's neck.

'Oh, I don't think he left a name.'

'No name?'

'No, I don't think so.'

'Can you check, please?' Kenton thought the PC must be simple. Jennings unbuttoned his uniform breast pocket and pulled out his notebook. Licking his thumb, he placed it on the counter and flicked through the pages.

'Nothing, mate. Sorry.'

'What about the car? Can you remember what type of car it was?'

'Nah, I didn't make the car out. It's pitch black on that road in the middle of the night.'

Even Bradley was stirred by this dismal lack of standard information. He came to stand at the lad's shoulder.

'You would have picked the call up here on Friday: you'd've been here – on call.' He winked at Kenton. 'Friday and Saturday nights we're open twenty-four hours. Check the incident book. 'Ere, budge over.'

Bradley elbowed Jennings aside and pulled forward the large desk ledger. Kenton was pleased that the sergeant was proving agreeable. 'Now, where are we? January one.'

Kenton wondered how they filled their days as the mainly blank pages flicked by. Small community stations like this one – their days must be numbered.

'There's bugger all there!' Bradley exclaimed to his junior colleague.

Jennings shrugged his lanky frame. 'I was in a hurry – it's not every day a body washes up on the road. I dashed out sharpish.'

''E 'as a point. Last one were '74 – a fisherman by the name of Munson . . . got tangled in a net and swept overboard. Or were it Moore?'

'Err . . . we're straying from the point. Can you talk me through exactly what happened that night, from when the call came through?'

'It weren't a phone call – there's no phone on that road. A driver came by the station and said the fella in front of him had skidded on something in the road. Looked to be a body. So I went down, and there he was, headless on the side of the causeway.'

'You say, "there he was" – could you see him on your approach?'

'Yep. Just lying there like a sack of spuds in the fella's headlights.'

'If you could see him, how come the motorist that hit him didn't?'

'The tide was still partly over, but as it starts to ebb, people drive down the centre of the causeway, over the camber in the road. He and the first fella drove down the middle. He caught it on his near side.'

'It'd be about six inches of water,' Bradley commented, opening the side door and joining Kenton in the tiny reception area, 'and, what with the spray, he'd more than likely not have seen the body.'

'What sort of speed was he travelling at?'

'They all tonk along that causeway, even in the dark, depending on the water level, to avoid stalling. What's the fuss? Ain't 'e reckoned to be a German fisherman or summat that got ripped up by the propellers?'

The discovery that the body was that of Freddie Cowley had not been made public, but Kenton decided to tell them something of what they'd found out. There was a chance it could prompt sharper thinking, although he doubted it. 'We believe the man – an Englishman – was murdered and then dumped on the road. So we need to interview the gentleman who found the body.'

'Are you sure?'

'We know the body was moved, for sure.'

Bradley looked at his subordinate with what Kenton hoped was disappointment, and said, 'Come on, lad, give the CID a hand.'

'I've told all I can, sarge,' he said plaintively. 'I got down there about twelve thirty and radioed the desk at Queen Street, and then shut the road, while I waited for assistance. I parked across the road on the Colchester side, and stood on me Jack Jones, halting traffic, waiting for Colchester police to turn up.'

'And how long was that?'

'About twenty minutes.'

'And what was the driver doing – the man whose name eludes us – while you were standing on your Jack Jones?'

'He was sitting in his car until Uniform from Queen Street turned up. It were bloody freezing. I'm sure he gave them a statement.'

Bradley shrugged apologetically. 'Try Colchester Uniform,' he said.

4.40 p.m., Queen Street HQ

Once his initial outrage had subsided, Oldham appeared stoic and came without a fight, looking impeccable in his uniform.

Lowry assumed it was down to his military training. He was escorted from Abbey Fields and brought to Queen Street to be questioned over the double murder at Greenstead and the kidnap of Patricia Vane. He was not as yet accused of Freddie Cowley's murder, which was still under investigation. Indeed, there were many gaps and unknowns, high among them what had happened to the drugs – were they still on the marshes? And there was no evidence of the cash; a drug deal that went wrong would usually throw out money somewhere. But a timeline was slowly forming, and Sparks was sure all would flush through once charges were pressed. And there he was, the captain of the military police, immaculately presented in dark green uniform and red-banded cap, refusing assistance down from an unmarked Commer van. Lowry and Sparks observed from across the road, outside the haberdasher's. Sparks, though bold, was nervous, and had opted to witness Oldham's arrival at a distance – on the lookout, as he put it. For what, Lowry was unsure. Military vigilantes? The press?

'What have you said to the Beard?' Lowry asked, his toes beginning to feel the cold again.

'Haven't told him yet. See what Oldham has to say for himself first.'

'If you think that's wise.' It struck Lowry as spectacularly foolish; if he wanted the regimental commander's support, why not communicate with him from the start? It seemed to Lowry that Sparks had been impetuous, caught up in the heat of the moment.

'Wise? Who has time to be wise in a situation like this?' Sparks said sharply, sensing disapproval. 'Oldham was in Germany with the rest of them, remember. C'mon.' They crossed the road and entered the building, passing two uniformed constables at attention on either side of the door.

A further two uniforms had been posted outside the interview room. This indicated more about Sparks's state of mind than he was prepared to let on. He must be fearful of reprisals, thought Lowry. If this got out, it would make the national news.

'Evening, Captain Oldham. Thank you for cooperating and helping us with our inquiries,' Sparks said coolly.

'Ha. Is that what you call it? Practically strong-arming me into a vehicle.' He spoke in his usual clipped tone, betraying nothing. 'May I ask what I am supposed to have done?'

'In the first instance, abduction.'

'Abduction?' A ripple of confusion passed over the captain's face.

'Yes, abduction. We'll come on to the serious stuff later on.'

'Drug trafficking, you mean?' The smaller man edged his chair back and crossed his legs. 'Yes; that, I get. A natural assumption. The firing ranges were used to hide drugs and I was the last to sign in before the end of the year. You neglected to mention this yesterday because you were – how do you say? – "building your case". Testing me for my reactions.'

Sparks waved this remark away, circling Oldham, who sat neatly at the crooked interview table.

'Too subtle for me, captain.' Though of course Lowry knew

that had been exactly what he was playing at. 'No, hard facts are all I'm interested in.'

'Enlighten me, please?'

'A nurse was found handcuffed to the lavatory in your boat.'

Oldham glanced at Lowry in surprise. Lowry winked back.

'A nurse? Forgive me, Chief Sparks, but what use would I have for a nurse in matters concerning drug trafficking?'

'You tell me, sonny Jim.'

Sparks placed his knuckles on the edge of the table, which moved awkwardly underneath his weight. He puffed furiously on an Embassy that hung from his lips.

'Words fail me,' Oldham said.

'We have two dead bodies on a council estate in Colchester, captain,' Lowry said. 'Miss Vane had been in contact with the men on the night prior to their death.'

'I see. Does the young lady in question know me?'

Lowry took one of Sparks's cigarettes, waiting for the chief to elaborate. He wasn't sure what to make of the captain. Given the gravity of the accusations, he was remarkably unruffled; if anything, he was faintly amused.

57

5 p.m., Thursday, Queen Street HQ

Dejected, Detective Constable Daniel Kenton straightened his tie and tidied his hair with his hands. He had departed Mersea flummoxed and disheartened. What would Lowry have done differently? He felt his inexperience keenly. And now, as if he wasn't feeling insecure enough, he faced the prospect of interviewing his boss's wife's best friend. Sparks had briefed him to keep it low key, and to have no other officer present. This was 'fact-finding only'. But despite the reassuring words, the tension in the chief's voice had made Kenton nervous. With a deep breath, he pushed open the interview-room door.

Patricia Vane had changed her clothes and now sat, her hair tied back, in jeans and a baggy white cardigan with the sleeves pushed back to the elbow, as was the fashion. She was a few years older than he was, and good looking – the sort of woman he'd be terrified to approach in a pub for fear she'd laugh in his face. He pulled up a chair and folded over a new page in his notebook. His brief was to ascertain information on the kidnapper. The woman sat calmly, playing with a pink lighter on the table. He watched her turning it over and over. There was chafing around her wrists.

'Would you like someone to look at that?' he asked.

She touched the red inflammation, which marked a very pale forearm. 'No, it's okay.'

'I hear they were police handcuffs,' he remarked. 'I wonder where he got hold of them?'

'The back of the car,' she said, sipping her coffee. 'They're . . .' She looked away.

'They're . . . ?'

'Detective Inspector Lowry's . . . Jacqs lent them to me. For a bit of fun. You know?'

'Oh.' He didn't ask her to elaborate. 'Okay. Let's proceed. Could you talk me through the last couple of days – starting with when you left for the hospital in the morning. Did you see your abductor?'

'No.'

'Can you tell me anything about him?'

'He was rough.'

'Rough? You mean the way he manhandled you?'

'No. Well, yes, he shoved me about a bit, but I didn't put up much resistance – he had a gun at my neck. His hands were rough, calloused. And there was a familiar smell about him. Perfume, hair spray or gel. Cheap.'

That didn't sound like Oldham or any of Daley's unit. Hair product was not standard issue, as far as he was aware.

'Did you hear him speak? Any accent?'

'From round here. Essex.'

'Do you think you'd recognize this man if he came through the door now?'

Her eyes flicked anxiously to the interview-room door.

'Nah.' She fumbled with a crumpled pack of menthol cigarettes.

'Is there any reason you can think of why someone might want to kidnap you?'

'My ex, to get his own back.'

'Really? His name?' Kenton sat poised.

'Nah,' She shook her head. 'Andy'd not do that,' she said, sadly he thought.

'Are you sure?'

'Positive . . . Jacqs will tell you. Have you spoken to her?'

Kenton felt uncomfortable at the mention of Jacqui Lowry. An image of the inspector's wife in a kimono flashed across his mind.

'Not yet,' he replied cautiously. 'Let's keep the focus on what you yourself remember over the week. Anything strange happen in the hospital recently, say?'

'Okay, well, I don't remember anyone on the ward – I was tired, you see. Shift work.' She smiled wanly. 'Anyway, why would any abductor appear publicly like that?'

'Okay, maybe not on the ward; think – where else have you been?'

She tapped the lighter on the table. 'Saturday night.' She paused. 'Has Nick – sorry, Detective Inspector Lowry – told you about Saturday night?'

'Only that you went nightclubbing.'

He was aware they'd not made eye contact. She reached for a cigarette.

'Yes, we did . . . It's possible he – whoever it was – might have been at Aristos. I'm sorry, but my memory of the night is very hazy.' Then, looking at him directly, she said, 'What we do for the sake of a good night out, huh?'

5.30 p.m., Colchester CID, Queen Street

'All the men in question were in barracks on the morning of the kidnap!' Lane barked down the phone. 'What the dickens does Sparks think he's doing?'

'But Captain Oldham is not stationed at the cavalry barracks,' Lowry argued.

'This is the British Army, goddamn you – we know where every bloody soldier is at all times!'

Lowry held the receiver away from his ear. He knew this wasn't entirely true, as a lot of men lived off barracks, but now wasn't the time to cross-question the brigadier.

'I understand your consternation, brigadier, but a woman was discovered bound and gagged in the captain's houseboat.'

'I don't care if Princess Diana herself was strapped to the prow naked! I shall be on the phone to the chief constable!' And with that he slammed the phone down.

Kenton glanced over. 'Sounds like he took that well.'

Lowry got up and read Trish Vane's statement, taken by Kenton. There was nothing in it that remotely implicated Oldham or his soldiers: workman's hands, local accent, cheap scent. Headless Freddie Cowley in the morgue was all that was on his mind. He just couldn't see Oldham using Philpott or Nugent.

'You're not convinced, are you?'

'About Oldham, no,' Lowry confessed. 'And the brigadier has added another layer of doubt. If you think about it, anyone could access those boats. Security is non-existent, especially as Oldham's is only occupied part-time. And there are plenty of people who would hold a grudge against a military police captain . . .'

'Derek Stone, for example?'

'Possibly, but he's dead. I bet if we probed deep enough in the military police files we'd find a catalogue of ex-servicemen with grudges.'

'But that avenue of inquiry is currently closed to us.' Kenton thumbed downwards: Sparks had incarcerated Oldham below and was personally interrogating the man.

'Yes, for now, but I suspect not for long. I imagine it's only a matter of minutes before Lane gets hold of Merrydown. But if we rule Oldham out, where do we find our man?'

'Maybe a stalker; she's very pretty? Maybe someone she met at the nightclub on Saturday night?'

'Maybe. Maybe. Everything is maybe. What news on Mersea?'

'A blank, I'm afraid.'

'You what?' Lowry said, surprised. 'Did you tell those clots the reason we need to see this man, ask them for the name of the driver who hit Cowley's corpse?'

'I said that it was now murder, but didn't say why. They had no record of who he was.'

Lowry rubbed his temples. 'But Jennings was there when we turned up.'

'I know; he didn't log the call.'

'What exactly did Jennings say?'

'He said Queen Street Uniform might have details.'

'And do they?'

'No.'

'Did Jennings know what type of motor it was?'

'No. He said it was too dark. He's a pretty low-watt bulb.'

'What?' Lowry said, amazed, and then it all fell into place. He had it. 'Bollocks. Nobody's that fucking stupid.' He picked up his donkey jacket. 'Come on – quick.'

'Where are we going?' Kenton said.

'Records. For Jennings' home address.' Lowry span round. 'By way of the cells and a final word with Mr Nugent, and then to Mersea for one last trip.'

'*Last* trip. That I'd like to believe – I'm sick of the place. Why? You're on to something?'

'Maybe.' Lowry smiled faintly. He knew that, if he was right, they didn't have much time.

58

5.35 p.m., Thursday, basement cells, Queen Street

'Now then, Ted, what if I told you that the person you saw through Derek Stone's window was the last person you'd expect to be skulking around a low-rent flat in New Town?'

Nugent looked up sullenly from the bunk. He'd been down-stairs for nearly four hours – long enough for a musty bodily odour to fill the tiny cell. Kenton had no idea where this line of questioning was heading, and stood back, leaning against the cell bars. Lowry nodded to dismiss the duty PC and sat down on the bunk next to Nugent. He pulled out a pack of Player's Navy Cut.

'Don't know what you mean – barely know the geezer.'

'All right, let me be more precise. I'm suggesting you saw someone who could influence your parole in a dubious situation.'

This remark grabbed his attention. 'I don't know what you mean,' Nugent repeated, his tone stiffening.

'Okay, let me spell it out for you. And you – you try and think clearly before you answer, because time is running out. Your parole is screwed, anyway, but let's see if you can limit the damage. Listening?'

'I am.' The man's composure had changed. He was no longer the cocky little handyman caught out. Here was a man with his freedom on the line.

'When you were up your ladder on Artillery Street, you saw another face you recognized, one more troubling than a druggy no-hoper like Stone . . . the face of a man usually in uniform. A policeman.'

Nugent turned to face Lowry, then shot Kenton a look.

'I don't know who to trust,' Nugent said quietly.

'Trust me,' Lowry said.

'Ha! Right.' Nugent shook his head.

'It's you we're talking to, not Jamie – you're safe. I give you my word.'

A man with few alternatives, Nugent sighed. 'Most of what I've said is true, like. Minding the window-cleaning round and that. I never wanted to get mixed up in all this. Imagine, first job I do and there in front of me is Stone waving a shooter around, shouting at that Mersea copper and Jamie Philpott.'

Lowry thought of the smeared window again. He could envisage the scene. 'Carry on.'

Nugent hesitated. He needed reassurance.

'I promise you're safe.' Lowry shucked him another cigarette, taking one himself.

'PC Patrick Jennings is yer man,' said Nugent in a voice barely above a whisper. 'He planned the post-office job and was after the drugs drop.'

'How?' Kenton crouched down.

'Jamie and Derek Stone had heard from a soldier pal of Stone's. Jamie is Jennings' cousin.'

'Jennings is bent?' Kenton hissed, barely containing his naïve surprise.

'And the rest. Jamie had been bragging how he and Pond had had safe conduct, like, from your mob, for years with the weed . . . The temptation was too much.' Nugent nodded. 'Especially when 'e 'eard it was coming in through his patch, Mersea. They thought they could muscle in there.'

'What did they want exactly, Jennings and Philpott? Drugs? Money?' Lowry asked.

'Not the drugs; they ain't set up for distributing a hundred kilos of speed. It was the money. The post-office cash was to buy Stone a way in, cash down, like, but it also gave him the power over the others. And although Jamie remained on the outside, he was still in Jennings' pocket. The only problem was they weren't sure exactly when the stuff was arriving.'

'Go on.'

'Jennings leaned on Stone to find out when the gear was coming in, but his pal wouldn't say . . . so Jamie, who turns out to be a bit of a headcase when wired, squeezed him, but all he managed to get out of him was New Year's. But when

455

that wasn't enough, Jennings sent Jamie round to Del's flat to confront Freddie Cowley, and they fell out, good and proper.'

Now Kenton could see the picture. 'Fell out? It was a little more than that.'

'I dunno what happened exactly. Jennings overstepped it, thought he could slice a wedge for providing safe conduct across the island, or some crap like that, I dunno . . . I only know what happened next. They knew when it was coming in – roughly – but not where or who with, or where it was going. And with Cowley out of the way, they weren't going to find out any time soon. But they knew it had to come off the island.'

'Ingenious,' Lowry said. 'Who else, other than a copper, could check everyone's comings and goings from the island? Even better, close the road, and, while they're at it, dispose of a body under everyone's nose.'

'I don't know nothin' about that. Promise me I'm in the clear? I 'aven't hurt anyone.'

'You have my word,' Lowry said. 'We'll have you out of here just as soon as we tidy up some loose ends. When was the last time you spoke to either Jennings or Philpott?'

'Jennings, when I called him to get you off my back. Fat lot of good that did. And Jamie gave me the finger as he left, just now.'

'As he left?' Lowry said.

'About an hour ago – I assumed you'd moved him.' He looked from one of them to the other. 'You don't think I'd be dumb enough to gabble away with him in the next cell, do you?'

'Of course not.' Lowry feigned a smile. He thought Jamie must be upstairs with a solicitor. 'We've got to run. Now, Jennings – any idea where he lives?'

'End terrace on that row of fishermen's cottages behind the yacht club – off Coast Road – right past the harbour, looking across the Blackwater.'

Lowry beckoned to the duty PC. 'One more thing: does the name Oldham ring any bells?'

'Oldham? Who's he? A druggy?'

5.45 p.m., Sparks's Office, Queen Street HQ

Sparks was listening hard to the woman on the other end of the line. He locked on to the blonde WPC opposite him. He'd forgotten her name.

'Let him go,' the voice said.

Sparks didn't answer.

'Hello? Sparks, are you there?'

'Yes, ma'am.'

'You have no evidence. Has it not occurred to you that you're being played with? Someone wants you to believe the army's behind the whole thing.'

'But there are traces out on the ranges. Oldham had—'

'I'm well aware of that!' The nasal rasp stopped him in his tracks. 'Let him go. Philpott's fingerprints were found at the house, which is more than can be said of Oldham's. You can't place him anywhere other than at the ranges, where the drugs happened to be; place him somewhere he *shouldn't* have been and then I'll listen. In the meantime, charge Jamie Philpott. You've nothing to lose.'

Sparks just couldn't credit Philpott as the ringleader, knowing him as he did. But if that's what she wanted, so be it. They had him banged up downstairs for the armed robbery, anyway.

'You cannot imagine the shitstorm it would cause if the captain was wrongly charged. How is he?'

Who gives a toss? thought Sparks, but instead he replied, 'Stoic, ma'am.'

'Well, let him go immediately.'

Sparks looked again at the WPC opposite.

'Tell Lowry to charge Philpott with murder,' he said blankly. She didn't respond. 'What's the matter?'

'Uniform took Philpott away, sir, at Sergeant Bradley's request.'

5.50 p.m., Colchester Road

Lowry floored the Saab out of Colchester. He didn't have time to wait for back-up. West Mersea had requested Philpott for questioning the minute Kenton had left the island: the Dodger had put the call in. The desk sergeant hadn't thought to check with CID and, in a very slim window of time, Jennings had convinced the old fool that Jamie was the driver who had hit the body on the Strood, and thus facilitated his escape.

'And the irony is it was Philpott that laid Freddie in the road.'

'Got to say you've lost me, guv.'

'Think about it. Jennings remembers turning a Land Rover back that night, but can't give you the name of the man who ran over the body. When you went back this afternoon, you caught him out. He wasn't expecting that. The man who "hit" the body was Philpott, but he didn't run him over, just unloaded it once they'd spotted their men.'

'How could they be sure they had the right men?'

'Two men in a Land Rover in the middle of the night, covered in mud? Felix said the police advised them where to spend the night – at the Dog and Pheasant – so they knew where to find them in the morning, and followed them into Colchester for the drop.'

'But Philpott, a murderer?'

'Drugged out his mind, anything is possible. We'll find out . . . Explains why Stone went to the house unarmed. He knew his murderer.'

'And Patricia Vane in Oldham's houseboat?'

'Jennings would have seen Oldham coming and going and have figured it out as the ideal place to hold her to keep an eye on her. At the same time, it would implicate the good captain, as Jennings would know the military connection with the ranges.'

'What, and have us barking up the wrong tree, as the chief's been doing?'

'Yes, it would appear so. Jennings. Jennings is the mastermind.' Lowry dipped his beam as he followed the road round to the right towards West Mersea. 'Clever lad, all along; playing the lackey PC.'

'I still don't get it – you've given Nugent your word that you'll help him out, after he tried to run you down. Why trust him and not Philpott, who, until lately – let's be honest, guv – was practically on the payroll?'

'His behaviour.'

'What, the swearing and cursing? I can see there's an honesty—'

Lowry interrupted. 'Ted Nugent is the epitome of a man in jeopardy, and I don't just mean because he's been nicked – he didn't know which way to turn or where to find safety. When we spoke with Nugent the first time, wild horses wouldn't have dragged him from the island, remember? Yet the second time, when I nabbed him up the ladder, he knew the situation had shifted up a gear – he was in trouble with us, and that meant with Jennings, eventually, who was the bigger danger. That's why he was practically begging to come to Queen Street; that energetic episode with his XR3 – as if he'd get away? And then telling us about the cash in the glove box. Compare him to Jamie with his eyes gone crazy – who'd you trust? It's not always straight forward.'

'Straight forward,' Kenton muttered as they passed through

the small town centre, its ancient church reaching up into the night, and descended into the harbour.

'Jesus, it's dark down here. Worse with the snow,' Lowry said as huge flurries swirled down, covering all in their path. 'I can't see the name of the road, but I'm sure that's the lane – at the end there next to the yacht club, through the arch. Too narrow for a car.'

By a large white building with large black windows on the upper floor, the road slipped away into the dark.

'Right, we'll park up here.' Lowry edged up to a chain-link boundary, on the other side of which large white hulls loomed, quiet and majestic, the lanyards clinking invisibly above them.

'I used to be afraid of the dark,' Kenton said across the car roof, which was already white.

'Really? Not now, I hope.' Lowry's breath caught in the weak orange gloaming surrounding the solitary street light.

'Of course not.'

'Good. It'll be pretty black down there. And be aware, to the left, the path falls away to water, like the edge of a pier. Now, keep quiet.' They each carried a torch but would hold out on using them unless absolutely necessary. A second later, a gull screech pierced the dark from amidst the boats, confirming Lowry's warning of the sea's proximity.

As the street narrowed, the rapidly disappearing tarmac gave way to cobbles. The street light didn't reach beyond the stone archway, so having passed through they found themselves in total darkness. Lowry had stopped – or Kenton could no longer hear his footsteps, lost in the snow perhaps. Instead, he heard water lapping below and to the right of him. Kenton found that this affected his balance. The closeness of the sound compelled him to reach out blindly for a secure surface. He could barely move his feet; an atavistic fear, something akin to vertigo, had him rooted to the spot.

'*Guv? Guv!*' he whispered urgently into the void.

'What?' Lowry's voice, soft and barely audible, came back through the dark. 'Don't panic; your eyes will adjust. Listen.'

He stood still and listened as hard as he could. Footsteps.

'Who's that?'

No reply.

Then voices, urgent, cracking the silence ahead. Gradually, Kenton's spatial awareness came back as his vision adjusted. A weak moon flickered on the water.

'I should have let you drown that night,' came a voice out of nowhere, a second before he felt a truncheon smash across his jaw.

By keeping close to the cottages, Lowry, by dint of a sliver of moonlight, had caught sight of the silhouette lunging out at his younger colleague. As Kenton went down, Lowry swiftly leapt in and rabbit-punched his assailant across the neck. Jennings' pasty face spun round and met with a left hook, which sent him flying into the water and the truncheon rattling on the cobbles.

Kenton lay groaning at his feet. Further off, an outboard motor sputtered into life. Lowry flicked on his torch and shot it down the jetty path; thickening snowflakes caught in the beam. At the very end, there was movement.

'Keep him in the water – it'll cool him down,' he said to his prone colleague, and ran down towards the boat. Snow caught in his eyes as he went, but he could just make out a dinghy casting off. He broke into a sprint and launched himself off the jetty and into the boat, landing squarely on the figure who was steering the outboard motor. The two men went crashing to the wooden hull, the decked pilot bucking violently. Lowry pressed down against taut muscle and sinew underneath the man's overcoat – this was no weakling like the stringy policeman. Philpott thrashed hard again, this time dislodging Lowry, who was thrown back and cracked his head against the gunwale. The boat circled out of control as Philpott tried to pin Lowry by the neck; he was searching for something within his coat – a knife perhaps. Lowry struggled but couldn't escape his surprisingly vice-like grip. Reaching blindly to his side, he grasped what felt like a fuel can. He fumbled to tilt the metal container and grab the handle, then swung it up with all his might, clouting the seething, bristly face above him and sending the lighter Philpott sideways. He shot up, abruptly buckling as the boat keeled inwards, then swiftly righting himself as he caught a glimpse of a blade. Philpott was still on the floor, so Lowry tossed the fuel can at his head and trod forcefully on his groin, causing him to bellow with pain. Crouching to steady himself, Lowry was suddenly blinded by torch beams. 'The cavalry,' he muttered to the four or so uniforms who had appeared on the jetty. After a sharp kick to the whining man's ribs, Lowry took control of the outboard and brought the dingy to dock.

7.15 p.m., Queen Street HQ

Oldham had been released.

Jennings and Philpott now swallowed all the attention. The latter was raving in the furthest interview room, his voice echoing down the corridor. Lowry pulled the door shut and took a last look through the glass at Jennings. The man caught his eye. Wrapped in a blanket, his pale face was indignant and said, 'I'm as good as you.' And Lowry thought, Yes, you probably were; it was a shame his intelligence had not found a better outlet. Jennings had hidden all this time working under the Dodger, and Lowry wondered what drove a man like him to crime. Surely it was more than frustrated ambition? He couldn't help but think that, if Jennings had had a more capable number two, he would have inflicted some major long-term damage and gone undetected for some time, above and beyond the blood of the last week. He could have got away with killing Freddie Cowley, too, probably, if it weren't for Philpott's insanity on Sunday night at Greenstead.

Lowry blew his nose; he felt the onset of a cold. He had business to attend to home, but Jacqui had just started a rota of nights; it would be the briefest of interludes – make sure Matt didn't go to bed too late – with no time for a proper conversation. And he needed time to think how to approach the situation. But if he wanted to catch her before she left for work tonight, he'd have to leave Queen Street no later than eight.

Corporal Quinn was still in custody, and probably feeling abandoned now his chief had been freed. Lowry took advantage of all the commotion to slip down to the cells and run a scenario past him.

He presented Quinn with the facts as the police interpreted them: Daley, Jones, Quinn and Cowley had imported one hundred kilos of amphetamines from Germany. Freddie Cowley had arranged the deal. Quinn had avoided much of the trouble by being in the Glasshouse on New Year's Eve for some minor offence (which had possibly saved his life; otherwise, it might have been him at the bottom of the wall at Castle Park), so, with less of the heat on him, Lowry hoped he might cooperate.

'Patrick Jennings did not know who Freddie's contacts were, this side of the channel; Freddie wouldn't tell them, and so he was killed for protecting you lot. Admirable, don't you think? But the question remains – Daley and Jones; who chased them?' he asked as they sat alone in a cell.

'I dunno,' Quinn said. He looked tired.

'The witnesses – one, the girl from the video shop; you know who I mean – said they were meeting people from out of town. Were they dealers? What was the plan? Where were they going to sell it?'

Quinn frowned. 'There were no dealers. They were looking for those boys from Brightlingsea, you know that . . . and no plan, neither – it was just for us and our mates.'

Lowry didn't believe it for one minute. There might have been no dealers, but he reckoned on some kind of distribution within the army – possibly nationwide, given the quantity. But there was one question he needed an answer to: the financing.

'So, no money changed hands at Beaumont Terrace?'

'No money was ever to change hands – we'd bought it outright, with our active-service bonus. The plan was to ship it halfway from Germany and get some local boys who knew the water to bring it in.'

'So, if it's just for you, why were two of your gang chased across town, ending in the death of one of you?' Given the subsequent course of events, Lowry believed there had to be a connection.

Quinn scratched his cropped ginger scalp. 'Freddie was staying with that scumbag, Stone – he should never have let him in. It was contained until then, but then Stone came into some money and wanted a piece of the action. We thought, why not? But he couldn't keep it to himself and told that smartarse, Philpott. And then Stone kept asking about the deal,' he continued. 'Like you, he thought there was somebody else.'

'How do you mean?'

'He thought we were middlemen. After Felix and Boyd landed it, he thought we were going to sell it on . . . but Boyd was a day late – nobody knew where they'd got to – and then what happened happened at Castle Park.'

'Okay, and who else would know? It wouldn't be Philpott who chased them across Castle Park.'

'No way. Jones and Daley wouldn't run from no one, 'cept maybe the Red Caps.'

And then it clicked. 'Do the Red Caps ever operate in civvies?'

'Aye, for covert ops, so as not to attract attention, but you can always spot them a mile off. Solid hard bastards.'

'Tell me, Quinn, why were you detained on New Year's Eve?' As Lowry asked, he could hear footsteps approaching down the basement aisle. He wouldn't get his answer now, tonight, from Quinn. But that didn't matter. He knew the answer. He stood to pre-empt the PC now standing at the door. 'Ah, constable, about time. We need to let the corporal here return to base.'

Quinn looked up, surprised.

'Thank you for your time, Corporal Quinn,' he said re-assuringly. 'Try and keep out of trouble, eh?'

Friday, 7 January, 1983

59

8.30 a.m., Friday, Great Tey

'But Jacqui, don't you see, it's because you're unhappy that you're so reckless?'

'Not now, Paul. I just started on nights. I need to go to bed.'

She twirled the telephone cable, listening to Paul plead with her as she sat on the bottom stair in the empty house. He repeated the same line, or variations of it, over and over – that she pursued these stupid, childish antics because her marriage was unfulfilling. Was he right? She didn't really care; she'd just been having a giggle with her mates. It was pointless Paul saying that if she thought about it 'deep down' she'd feel differently: she felt how she felt. Besides, Trish had had an unhappy marriage, got divorced; that hadn't changed her 'antics'. And it was her, poor Trish, that was kidnapped, not Jacqui – in fact, she wondered if her marriage to Nick had saved her from that horror somehow . . . Then there was Nick. Nick had arrived home just before she left for her shift

471

last night. He said that he'd be home when she woke up this evening for a proper conversation that was long overdue. She needed to get herself into gear; he sounded serious.

Paul was still going on: 'You have to leave Nick.'

'I don't *have* to do anything, Paul.'

'But I love you, Jacqui. I *really* love you.'

She didn't love him back – it was just a laugh, a bit of fun, and something to give the endless night shifts a kick. 'Oh, you're so sweet, Paul. Really . . .'

And, as she said this, she knew she had to end it. Love was not fun.

9.30 a.m., Queen Street HQ

Sparks scratched his chin thoughtfully. What a week. He topped up his coffee with Scotch. After the week they'd had, to his mind, it was perfectly okay to drink alcohol after breakfast and he needed a nip before facing the press. Even when victorious, the Colchester chief suffered from nerves. He wished Lowry was at his side.

Lowry was bracing Oldham over the Castle Park incident. Sparks had asked him to stop for a pint afterwards, when the press had been dealt with, but Lowry had tried to duck out, pleading family matters (and, in fairness, who could blame him?), but it was approaching the first game of the new year and Sparks reckoned he could persuade him to see the U's train the day beforehand. There was cause for celebration, after all: they had solved three murders in under a week! And although there were still some loose ends – they had no idea where the drugs were, for one – Lowry was convinced he could get Oldham to square things with Lane, thus allowing Sparks to save face over the arrest. (Lane would then phone Merrydown and explain it was all a misunderstanding.)

Merrydown. Sadly, there was no escaping her. They were due to have dinner on Monday evening to discuss a shake-up at West Mersea. Dodger Bradley would certainly have to retire. Shame; Sparks liked the old toad. He might be crap at paperwork, but in his day he'd been a damn fine policeman.

He took a sip of his laced coffee as he pondered the afternoon's Division 3 football. Shame about young Jennings, too, with his long legs – would have made an excellent winger. The police had now traced phone calls from the West Mersea cottage to Germany. Whatever disagreement had taken place, it had been enough to prompt Freddie to get on a plane and meet Jennings. He hadn't realized it would be the last trip he ever made.

Sparks didn't know Jennings and cared little what happened to him. No, the big surprise was Jamie Philpott, who had killed Boyd and Stone. The fight with Quinn had sent the man crazy – paranoid and psychotic, according to the doctors, for Jamie Philpott was entering a plea of insanity. After doing a bunk from Colchester General, he had indeed holed up with his mother for a spell, but after refuelling on more powder, he had taken it upon himself to return to Greenstead on Sunday evening. There, the domestic simplicity of two men jabbering away over a curry sent delusional signals of conspiracy pulsing through his temporal lobes. He was convinced they were plotting against him. Philpott waited until one man went to use the toilet. He picked up a combat knife and killed one while he ate, and then followed the other upstairs to the bathroom.

Sparks was surprised that Philpott had it in him to murder, and found it equally unlikely that a pasting from a giant Irishman could send a man mad, even if he was whizzing like an Apollo rocket. It was one thing to have taken leave of one's senses when the incident happened, fully loaded, but then to spend a night at his mother's, in Tiptree, craving revenge on his pal and a simpleton from Brightlingsea? But that's what had happened. Still, not his problem: the lunatic had confessed, leaving Sparks with nothing to worry about. That was drugs for you. The phone disturbed his thoughts.

'Sparks.'

It was the front desk. 'There's a doctor here to see Detective Inspector Lowry.'

'He's not expected back until midday.'

'I've said that, sir. The gentleman said he'd wait. I said not to . . .'

It would be about Kenton, no doubt – truncheoned across the jaw last night. He might be a crafty bugger in the ring, but every time they let him loose outside, somebody took a swing at him.

'All right, send him up.' Poor sod might have concussion.

He could ill afford to be a man down this early in the season. Lowry had better shake himself out of this no-fighting nonsense, with Kenton idling in the General. He folded the *News of the World* and topped up his coffee again.

In less than a minute, there was a rap at the door.

'Come.'

In walked a handsome blond fellow with a gingerish beard. Well-built, broad shoulders.

'Ah, doctor, sit down. Can I interest you in a snifter?'

The man frowned and hesitated before pulling up the chair. 'Err . . . no, I won't, if it's all the same to you.'

Sparks replaced the cap on the Teacher's. 'I always thought you chaps started at dawn,' he joshed. 'Now, how is he? He's used to receiving a stray right hook or two, so he needn't take a week off because of a poke with a truncheon.' Sparks smiled.

The doctor looked baffled. 'I'm sorry, but who are you talking about?'

'Detective Constable Kenton, champion boxer. I assume that's why you're here?'

'No, no, Chief Sparks.' The doctor grimaced. 'I'm after your birdwatching inspector.'

'Ha!' Sparks boomed. The Scotch had made him rather jolly. 'I fear you have the wrong police station – we have no one fitting that description here!'

'Detective Inspector Nicholas Lowry – he's CID, I believe.'

'Why, yes, but—'

'It's about his wife. I'm in love with his wife.' And with that, the doctor put his head in his hands and sobbed.

'Well, I'll be damned.' Chief Sparks slumped at the desk, stunned. 'He's become a bloody twitcher.'

60

9.50 a.m., Friday, Abbey Fields, Military Police HQ

Oldham sat at the piano, his back to Lowry as he entered the captain's office. The DI had little knowledge of classical works but, whatever the piece, it was pleasant on the ear.

'Very nice, captain.'

'Ah, Detective Inspector Lowry, I wondered when you might show,' he remarked over his shoulder.

'Were you expecting me?'

'Yes, I figured it was your turn this time.'

'This time?'

'As opposed to your hot-headed chief, hungry for a collar.'

Lowry settled into the leather chesterfield. He was in no hurry. The piano playing ceased, and Oldham brought the lid down gently. Rising, he asked, 'Sherry?' It was a bit early in the day, but it had been a long week for them both.

'Love one – thank you.'

Oldham placed a coaster neatly on the edge of the antique

477

octagonal table next to Lowry before handing him a crystal schooner. Here was a precise man who would not tolerate disorder, or untidiness, in any shape or form.

'Of course, you won't be able to prove anything.'

'Of course,' Lowry agreed, and swallowed the fino in one. He could drink this forever. 'But an admission would be sporting on your part.'

'Sporting? As in "a sporting chance?" That has no meaning for me, inspector. There are rules and regulations; a code of practice. That is my law, the army's law. Our jobs are not dissimilar.'

Lowry made for the decanter and helped himself. 'Yes, of course. But your rules fall within my community, and when people get hurt, then it's my concern.'

'Are you seriously telling me you've never had to bend your own regulations for the good of the whole –' a slight pulse became visible at Oldham's temple – 'such as when you see the fabric of your community under threat?'

'I'm not doubting your intentions,' Lowry said, meeting his gaze, 'but I need to hear your account, and then we'll say no more about it.' He was careful in his phrasing – 'account', rather than 'confession'.

'Very well.' Oldham clasped his fingers behind his back and stood behind the large desk, perhaps to feel in command. 'In Germany, a number of men were caught dealing in illegal substances. Corporal Frederick Cowley was under surveillance long before he left the army, and the German police kept an eye on him following his exit from the forces. It was they who alerted me to the drug trafficking. A new type of recreational drug was being made in central Europe – as I'm sure you're aware, it was a German who invented LSD. Anyway, we intercepted correspondence from Cowley to Daley.'

'So why not arrest them?'

'We made a deal with the German police to catch them – we knew who and when but not where, which made it difficult; we had to follow them, and civilian clothes disguise a military policeman only up to a point. When Daley and Jones paused in the high street outside a hotel, a civilian told them they were being watched, and that's when—'

'When they ran for it.' Thanks to a shifty Tony Pond, who clocked the military police surveillance.

'Correct. And nobody was more surprised at the outcome than me. Whether they fell or jumped, I have no idea.' He sat, elbows on the desk, fingertips now forming a triangle. Lowry waited for more.

'The unit in pursuit reached the bottom of the hill but, on hearing cries of pain, retreated. There's little more to say, other than that we expected them to make a deal on New Year's Eve. When they didn't, we thought they'd slipped through our fingers. We didn't know about the hold-up with the delivery.'

'Why was Quinn out of the picture?'

'Ah, well, Corporal Quinn is not as daft as he makes out. He smelt a rat, so we had to detain him just to make sure he understood on which side his bread was buttered.'

'I see. So that would explain why he was rather fractious the following night. And why you turned up in person following the disturbances.'

'Yes, it all grew rather emotional.'

'I'm surprised you let him out again.'

'It wouldn't do not to, having pulled Jones from your clutches ... and though, ostensibly, Quinn may appear a loose cannon, he follows orders. After a quiet word, we let him out, needing eyes and ears on the street, given what subsequently happened at Greenstead.'

'We'll get to that in a minute,' Lowry said, savouring the fino.

For the first time, everything slotted into place. The couriers had arrived late and there was nobody there to receive the shipment with Daley dead, Quinn detained, and Jones AWOL. A picture formed: Derek Stone minding the house, clueless, not sure what to do, with Jennings breathing down his neck, and Philpott making a nuisance of himself.

'Jones disappearing did raise eyebrows,' Lowry agreed, 'but I wrote that off to bureaucracy.'

'And it very easily can be. Best bet, though – young Jones would have cracked under pressure. Knowing Daley had died, the cat would be out of the bag in no time that the military police had chased his friend to his death.'

There, he'd said it.

'So where is he really?'

'Oh, he really is Falklands-bound.'

Lowry was satisfied with Oldham's frankness; the conversation would go no further.

'And is it true that a policeman was responsible for the murders?'

'Indirectly, yes.'

'What a state of affairs,' Oldham said without conviction, leaving the desk and helping himself to a refill.

'Of course, had Daley, Jones and Quinn been at the house to collect, two lives may have been spared,' Lowry said. Freddie Cowley would still have been doomed, but Lowry believed the other two would have lived.

'Who knows, inspector?' The captain returned to the piano. 'And if there'd been no fog, half the armed forces would be high as a kite. It's still my view that it was the involvement of civilians that caused bloodshed at Beaumont Terrace.' Oldham placed the sherry glass delicately on the piano, assuming the matter closed, and resumed playing.

And then Lowry made his final move.

'Of course, you know why it ended that way, with two men dead?' The piano stopped as abruptly as it had started.

'I have not the faintest idea, nor do I care.'

'But you do know the drugs were never recovered.'

The captain turned on the stool with an impressive air of polished patience.

Lowry continued. 'On Saturday night, Jamie Philpott runs into Corporal Quinn at the other end of town, having visited Beaumont Terrace. A conversation takes place before the fight. Quinn discovers the whereabouts of the shipment and passes the information on.' Lowry paused, purposely not saying where. 'The next evening, while the occupants are out to fetch a curry, the rucksacks disappear from Beaumont Terrace. Philpott returns to discover this and, after nearly two days observing these hopeless tossers, finally cracks and kills the remaining two men, thinking he's been shafted.'

'I see,' Oldham said. 'And the drugs . . . ?'

'Taken out of circulation, destroyed.'

'Hmm, for the best, wouldn't you say?' He looked on archly, wanting to confirm they were on the same page.

Lowry nodded. 'The marshes?'

'It should be easy to move about unseen on one's own territory, but it appears that the military are not the only ones to use binoculars.' He stood and picked up a gold cigarette case from the piano. 'That men have time to traipse about looking at *birds*.' He winced as he lit the cigarette. 'I mean, can you believe it?'

'Doesn't bear thinking about.' Lowry couldn't help but smile. Oldham's men had obviously stumbled across Doug Young, looking for his peregrines, while trying to dispose of the drugs. Two large rucksacks of amphetamines couldn't just be binned – they'd obviously had to have been parked in the hut, until Doug and his birds had gone. Oldham passed the cigarette case.

'Can I be frank?' he said, proffering a lighter.

'Please.'

'I must admit, I was in hot water.' He smiled for the first time. 'Heavens, I'd clean forgotten we'd been out on the marshes taking pot shots before Christmas – and there's my name chalked up for all to see. Have to hand it to you chaps, how the devil did you catch on to the ranges?'

Too coy to admit to being one of those who traipsed about looking at birds, Lowry said, 'We had a telephone number we thought might be a military field line, which put you in the frame. But if it was, it was incomplete, and the brigadier—'

'Do you have it on you? May I?'

Lowry reached inside his suit pocket. 'Be my guest.'

'Thank you, and talking of the brigadier, it goes without saying he's completely in the dark about the aforementioned situation.' Oldham scrutinized the scrap of paper. 'This is indeed a phone number.'

'Oh, really? We assumed there must be a number missing at the end, but we tried every permutation and came up with nothing.'

'There is indeed a number missing, but it'll be in the middle – an old army trick. There should also be a zero at the front for the international code. For, correct me if I'm wrong, but this is a German phone number.'

Cowley's contact number in Germany, of course. Less a digit, should it fall into the wrong hands – in this case, the hapless brother. The contact would be out there now, in Europe, wondering what the hell had happened. Lowry tipped what remained of his sherry down his throat. That was for someone else to worry about. He left the number with Oldham, suggesting he may wish to make inquiries, and said goodbye.

Lowry knew the system well enough to know that no good would come of divulging what he'd confirmed this morning. Besides, he rather liked the captain; he was a brave and principled man. He rose. A swift trip to Colchester General to check on the wounded Kenton, then . . . then what? Jacqui wouldn't be up until five. He was determined to have it out with her; he'd thought it through overnight. He'd been compromised, and refused to accept that sort of behaviour. And Matthew; he needed to talk to his son. That bruising . . . So, in the meantime, what? Watching the U's run around Layer Road with Sparks? It would be a break, and maybe go some way to reassure the station chief that Lowry wasn't losing the plot completely.

ACKNOWLEDGEMENTS

Thanks to Jon Riley, Felicity Blunt, Sarah Neal, Deborah Treisman, Sarah Castleton, David Shelley, Andreas Campomar, Natasha Fairweather, Richard Arcus, Sarah Day, Penelope Price, Mike Bulmer-Jones, Steve Moore, Alan Munson, Clare Worland, James Oldham, Katie Gurbutt.